TRUE LOVE NEVER DIES

Carmen Rosales
Erotic Quill Publishing, LLC
www.carmenrosales.com
carmen@carmenrosales.com

3020 NE 41st Terrace STE 9 #243
Homestead, Fl. 33033

Special Edition cover and interior art by Jay Aheer

Paperback ISBN 978-1-959888-48-2
Hardback Edition ISBN 978-1-959888-49-9

Manufactured in the United States of America
First Edition September 2024

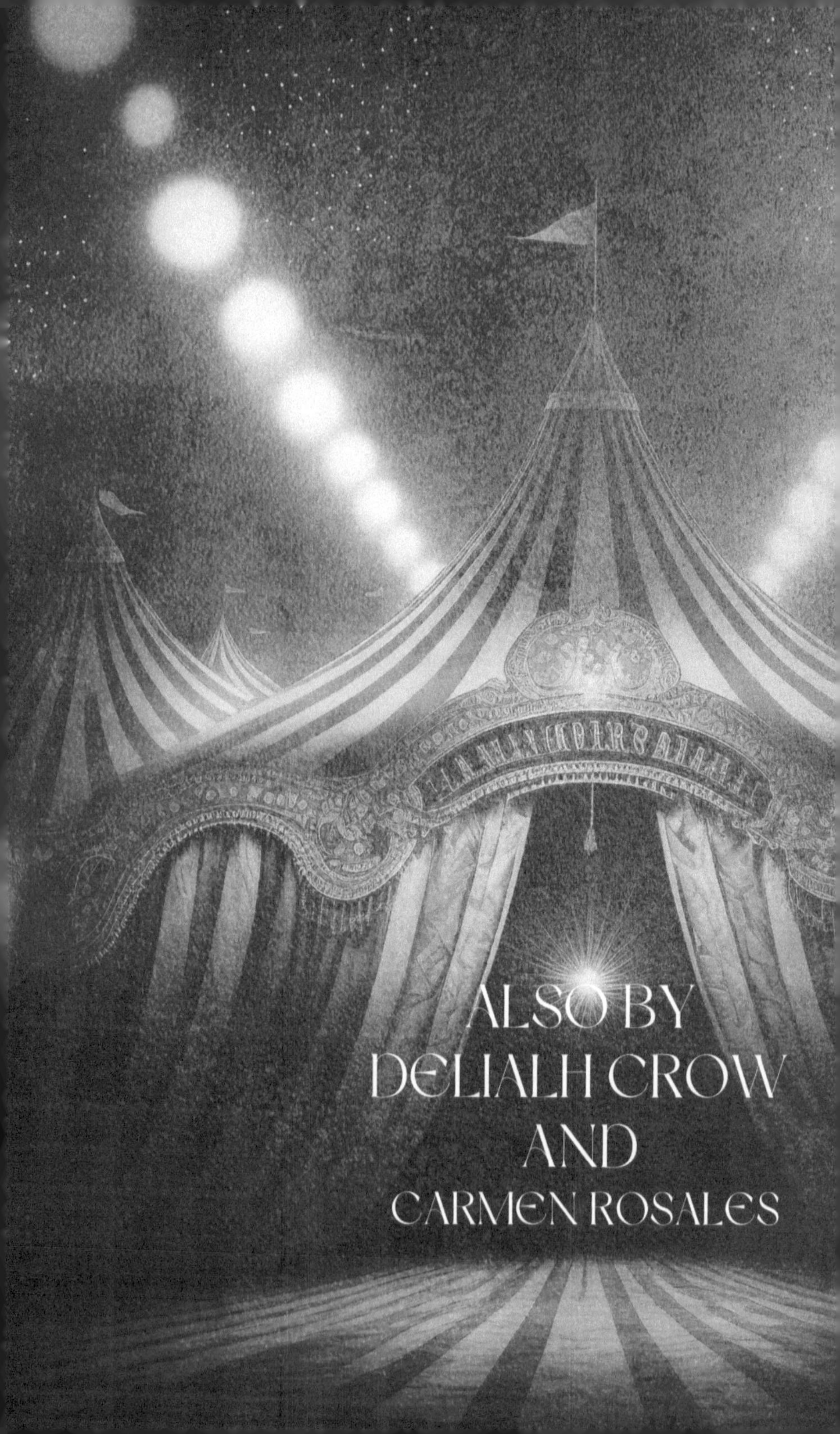
ALSO BY
DELIALH CROW
AND
CARMEN ROSALES

LOVER'S FATE

I could die a million times, and our love would always bring me back to you.

— DRACO

There is one and the same soul in many bodies.

— PLOTINUS

WHISPERS IN THE DARK

Is he real, or was it all in my mind?

Alice

After my mother remarried, my stepfather convinced her to move us into an abandoned estate, but I knew better. From the moment I stepped inside, I could feel the dark energy that permeated the walls. It wasn't long before I heard whispers, a haunting voice that seemed to be calling to me, or noises coming from the walls.

It's my senior year of high school. I want to go out, have a boyfriend, and avoid my mother's overbearing existence because she thinks I'm making things up. I want to explore my sexuality, but it's like the house smells the need for me to leave.

At night, it gives me what I crave. The more reckless I become, the more it becomes real, but I want the truth. I want to know if I made it all up. The only way is to find out the house's history, but I never imagined there were secrets from the reality haunting me for so long.

The truth was right in front of me.
I could feel it.
I just couldn't see...him.

CHAPTER
1

I peel my eyes open when I hear a rattling noise from the door. Then it stops. I sit on my bed, but I'm not imagining it. It happens again. The doorknob from my room turns halfway and rattles, but it doesn't open.

Reaching to grab my phone from the nightstand, I check the time—3:15 a.m.

The doorknob continues to jiggle. I draw my knees up, hoping it will stop. It must be a dream, or my mother is right. I'm seeing and hearing things that aren't there. When I fell asleep last night, I remember leaving my door open.

I never locked it.

It continues to rattle.

I shut my eyes.

"Stop it," I whisper, covering my ears. My heart thuds like a frantic drumbeat.

Someone is trying to get in, but I know it's no one. It always happens around three o'clock. Not before or after. And always when my mother and stepfather are out of town. I can't tell them what I see or hear anymore because they warned me they would put me in an institution if I kept it up.

It's all in your head, Alice. It's all in your head.

The noise stops.

I look up, dropping my hands. The shrouded eerie silence

envelops the room. All I hear is the thumping in my ears from the blood pumping in my veins and the occasional rustling of leaves from outside.

The tree outside my bedroom window sways, casting long, menacing shadows across the mint-green walls. The shaded lamp I found in the attic when I was nine lit the room.

A loud thump comes from behind the wall near the closet.

I pull the sheet, walk over to the wall, and place my ear against it, looking toward my bedroom door, letting out a trembling breath. *It's all in your mind, Alice. It's not real.*

Thump! I rear back like something hit me, but it didn't.

I step back, looking at the mint-green wall like something will manifest right before my eyes.

Thump! Thump!

"Stop it," I say aloud, my voice echoing around the room.

My eyes scan the bedroom door to the window, the closet, and back to the window. The sound of an iron gate slams from outside.

I run toward the window and peer out between the thick, cream-colored curtains. Scanning below, I sigh in relief when Wilfred comes through the gate.

Wilfred oversees the estate. The family who used to live in this house died in a terrible accident a year before my mother and step-father rented it. I remember the first time I laid eyes upon this house. I was nine years old. I exited the car and looked up at the Gothic-styled manor. The family who lived here put it in a trust named Hades Manor. With that name, the place seemed haunted.

When my mother asked me what I thought, I told her the house felt alive, like it was waiting for me. My mother said I had an overactive imagination. But something always nagged me in the back of my mind whenever I crossed the gates onto the prop-erty, and the feeling only intensified once I was inside. My heart-beat would race by unseen eyes. When I told her I thought it was haunted, she said I was imagining things because I was nine and to stop making things up.

When I turned thirteen, things got louder. Weirder. Doors would shut on their own. Voices coming from empty hallways. I felt isolated because no one believed or understood what I was going through. I wasn't a kid with an overactive imagination. I was Alice, the daughter who wasn't right in the head and needed a psychiatrist.

The doctor listened for five minutes, wrote a couple of things down on a piece of paper, and handed my mother a script for medication that made things worse. He also recommended a therapist. It all went downhill from there.

Now, I was unstable, and no one would take me seriously because I was labeled crazy in layman's terms or I couldn't cope after my father's death. He died from a heart attack, and not even a year later, my mother remarried and was having trouble adjusting.

Wilfred, with his slow gait, reaches the black metal gate, making a creaking sound when he locks it. It might cause the thumping noise coming from the wall. This house was built in the late seventeen hundreds. It's historic. There may be several reasons. The gate. A door from the back of the house opened, causing things to shift from inside the walls. Rats.

My stepfather told me Wilfred had been the caretaker since he was a teen. His late parents lived here, and their parents before them spanning generations. It is why the family kept him on, given the history dating back to when the first family moved here from England and brought his family along. It was a stipulation left by the previous family. Wilfred is to live here until the day he dies.

Wilfred pauses, his back facing me. His white hair peeked out of the bottom of his hat. The black outdoor jacket does nothing to hide that he is hunched over a bit. He turns and looks up as if he could sense me watching from my window on the second floor.

The deep lines etched into his weathered skin make him look like a walking ghost. His eyes, shadowed by the moonlight, glimmer with an eerie glow when he nods his head in acknowledgment.

I lift my hand, placing my palm on the cool Victorian windowpane like I've done since I was ten to say hello when I would catch him walking the grounds.

After a minute, he turns and continues walking toward the cottage he lives in at the edge of the estate with a shotgun in his hand.

The gate rattles when the wind picks up. It could explain the thumping from behind the walls but not the rattling doorknob.

I walk over to the nightstand, open the bottle of pills prescribed by the doctor, slide one out, and drink it back with the small glass of water to relieve my anxiety. I don't like to take them because they make me drowsy, reminding me of the date rape drugs they talked about in health class. Psychoactive. But when I can't sleep, like tonight, I'm left without a choice if I want to function the next day and not walk around like a zombie from lack of sleep.

I slide under my sheets and stare at the door, zeroing in on the doorknob, but it doesn't rattle. I must have thought it did.

Whether it did or didn't, the medication will take effect. It doesn't matter when the house messes with my sanity. It knows my state of consciousness and does whatever it wants. Like it's inside my head, or maybe it's...me.

"Mmm..."

I squirm, feeling something wet between my thighs, a shock wave of exploding nerves.

My eyes open and I try to refocus, but it's too dark, and that's when I realize something is over my head. It smells of rich leather.

I try to touch my face, but my hand stops midway, chains

rattling when it meets resistance. I try with my other hand, but my wrists are bound, and I can't pull them free.

I've thought about sex a lot lately. The few times I have before I fall asleep. I've felt a touch. Something between my legs, but it always happens when I take the pills. I've thought of having a boyfriend––of how he would fuck me. Taking me over the edge in a way I couldn't do myself.

I googled the side effects of the medication for anti-anxiety and found that it increases my desire for sex. Sometimes––sometimes I dream about it. In my dream, a guy does things to my body, but I can't see him.

A low, seductive voice whispers into the darkness, sending shivers down my spine. "You've been craving this," it purrs, its words dripping with desire. Suddenly, I feel a feather-light touch tracing from my ankles to the sensitive skin behind my knees. A gasp escapes from between clenched teeth as pleasure surges through me like an electric current.

A flick of a tongue glides over my slit, sending waves of pleasure through me. "Mmm..." I moan, lifting my ass off the bed. It feels so good to have a man's hot breath between my thighs. My taut nipples strain against the fabric of my T-shirt. I grind my hips, seeking more. Goose bumps snake over my skin like wildfire. "More," I whisper, closing my eyes. I want more.

If this is a dream, I don't want to wake up.

I'm floating in the dark with the gift of feeling but can't touch *it*.

The feeling intensifies like I'm about to fall off a cliff into a never-ending darkness of pure bliss. Large hands grip my thighs, holding me in place. Another flick of a tongue slides in and out, fucking me faster and faster and pushing me closer to the edge.

"Oh God. Yes," I hiss. My face is hot, but I keep my eyes shut, fearing the glimpse of light. If I wake up, it will be over. And I want to come. Hard.

There's pressure on my clit like it's being sucked and then a tongue dips inside me, taking me over the edge. I writhe when my orgasm slams into me like a tidal wave crashing against a rocky shore. When I pull, the chains grind against the wood bed frame, my hands squeezing into fists. My back arches, and the wet sounds echo in my mind with each breath I take. The backs of my eyes flash with white lights like fireworks.

"Mmm... yes," I mewl, grinding my hips, loving how it's drinking me in. "Don't stop... please."

My legs shake like fragile branches swaying in a storm. I'm being struck by a lightning bolt, causing another breathless moan to escape my lips. My heartbeat pounds, mixed with rapid breaths. Strong fingers grip my hips when my thighs close on the head between my thighs. My clit pulses in a rhythm with my heartbeat until I'm spent.

A chill slides over my sweaty skin when it's over, but something isn't right. I open my eyes, and it's still dark. My face drips with sweat, and I taste the salt. I'm wide awake. My heart pounds in my ears. And that is when I realize a leather mask is over my face. But how?

I give a hard tug with my hands, hearing the chains rattle. A strong grip is on my wrist, causing me to panic. "Who's there?" I ask in a shaky voice, but no answer.

The eerie silence is broken by heavy breathing––a wave of terror snakes around my chest. My tongue is stuck on the roof of my mouth. I'm wearing a mask over my entire head. Someone is in my room, and I'm chained to my bed, so it could...

It is too late when realization dawns. A hand unbinds the cuffs on my wrist. I reach out, but nothing. I'm about to scream, but remember, I'm alone. My parents aren't home, and Wilfred is too far away to hear me.

I swing my hands once again to only air. I reach to remove my mask from my head but come up short with a gasp. A strong grip wraps around both tender wrists.

"Who are you?" I croak. "Please, don't hurt me." He tugs me forward. The strong grip tells me I don't stand a chance. My eyes sting from the tears threatening to fall. "Please," I beg in a quivering voice. "What do you want?"

His hot breath fans my neck. The eerie silence stretches for a beat. "You," he whispers––"you'll get hurt." A tear trickles down my cheek

How can I get hurt?

I reach with my other hand to pull the mask off, but he squeezes harder. He takes two of my fingers, and I touch something sharp, like metal spikes that tug the mask.

I swallow the lump in my throat and ask, "What are you going to do to me?"

No answer.

Seconds bleed into minutes.

My body begins to tremble. I don't know how many spikes are attached. If I thrash or try to fight him, I could hurt myself. It will give him time to run and get away, which he most likely will.

What will I tell my mom? A man was in my bedroom, tied me up, placed a spiked mask over my head when I was knocked out cold from my sleeping meds, and ate my pussy? She wouldn't believe me. No one would because no one thinks a person who claims to hear and see things no one else does tells the truth.

They say the mind is a powerful thing. It can create. It can lie. It can dream. It can die or trick you into thinking you are in a place no one believes in. All you need is the push that triggers it.

When I realize what is happening, the cold air hits my skin, and the mask is pulled off my face. My eyes try to adjust, but the room is dark, and my lamp is turned off. With trembling fingers, I wipe the wetness from my cheeks.

A small stream of light comes from the hallway under the bedroom door. My eyes dart around the room, looking for a man, but there's no one. How is that possible? I didn't hear the door open.

I swing my legs and plant them on the hardwood floor. The sinister silence is like a cruel joke when I reach the hallway. I poke my head out, looking left and right. No one. No sounds of doors opening or closing. No footsteps or creaking from the floorboards.

I walk back inside my room, grab my phone, and check the time--5:00 a.m. I'm tempted to call the police, but looking around the room, I see no evidence except the indents on the wood of my headboard from the chains. I have a history of mental instability, according to my records. When the police arrive and I make a report without evidence, it proves everyone is right. I'm crazy.

I scan under my bed and then my closet, but nothing. I inspect the latch from my window--no signs of forced entry. No one could climb into my bedroom window this high up anyway. The tree is too far to climb on and has no edge to walk on. No balcony.

Swallowing the metallic taste of my fear, I find nothing after checking every room in the house for the next hour. The alarm my mother had installed never went off and is not disarmed. Reviewing the history of the last entry door opened, it was when I came home from school. The time stamp has me questioning everything.

With shaky fingers, I reach between my thighs, swipe at the sticky moisture, and bring it up to my nose. My bottom lip trembles when I smell my arousal mixed with his scent. A man's cologne. A rich and exotic scent I don't recognize clings to my folds.

Whoever it is, he's here.

I heard him.

I felt him.

But I can't see him.

He's playing with my mind, and no one would believe me if I said he was real.

CHAPTER

2

"Hey, Freak?" I look up, walking from the student parking lot. Jason sits atop the outdoor bench.

When I was thirteen, I begged my mother to move after the first therapist appointment. I told her we could move anywhere but Hades Manor. My mother screwed up my reputation at school. It started in middle school, but thank God it never stuck. However, in high school, everything sticks. Everyone tries to find shit on anyone. In my case, word got out. I see and hear shit that isn't there, and I'm on medication. Labeled a Freak.

The counselors talked about me among the faculty. They did it where other students could eavesdrop. It's the only thing that made sense when I tried to wrap my head around it. They couldn't care less how a rumor would ruin someone every day they set foot in school. It's not their life. People love to jump on the opportunity to talk about something other than themselves, and I've never said or given them a reason to believe it.

I see Ivy looking behind me at Jason and the assholes he loves to hang out with, mainly the football team and the cheerleaders needing attention. They have it out for Ivy since she started her sophomore year and mistakenly went out with Tommy Hill. Tommy wanted to test the new girl and fell for it, but Tommy was the one who face-planted. According to him, she slept with him on the first date. He called her a slut, but I didn't miss the regret pasted on her face the next day at school after their so-called date. Not because he was slut-shaming her but because it was obvious she didn't like Tommy. Whatever happened between them was bad, and he knew it.

Since then, Ivy Sloan has been called a slut and bullied by everyone. Especially Jason. He never lets up with his crude remarks, and it irritates me. Tommy watches it happen with a smirk, but you can see it if you get close enough. Tommy has a thing for Ivy.

I'm about to pass Ivy when Jason says, "Hey, Ivy. Do you and the Freak want to suck me off after school?"

I see her roll her eyes and wait for her to fire back. "I thought we talked about this, Jason. You can't find your dick in the morning when you get a hard-on, remember? It's too small." Everyone around him laughs.

"That's because a slut like you needs to have a huge cock inside your loose pussy."

Lame. He's such an insufferable prick. He never leaves her alone. I can handle being called a freak, but with Ivy, he goes too far. I turn around and flip him off.

"Anytime, Freak." He gets up from the bench. "I'll throw in a pity fuck after you watch your friend Ivy take my cock."

Ivy isn't my close friend, but I wish she were. I find it hard to trust someone. I have no friends since my mother moved us to Hades Manor. No friends outside school, either. There was no way I would invite friends over--with the creepy sounds. Doors locked when they were left open. The grand piano in the living room playing when I was home alone. When I started middle school, it got worse. The house got worse, and so did my mind.

I turn around, not wanting to throw gas on an already lit fire heading inside the building, but I don't miss Ivy's last parting shot with a smile.

"Hey... Jason? Good luck finding your dick."

Not wanting to hear his last remark, I walk inside, moving

through the throng of bodies filling the hallway like ants in a pile of dirt.

"Hey, thanks," she says, catching up with me when I reach my locker, turning the lock to get my books for class. "For what you did back there. I'm not what they say I am."

I nod. "I know."

Why would she be? They don't know her, and I've never seen her around another guy at school. Who are they to judge anyway?

"You do?"

I have my first class with her and don't want to brush her off. Ivy doesn't deserve the shit she gets here. She bothers no one and keeps mostly to herself like I do.

I pull my textbook out of my locker. "You went out with Tommy on a date after he kept asking you repeatedly your sophomore year. I was a freshman, but everyone knew you went out with him one time. He made sure everyone knew you slept with him and made up crap slut-shaming you. Guys act stupid when they like a girl and know she doesn't feel the same way. You found him lame, and you don't like him." I shut my locker. "It doesn't make you a slut. Besides, I have never seen you with another guy since my freshman year. Not one."

"I don't think you're a freak," she blurts, making me smile.

"Thanks, I guess."

It's nice to hear the opposite of what they say for a change.

"I guess we both have something in common."

I pinch my brows together, wondering what she means. What could we have in common? "What do you mean?"

"We both have people saying things about us that are untrue."

I keep smiling when I take my seat inside the class. No one has ever told me that what they thought of me wasn't true. No one has ever said I wasn't--a freak.

I also never believed what they said about Ivy was true. Ivy Sloan is stunning. Her platinum hair is gorgeous, with her complexion, and she has a body to die for. They are just jealous assholes.

Everyone thinks Tommy Hill is God's gift because he's the starting quarterback and comes from money. He's a good-looking snob with a football up his ass. He thought he had Ivy all to himself. I suspected he spread the rumor after their date so no one would take an interest in her. He knew she didn't come from the same circle he did. He also knew she didn't find him as attractive as he thought she did.

"I agree. It's when we believe what people say when it becomes a problem."

I watch her turn and stare at the wooded desk where they carved IVY SLOAN IS A SLUT. I hope she believes me. I hope she thinks it's true. If not, it would give everyone else power over her. When someone has power over you, they make you do things you normally wouldn't. It's a tragedy to the soul.

I pass through the gate from school and notice my stepfather's black Mercedes in the circular driveway under the leaves strewn across it, hinting at the beginning of the fall season. They must be back. I park my Tesla inside the single garage to the right.

When I enter the house, it's quiet. I don't hear my mother's voice like usual and go to the kitchen. The walls feel like eyes watching me everywhere I go.

I lick my dry lips like I've been walking through a desert and need water. Opening the stainless-steel refrigerator, I feel the cold blast of air on my heated face, reminding me of the horror from this morning mixed with the intense pleasure I secretly craved. I grab a bottle of water, twist the cap, bring it to my mouth, shut the refrigerator door, and jolt. The bottle slips from my fingers and hits the floor with a thud.

"You scared me."

My stepfather leans against the black marble counter in the Gothic-styled kitchen, watching me. His blue-eyed gaze is cold like the ice in the Arctic.

"I'm sorry. I thought you saw me in the kitchen."

He knew I didn't because he watched me like he always does, trying to find a crack in my behavior.

I grab the paper towel and bend to pick up the water bottle. "When did you guys make it back?"

"I just got back."

I straighten and drop the paper towel on the dark hardwood floor, placing my boot so it can soak up the small puddle of water. Picking up the soaked paper towel, I pinch my brows in confusion. "Where's Mom?"

They both went to Chicago for a business meeting. My mother *was* my stepfather's secretary before my father died. Not even a year after my father passed away, my mother married Nick Giles. Nick is a business developer and has developed buildings all over the country. His goal is to buy the estate, but he cannot convince the trustee to bend. He thinks living here and paying rent will give him an advantage.

Sometimes I suspect my mother had an affair with Nick when my father was alive. It was too much of a coincidence. The pieces fell perfectly. My father died, and exactly a year and a day after the anniversary of my father's death, she married Nick. I don't remember my mother bringing him to our small house in Boston, and when I asked, she said I wasn't ready to meet him. She didn't want to hurt my feelings because I was my father's baby girl—Seth Grayson's pride and joy.

"She got held up today with minor details that need sorting out, and I flew into Boston this morning. I had an issue at the office. I'll pick her up when she lands later today."

"Oh," I say, mindlessly taking a sip from my water bottle.

I can feel him watching me from the corner of my eye. I was always nervous around Nick like he knew something I didn't. He's always been nice to me and respectful. Cordial, if I want to be honest, but something in his gaze is off. I could never pinpoint what it was or why.

"Did everything go okay while we were gone?"

He means did I hear and see shit. I would not tell him about last night or this morning. *A man chained me to the bed and put a spiked mask over my head, and fucked my pussy with*

*his tongue until I came hot in his mouth. Then he disappeared
into thin air.*

"Yeah. Everything was fine."

He sighs, pushing off the counter. "I know you hate living
here, but it's your senior year in high school. It's an important
year for anyone. If you focus on..."

"I asked Mom if I could go out with friends or have a
boyfriend."

"Is that what you want?" He arches his brow. "A boyfriend?"

I feel weird talking to Nick about this, but my mother is stub-
born and asks the therapist for her guidance on everything I say. I
can't even take a shit without her all up in my ass. She questions
everything I do. She probably asks the therapist if taking a shit
every day is normal.

If it weren't for Nick, I wouldn't have a car. I'm grateful
for him.

I look away, embarrassed, when I answer, "Yeah. I want to
date. Like normal teenagers do their senior year. What about
prom or if I get invited to a party?"

I don't tell him it's highly unlikely anyone at school would ask
me. But it doesn't mean I can't go out and find someone who
would. I turned eighteen last month. It's not illegal. I can't be
held hostage in this house forever.

He steps close and places his hands on my shoulders. "I'll talk
to her." I look over at where his heavy hands are and meet his gaze.
His eyes darken for a fraction of a second before he pulls his hands
away.

"Okay."

"You're eighteen." He grins. "It counts for something, right?"

I give a half shrug. "I hope so. I'm an adult, but you know
how Mom is."

"She just wants the best for you." The grin slides off his lips.
His expression goes blank. "I want the best for you." His eyes are
like two cold pieces of ice, traveling from my feet to my face. "Go

freshen up. When I pick up your mom, I'll bring back Chinese. No vegetables. Just the way you like it."

An uncomfortable feeling creeps up my spine. I'm aware of him. We're alone in the kitchen, and I suddenly feel like running. It wasn't what he said about the food. It was how he said it and how he looked at me when he said it.

I blink rapidly, pushing unwanted thoughts from my mind. I'm overwhelmed by what happened when I was home alone. Nick is my stepfather. He wouldn't overstep. He loves my mother.

I turn toward the staircase to shower but turn back around, walking backward. "Remember to arm the house on your way out, please," I say hastily, trying to hide my unease.

He gives me a half grin, but it doesn't reach his eyes. "Of course."

I swallow thickly, feeling suffocated from his gaze when I climb the stairs while he's standing near the kitchen.

CHAPTER 3

The bathroom was cloaked in silence when I stepped into the glass shower. Steam billowed from the shower head, quickly filling the space with a dense foggy atmosphere. I step under the spray, watching water droplets dance like phantom tears against the glass. The bathroom was modernized but still maintains the bones of history––the old mixed with the new. The warm water cascades over my body, hitting the tile in a cacophonous symphony, masking the distant sounds from the rest of the house.

When I close my eyes, letting the warm water envelop me, a sense of unease washes over me. I dismiss it as irrational fear and remember I've locked the bathroom door and checked it three times. I wash my body and my hair and keep my eyes closed to avoid the sting from the soap, ignoring the feeling of being watched. I look out the glass shower, but the glass has fogged up. I rub my eyes, trying to focus. It seems like a dark silhouette is flat against the wall behind the door.

I shiver, and it's not because I'm cold. I hesitate before swiping my hand over the glass. I lick the water from my lips and reach out with my palm. A whiny creak comes from the door–– the same sound it makes when it opens. Could it be Nick walking up the stairs and making the door pull because of the draft from another door opening inside the house? I touch my palm flat against the glass. When I swipe my hand to remove the condensation, the lights go out, and I'm basked in darkness.

A loud bang, like the door was pushed shut, and then footsteps.

"Who's there? Nick?"

My eyes try adjusting to the darkness, and I hear the sound of the water mixed with heavy breathing. With a trembling hand, I shut the water off.

"Hello?" I call out, but nothing. "Shit," I mutter.

I push the shower door open, wondering why the lights went out. It must be a blackout. That must be it, but I know it isn't. Another thing I can't explain.

I try not to slip on the tile when I reach for my towel. When I finally feel the cotton hanging on the hook, I wrap it around my body but still hear breathing. I hold my breath to make sure it's not my own.

It's even. I feel the sharp sting of tears in the back of my eyes every time I blink as fear curls around me, hitching my breath.

"Who are you?"

I know I sound crazy, but I feel him. Whoever it is, he's in here with me. I step forward. Another step. Then another. I can smell him. The same scent as last night. It's...him. It's like he lives inside the walls of this house and only comes out to torment me. *And touch me.* My mind starts flipping back, piecing every sound and slammed door or the Steinway piano that plays when I'm alone. Was it him?

"I know you're there... I can hear you breathing. I-I can smell you."

I reach forward with my hand to check the light switch when suddenly the bathroom door opens. Before I grasp what is happening, strong hands shove me out into the hallway, the door slamming shut behind me. I turn around and look at the bathroom door looming ominously like I'm in a horror movie and the killer is on the other side. I begin backing away instead of being stupid and trying to see who is behind the door. I run into my room, shut the door, flip the lock, and back away until the back of my knees hit the edge of the bed. My hair drips all over the floor.

I'm trying to make sense of what happened. I run to my window and look out to see if Nick left or if he is still here, but his car is gone. If the man from the bathroom wanted to hurt me, he would have done it. I'm creeped out that he was in the shower watching me, reminding me of Alfred Hitchcock's *Psycho*. Who knows how long he's been watching me or if all I have seen or heard inside this house is because of him? I'm not crazy. He's inside this house, but who knows how long or where he came from?

NINE YEARS AGO

"Mom, I heard a noise coming from the wall."

Her eyes meet mine while she blows at the steam from the coffee cup in her hands.

She places it down with a thud on the island in annoyance. "Alice. This is an old house. You probably just heard the pipes."

Wringing my hands in front of my blue plaid skirt, I reply, "It wasn't a pipe. It was someone inside the walls. I was playing in my room, and I heard a loud thud. Three times."

Since we moved here, Mom doesn't believe me when I hear a door close, and there was no one there, but I heard it.

"Nonsense. Go back to your room and play. It's eight o'clock in the morning. I don't have time for this."

"What's wrong?" my stepfather Nick asks, stopping behind me and placing his large hands on my shoulders. He rubs my back with his thumb.

My mother waves her hand, the diamond ring catching in the light from the sun streaming from the glass window. It just reminds me that my father is dead because he would never give Mom a diamond ring like that.

"She says something is inside the walls, making a thumping noise. The other day, she said someone slammed the door closed. I checked to see, but no one is there, Nick." She glances at me with disappointment. "Ever since we moved here, Alice, you keep making things up. I know it's hard when you move from what you were used to, but you have to accept it. We live here now, and this is your home." I nod.

My eyes burn, but I know she will get upset if I cry in front of Nick. Ever since she married Nick, my mom hasn't been the same. It feels like she died with Daddy. She doesn't tuck me in at night. She doesn't take me anywhere except for school. The only one nice to me when Mom is not around is Nick.

"Give her a break, Lynn. She's nine years old. It's a big move."

"It's been four months, Nick. She can't be making up this nonsense. Doors slamming, thudding inside the walls. The next thing will be that she sees ghosts."

"This house is haunted," I blurt.

Her eyes narrow, then dart to Nick. "You see. That's what I'm talking about."

"She's a kid," he argues.

"She is driving me crazy with this haunted house crap. I'm not entertaining it. She can't go around saying that stuff. What if she says that at school? I'm going to get a call from the principal, and then they are going to have me take her to a counselor about her living arrangements. The last thing we need is people prying into us living here." As soon as those words leave her mouth, Nick tightens his hands on my shoulders.

I try to wiggle away from his grasp, but he turns me to face him. Hard blue eyes cause me to flinch. "Go to your room and listen to your mother, Alice. She's right. You have to stop this. There is no one in this house except us three, and Wilfred does not come inside this house unless I allow it." I blink, trying to avoid crying, refusing to look at my mother so I don't see the triumphant look in her eyes.

I ascend the stairs, and when I'm sure they can't see me, I turn to see my stepfather and mother kissing, churning my stomach. Gross. Mom never kissed Daddy like that. Daddy would never talk to me like that either.

When I shut the door to my room, another thud comes from behind the wall. Angry, I march and bang it with my fist, wincing at the sting. "Quit it," I yell––another thud. I close my eyes, telling myself it's the pipes like my mother said.

"*Soooorry.*"

My eyes pop open. I heard the faint whisper. Barely audible. The tiny hairs stand on my arms as I stare at the mint-green wall with wide eyes. Someone whispered *sorry*.

I place the palm of my hand over my chest. My heart races under my trembling hands, taking another step away from the wall. The room closes in around me, telling me its secrets. Secrets that want to be revealed.

I listen, helpless, to the haunting whisper, unable to escape the horrifying realization that the house holds something lost. I just hope it doesn't hurt me before my mother believes me.

CHAPTER
4

After school, I pull into the driveway of Hades Manor like it's my first time, looming between the surrounding landscape like a dark sentinel of dread. Its towering facade, composed of ancient, weathered stone, is a testament to a forgotten era. The mansion's architecture is a haunting blend of Gothic and Victorian styles, characterized by imposing turrets and ornate wrought-iron gates.

After I parked my car inside the garage, I wondered how it had full charge when I forgot to plug it into the charger the night before. I keep forgetting to charge the damn thing.

Opening the door, I disarm the alarm, and once regal and majestic, the grand entrance is now welcome with marble steps and a tarnished brass knocker resembling a twisted demon's face. The front doors, heavy and imposing, creak reluctantly as if resisting the intrusion of the living into its malevolent domain— the heavy silence when no one is home. I'm glad my mother and stepfather aren't here, and to be honest, I like to avoid them. They always hit me with twenty questions and questionable looks, like they were waiting for me to come up with another crazy omission of what I heard or saw the night before. It's exhausting, and I prefer to keep my mouth shut and act like they don't exist.

The manor is a labyrinth of winding corridors and shadowed alcoves. The walls, adorned with faded, macabre portraits of long-dead residents, seem to watch and whisper secrets to one another. The grand staircase spirals upward toward the upper reaches of the mansion, where darkness dwells.

Candle sconces line the hallways with ghostly glow despite the upgrades from candles to electric lighting, casting eerie, dancing shadows that seem to have a life of their own. The air is thick with an ancient, oppressive presence, as though the walls are saturated with history. It feels like a curse ever since I moved here.

I'm about to climb the second step when the sound of music being played is coming from the piano. I know it's real because I have an app on my smartphone that tells me the artist of a song being played. It only plays when I'm alone and stops when I walk toward the living room. The music sounds like a mournful dirge or a chilling, otherworldly melody but romantic simultaneously.

The music floats like a caress all over my skin. I smile. I pull my phone out of my bag and unlock it. Pressing the app, I wait until it circles, capturing the sound. It stops and says "Liebestraum No.3." The music slows and then picks up, bringing tears to my eyes as another melody begins. I press my thumb over the app, and after a few seconds, it stops. It recognizes Beethoven's "Moonlight Sonata."

I sit on the lower step, resting my head on the wood balustrade, listening to the hauntingly beautiful piece. Whoever plays makes it feel like the notes are flowing like moonlight on the water with longing and emotion. When it stops, I wipe my face from the tears that have run down my cheeks.

After showering, I dozed off listening to both music pieces on my phone. I reach over and check the time. It's almost seven. My mother's voice sounds faint, then footsteps. I can hear the deep timbre of Nick's voice answering her but can't make out what they're saying. After a few seconds, a door slams shut.

I picked out a wool skirt with dark tights and a V-neck sweater. I grab a small wallet with my keys and open my bedroom door. I breathe and ease the door, praying it won't squeak. With the door just wide enough for my slender frame to slip through, I venture into the dimly lit hallway--my heart pounding, locking my door. My mother doesn't bother me if she sees my door shut.

Every shadow seemed like a lurking enemy. I move stealthily, one foot in front of the other, as if the darkness conspired to keep my secret of sneaking out. I take measured steps down the stairway, each one a small victory until I reach the bottom, letting out a breath. When I made it outside, my pulse is racing like it would jump out of my skin from the thrill, the exhilaration of freedom drawing me closer to escape.

It isn't the first time I've snuck out. I did it in the summer when my mother told me I couldn't leave the house and went driving in the Tesla they bought me at the beginning of the summer or, rather, Nick bought me. She had groceries delivered like I was incapable of driving to the store myself. The advantage of an electric vehicle is that you can't hear it. There is no sound because there is no engine. Checking the battery, I have enough to drive around at night and hit the main highway.

The sun is setting, and it's almost dark. After five minutes, I noticed someone walking on the grass on the side of the road. As I drive closer, I see it's Ivy. What the hell is she doing walking on the main highway by herself? There have been reports of teenage girls being abducted and found dead all over the news. Pulling over, I honk the horn to get her attention.

She stops with a look of terror pasted on her face, like she is running from a murderer, reminding me of a *Friday the 13th* movie, where the girl runs through the forest away from Camp Crystal Lake.

I roll the window down. "Do you need a ride?"

Her shoulders sag in relief, and she nods. "Yes, Alice. Thank God." She runs up to my car and gets in like something is after her.

"Is everything alright? It looks like you've been running from Jason Voorhees."

"Close. This couple stopped to offer me a ride, and something was off. I told her my boyfriend was picking me up, and the way she smiled before they pulled away gave me the creeps. All the talk about teenage girls missing has me thinking everyone is a body snatcher."

"That must have been scary. It's dark out." I look up at the glass moonroof. "The moon is full. You know what they say, weird people come crawling out when the moon is full."

She looks around inside the high-tech car. "Thank you for pulling over. Nice car, by the way."

It is, but she doesn't know it's useless if you don't charge it. The time it takes sucks. You're like a sitting duck waiting for it to have enough battery power. Anyone can run up on you while charging it away from home. I don't think Nick and my mother thought that through when they bought it.

"Trust me, it's not nice when you have to wait inside to charge it when the battery runs low after driving it all day. I'm lucky it's charged every morning because I forget. I think my mother or stepfather remember, or I wouldn't make it to school on time. They keep giving me shit about it."

I thanked them one day, and they looked at me the same way when I told them I heard something they didn't. Then they both played it off, giving me shit for not remembering to charge it and that it's my responsibility. I get that it is, but I haven't run out of battery or called them because I was stranded somewhere.

"Mine can't make rent." She points at her uniform shirt I recognize from the grocery store in town, the Big H. "It's why I'm walking home. I had to stay late and missed the shuttle."

I pull out onto the road. The bell chimes from the screen when I drive in the opposite direction. I hope I can convince her to hang out with me so I'm not alone.

"I needed to get out of my house. My parents don't want me out, but I couldn't take being stuck in my room, so I snuck out."

I want to tell her I don't want to be alone anymore, but I don't want to sound needy and pathetic.

"Have you been to the haunted fair?"

I wish. I've been trying to convince my mother to let me go, but she thinks I will tell people about the house. She got the therapist to agree and blamed it on too much stimulation because of the fact it's a haunted fair. She doesn't tell me the real reason, but my mother hates gossip and looking bad in front of people from Stockbridge. Being married to Nick inflated her ego because he has money.

"I'm not allowed to go. My mother doesn't think it's a good idea. Too much stimulation."

She snorts. "What does she say about sex? That's stimulation."

I laugh. If she only knew. "I asked if I could have a boyfriend, and they said they didn't think that was a good idea either."

"What? Are they going to send you to a convent or something?"

"Doubt it. They might think I'll appear like that diabolical nun in the movie."

I shouldn't have said that because it opens a door to questions as to why, but fuck it. I said it.

She scrolls through her phone, and the Circle of Freaks page appears. I want to at least go to the fair. I'm pushing my luck by sneaking out and asking to date as it is, but maybe Ivy would go with me. I'm surprised she hasn't gone.

"Are you going?"

"I want to, but it costs three hundred bucks. That is what I make in a month working at the grocery store, and I need it to help my mother with rent. I signed up to see if I could win a free ticket on the website."

It is a little pricey, and if Ivy is working because her mother can't make rent to cover the bills, I doubt she can go. I overheard Mich telling Jason from the football team that they give fairgoers free tickets for the first few weeks on weekdays at the haunted fair. You have to be eighteen, but Ivy repeated her junior year, making her eighteen or maybe even nineteen.

"If you go to the haunted fair during the week and wear an eighteen and over orange band, they hand out free tickets."

"Really?" she asks excitedly. "How do you know that?"

"I heard Mich from the football team tell Jason. I think they were going to go since they turned eighteen."

I watch her search for free tickets for the Circle of Freaks circus. "He's right. There's a blog. It says the Circle of Freaks will hand out a few tickets to fairgoers if they enter the haunted carnival during the week for a special weekend ticket to their show."

"You want to go that bad?"

She glances at me with a hopeful expression. "Yeah, I've loved the circus since I was a kid but figured I was too old to go now, but this one... this one I want to check out."

I drum my black-painted fingernails on the steering wheel, contemplating whether we should go now. Fuck it. If I don't go now and Nick doesn't convince my mother to let me go out and date, I'm screwed. Fuck it.

I slow down, turn the wheel, and drive in the opposite direction when I reach her apartment complex. Everyone at school knows where Ivy Sloan lives. Tommy made sure he let the school know that she doesn't come from money and that he fucked her in the Coyote Drive-In because he's a loser.

"That was my stop," she says.

I grin. "I know." I press the search icon on the screen and type in Carnevil, and the address pops up, routing the car to the destination.

Butterflies swarm inside my stomach. I'll even offer to pay so she won't say no. "The ticket to the haunted fair is twenty-eight dollars, including all the rides. I could loan you the money."

I have money in my account. I needed it for something at school, or they wouldn't even notice. Nick started giving me an allowance when my mother embarrassed me and told him I got my period. I wanted the ground to swallow me whole. He raised a brow like he knew something I didn't and opened an account to buy personal items.

"Thank you, but I have enough," she says, knowing it was her pride talking.

She looks down at her work uniform top and takes it off, sliding it into her bag, and fixes her blond hair.

"You never know. Maybe you'll get lucky, and even if you don't, you'll have fun trying. The tent shouldn't be far away. No one knows what happens inside unless you pay to go."

It's true. No one knows what goes on inside the tent or what happens. It's like one big secret, but it's a great marketing tactic, or it wouldn't sell if everyone knew what the show was like.

"I think that's why I want to go so bad."

"You like the dark paranormal circus stuff?"

She shrugs. "Yeah, why not? I've never gone to a circus, but it beats work, school, and where I live."

She couldn't be more wrong. I feel like I'm in prison, and the only highlight right now is the man who secretly excites and torments me.

"Trust me, I know the feeling."

CHAPTER
5

There is a line to park when we arrive. Once I find a spot on the left side of the parking lot, the line is due to the carnival on the right. Parents with little kids in their strollers walk toward the entrance. The booths have bright lights with children painted on them. It reads FUN FOR EVERYONE.

To my left is the haunted fair. The light from the moon is a backdrop behind the huge sign over the rusted ticket booths with red lights. The sign says, "Welcome to Carnevil: Where Fear Meets Fun." It's a complete contrast to the regular fair. Instead of little kids, there are teenagers, and most are not with their parents.

We walk toward the ticket booth with the least number of people. Middle and high school kids line up at the one closest to the right. Some I recognize from our school, but I hope they don't see us in line at the booth to the far left.

"Are you sure you won't get in trouble for bringing me here?" Ivy asks.

"I don't think they'll find out I snuck out. I closed the garage, so they think my car is inside. My stepfather is away on business, and my mother is fast asleep. How about you?"

I lie on the last part. I don't know why, but I don't want her to ask me to take her home. I'm excited and want to do something my mother won't approve of.

"My mom could give a shit as long as I bring her the other half of the rent."

We step up to the front of the line. "That bad, huh?"

"You have no idea," she says derisively.

It sucks to have a mother who doesn't care about you, but it sucks when they act like they care for all the wrong reasons. It's worse when they don't believe in you. Ivy's mother seems to care less about Ivy if she brings money home. I bet she doesn't care if she finishes high school.

We pay for our tickets and get our bands. We walk in, the fog floating like clouds around us. The dim lighting gives the sense that you're in an abandoned carnival.

The Ferris wheel moves slowly––the creaking sound of the gondolas swaying in the night sky under the moon. Skeletal figures and people wander mindlessly, alone, wearing costumes. A group of kids ahead of us disappear in the fog, but you don't miss their screams, causing a chill to slide down my spine.

The Ferris wheel increases speed. A creepy laugh and a high-pitched scream make my heart beat rapidly inside my chest. A sinister clown pops out of nowhere, causing Ivy and me to jolt. The clown has a sinister smile with wide teeth.

"Come, play with me," it hisses, gesturing for us to come over.

We walk farther into the carnival, and more disguised characters pop out from hidden spaces, startling us. The vendors sell popcorn and cotton candy that appear to be dripping in blood. One vendor holds a bloody cotton candy, watching us pass, and hisses, "Hungry?"

I'm tense, trying to remind myself that it's not real. It's easy to say that when you're not here. Once inside, it's a different story. The characters. The makeup. The food resembles something grotesque.

We pause in front of a roller coaster that reads, Roller Coaster of Evil. It's tinged with rust or seems to have rust like it has been there for centuries, making you wonder if the track will collapse.

The coaster dips at breaking speed with a peal of sinister laughter. Screams echo with a whoosh of air from the G-force, leaving you with dread and excitement. The ride stops, and people step off with their hair sticking up and smiles on their faces from the rush.

"Do you want to ride it, Alice?" Ivy asks, holding up her left hand with her orange band. "We can ride everything. Let's have fun."

My lips break into a smile because that's the point, right? To have fun. To rebel.

"Alright, fuck it. How bad could it be?"

The line is long, but people are being let on and off, so it moves fast. I notice characters from the park wearing costumes sliding in with the park guests on the ride. "Are they letting the people in costumes ride with random people?"

Ivy follows my gaze. "Yeah," she says.

"That's...crazy."

"This place is crazy," she admits under her breath.

I couldn't agree more.

A group of cloaked figures walk in like a mob with masks on their faces. A taller one in the center of the group with a creepy white mask looks dangerous.

"Whoa," I say softly, leaning close. "Where did he come from?"

"I think they are part of the circus." She points. "They came from there."

I follow her gaze to the entrance of the Circle of Freak, spotting a cloaked figure with a black mask walking out. Craning my neck to take a better look, I see the area blocked off is the entrance to the Circle of Freaks. She's right. They must be part of the circus.

"You're right."

We're finally at the front of the line, waiting to ride, when Ivy tugs me forward. The characters are sliding inside the cart with random people. "Have fun dying," one of the characters jeers.

My stomach is in knots as I'm about to get on the ride with

Ivy, but it's short-lived. A woman dressed in a sexy costume and fishnets steps forward. She has fake blood splattered between her breasts. The other masked, cloaked performers are behind her.

"I'm hungry," she says with her teeth bared, looking at the next group to get on. "Women are my favorite. So soft." She tilts her head while mine pounds like my pulse is ready to cause my head to explode. "So pretty." She licks her crimson-painted lips. She jerks her head and straightens when the guy in front of us moves forward to sit. "He'll do," she says, sliding in beside him.

His eyes widen in horror. His reaction causes her to laugh when she secures the lap bar shut.

"She's awesome," Ivy says. *Yeah, she's great if you want to die.*

Ivy slides into the next cart. But I'm pushed out of the way by the tall man wearing the white mask with black tears painted under his eyes. What the hell?

The ride operator motions for me to sit in the cart behind. When I slide in, a man in a black mask and a dark hooded cloak sits beside me.

"What are you doing? Get out." It's bad enough Ivy is sitting with one of them, but he doesn't move and stares straight ahead. I let out a sigh. "Fine." I pull the lap bar, but he stops me, placing his gloved hand over mine. His hand causes an electrical pulse to shoot right through me, making me squeeze the bar in the palm of my hand.

He pulls the lap bar shut before the operator passes by to check, causing me to tense. This is happening. I'm going on a haunted roller coaster with a stranger. What if I scream, or I'm thrown into him by the twists and turns?

The wind picks up. My wool skirt is mid-thigh with black tights, and my sweater is high enough not to show cleavage. I'm grateful I'm not showing too much skin. But it does nothing to calm the rapid beat of my pulse or my stomach clenching.

"What's your name?" I ask. But he remains still like a statue. I pull my hand in my lap. "Okay, fine. If you touch me, I'll scream."

Which is stupid to say because I will scream anyway. I kind of set myself up for that one.

The roller coaster makes a clunking sound from the chain as it climbs to the crest. I grip the bar. The wind gets colder as we go higher and higher. The anticipation burns inside me because of the huge drop. The coaster makes a hesitant sound, the chain clanking louder. "Oh my God."

We are high up. I see Ivy up front, looking straight ahead, probably nervous like I am. There is a charge in the air. A fear mixed with the unknown but, most of all, excitement. The rush of falling without control of your body. The only thing you can do is embrace it. The roller coaster stops, and I squeeze my eyes shut. The ride pushes forward. A sinister laugh comes from the speakers. The ride tricks riders by pausing before it lets go and plunges down the track at breakneck speed.

I feel the pull of gravity, and a strong hand grips my thigh. My eyes fly open. I turn my head to see the black mask staring at me. My throat has seized, not letting me yell at him to move his fucking hand.

I move to push his hand off, but it's no use. The ride lets go, and he wraps his arm around me, holding me to his side. The cart moves and twists, but he doesn't let go. All I can hear are distant screams, the sound of his pounding heartbeat against my ear, and feel how solid his body is. The roller coaster takes another turn, my hair whipping in the wind. I grip his arm to keep me from jerking forward. His hand slides over my thigh, and his thumb caresses me in circles, wreaking havoc between my thighs.

The roller coaster comes to a full stop, and the lap bar automatically goes up. He releases me and jumps off the ride without a backward glance.

I slide out, about to go after him, but pause. What am I doing? He preyed on my being stuck on the ride with him and touched me. *You liked it.* I look around for Ivy but don't see her until she calls my name.

"Alice!" I turn, and she is waving at me to go over.

"That was insane," I tell her, hoping the guy who sat with her didn't do anything weird.

"Did that guy say anything to you?"

"Not a word. He...sat there. He made sure I didn't jerk around, so that was a relief. I'm unsure, but if we rode together, we wouldn't have flown out of the cart. It was so fast."

She laughs. "I thought my heart would pop out of my chest when the ride stopped, and the red-eyed clown started laughing." *I didn't notice the clown because I was too busy paying attention to the man's hand on my thigh.*

We walk over to a jester with an ominous smile, selling a drink with smoke coming out of the cup. "Want some blood?"

"How much is the blood?" Ivy asks while we both pull out money, but I don't miss the way his smile falls when he looks at something behind us.

We both turn in tandem but see no one except people running to another ride with excitement. We turn back around to see him holding out two fresh drinks to us.

"Have a bloody night, and be careful. You never know what follows you," he says in a high-pitched nasal voice, like the creaking of an old, rusty gate. It carries a disconcerting, singsong quality as if he's teetering on the edge of madness. Each word is drawn with a deliberate, unsettling cadence in a nightmarish rhyme.

"Funny," I say sarcastically, grabbing the drink and taking a sip. My eyes light up, surprised it tastes good as it fizzes on my tongue. I look at Ivy. "It's good." I take a bigger sip, liking the sweet, carbonated fruit punch.

I almost forget to pay when Ivy holds out a ten-dollar bill. "How much for the drinks?" she asks, but he ignores us, staring straight ahead with black eyes that cover the white parts of his eyes.

"Fine," Ivy says, pocketing her money, and I stuff mine into my wallet.

We walk away toward the crowd, sipping our fizzy drinks.

"Funny finding you here?" Ivy turns around, but I recognize the voice. Jason. He's hanging out with Matt and Tommy from the football team. I also noticed Emma and a couple of other girls from school. "You two a thing now? You know we don't mind a little lesbian action," he says, making me cringe.

One day someone will kick his ass, and I'll pay to see it.

Ivy glares. "Fuck off."

"Fuck we can do, baby. You name the time and place, and I'll slide right in," Jason says, stepping closer to her. I wish I knew why he was so crude to her. She has done nothing to anyone, but I don't miss the lust in his eyes.

"Oh, you finally found your dick?" she retorts.

"You want me to show you, Ivy?" He pierces her with his gaze. "Do you want to see how big my dick is so you can ride it? I promise to make you scream louder than any ride here."

Pig.

"Let her go, Jason. Stop fucking around," Tommy scolds.

I glance at Tommy, not liking how close Jason is to Ivy. He looks jealous. I wonder if he would kick Jason's ass if he were to lay a finger on Ivy.

"I don't do kiddie rides, Jason. I like real men," Ivy says, then glances at Tommy. "The kind who finish the job."

"Spoken like the true slut that you are," Tommy sneers.

I guess I got ahead, thinking he had a soft spot in his black heart.

I glare at Emma when she sniggers. "You're such a ho."

I want to tell her she almost has sucked off the entire football team like a hoover, but I don't have to.

"At least I don't pay for a guy's condoms so that he can fuck me. Tell me, Emma. How was your three minutes in hell?" I almost drop the drink, watching Emma's mouth hang open.

I was right. Tommy is lame at sex and doesn't last. He probably can't get a girl off, and I can't believe Emma paid for Tommy's condoms.

"I can go all night," Jason fires back.

"Pfft. Yeah, annoying everyone," Ivy says, turning around, annoyed that they're here on the same night. "Assholes," she mutters.

"They're insufferable. All guys do is think with their dicks. It's all that asshole Jason talks about. Sex."

"That's because he can't get laid."

He probably can't. I wonder if what she said about Emma and Tommy is true. I never thought about a guy unable to last more than three minutes or how it would feel to lose your V-card. I'm eighteen, and most girls have had sex. I'm determined to experience it. I'm tired of my mother dictating my life and want to start living mine.

"Is it true?" I ask. She pauses before the trail to the haunted houses, but I continue, "What you said about Tommy?"

"Yep." She sighs. "Awful. I didn't feel it, and it was my first time. He lasted three minutes. I counted."

We step in the line to the first house. "Damn, that must suck."

"I faked it," she says with a laugh. "Then he called me a slut."

She looks like she wants to tell me more but doesn't. We don't know each other that well, and I can't believe it's taken me this long to hang out with her.

We toss our drinks in the trash by the line before entering the haunted house. My eyes try to adjust to the darkness. Noises are coming from deep inside. There is shuffling in the next room, people screaming, and the sound of chainsaws. I chew the corner of my lip. *It's a fake haunted house. This isn't real.*

We turn a corner. There are beds with props of human bodies opened, spilling their guts. I take measured steps, walking farther through the maze of hallways. I scream when a man jumps out with a grotesque-looking costume, making animal noises. Doors slam ahead. A dark figure pops out, making a noise that causes me to jolt. I'm about to jump out of my skin, but it's supposed to be fun.

I laugh along with Ivy when another one pops out.

We walk farther into the maze down a dark hallway when the

ground shakes. Ivy tries to grab me when the floor under us gives way. I jump to the right, hearing her call out my name, fading until there's silence.

"Aliiiiiice!"

"Ivy!" I reach out, but the floor raises like a trapdoor. "Ivy!" I call out.

I look around, but I'm shoved into a room. I let out a shrill scream, but a hand clamps over my mouth. It's so dark I can't see. *It isn't real, Alice. It isn't real.*

They are not supposed to touch you, but not everyone plays by the rules. I think about the guy wearing the mask on the ride, but he disappeared.

"Shhh..."

I try to move, but he has me pinned against the plywood wall. "What do you want? Let me go... This isn't funny." I swallow the lump in my throat. "You're scaring me."

"That's the point," he whispers. His breath fans the skin under my ear. His leg wedged between my thighs. "You asked what I wanted. I want... you, Alice."

"H-how do you know my name," I stammer.

"I know a lot of things," he rasps against the skin on my neck. "How you taste." I freeze.

It's him!

"Who are you? Why are you doing this?"

"You know why." He slides his hand between my thighs over the fabric of my black tights. "Did you like it, Alice?" I whimper. "Did you like me fucking you with my tongue? You came all over my face, and I sucked you dry." His fingers find my clit and rub it in circles, causing my insides to clench. "Mmm... Alice. I'm going to keep coming for you. Nothing will stop me from taking what is mine."

"What is yours?" I ask breathlessly, trying to figure out what he means.

Sweat drips down the center of my spine. My slit is wet from his touch. I like what he did. I'm sick for liking it. Being tied up and not seeing.

His hand between my thighs cups my pussy with his thumb pressed on my clit. "Everything." His nose kisses my skin, followed by his tongue. "Your fear is addicting, Alice. I feed off it, but when you come, when I'm inside you, that.... is my favorite drug."

I whimper when he rubs my clit faster. "Please," I beg. He knows what I want. It's like he manifested from the thoughts in my head.

He chuckles. "You're dying, Alice. This is what dying is like." I moan, holding his hard shoulders. If it is, I want to die again, and again.

I grind my hips, needing more.

"You're dying for me to fuck you." His thumb makes circles over my clit while his index finger teases my entrance. "Soon. If you behave and take what I give you."

I tilt my head and close my eyes, arching my back. He dips his head and pulls the neckline of my sweater, releasing my left breast. His mouth moves over my nipple, taking it between his lips and sucking hard.

"Mmm..." I gasp when he slides his hand inside the band of my panties.

"You're so wet for me, Alice. Are you going to tell Mommy what you heard and felt?"

My blood turns cold. I try to push him off me, but his grip tightens. He is so strong. There is no way I could overpower him. "Get the fuck off me," I grit. The memory of the bathroom. The things I have said to my mother. The fear. How did he know?

"Was it you in my bathroom?"

He steps back, releasing his hold, pulling out his hand, hearing him suck his fingers. I look to my left and right, trying to find a way out, but I can't.

"What are you talking about? What bathroom?"

My bottom lip trembles, and a cold chill snakes through my

veins, sobering me up. *If it wasn't him, then who was it?* I think nervously, fixing my sweater.

"Show me the way out," I demand in an unsteady voice. *I need to get away from him.*

I hear him move around the room. The sound of a door pushed open to screams and laughter from a distance. Relief washes over me when a small stream of light shines through, but he remains in the shadows.

I walk out but pause and turn my head over my shoulder. "Don't know what game you're playing or where you came from, but don't ever touch me again."

I run through the back hallway and exhale a shaky breath toward the exit.

He followed me. I don't know where he came from. But I need to find out who he is and how he gets inside the house.

CHAPTER
6

"Ivy!" I turn three hundred and sixty degrees calling her name, not caring that people give me strange looks. I spot her platinum head between two people rushing out of the haunted house laughing. "Ivy?" She turns at the sound of my voice. I run up to her and notice she has this stricken look on her face. "I've been trying to find you everywhere. Are you okay? You look flushed."

"I was trying to find a way out. I called for you."

I didn't hear her, but I'm guessing that a guy in a mask cornered her like they did me.

"Did a guy in a mask show up and freak you out?" she asks.

I nod. "Yeah. You?"

"Yeah, the same one from the roller coaster ride?" I want to go home. If he's here, he is not there. "I think we better call it a night."

"Yeah," I agree. "This place is insane."

"Now, I know why they stress on the age limit," she says, sliding her hand through my elbow and tugging me toward the exit. "I've had enough for one night."

The fog is thick. You can barely see the ticket booths. I tense, locking my arm with hers, waiting for someone to pop out and scare us.

We're about to make it to the exit, but the man in the white mask appears. Ivy ignores him and keeps walking, but he bows, holding a ticket out to her.

"Oh my God," she whispers, looking at me. I grin because that was the point of coming. I hoped she would get one.

"Take it, Ivy. He chose you. Don't think about it and... take it."

She slowly reaches and takes the ticket. He looks up for a second, and to my surprise, he places a kiss on the top of her hand. The ticket is the only thing keeping their fingers from touching.

"Thank you," she says, and I know she means it. If only the guy knew he was giving it to someone who loves the circus.

A clown hobbles over with big red shoes and blood dripping down his multicolored outfit. The corners of his mouth curl upward, showing yellow teeth.

"Thank you... for playing with us tonight," the clown says in a screechy voice. "We're DYING to have you back." The clown stares at Ivy with hunger in his gaze. "We can play a game... if you want. Do you like games?"

Ivy takes a step back. "T-that depends," she replies. I know she is trying to appear unaffected, but the way he's looking at her causes the hair on my arms to stand.

"On what?"

"How it ends."

"Come back and find out," the clown quips, causing the man with the white mask to straighten to his full height. Dark and imposing.

I don't miss the fear in the clown's eyes. Someone fucked up, but I don't want us to fuck around and find out.

"Come on," I say softly, tugging her toward the exit. "They're messing around."

I say that to calm her down and get the hell out of here. We both know more than carnival rides and haunted houses are going on here.

Locking my car, I parked on the street behind the line of cars. I avoid people walking from the house party on the sidewalk. I have never been to a party from school, but the flyer fell out of my locker, and I saw an opportunity to go.

After I dropped off Ivy last night, my mother didn't notice I had left. When I got home from school earlier, my stepfather said he needed to take care of something in Boston and had to leave. My mother passed out in her bedroom after a bottle of wine. I didn't want to be alone inside my bedroom. I was tempted to call Ivy, but I don't want to seem clingy. I'm not sure she would come to a party from school, given how everyone treats her.

I pull the hem of the black spaghetti dress down lower. It was not that short when I tried it on in front of the mirror. Then again, I wasn't walking in it. Every time I step, it rides up, but I can't do anything about it now. Pulling my jacket close together, I'm conscious that the swell of my breast is showing.

I wanted to look good when I finally went out. I want to feel pretty and hope I can attract attention. Maybe people wouldn't see me as a freak outside of school. I heard that other kids from other schools go to these things. College kids that used to go to Stockbridge High in their freshman year in college. I thought of going to a dance club, but I'm eighteen and not twenty-one and didn't have time to find one eighteen and over. If I want to meet someone, this is my best bet.

I slide my hair forward when I enter the massive house. I don't know whose house this is, but it doesn't matter. Their parents are not home, judging by the blaring music. Solo cups are in the hands of different people dancing and talking in groups.

The air is thick with the smell of sweat, perfume, and beer. It is so loud I can't even think. I walk toward the back. The smell of vape with a tinge of marijuana floats in the air. Four guys sit in the large family area with modular sofas playing *Call of Duty*. Girls are seated almost in their laps. One guy I recognize from the baseball and football team. His name is Jake.

To my left are coolers with different beers. Liquor bottles line the marble island. It looks like they raided their parents' liquor cabinet and pulled out whatever was in there. I doubt kids from high school drink bourbon or scotch. I don't think they have options, but these are not your typical high school kids by any means.

The patio door swings open, and three girls stumble inside, giggling.

"He's so hot. Jenna said his dick didn't fit when he fucked her on the hood of her car two weeks ago."

The brunette's eyes light up like she would make it fit if given the chance. "You think I have a chance with a guy like him?"

The girl next to her gives her a look like she's high for thinking she has a chance. The way they talk about him has my curiosity piqued. Who is this guy?

As I wait for them to get out of the way, I'm glad no one has noticed me yet and slip outside to the back patio. More groups of people are drinking, sitting near a firepit. A girl moans while she fucks a guy on a lounge chair behind them. Getting a room doesn't apply here, but they call Ivy a slut.

My eyes swing back to the firepit, the flames lighting up the backyard. People are drinking and smoking. Emma tilts her head back, laughing at something the tall guy standing straight ahead said. I don't miss the way the light from the fire kisses his skin, highlighting the perfect angle of his face. A straight nose, full lips, and the bluest eyes I have ever seen. His hat doesn't hide the fact that his dark hair is straight. The dark, long-sleeved sweater he wears molds to his ripped frame. Dark gray jeans hang on his narrow hips. Every time he takes a swig of his beer, his jeans slide lower, revealing an inch of smooth skin and the band of his underwear. He's the most gorgeous guy I have ever seen.

"What are you doing here?" I turn to see Mich with a Corona light in his hand.

"It's a party. Everyone was invited."

He tosses the bottle cap in the trash with a clink, his eyes watching me when he takes a pull. The sound of his lips sucking the rim of the glass bottle after he swallows. "Want a beer?" He tilts the beer in my direction.

"I don't drink beer."

"What do you drink?"

I don't know, but I don't want to act like I'm a prude and sound stupid. So I go with, "They don't have what I like."

He steps closer. I'm at a disadvantage if he draws attention, and they start messing with me, calling me a freak, and I just got here. I don't want to go home.

He stops a breath away from touching me. My eyes meet his honey brown, and I watch as they stop at the swell of my breasts and pause on my thighs and back up to my face.

"Well, well. You're a surprise. I didn't think this was under what you wear at school. If I didn't know better, you came here to hook up."

"I came to hang out. Not hook up."

He chuckles. His eyes study me, taking another pull of his beer. "You're missing the point, Alice." *Alice?* "Everyone who comes to these things hooks up. Like that girl over there riding Travis." He leans close and lowers his voice, the smell of beer on his breath burning my nose. "Jason's next, Alice." I turn my head toward the crowd around the firepit, finding Jason watching them.

He senses me watching him because his head turns. My stomach bottoms out when he looks my way, the light from the flames making his eyes appear black. Full of lust. "All the girls who come here want to hook up. They want to fuck as much as we do. The way you're dressed tells me one thing."

I look away from Jason and find blue eyes the same color as blue flames from the fire meeting mine. He tilts his head like a cowboy with a Stetson. I'm unsure if the acknowledgment is for me or because of Mich. His words swim in my mind because he is not wrong. Why do girls go to parties? To get drunk and fuck a good-looking guy or girl, hoping he could be the one. But deep down there is a slim chance of that happening. The same way guys are not interested in anything other than sex.

Mich raises his hand, holding his beer out to the gorgeous guy looking our way. "Hey, man." Everyone looks our way, and I want to die. My heart bangs in my chest, telling me what the fuck were you thinking coming here. "Look who came to have fun."

But the mystery guy doesn't smile. He doesn't wave back. A girl whispers something in his ear, but he doesn't flinch. He stares at me.

Mich tugs me along toward the crowd. "The freak wants to get freaky," Mich says with a chuckle. I'm a lamb in a slaughter-house when the guys from the football team leer at my chest like starved wolves. I wish I had chosen something else to wear.

"Oh my God, she has boobs," Emma sneers. "I bet she thinks she's going to get lucky."

I want to tell her she has none, but it's me against everyone else.

"Damn, Freak. You look fuckable. I'm impressed," Jason says.

The girl gets off the guy from the lounge chair, sliding her skirt down. While he disposes of the condom like it's a gum wrapper.

"I think it's your turn," I retort, watching Jason's jaw tick when he gets up from his chair.

"What's your name?" My head lifts, meeting blue eyes. His voice ignites an awareness between my thighs. The girl standing next to him gives me a dirty look. I can't place her as I can't place him. He doesn't go to Stockbridge because I would have remembered him. There is no way you could forget a guy with a face and body like that.

"Alice."

Jason forgets about the girl who finished fucking Travis when he sits back in his chair and looks between the beautiful stranger and me. He must be important because no one cracks a joke or interrupts him.

"What's yours?"

"Come over here, and I'll tell you." He grins. "Don't worry, I don't bite, Alice." He lowers his gaze but doesn't leer at me like the others. "Unless you want me to."

"I thought we were going somewhere?" the girl next to him whines.

Jealousy rips right through me thinking about them together. Her on top of him, him on top of her. Between her legs, making her come. That sounds crazy because I don't know this guy. I think about the man from the fair, the same one who breaks into my room. He hasn't come back, but I secretly want him to. I want him to do things that I should not allow. He gave me a taste of something I didn't know I needed, like oxygen.

I've been researching sex, BDSM, and bondage. I've watched porn while touching myself, thinking of him. I came here hoping to forget him and meet someone. I know it's stupid coming here, but there are not many options in a small town. If I dressed differently and blended in like most girls, they might look at me as more than a freak.

A girl walks out the patio door, rummaging in the outside cooler, and I spot her grabbing a wine cooler. I heard it's better than beer and lighter than hard liquor. Making my way to the cooler, I lift the lid and grab a red one once she walks back inside the house.

I try to lift the cap with my hand and gasp when the ridges dig into my skin.

"Careful." I look up, meeting blue eyes gripping the cold bottle, hoping it could cool off how hot he makes me feel when he looks at me.

I point toward the firepit. "I thought you had plans to go somewhere?"

His gaze slides over me. This time, he does not hide the fact that he is openly staring at my breasts. "I did." His eyes lift. "Until you showed up."

I snort. "I'm not like those girls over there or the ones inside."

He steps closer, taking the bottle from my hand and twisting the cap effortlessly. "I never said you were." He hands me the bottle.

"Thank you," I say, bringing the bottle to my lips. The red wine cooler makes me squint at the taste. It burns as it goes down my throat, and I try not to cough like an idiot.

He raises a perfect brow. "First time?"

I swallow. First time for what? Is he asking me if it's my first time at a party? My mind goes straight to the gutter. Is that something a guy would ask me if I want him to have sex with me?

He points at the bottle. "Drinking."

I must have looked stupid trying to open the bottle. *Get a grip, Alice.*

I nod. "I'm not much of a drinker." I don't drink. I tried my mother's wine once and spit it out in the sink, sputtering at how thick it tasted on my tongue. It was red, and it tasted dry.

"What do you like to drink?" Water or soda but I can't tell him that without sounding lame. So I say, "Whatever tastes good."

He pierces me with his gaze. "I couldn't agree more. If it doesn't taste good, why drink it." He isn't talking about drinks anymore.

"What do you like to drink?" I volley back.

"That depends."

"On what?"

"How it tastes when I drink it the first time."

My cheeks flush, and I let out a nervous laugh, but he doesn't smile. The silence between us stretches full of tension. His gaze is fixated on mine, and I can't deny the magnetic pull. Everything around us fades away.

The music.

The distant conversation.

The eyes cast our way.

All I can feel is him. There is no mistake he was the one the girls were talking about inside. He has a way of making you notice him and no one else. It's like nothing or no one else exists. He's the guy you remember. The one who made your heart somersault when you steal a glance. The one who makes your heart race. The one who makes your palms get clammy when he's close. The one you think about when you touch yourself needing to come.

"Where are you from?" I ask, taking a pull of the wine cooler, welcoming the burn and rich taste of alcohol needing the courage.

"Here."

"Where do you go to school?"

"I'm a senior at Stockbridge."

I pinch my brows in confusion. I've never seen him before, and I've been there all four years. "How come I've never seen you there?"

"Come with me, and I'll tell you." He takes my hand and tugs me over to the side of the house. There is a bench hidden in a medium-sized garden. The evidence of the fall season is all around us. The leaves have fallen from the trees. The brisk air on this side of the house cools my overheated skin. He takes a seat. I can feel the heat coming off him when I sit. The smell of his citrusy cologne floats over me. "I'm an online student."

"Oh." I try to pull the hem of my dress down my thighs but give up because I would have to lift my ass off the bench to tug it lower. "I didn't know Stockbridge had an online program."

"They do," he says, burning a hole with his gaze on my thigh. That is how he knows Jason and Mich from school.

I take a sip of the wine cooler, kicking myself because my dress rises higher on my thighs when I raise my arm to take a sip. "What's your name?

He shifts his weight to face me and pulls my chin so I can look at him. With his mouth inches from mine, he says, "My name is

Lazarus." His heated gaze is on my lips while I process his name. "Some people from school call me Laz."

"I like Lazarus." It means God has helped in the Bible. It suits him.

"If you wish." I pull my brows in because I could have sworn I heard a hint of a British accent. But when he continues, I must have misheard. He speaks perfect American English. "Who are you here with, Alice?"

"You," I blurt. My face heats. I can't believe I said that.

I'm relieved when he smiles, but his eyes are on my lips like he wants to kiss me. He's in the heat of the moment type of guy. He promised the girl by the firepit to go somewhere, but he is here with me instead because I'm unfamiliar. I'm a mystery to him, and he will move on once he figures me out. He will be my greatest memory, while I'll be a distant one.

"That means you'll leave with me."

"W-why is that?"

I could only imagine where he would take me, but I bet it would involve a smooth surface or even a bed.

He closes the distance, his lips brushing mine in a feathery kiss. "Because that's what people do when they first meet and don't want the night to end." His tongue peeks out, licking my bottom lip like I'm sure he would my pussy. Full of wet heat and promise. "They leave together. Alone."

His lips press against mine. Soft at first, then rough and demanding. Hungry. Our tongues meet. A low whimper hums in my throat.

I fist his black sweater against his chest, pulling him closer. His fingers slide in my hair and pull, tilting my head back to deepen the kiss. His other hand is on my bare thigh, teasing the skin right under the hem of my dress.

Our lips break apart to catch our breath, our foreheads resting against each other. His hand moves to the inner part of my thigh, and the other slides behind my neck.

"Come with me, Alice. If it's what you want because it's what I want." My palm rests flat on his chest. This is my chance. The little voice in my head tells me to be careful. You don't know him, but he doesn't know me either. He doesn't know about my past.

I nod. "Okay."

CHAPTER
7

Twigs and rocks crunch underneath my tires following Lazarus's blacked-out classic SS Camaro. The path leads to a beautiful house with glass windows surrounded by trees. The house isn't big like the manor by any means, but it's like a modern cabin nestled deep in the woods.

White lights surround the landscape. There is glass instead of walls between wood panels in a sleek design. The architecture captures peace without sacrificing luxury. A big contrast to the houses in Stockbridge.

I park behind his car. The rumble of the powerful engine shuts off. I shut the door of my car. Lazarus's black boots hit the ground when he steps out of his car. I take him in when he stands, shutting the door of his car with a thud. Jeans mold to his muscled thighs. The black sweater shows off muscled biceps and broad shoulders. He's gorgeous. I love the small piercing in his nose with his straight black hair on top.

He arches a brow when I get caught ogling him like an idiot. "Do you want to come inside?" he asks.

I blink, trying to get a grip on our differences. He's attractive, and I'm plain. Guys like him don't invite girls like me inside or ask me out on dates. I'm unapproachable at school for obvious reasons, and I'm nervous.

"Yeah."

He nudges his head toward the oversized wood door, and I follow him inside. The blast of cool air hits me once I step inside, causing me to shiver. The smell of bergamot greets me. The space has white walls, dark wood, and glass. It's clean and simple. His parents must have money like most kids that go to Stockbridge High. There are no family pictures on the credenza against the wall.

I didn't ask if he had a girlfriend, and he didn't ask if I had one either. He might assume with the way the guys at the party treated me, that meant I didn't have one. If he had a girlfriend, I would leave. It would give me a reason.

He pauses and places his keys on the marble counter. It's a direct contrast to the rest of the kitchen, with the butcher block a shade lighter than the wood flooring. When he moves, the kitchen lights flicker on, sensing his movement. The house is impressive. In the daylight, I bet you feel like you're standing in a forest but protected from the weather.

"Do you have a girlfriend?"

He looks up, blue eyes surrounded by thick black lashes. "Don't you think it's a little late to be asking me that?"

"You didn't ask if I have a boyfriend," I counter.

He leans over, placing his elbows on the counter to study me for a second. "I didn't ask because it's not important."

I lick the corner of my lip because my mouth has gone dry. He's confident and cocky. A guy like Lazarus wouldn't give a shit if a girl has a boyfriend or not. I suspect being with a girl is a one-time thing.

"You're not afraid some guy would want to kick your ass for inviting his girl to your house?"

He laughs through his nose, and the way his lips twitch makes him even more attractive. He licks his bottom lip. My eyes track the movement, desperate for them to be on my skin. What is it about this guy with me losing my mind?

"Why would I be afraid? I didn't force his girl to come over. She drove and followed me home. It's not my problem, it's his.

He should have kept his girl interested. She wouldn't be kissing a guy she met at a party or...it means she doesn't have a boyfriend at all." He turns and grabs a bottle of water from the fridge, opens it, and stands in front of me, holding it out. "Thirsty?"

I nod. Anything to match how wet I feel between my legs. He slowly tips the bottle over my lips. The cool water in my throat causes my nipples to strain against my bra.

I stop swallowing, and the water fills my mouth, causing it to spill down my chin before he has enough time to pull it back.

"Shit. I-I'm sorry," I sputter, stepping back. The cold trail slides between my breasts.

He steps back and drinks from the bottle. My eyes are fixed on the smooth column of his throat while his stare down at me.

When he disposes of the bottle, he comes back and slides my bag from my shoulder, placing it on the counter. His fingers slide under my jacket, pushing it over my shoulders. I stand frozen. My pulse pounds in my ears. I inhale his scent mixed with his cologne.

"I don't have a girlfriend, Alice. And we both know you don't have a boyfriend." I watch his full lips move, holding on to his every word keeping me from falling off the edge. "Does that make you feel better, Alice?" His teeth scrape over his bottom lip. His finger trace the trail of water between my breasts, snagging the neckline of my dress. He pulls it down enough that the straps slide down my shoulders. My bra goes next. He leaves my breasts exposed to the cool air, and my hard nipples ache for the heat of his mouth. My eyes locked on his like I'm in a trance. Hypnotized by him, and nothing is telling me to stop him. "Do you want me to fuck you, Alice?"

"Yes."

He nods, eyes locked on my nipples. I gasp when he grips the back of my thighs and lifts me off the ground like I'm weightless, setting me on the island. He pushes my thighs wider, and I lean back, placing my hands on the cool marble.

"You're beautiful, do you know that?" I don't. I've never had a guy tell me I'm pretty. I look away. "No one has told you, have they?"

"Told me what?" I ask, playing dumb.

His hands slide up my thighs. A whimper escapes my throat when his fingers grip my panties and tug. I lift my butt, and he pulls them down my legs. He holds them in his hand, bringing them to his nose. *It's hot.*

"Your panties are drenched. I love the way your pussy smells." My dress is bunched around my waist like a belt, his gaze focused between my thighs. I almost slide off the island when his thumb presses against my clit. A charge of electricity ignites within. He circles his thumb in a rhythm, making wet noises by how wet I am. His eyes flick up. "Have you ever had your pussy sucked, Alice?"

My thoughts go to Hade's Manor and my room. The chains on my wrist. A mouth with a wet tongue waking me up from a deep sleep. My masked stranger.

I nod. "Yes."

"Did you like it?"

"Yes."

"Was he good?" I nod again. "Did he make you come?"

"Yes. The same way I heard those girls at the party say the same about you." His thumb stops mid-stroke, and he pinches his brows.

I don't know why I said that, but I don't want to think about my masked stranger or the way he made me feel.

He doesn't move, and I'm self-conscious. My self-esteem, along with my courage, takes a nosedive. I feel exposed. I don't look like those pretty girls at the party, and I'm not popular like them, making me question why he asked me to come.

There's an awkward silence, and an expression of guilt moves across his features.

My eyes sting.

They call you a freak for a reason, Alice. He didn't use the front door where everyone could see him with you when you two left.

My bottom lip trembles, causing me to straighten and making him step back. "I gotta go," I say, pulling the straps of my dress and bra over my breast.

I jump off the island, glad my shoes are still on as I try not to let my tears fall while I pull my dress down. Shame burns me up like flames. I almost fell for it. There is no way a guy like him would give me a second of his attention unless he has an ulterior motive.

He says nothing or stops me, but he doesn't have to. His reaction when I mentioned those girls is clear. He could have brought one of them here instead of me.

This was a setup.

I grab my bag and rush to the front door. I turn before I close it, watching him standing there staring at the floor. "You didn't have to lie to me. I know I'm not beautiful. I know I don't look like those girls. Whatever game this is, you need to stop because I won't fall for it. In my eyes, you're one of them."

Silence.

My eyes blur, and that's the push I need to shut the door behind me. I rush to my car and slide inside. The dash lights up, and I'm glad it's easy to place it in reverse. I look up one last time and see the front door is still closed. *He will not go after you, Alice. He got caught.*

"I am a freak," I say out loud, a tear sliding down my cheek. The look on his face said it all.

CHAPTER
8

I snuck back in last night and cried myself to sleep. My mother didn't argue when I told her I wanted to stay home from school today. She must think I'm about to have an episode, as she calls it. In her eyes, I'm unstable. The thought of me being sick never crossed her mind. It's always a mental issue with her. She prefers for me to stay home from school than to embarrass her. If she only knew that it was the opposite. If she hadn't opened her mouth, I wouldn't have been bullied at school or called names.

Honestly, I'm not ready to return to school after last night. I need a day to get over what happened and how it would blow up in my face.

A sound comes from within the walls, but I ignore it. I don't care about the noises I hear or think I hear. Not anymore. I'm tired of it dictating my life for so long and molding me in a way I can't control. The best thing I could think of is to act like it isn't there.

I wake up after dozing off. I grab my phone, and check the school's social media page, scrolling through posts, pictures, and comments. Cheerleaders, jocks, and popular kids posted pictures from parties and football games. Some are from last night, but none of the posts have Lazarus. Not one.

It's nine o'clock, and the moonlight streams through my

window. The trees cast shadows on the walls like growing vines in my room.

An alert catches me by surprise on my phone that reads. "CLUB MEADOW 18 AND OVER. GIRL'S GET IN BEFORE MIDNIGHT. I've seen this place before. It's located near a gas station with a charging station for electric vehicles right on the edge of town.

It is the only dance club in town that allows people under twenty-one. I forgot all about it. I'm sure you have to show ID to get a special band to drink liquor, but I don't want to go there to drink.

My stepfather isn't back from Boston. My mom said that something held him up, so she said she was heading over there to stay with him at a hotel.

I could go, and they would never know. Sneaking out has become a norm as of late. It's not like they could do anything about it except maybe kick me out. They would do me a favor if that happened. I wanted to move out after I graduated for so long, but my stupid mouth has hindered my chance. Any hope of that has evaporated like smoke. My mother thinks that I wouldn't be able to handle it because of my fragile mind. Sometimes I feel like a chained dog given enough slack to wander out but pulled back if I go too far.

I check my reflection in the mirror for the tenth time. I hear a banging behind my wall, but I ignore it. The faster I get the fuck out of here, the clearer my mind would be.

A door slams, making me jump. *Ignore it. Alice.*

My hand shakes when I check the back of my short skirt. I'm wearing fishnets with black boots. I saw the look online and ordered something similar from Amazon. I tug the cropped jacket and zip it over the cropped top that matches the black skirt. I made an effort with my makeup. I watched tutorials the other night until I fell asleep trying to get the cat-eye effect look. My hair is loose down my back and hits right above my waist. I look different, but that's the point. I want to look sexy and feel free. I'm tired of feeling trapped.

After the twenty-minute drive, I locked my car after finding an empty spot in the back of the club. I head to the entrance, where a huge man wearing a black suit with a flashlight checks ID before letting people in. My hands are sweaty when I head to the back of the line, ignoring the curious stares aimed my way.

When I hand him my ID, he shakes his head. He waves his hand, gesturing me to go right in. I pocket my ID behind my phone, along with the money I pulled out of my account. The place smells like sweat and smoke. The writhing bodies rub together on the dance floor to the beat of the dance music. It's hot, so I unzip my jacket, moving through the throng of bodies toward the back, where there is more space to stand.

A guy walks up and leans in close to my ear. "Want to dance?"

I'm not much of a dancer, but there are so many people here no one would notice if I make a fool of myself. There is hardly room to dance. Except to take two steps side to side or forward like the woman and the man next to me dry fucking each other.

I look at his face. He has brown eyes. He isn't Lazarus, but he's cute. He's wearing a pair of jeans and a blue T-shirt. I give him a half shrug. "Sure." He smiles.

After the third song and telling him I needed the restroom, he tugs me toward the back of the club. He said his name is Lance, and he works on motorcycles like Harleys.

After the next turn down the dim hallway, I noticed no restroom sign. I'm about to tell him that, but he pulls me into a room with pink lighting and graffiti all over the walls. He takes my lips in his.

I could smell the alcohol on his breath. His hands slide up my skirt, gripping my ass. "You're so hot, Alice," he breathes over my lips, pressing the evidence of his hard cock between my thighs. I blink. "See what you do to me?" He grinds his hips. My stomach tightens when his kisses turn rough and frantic. He wraps his hand over my throat. I'm about to pull his hand off, but Lance is flung into the air like he was sucked by a tornado and lands across the room.

My mouth drops open.

He's here. The man from that night in my room and the haunted carnival. He's dressed in all black, wearing a black mask over his head.

An unease settles in the pit of my stomach.

"What the fuck, man?" Lance looks up, sliding down to the floor. "Who the fuck are you?" He tries to get up, but the masked man grips him by the throat. Lance is wheezing, trying to breathe.

If I run out of this room, I won't forgive myself if something happens to Lance. Yes, he took advantage of me by bringing me back here, but I was leading him on the entire night. I would tell him to stop. "Stop it." Lance's eyes are bulging out of his eye sockets, but my plea falls on deaf ears.

"Please, you're choking me." Lance squeezes out between breaths.

I walk up to the masked man, trying to pry his hands off. "Stop, you're going to kill him."

He leans down and whispers, "And you're going to watch."

He releases Lance and pulls out a knife, holding him up by his brown hair. Lance tries to take in air in his depleted lungs.

"Tell me, would you still fuck her if she told you to stop?" His voice sounds changed like he is speaking through a device. But his question has my attention.

Would he have stopped? I don't know why, but the thought crossed my mind when his hand wrapped around my throat to tell him to stop. I wasn't aroused. I wasn't ready.

Lance tries to get away, but the masked man points the knife near his eyes. "I'm not going to repeat myself. Answer the question. If your cock was out and about to plunge into her tight cunt, and she said no, would you have stopped? The truth shall set you free."

I glance at Lance, his eyes meeting mine. "No."

Disgust causes the bile to pool in the back of my throat. He would have raped me.

Lance's eyes swing to my right. The point of the knife stabs Lance in the eye and then the other. His body begins to twitch, not letting him scream, but instead, blood gurgles out of his mouth. A scream is lodged in my throat.

My hands cover my ears, hearing his grunts as he stabs Lance's face repeatedly, holding him by the hair like a rag doll. The knife is full of blood. When it's over, he begins to stab his groin area repeatedly. There is blood everywhere. Splattered on the walls and pooling on the floor.

I can't stop shaking.

When he's done, Lance's eyes are missing, and nothing is left of his face. He stabs his head one last time, letting him drop on the floor bleeding out.

I cover my face. "Please," I beg. He grips my arm and drags me out by the back exit after closing the door to the back room. "Where are you taking me?"

He doesn't answer and pushes me toward my car, opens the passenger side, and pushes me inside. I reach over to the screen to lock the driver's side, but I'm too late. He gets in.

"I'm not going to hurt you."

"Who are you? Why did you kill him?" My voice shakes in fear.

"He was going to rape you, and he touched... touched you. If you were so horny and dying to fuck, you could have waited for me in your bed with your legs wide open."

"You're crazy."

"Last I heard, so are you."

"Fuck you."

"I am going to fuck you, Alice. If anyone touches you, they will end up like that piece of shit back there."

"Is it you? In the house? The noises."

"I don't know what you're talking about."

"Why are you doing this to me?"

He doesn't answer, but I know where he's taking me--back to Hades Manor.

CHAPTER 9

The door to my bedroom slams behind me. I'm shaking and don't know what to do. If I call my mother, she won't believe me. If I call the police, it will be the same as last time. He will leave, and given my history, they will think I'm having one of my episodes.

"I'm not going to hurt you, Alice, but you already know that by now."

It is true. He could have killed me back there at the club or taken me somewhere, killed me, and dumped me in the woods.

"Why did you have to kill him?"

He tilts his head and steps closer. "So he wouldn't rape the next girl when she says no. He was going to force himself on you, Alice. And...he put his filthy hands on you. His dirty mouth on you. I need to cleanse the filth off you, Alice."

"Get out and leave me alone." My voice shakes. Images of Lance's face play in my head like an infomercial.

"I'm afraid that won't happen. You want to spread your legs so badly, then you will do it for me." He undoes the button of his pants and takes himself out. His cock is big. The head is red with a piercing on the tip. He strokes himself from base to tip. "You want to feel or do you want to see, Alice. My mask or yours? Either way, you will be chained to your bed like last time. The choice is yours, but tonight, I will not leave until your cunt drips with my cum."

I shake my head. "I'm not on the pill, and you can't force me."

He chuckles. "I don't think you will kick me out when I'm pounding you into the mattress, Alice." He gets closer until I'm at the edge of my bed, jerking his cock. "Open that pretty mouth and taste me."

He smells like man and sex. I feel a trickle of my arousal drip between my thighs. He makes me so wet when he talks to me like that. He radiates danger, sin, and sex. I'm convinced I'm sick because this man murdered someone right in front of me, and I want him to fuck me.

"Suck my dick, Alice." I grab the smooth skin of his cock and sit on the edge of my bed. I look up at the mask covering his face. "Take off your jacket and spread your thighs before you wrap those pretty lips on my dick."

I do as he asks.

I look up when I take him in my mouth––the softness of skin and the metal on the tip of the flat part of my tongue. I feel powerful. More powerful than he must have felt when he killed Lance. I suck and twirl my tongue, hearing him groan. His hand fists my hair.

His grunts break the silence in the room. The tip of his cock hits the back of my throat when he increases his speed, causing me to gag. "Relax your throat. Take it, Alice. All of me." I ignore the pain when he tugs my hair and fucks my face. I can taste the saltiness of his pre-cum on the back of my tongue. Drool slides down my chin.

"So pretty," he rasps. "So innocent. It feeds the demon inside me, Alice. The one that wants to break you." My lips pull tight, wrapped around his big cock, loving the way he tastes. "I own your mind, your soul, the clit that throbs every time you think of me when you play with your cunt." Tears leak down my cheeks from the truth of his words. My throat is already sore. "Play with your pussy," he demands.

I slide my cold fingertips between the fishnets, feeling the evidence of my arousal–how wet I am. He continues to fuck my mouth rough without apology. He grunts with each tug of my hair. I'm wet everywhere. My pussy. My chest from my saliva sliding down my neck. I moan and hum on his cock.

When he's close, he pulls out. He leans close to my ear. "I need your consent to fuck your virgin cunt, Alice. That's what you want, isn't it?" I wipe the drool off my chin. His hand replaces my fingers between my thighs. "You want me to break this pussy open and feed it my cock. It's what you wanted at the club. The other night when I was sucking your greedy pussy, and it's what you crave right now." I whimper.

It is what I want. This man makes me feel things I never thought I could feel. Fantasies I've thought about when I think of sex. The way it would feel different with a cock inside me instead of my dainty fingers playing with my clit. I don't care if I don't know him or know what he looks like. He doesn't call me a freak or think I'm crazy. He's crazy enough for both of us. He killed for me because Lance touched me. I could have said no to Lance, and my night would have ended differently.

"Yes. I want you to fuck me."

His thumb presses on my aching clit. "Mask or no mask?"

"Huh?"

Was he going to take it off?

"I wear it, or you wear it, but I will chain you to the bed. Your choice."

"I-I want to see you."

I want to see his face. I want to know the man who will take me for the first time, but I would do it if he refused. There was a reason I ran out of Lazarus's house. He's the reason.

"In time." He bends and pulls the chains I didn't know were under my bed. "But not yet."

I scoff. "I can't see the man who fucks me for the first time?"

He loops the chains on each side of the headboard like he's done this a hundred times. Three, if my mind wasn't playing tricks on me. Three times, he has come during the night to eat my pussy when I thought it was a dream. The other times, I don't know if it was him or if I dreamed it.

He grips me by the throat. The black leather from his gloves against my wet skin. "It doesn't make a difference."

"Why not?" I challenge, my chest heaving. Saliva runs down my belly button.

"Because I'm the only man who will fuck your pussy."

"Cocky much? You're full of yourself, aren't you?"

"Try me. You've seen my work."

I have.

He grabs my hand, pulling me toward the headboard. "Lie down. Hands up."

I place my hands above my head, lying on my pillow. He fastens each wrist, giving me a little slack from the chains.

The bed dips. My pussy drips like a faucet down the crack of my ass. He removes my boots but leaves the fishnets. He pushes my skirt around my waist. His fingers slide between my thighs. "Fuck," he mutters. I look down, and he pulls the fishnets roughly. My panties go next when he tosses them across the room.

The only light in the room is from the moon filtering from the window. He must have removed his gloves because I feel his fingers cooler than my hot slit. I jerk when he plunges two fingers into my soaked cunt. "You're so wet for me, Alice. You want me to turn you into a filthy whore."

I moan. "Yes."

I do. I don't know shit about having sex, but I know that I wanted to be dirty for him. I want him to own me like he wants to.

He stretches me with his two fingers. My pussy makes squelching noises every time he slides them in and out. He reaches up and pulls my top down, releasing my aching breasts. My nipples beg for his mouth.

My eyes roam over his frame. Black hoodie, black jeans. The

carbon fiber of his mask looks at me like a slasher wanting to fuck his prey before he ends her.

"You look so beautiful, Alice. Desperate. Begging for what I give you." He grips his thick veiny cock. It's huge, the shadow of his cock on the walls. The head is so big, I hope he won't make me bleed out. My breaths come hard and fast. My pussy throbs when he brushes the head over my slit.

"This is the only time I will have mercy on your cunt because this will hurt, Alice. It's going to hurt so fucking bad, but then it's going to feel good. So good you will beg me to leave my fat dick inside your pussy and never take it out." I swallow and open my thighs wider. He looks down, lifts his mask just enough to keep his face obscured, and lets go, a string of spit landing on my clit. I moan. "Greedy little whore." He brushes the tip of his cock, smearing it.

I grind my hips, wanting to come.

I watch him. I can't see his face, but he's watching me. I've watched porn on my phone, wanting to learn how to pleasure myself. The last time, it was a woman taking a man's cock in her pussy, and then he put it in her ass. I saw how she moaned, grinding her hips and teasing her nipples. It's where I learned to play with my clit. The man in the video was wearing a mask, and he was ramming his cock in her ass hard. You could see the ripples on the skin of her ass when he pounded her from behind. His fingers were rubbing her clit in rhythm as she dipped her middle finger inside her pussy.

The tip of his cock slides in, and I gasp from the burn pulling my hands and hearing the chains rattle. "Ow," I cry. He pauses. I lick my lips. "Don't stop."

"Give in to me, Alice. Don't fight me. You need to relax."

Then I remember. Tilting my head, the fat head of his cock with a piercing on the shaft penetrating me, I stammer, "C-condom."

He laughs. The small line of hair on my pussy stands. A resonant, low-pitched chuckle reverberates, making my heart beat fast.

It reminds me of rolling thunder on a stormy night. He spreads the lips of my pussy with two fingers and pinches my clit.

"Mmm..."

"This cunt is mine. It's going to drip for me. Milk me dry. Weep for me. Now, it's going to bleed for me. You're on the pill, Alice. Mommy made sure. Skip it. And your pussy will breed for me. The choice is yours."

"How..."

He pushes deeper, and my ass lifts off the bed. I'm so full. So tight. The only thing I can do is squeeze my hands.

"More?"

"Yes," I hiss. "Give me more. Give me your name."

"Hades."

"Like the house?" I ask breathlessly.

"Yes, it's what brought us together. The house you hate so much but will learn to love after tonight when you bleed all over my cock."

Fuck, he's dirty.

"Hades, fuck me. Please."

He growls and pushes farther. I gasp and take lungfuls of air, breathing through the pain.

"One more push. One more push, and I'm going to fuck this cunt hard. You can scream. You can fight. You can't break free, and I won't stop."

He grips my hips, holding me still, and pushes the rest of the way in. "Ow, shit. It hurts." I see white spots behind my eyes, but I welcome the burn.

He pulls out. My head angles, confused. He swipes the palm of his hand over my swollen cunt. He holds it up to the moonlight, turning his head to the side, and slowly slides his hand under the mask and licks it.

He licked the blood.

"Mmm... your innocence tastes so good, Alice." He turns to face me, and without warning, he shoves his cock hard inside me, causing me to slide up the bed. He fucks me hard. Like an animal.

It feels raw and primal. My pussy grips his cock. A dirty moan escapes my throat over the sopping noises my pussy makes with each thrust. "Fuck. Your cunt is so tight," he growls, grinding his hips and stretching me with his cock.

He lifts my legs over his shoulders, bracing his hands on the bed. My hands brace the headboard, my nails scratching the wood for the brutal fucking he will give me. He thrusts hard. Digging his cock deep. I can feel him in my belly. Hard and powerful. My tits bounce. My pussy spasms. My screams bounce off the walls of how good he feels inside me. I yelp when he slaps my tits hard––the sting causes my orgasm to crest.

"Again!" I scream.

"You like it, don't you?"

He slaps my other breast again.

"Yes. Mmm...Fuck, yes, Hades." I can feel my skin bloom. The heat spreads over my chest like wildfire, sending a message straight to my clit. I grind my ass, seeking more of his cock.

His hand wraps around my throat, squeezing my air, but I can still breathe. I moan, and he slides his other hand down to where we are joined. His fingers teased my clit. Is he? He slides a finger inside with his cock teasing my clit at the same time.

"You're so beautiful, Alice. Come for me," he says between breaths. "Look at your pussy spread open, taking my big cock in that virgin cunt. Ready for my hot cum." I'm about to come, and he knows it. My legs are stiff over his shoulders. I reach to touch him, but the chains pull tight.

I groan. "Fuck, Hades. Harder! I'm going to come." His hand dips between the crack of my ass until he finds my forbidden hole and slides his thumb inside. I see stars—explosions behind my eyes. I come hard. Harder than I thought I could ever come.

He doesn't let up fucking my ass with his thumb and my pussy with his cock. "Open your legs, Alice," he demands. "Wider!"

I do. His thumb slides out, and two fingers slide back in with his cock, filling me. My pussy will be useless when he's done. He's ruined it.

He rubs on my clit and feels the need to come again. My head whips from side to side. The sensation is too much. My legs begin to shake. "H-Hades," I sputter. "I..."

He comes on a roar. Hot cum spills inside my battered pussy. My bottom lip trembles before a dirty moan escapes my lips. I'm coming again. My pussy clenches, soaking his cock.

My legs are limp and fall to the side. I'm spent. A tingling sensation begins to creep up my skin. I can't feel my legs. He slides out of me, and I wince. My pussy feels sore and used. His hand dips between my legs. I'm positive I've ruined the sheets. He cups my pussy. I can feel it leaking. He brings his hand to my mouth. "Lick us."

My nostrils flare. I lick his palm with the flat part of my tongue. The taste of copper, metallic, salty cum, and musk. *Us.*

His head dips near my ear. My breaths are shallow, and my pulse is heavy between my legs. I reach for him again, only for my hands to be pinned above my head. "We're not finished, Alice. I'm... not finished."

CHAPTER 10

The cold wind bites my ears as I venture deeper into the back of the property. I breathe in the fresh, cold air. The silence was eating me for the past two days inside the house. After Hades was done, my eyes rolled back in my head, and sleep took me under from exhaustion. He cleaned me while I was chained up. He ate my pussy and then fucked me again. I didn't know where I ended, and he began. One orgasm blended into another. My legs were numb, and my insides were raw, but that was how he wanted me. I also knew he would pop out whenever he wanted. When I least expected it.

The Hades estate has thirty acres, maybe more. I never ventured out this deep. Wilfred said there was a creek, but my mother warned me to stay within a safe distance for fear I would get lost. I used to listen to her paranoia, but not anymore. Sometimes I think she needs therapy instead of me.

A twig snaps, and I catch my step. I push a branch out of the way. My eyes widen when I notice a small Ferris wheel in the mist of overgrown grass. The kind they have behind a church in the summer when they try to raise money. There's a merry-go-round. A mechanical swing that raises in the air with five swings with rusted chains on each side. It looks like it's frozen in time.

The old Ferris wheel has missing seats and creaking joints. It looms like a skeletal sentinel over the grounds. Once-colorful gondolas are now faded and cracked and sway in the breeze.

Amid the forgotten rides, nature has reclaimed its territory. Vines and weeds snake their way around the rusted metal. A forgotten gem of nostalgia but silent, abandoned, and steeped in memories. Telling a poignant story of joy and the relentless march of time.

Walking up to the Ferris wheel, I push the gondola to see if it will come off. I smile, wondering if the family that used to live here built it for their child. I sit in the gondola. My hand swipes at the vines and rust, revealing two letters engraved over the metal. L.H. H must stand for Hades. L...

"What are you doing here?"

My head whips around. My heart is in my throat, and I sigh in relief. "You scared me."

"Wilfred said he saw you venture this way alone."

"I wanted to get some fresh air." I pinch my brows, staring at the letter L. "When did you and Mom get back?"

His eyes gleam. "About an hour ago." He looks up at the Ferris wheel and then at the swings. "Cool, isn't it?" He checks the sturdiness of the metal. "The estate lawyer mentioned the small fair when I rented the place." His eyes meet mine. "The late family built it. I think they had a son or two. I'm not sure."

"He built this?"

He nods. "It appears so. It hasn't been used in years. Obviously, from the looks of it. Maybe more than that. That's why I never told you about it. I thought it would be dangerous since no one cared for it."

I look around the small fair and imagine a little boy or two laughing. The parents must have loved their children. The father loved his sons from the looks of it. Nostalgia from my own father bites at me.

"He must have been something," I mumble.

My stepfather looks up. "What was that?"

I shake my head. "The father. He must've been something. He loved his son or sons."

"Rumor has it..." I stand, hearing the metal groan, cutting his words when I move to step off. He grabs me by the waist with two hands so I don't fall, carrying me to the ground. I falter a bit from the soreness between my thighs. His fingers tighten for a second around my hips. His hand was almost on the swell of my ass, making me cringe. "You okay?"

I turn my head over my shoulder where his hand is. I look up, his blue eyes dark like the sea for a second. He lets go and continues, "Rumor has it, the Hades family owned theme parks all across the country. They also own the fairgrounds and provide all the rides for fairs in different states."

Sometimes, my stepfather looks at me in a certain way that doesn't sit well with me. He's an attractive man. There is no doubt. Since I was little, he would defend me against my mother unless it involved this house. The way he would look at me a certain way. A hand that lingered a second longer than necessary. The car. The allowance. I didn't ask for those things, but he provided them. I was grateful he did it, but not for the looks or the lingering touches.

"They were very wealthy."

"Not from the theme parks. That was a hobby. The Hades family is insanely rich or was."

"High millions?"

He laughs. "Try high billions."

"How come no one knows about them?"

"Because they originated from England."

"How do you know all this?"

"Not from the lawyer, I assure you. I did some digging."

I pause right before we enter the garden that leads to the patio. "They don't want to sell you the house, do they?"

His jaw tightens. I struck a nerve. "They will," he says, clenching his teeth.

Not wanting to piss him off, I smile. "Of course, they will. Why wouldn't they?"

"Positivity. That's my girl."

I'm not your girl, but I don't say that. The only thing we have in common is my mother. I look around but don't see her through the kitchen window. He pulls the French door open. "Where's Mom?" I ask.

"She is on her way from Boston."

He walks inside, but I don't follow him. He lied. He said they both got in an hour ago. But why?

"Is everything alright?"

I jerk like I got electrocuted. "Jesus, Wilfred."

The old man smiles at me with his white teeth. Dentures. "I'm sorry, Alice," he says in his British accent.

I smile. "It's alright, Wilfred. I didn't hear you walk up behind me."

I love his British accent. I could talk to him for hours to hear him speak. It's different and proper. When I was ten, I tried to speak with a British accent in front of the mirror. I would hear faint laughter inside the walls and stop. It got worse. The whispers and noises. A laugh from a little kid. Like the ghost of the boy who died in the accident.

His expression looks guilty, like he made a mistake or said something he shouldn't have. "I'm sorry. I told him you were out there. He came to me asking for you. He looked worried and didn't know what to do."

"I'm fine, Wilfred. I needed fresh air. I'm not mad at you or anything."

He looks toward his cottage and then back at me. "The swings work."

I blink, hoping I heard right. "The swings?"

"Yes, the swings. The Ferris wheel needs some polishing, but the swings work fine."

I look at the door and then back at Wilfred with a grin.

Feeling like a little kid sneaking off to play after their parents told them they were grounded, I say, "Show me."

I WANT TO ASK HIM SO MANY QUESTIONS WHEN I follow his steady gait back to the little fair. Why didn't he tell me about it? I get why my stepfather and mother would keep it from me. But Wilfred didn't seem like the type not to tell me about it since I was a little kid. I would have loved to play on it. A secret place no one else went or knew about because they were dead.

"How come you didn't tell me?"

He pauses and turns, giving me a side profile of his weathered cheek. "They told me not to." *They* meant my stepfather and mother. "Estate rules. No one is allowed to be back here."

"Why? Because it's unsafe?"

"No. The fair was built for the Hades boys."

So there were two.

"Did they die?"

He nods. "Yes. They died with their parents in that horrible accident. Everything went into a trust. The lot of it. It was the saddest thing. The boys were about your age. What age..."

"Here we are," he says, cutting me off.

He walks to a generator and flicks a breaker switch. The swing lights up with a melody. The lights flash. It's no different from the real thing but on a smaller scale.

He walks over and pulls up the metal bar of the swing, double-checking the chains. "Here." He nods. I take a seat, and he slides the metal bar, and I clip it between my legs to the seat. "The ride goes on for about five minutes and then lowers so you can get off and start back up again. It doesn't go very high in case something goes wrong. I'm going to check something and be right back." He walks away, his back hunched under his black outer coat.

"Thank you, Wilfred," I shout. He raises his hand above his head.

The swing lifts and takes off. The cold air whips my hair. The butterflies in my stomach flutter in excitement.

I smile, feeling like a little girl. It's a kiddie fair, but I don't mind. It brings me back to memories with my dad when he took me to the fair for the first time.

The sky is overcast. The wind gets a little colder as the sun begins to set. I raise my hands with a smile while listening to the melody playing. *A little longer*, I tell myself. Wilfred said the swing stops with enough time to get off.

The swing keeps going. After a few minutes, the sun dips behind the tall trees and blankets the small fair in twilight.

The swing begins to slow down. I make sure my boots hit the ground in a firm landing. I unlatch the metal bar. It climbs the chains as I get out. The lights from the ride are bright under the sky, turning dark by the second until it shuts off. I whip my head toward the generator.

"Wilfred?" I shiver under my sweater, thankful that I'm wearing wool leggings. "Wilfred?" I call out again. Nothing.

CHAPTER

11

I should turn around and head back before it gets dark, and I won't be able to see anything. I don't know my way around the woods surrounding the estate. The leaves rustle from the wind. Twigs snap in the distance. There could be bears or coyotes out there.

Wilfred said he would be back, but I will not stand around like an idiot and wait for the old man to remember. He probably forgot, but it doesn't explain why the generator shut off. I saw the switch he had to lift to turn it on. Someone must have flipped it off, or it doesn't work like it used to.

Not wanting to ponder the what-ifs, I return to the house, trying to remember the way. I pass the branch I pushed out of the way, revealing the kiddie fair for the first time. The problem is I can't see shit. Heavy clouds pass over the moon and set high in the sky. The bite of the cold air causes the leaves to fall off the trees. I keep walking, treading through the trees. One tree, then another, and another. They all look the same up close.

I stop. A branch snapping off the tree has my ears sharp. It sounds like footsteps. It's funny how your ears play tricks on you, and it's your footsteps that you keep hearing.

I pick up my pace, moving through the trees. The silence feeds fear. The fear of being alone. The feeling of being something's prey. In the darkness of my room, I know the monster is the house feeding my mind, giving me nightmares. Nightmares that have turned bittersweet between my thighs. Feeding my cravings and fantasies. Maybe they are right for calling me a freak at school.

But I'm out here, and I'm not in my room. The house is somewhere I can't see. Out here, my monster could be anyone. It could be anything.

My hands reach out, moving the branches out of my way, but it feels like I'm going deeper inside instead of out. I should have been at the house by now. I stop and look around. Dread surrounds me like the darkness moving in.

The feeling of being hunted snakes its way into my thoughts. I blink hard, trying to settle my nerves. I feel vulnerable. I feel naked, like a dream I had once. I was at school, and everyone was calling me a Freak. I looked down, and I was naked. No clothes on any part of my exposed skin. I could feel nothing except the tingle from my hand when I touched myself.

I woke up gasping for air with my hand between my thighs wet to the touch. I was naked. My pajamas on the floor. My sheets crumpled at the foot of my bed. My legs spread with two fingers between my slit, rubbing myself.

"*Aaaalice...*"

I stop, but all I hear are the sounds of cicadas and trees moving. I thought I heard someone whispering my name. Faint and ethereal, like the rustles of leaves in the breeze, I step. "Aaaalice."

The whisper feels intimate, filled with a dark appeal that sends shudders down my spine.

It's in my head. I've never been alone out here. *It's the wind, Alice.*

"Alice... Alice..."

I stop dead in my tracks, fumbling for my phone in the band of my leggings. I unlock my phone and turn on the flashlight. I look down, swiping the screen, listening for my name so I can run in the opposite direction.

I turn and stumble to the left through the thick underbrush, my heart pounding. It's a male voice growing stronger, more insistent, as though his voice guides my steps. My flashlight from my phone cast eerie, irregular shadows that dance before my eyes.

"Alice... Alice... you're mine..."

I run, but whoever is behind me is faster. My thoughts go to my tormentor from two nights ago. My pussy throbs shamelessly at being caught. The ground turns rough despite my boots slowing me down.

A hand clamps over my mouth, robbing me of my scream as the force of something solid slams me into the ground. My pulse pounds in my ears when my phone slips from my fingers. An arm snakes around my waist, lifting me off the ground. I struggle for breath, trying to fight back, but it's useless. The man with the mask overpowers me. He's a beautiful nightmare stealing my screams and heating my skin.

I'm stiff like an animal playing dead. My strength is depleted from running and trying to fight him off. I know he's strong, but I won't go without a fight. He hoists me over his shoulder like I'm still riding the swings, taking me deeper into the forest.

His steps crunch under the leaves. "If you scream, I'll make you bleed. Understand?" he says in a dark, threatening voice muffled by the device in his mask.

I nod. My pussy between my thighs is sore and throbbing. Hoping for more. I'm so fucked up. I want more, and the fear he gives feeds my need.

His hand slides off my mouth. I squeak when he pushes me against the rough bark of a tree. My braless nipples strain underneath my sweater, begging for his teeth. He presses his forearm against my neck so I don't move. He reaches behind him and pulls something out from the back of his jeans.

"Please...." I hiss, my voice trailing off.

"Quiet," he tells me, sliding a black leather mask over my head and tightening the strap underneath my chin.

I can feel myself leaking between my thighs. I've washed

numerous times. His cum dripped on my panties. I was so full of his cum. I thought it would never stop coming out of me. I even tasted it with my fingers to see if it was real. *It was us.* I played with my clit rubbing myself and getting off, not caring about the sting on my swollen flesh. It hurt so good.

The brisk air cools my aching nipples. His mouth is soft on my tender skin. His teeth sink into my soft flesh, stealing my breath. He sucks and licks, smoothing the pain, and moves to the other.

It's dark with the mask over my head. My fingers slide over muscled shoulders. He's hard everywhere. The heat of the smooth skin from his neck under my fingers. The hard edge of his jaw. His soft lips, the velvety wetness of his tongue when he sucks my fingers.

His hand roughly pulls the band of my leggings down my thighs. He plunges three fingers at once inside my sopping, tender cunt. My toes lift from the ground; he is so deep. His thumb rubs my clit. He's rough. Rougher than before. But he warned me. He said the first time would be soft, but we both know it wasn't. He made me bleed, and I loved it.

He continues fucking my cunt with three fingers stealing every breath from my lips. I grind on his fingers, about to come all over his hand, but he pulls out. I want to fall to my knees and beg for him not to stop.

His lips are near my throat, nibbling and sucking. "You have such a horny cunt. I like it," he whispers. My hands find his face. Smooth and chiseled. I may not see, but I can feel him in my hands. "What do you want, Alice? More of *my* cum inside you, leaking out of that bruised pussy begging for more."

"Yes," I hiss.

I do. I want more. Everything he wants to give me. No judgment. No regrets. Raw pleasure mixed with pain, feeding the adrenaline running through my veins. He makes me feel alive. Wanted.

"I see you, Alice—more than you think. I know things. Things I can't tell you, but I'm around when you think I'm not. Always watching."

"Why?" I whisper. "Why me?"

"Because...no one would believe you."

He grabs the back of my neck. My arms flail when he shoves me to the ground, losing my footing. I'm on my knees on all fours, thankful my leggings still cover my knees. My palms sting from the rough ground mixed with rocks and twigs.

My ass is in the air. I'm not wearing panties because it would rub on my swollen pussy, and they were all ruined. I hear a belt buckle. Tears prick my eyes, bracing for the sting I know is coming but know it will feel good right after. He will make me come like I wanted to this morning in the shower. My fingers are not enough anymore.

I need his big, pierced cock.

Inside me.

Filling me.

He spreads my ass. I can feel the cold air on my heated sex. He plunges his fingers inside me, spreading me open.

"Ahh..."

"So tender," he rasps. "So tight and pretty. So... mine."

My knees tremble on the rough ground when he pulls his fingers out. The tip of the cold metal from the head of his cock crowns my entrance. He grips my hips hard.

A mewl escapes my throat.

"This will hurt, Alice," he growls.

I tilt my head back. "I-I want it, Hades," I say breathlessly.

The tip sinks in, and I wince at the burn like he's searing my flesh. Marking me repeatedly, branding me.

This is wrong, but it feels so right. A fantasy I never knew I needed. Taking my breath away. Being fucked so raw out in the open with no one around.

He shoves his hips forward with more force, sinking in deeper. He pulls out, and I breathe through the sting, my pussy so wet it drips on my inner thighs. Then he pushes in again. Harder this time. Penetrating. Stretching my pussy tight.

He grabs the end of my hair, wrapping it around his fist and tipping my head back. One hand digging in my hip for leverage. I take a ragged breath. My fingernails dig in the dirt, feeling the cool soil and rough terrain.

"Hold on," he says in a gravelly tone. "Don't fight me."

His cock is snug inside me. The trickle of the wet tears on my chin and neck. His hips are tight against the cheeks of my ass, holding them open. His hot breath near my ear. His wet tongue licks my tears from my exposed neck.

"You're so beautiful when you cry, Alice. Your screams touch my soul. Your fear makes me come. The trembles from your body heat my skin. You're the match that lights my fire." His tongue licks my tears. "Now, I want to hear your cries so you can feel the pulse of my dick as you heat my blood."

He bites my neck and inches deeper inside me with his cock. I moan when he goes slow. It burns. My eyes roll back in my skull when my clit tingles, pleading to come. "Please... more," I cry softly.

He knows what I want, what I'm asking.

I can feel his lips curve on my skin. He rubs his nose like I'm a delicate flower he wants to inhale. Petals from a rose he wants to pluck. He maintains his grip on my hair and hip. I tense when his teeth mark my skin again. He pushes deeper, and I can feel the metal inside me. It's thick, like the girth of his cock stealing my breaths. "Give me your pussy, Alice," he croaks. "I want it."

I tremble and moan. I'm so full of him. He's inside me, filling me, and he hasn't even started. I know he hasn't. I feel the thrill-- the sense of excitement in the darkness of the mask. I buck against him, and he knows I'm ready. "That's my girl." The burn turns into pleasure. I'm so wet. I can hear the noises of my pussy milking his cock when he starts to move.

His hand releases my long hair, slides around my breast to my throat, and begins to pound me like a savage. I cry out. His cock is hard, growing thicker as he gets closer to his orgasm. I cry out again. The cicadas go silent in the background. The pounding in my ears from his brutal thrusts. He fucks me like an animal. Brutal. Unapologetically.

My clit throbs like an electrical current when I come. "Fuck....yes," I scream, spasming on his cock. Bright lights flash like a camera going off behind my eyes. I whimper when I'm coming down from my high. He doesn't last. His breaths are coming fast and deep, like he's running a marathon.

He thrusts hard. I swear he hits my cervix when he comes inside me. It's hot. I can feel his dick spasming as my pussy clenches his shaft.

He pulls out. I hear his belt buckle when he pulls himself away. The cold air hits my heated skin. I try to find my balance so I can stand. I feel lightheaded, but I manage. I can finally stand on wobbly knees and pull my leggings up. I wince when I step. The inside of my pussy feels like it is breathing fire.

I yelp when he grips my arm, pulling me to his side. The muscles from his abdomen and the warmth from his hoodie on my breasts when he removes the mask over my head.

The cold air cools my heated face. I wipe the remnants of tears from my cheeks. My eyes drink in the darkness surrounding us, with only the moon giving us light in the dark sky. He has his mask back in place with the hood from his sweater over his head.

He guides me through the woods for about five minutes and then pushes me forward. I stumble, taking precarious steps until I see the glow from the lights of the manor.

I turn, realizing I dropped my phone, but he's gone. I take a wobbly step to go after him but pause. I can try to find it tomorrow, after school. My mother and stepfather will give me shit about losing my phone, but I smile because it was worth it.

I wish I could kiss him on the mouth and see his face. I know it sounds crazy to let him use me, but I've never felt this alive.

When my father died, my world ceased to exist. Everything around me crumbled. I look up at the house in a new light. I hated it for so long, but it gave me something I would have never found. It gave me Hades. It was waiting for the right time or until I got older. Preparing me for something it knew I needed. Something I could never explain. Something a sane person would never accept. Something no one would ever believe——chaos inside madness.

CHAPTER 12

I wince when I slide into my car and head to school. I'm so sore. It hurts. Bad.

When I walked into the house last night, it was silent. My mother, probably too tired to seek me out. Instead, she left a note on the kitchen island under a blueberry muffin, telling me she missed me and had gone to bed. I took the note with me with a smile and ate the muffin. She used to do things like that when I was little.

I'm tired of being upset with her. I've stopped telling her the things I saw and heard for a whole year. I get that she was tired from working and traveling. The last thing she would want to hear is her daughter telling her she sees or hears things. I can't be ungrateful. My mother and stepfather work all the time. My mother has been his right hand since they got married, or even before that when she was married to my dad.

The Tesla powers up, and I notice it's charged. After pressing the button to the garage door and put the car in reverse, I see my phone. It rests on the dash with a small flower on top and a sticky note on the screen. I press my foot on the brake and pick up the note and smell the flower.

You dropped this.
H

That's it. Nothing more. I turn the sticky note in my hand, hoping there is more written on the back, but it's blank. What a romantic. A small flower with little white petals. No "you were amazing" or "I'm sorry for scaring you," but what did I expect? He hasn't shown me his face, and I know his name is not Hades. That's the estate's name he keeps breaking into. I shouldn't expect more. I would be crazy to think this is a romance. It isn't.

I power up my phone and see a missed text from Ivy.

Ivy: I got suspended from school for a fight in the girl's bathroom. I saw nothing, but you know how it is. Blame the poor girl until they can figure out what happened. I will go to the circus this week. I'll let you know how it goes. Oh, did you hear what happened to that guy at the club in town? Some crazy person stabbed him all over his face and body. They needed to use his dental records to identify him.

Alice: I got your message. That sucks. I'm on my way to school. I'll find out on my end. We'll catch up later.

My stomach drops, and I open the local news app. The hunt for the human traffickers killing teenage girls is still underway. What has my attention is the news story of the man at the bottom. It says they could not identify who did it, and there are no witnesses. It also says that the victim has a history of assaulting women. I could have been raped, but Hades saved me.

I take a deep breath and rummage in my bag for my birth control pills, remembering to take them every day. I must also head to the free clinic and get tested after school. Who knows how many women he does this to? I've been so wrapped up in each encounter I don't consider the consequences.

Shame douses me like a bucket of cold water. When your secret desires are met, reality is the last thing that crosses your mind in the heat of the moment.

I lost my virginity the way I fantasized. Even though the logical part of my messed-up brain wanted a boyfriend. Honestly, I want both. The fantasy and the boyfriend wrapped together, making the perfect package.

I want to fall in love because I've had none given to me since my dad died. He was the only one who showed me any. The cell phone with the note awakened the sane part of my brain. I need to stop thinking about Hades and wait for him to show up whenever he wants. I don't regret it, but I need to stop this. Whatever this is.

I want someone in my life I could spend time with––someone I could love and date and have safe sex with. I don't care if it's in the back seat of a car or by the lake. Cliché shit, I know, but I want the experience. The love notes the next day after hot sex. Not the crumpled yellow sticky note written in cold words.

I step out of the car after I park in the student parking lot. The wind picks up, taking the crumpled note from my fingers and onto the ground. I walk toward the entrance to the main building, not wanting to be late.

"You dropped something."

I turn and see the last person I expected. Lazarus holds out the crumpled sticky note. Remembering the night I ran out of his house causes a bloom to my cheeks in mortification.

My eyes flick to the paper and then meet his gorgeous face. Our gazes meet. Waiting.

"No, I didn't." I grab it from the palm of his hand, toss it in the trash, and keep walking toward the main building. I don't ask him why he is on campus, and it's none of my business.

He's one of them. He must have had a nice laugh at my expense. Rumors will fly around campus about how I ran out of his house like a scared little girl. A freak. If he only knew I could handle a monster.

He is probably here because he dropped off a cheerleader he screwed over the weekend. It could be his girlfriend. I'm sure he lied about that. I thought he was different the night of the party.

Common sense knocked me upside the head as a masked man. If he was invited and sought me out in front of the others, it was for a reason and not because I was prettier than the others.

"Are you always this grouchy in the morning?" he asks, walking up next to me, the thought of Hades disappearing from my mind.

I should be offended and tell him to fuck off, but I don't. I stop and see the grin pasted on his face.

"No. Only to fake people who think I'm stupid."

"Ouch. I want to apologize for the other night. It wasn't how I planned things to go."

I try not to notice how his jeans fit over his muscled thighs. Or the way his white long-sleeved shirt does nothing to hide how perfect his body is. It's hard not to notice him. He is so much taller than me and most guys at school. Staring at his chest doesn't help either.

He feels guilty. I'm not his type, and we both know that. A girl like me could never attract a guy like him.

I'm surprised he's apologizing. He probably has a conscience. Or I've been to his house, and he doesn't want me to show up like a crazy person. I'm sure he's had enough girls crushing on him already. I was a joke gone wrong. The crazy freak he's heard about. That must be it.

I half shrug. "I'm sure your plan was very different. You don't have to apologize to me to clear your conscience." Tommy and Emma are smirking with the cheerleaders looking our way seated on the bench. "That night was a mistake. I wasn't thinking."

He steps closer, and I look up. He touches the end parts of my hair between his fingers. "The first part wasn't a mistake."

"Hey, Freak!" I look over to see Mich with two fingers over his mouth, flicking his tongue back and forth. "I didn't know you were into cock. I'll make an exception for your crazy ass and take you for a ride on my dick Friday night. I don't mind sloppy seconds. I bet you give good head."

I roll my eyes and look at Lazarus. "I bet it wasn't. You can go laugh it up with your friends now." I turn and leave him standing in the walkway with a blank expression.

I feel so stupid for falling for his crap, no matter how gorgeous he is. He had me in the palm of his hand Friday night.

After the warning bell rings, I hear the rumors about Ivy flying around the hallway. Jason and Colin ended up in the hospital after they were beaten up in the girls' bathroom, and Ivy was in the stall. She said she saw nothing because she was locked in the stall, scared to come out. They don't believe her and suspect she saw who did it. What gets me is that they don't question what the fuck they were doing there.

"She was in there fucking them both, and someone got jealous," one cheerleader says across from my locker.

"Of course, she was. Everyone knows Ivy is a slut. She fucked Tommy in the back seat, moaning like a porn star." I recognize Emma's voice.

She has a thing for Tommy and hates Ivy for going out with him on a date. Jealous bitch.

"Did you hear about the Freak at the party last week?" She snickers. "She left with you-know-who."

"Girl, please. He loves to fuck and run."

I turn around, and they both give me a once-over from my black boots to my white blouse, pausing on my face. "So did you fuck him?"

"Why? Jealous, Emma? I thought Tommy was your type?"

Her lip curls, glancing at Melissa–Miranda or whatever her fucking name is. I'm feeling brave today. I don't know why. Probably, the brutal fucking I received from Hades gave me the courage to stand up to these catty bitches. I stopped caring a long time ago about what they think of me, but now, I will not let shit slide.

"You did fuck him."

"Why don't you ask him since you're so worried about it." I can see it in Emma's and her friend's eyes. These two haven't slept with Lazarus. I'm sure they've tried, but he didn't give them the time of day, or they wouldn't give me shit. I don't know if I should feel good about that.

I still remember the kiss and the way he touched me. If it wasn't for the people he hung around with, I would've fallen for him, maybe. I think of my masked tormentor. Hades. He's never kissed me, and I don't know if he's better looking or not, but that doesn't matter. He's giving me the part I crave in my mind.

He lacks the other part. The part I felt in Lazarus's arms. Two people with different intentions. One I can see, and the other I can feel in the depths of my mind.

"I will. We both know he was playing you." She snorts. "What do you have that he could possibly be interested in, you crazy bitch?"

"More than your lame ass. I prefer to be a crazy bitch than a desperate one. Everyone talks about how you're so desperate. Tommy let you pay for the condoms he used to fuck you with."

They didn't, but I took a page out of Ivy's playbook to slap back at this bitch. I love how she is turning red right now because it's true. Ivy scanned them at the grocery store.

She leaves with her bitch friend in a huff storming to her next class. The bell rings. I get my book and shut my locker in the nick of time, sliding past the teacher before he closes the classroom door.

I freeze. My mouth falls open like a fish out of water. Mich is nursing a busted lip, and his left eye is swelling up, turning a yellowish color. He looks up with his good eye when he sees me in the aisle and then looks away.

"Damn, Mich. He fucked you up bad."

"Not as bad as Jason and Colin. Whoever kicked their ass busted their faces and broke their hands. They're out for the season. We can kiss state goodbye," Jake says from behind him, shaking his head.

I don't feel bad for Jason or Colin for obvious reasons. It sucks that Ivy got suspended, though. She did nothing to deserve any of it. We've never reported the bullying or the name-calling.

What was the point? They get away with everything because they play football and can do no wrong. Their parents are sponsors and donate money to the school, which is also why they get off. It's nice to see it finally caught up with them.

Jake turns around to face me when I sit. "Is he your boyfriend now?"

"Huh?" I ask. What is he talking about?

Jake points at Mich. "He's never done that before. Not for a girl."

"I don't know what you're talking about. I wasn't there. I don't know him like that."

But I know. Lazarus kicked Mich's ass because of me.

Where has he been this whole time? It's like he appeared out of thin air.

"But it was because of you."

"What do you know about him?"

He shrugs and shakes his head. "He goes to school online. He's loaded, or his father is. He dresses like he came from New York's fashion week. Drives a nice car. No one knows much about him or where he lives. He keeps to himself most of the time. He shows up at parties and hangs out. Messes around like all guys do." He looks at me like he's seeing me for the first time. "But he's never gone apeshit over a girl." He lowers his voice enough so no one around can hear him. "I would have done the same." My cheeks flame when he gives me a wink and turns around.

When the teacher begins the day's lesson, my eyes swing to Mich. His face is tight. Not from the pain he must be in. It's something else, and I don't like it.

My mind begins to dissect Jake's words. I've been to Lazarus's house. I don't know why he brought me there or what it means.

Now, when I'm around Lazarus, I don't think of Hades, and when I'm with Hades, I don't think of Lazarus. It's like one cancels out the other.

THE FOLLOWING WEEK, I TEXTED IVY ABOUT WHAT happened and how I met Lazarus. She said to come over to the Big H during her shift so we could talk more. I also wanted to ask what happened in the bathroom at school. So many rumors are going around. The main one that sticks is that she was screwing one of them in the bathroom. The other got jealous, and they got into a fight. Another rumor is that she's a prostitute and gets paid to have sex.

I went to the free clinic after school last week on Monday. It feels like a weight has lifted from my shoulders. No pregnancy and no STDs. I've been taking my birth control religiously. It took four days to get the results back. It was four days of hell, but I'm grateful. Grateful to be clean. Grateful I didn't suffer from my stupidity.

"When will they allow you back?" I ask Ivy, standing in front of the bagging area at her register.

"Next Monday. I got suspended for two weeks so they could investigate."

"Did you see anything?"

"I didn't see anything. I was inside the stall. I heard them getting their ass kicked, but that wasn't good enough for them."

"Who was it?"

She's cleaning the conveyor belt at the register with a paper towel. Her lips set in a thin line. "I don't know." There's more, but I don't push. We all have crazy secrets we're afraid to share.

She tosses the paper towel in the small trash bin. She looks around to make sure no one is listening and lowers her voice, "He was wearing a mask."

I grab a chocolate bar, pick up a pack of gum, and place it on the scanner, trying to gather my thoughts. The guy from the fair. The one who gave her the ticket to the circus. He was wearing a mask.

"He…"

"Yes," she says, scanning the two items, but she told the truth. She didn't see his face or know who the man behind the mask is. In the same way, I don't know who Hades is.

"That's… crazy," I blurt the last part.

"Trust me, I know." She places the items in a bag while I rummage through my small purse for my bank card.

When I find it, the hair on the back of my neck stands. The belt moves forward, my head turns, and my bank card almost slips from my fingers. "That's twice now. Twice that I run into you stalking me."

Ivy looks at him and back with a raised brow. I told her over text what happened with Lazarus. She's got a keen sense to know this is Lazarus. I don't have friends and don't talk to anyone else at school.

His gaze lands on Ivy, sporting a polite smile. "I'm Lazarus, by the way."

"It's good meeting you. I'm Ivy." She clears the register and begins scanning.

He smiles. "I know," he replies. He motions to the popcorn, candy, and soda. "It's together." His eyes land on mine. "I got it." The pace of my breathing is in tune with the beeping sound from the register. I'm trying to calm myself down. My pulse beats faster when he steps behind me. "And it's three times… technically," he says. I can feel the warmth of his breath with a hint of mint near my cheek. "I was wondering…do you want to watch a movie with me tonight?"

My eyes flick up to Ivy. I don't miss the way her lips twitch. Her eyes beg me to say yes. I can feel his hard chest behind me when he hands Ivy the cash to pay for the items.

A man in his thirties walks in her lane, and her smile falls. "Hey, Ivy," he greets her.

Her shoulders stiffen. She doesn't answer him right away. Whoever this man is, she doesn't like him. Wanting her not to pay the man any attention, I answer Lazarus. "Sure." Ivy looks up with a hint of a smile, handing Lazarus his change. "What time?"

"Seven," he says.

"You need a ride home, Ivy?" the man asks with DTF written in big letters on his blue shirt. I recognize the name from next door. He's the owner or something from watching the local infomercials on TV. I don't know what he is to Ivy, but he's too old to give her a ride anywhere. The way he looks at her chest doesn't sit well with me, either. *Creep.*

"She already has a ride."

My eyebrows rise when Lazarus answers him for her. I don't miss the way the man's eyes harden or the way he places his grocery items on the belt harder than necessary.

Ivy rubs her lips together nervously, scanning the items one by one. The tension stretches thick like the conveyor belt every time it moves forward.

"I'm her ride," I tell him with a fake smile.

"You didn't tell me you had a friend, Ivy," he says, making a point that he talks to her outside of work. "I want to make sure you're safe, is all. All those girls are turning up the way they did."

What a dick.

"There are many things you don't know about me, Dean." The creep's name is Dean, and I suspect he gives three shits about those poor girls turning up dead the way they did.

I also don't miss the fact they're on a first-name basis, being that he is a shit ton older than her. I'm not against an older guy kind of thing. Ivy is an adult, and it's not illegal, but how he looks at her seems uninvited. The guy gives me bad vibes. He reminds me of my stepfather.

"I'm just looking out for you, Ivy. Taking the shuttle to the mall and walking home is not a good idea right now."

It seems genuine. Logical. But desperate at the same time.

She gives him a fake smile, handing him his grocery bags. "As you can see, I already have a ride. Have a good evening, and thank you for shopping at the Big H."

He grabs the bags, stares at her for a few seconds, and then leaves.

"Asshole," she mutters when he walks through the exit doors as they slide open.

"How do you know that asshole?" Lazarus asks the same thing I was thinking.

She points toward the sign you could see out the glass window that read DTF DOWN TO FLUSH. "That's how."

"Is he bothering you?" She shakes her head, but I know she's lying. "If you need a ride home, I can take you," I offer. She chews her bottom lip. "I don't need gas money. My car's electric," I add with a smile.

She grins. "Alright." I glance at Lazarus, and he's looking down at his phone, texting.

He looks up. "Are you two good?" I nod. "I'll see you at seven then?" he asks with a hopeful expression, melting my panties. They have evaporated by now.

Hades has made me into a sex-crazed idiot. I shouldn't fall for Lazarus's charm. But the way he spoke up for Ivy has me changing my mind about him and what he did to Mich that day.

Maybe I was quick to judge him and didn't give him a chance, or this is all a ploy. There is only one way to find out. Get to know him and hope it doesn't blow up in my face. I have nothing to lose except the heart beating in my chest.

"Yeah, seven."

His smile makes my clit flutter. "You remember the address?"

I have it in the recent locations saved in my car.

"I do."

He hands me a note from his pocket. "Here is my number." The way he says *number* gives me pause. He clears his throat. "See you later."

I watch him leave with the note in my hand as he exits with the bag like he owns the world.

"Where did he come from?" Ivy asks behind me.

I look at the note.

You look gorgeous today, and I can't wait to taste your lips again.
_413-254-6870_
Lazarus

"I have no idea."

"He's gorgeous, Alice."

I smile. "I know. He says he goes to school online."

"At Stockbridge?"

I nod. "Yeah." I glance at the bagging area and notice he took my chocolate and gum. He wants to make sure I show up.

"You look different."

I look down at my oversized sweater, leggings, and my UGGs. "How?"

She gives me a once-over. "I don't know. There is this...glow about you."

Yeah, I got fucked deliciously hard, but I can't tell her that.

"There is nothing to tell that I haven't told you." She doesn't buy it, but I can't tell her about Hades. I can tell no one.

CHAPTER 13

After dropping off Ivy, I head home to change for my date with Lazarus. I'm dreading the conversation with my mother. I didn't want to call to tell her my plans. To be honest, I hoped they weren't home. I hoped they were both out of town so I could sneak out, but luck wasn't on my side.

When I walk into the house, my mother sits in the kitchen by the window, nursing her usual glass of wine. My stepfather is across from her, scrolling on his phone.

"I'm going on a date," I blurt.

They both look up in tandem. "What?" My mother is the first to react like she didn't hear what I said.

"I'm going on a date," I repeat. "Tonight."

"Oh, so you're making decisions without consulting me now?"

"Calm down, Lynn," Nick says.

She gives Nick a glare. "I'm not going to calm down. I've discussed this with her before. She's not ready."

"I am, and I'm going. I'm eighteen years old. I'm not a child anymore."

Her eyes widen. "Watch your tone, Alice. Who is this person you are planning to go on a date with?"

"A boy. Obviously."

"Don't sass me, young lady. I've gone through a lot dealing with your issues."

Rage bubbles in my veins. "*My* issues. It wouldn't have been an issue if you would have listened to me."

"I did. I have," she retorts. "None of it was real or made any sense."

"You wouldn't think that if we hadn't moved here in the first place."

"This is our home now. Your...home."

"I didn't ask for this to be my home. This was your decision, not mine."

"Alice," Nick warns. "Don't speak to your mother that way."

My nostrils flare. "You're not my father, Nick."

"I never said I wanted to be your father, but you will respect your mother." He glances at her. She has a triumphant smirk across her face that turns into a scowl when he says, "Let her go, Lynn."

"What?" she screeches.

"Let. Her. Go."

She huffs. "I can't believe this. You're on her side. You need to stop pitying her, Nick."

My eyes swing to Nick like I've been slapped. "I'm not, but she isn't a child, Lynn. She's an adult, and you can't keep her in a gilded cage."

"She's unstable."

He shakes his head. "She hasn't said anything in almost a year. No strange noises. No voices in the walls. No pianos myste-riously playing. She's also done well on her own while we've been away."

"That's because you leave a couple of days early to check on her."

An unsettling feeling settles in my stomach. He leaves early to check on me? They don't trust me alone. But when I asked him where Mom was when he would show up alone, he always said she was coming the same day. Where did he go the day before or before that? He comes home the same day she does. Hours earlier but the same day like on Sunday.

Is he...?

No, it can't be. Hades is stronger. His arms are more muscular but I've never looked at Nick. Not like that. I back up. His eyes narrow. I need to get out of here.

Bile rises in the back of my throat.

I need to get out of this house.

Away from him.

Away from my mom.

Oh God. My mother.

"I'm leaving," I rush out. "He's a boy from school." I glance at Nick. "My age. I'll be back before midnight."

"Nick," my mother protests.

"Let her go," he finally says.

I sigh in relief and rush up the stairs before I break down in front of my mother. Guilt. Shame and disgust slice through me. I run to the bathroom and throw up, hoping the memories go along with it. *It can't be. Relax, Alice. It's not him.*

I WALK UP TO THE FRONT DOOR. LAZARUS'S CLASSIC car is parked in the driveway. The sun has dipped behind the horizon, creating a black canvas in the sky. The wind picks up and tousles my hair. The trees groan.

I'm about to knock with my fist in the air when the door swings open. Lazarus appears in all his glory. Sweatpants outlining the hard ridge of his cock hanging low on slim hips. The band of his designer underwear calls for my fingers. My eyes trail up his black T-shirt. His arms are inked with swirls of different designs in a kaleidoscope of colors. I reach for his face. His eyes are like storms, reminding me of lightning against the black color of darkness.

"You made it," he says with a smile. *Trust me, not fast enough.*

His eyes trail from the tips of my black boots to my face. I straightened my hair and took my time with my makeup for him.

He steps to the side so I can walk inside. The smell of his cologne mixed with fresh popcorn hits me. He points toward the living room. "I took the..." He clears his throat. "I took the liberty to set up a little picnic." Lush ivory couches sit in front of a modern fireplace below an oversized flatscreen TV on the wall. I look at the soda, candy, and popcorn on the contemporary coffee table. There are fluffy pillows and a black throw blanket over the couch.

"It looks amazing."

It did, but so did he. It's hard enough not to stare at him. I've never thought a guy who looked like him existed in Stockbridge. He belongs in a magazine. Jake had a point. He does look like he left the runway in New York City on fashion week. He has chiseled features like a male tattooed model. I never thought much about tattoos. I don't know anyone with any, but I like them.

The TV is already set on the streaming app. He takes the remote and motions for me to sit beside him on the soft ivory couch. The couch smells good, like someone sprayed a freshener on them. Not wanting to dirty the delicate sofa, I remove my boots, glad I chose leggings and a warm sweater.

He lifts his arm so I can lean closer. He feels warm and safe. When I feel his hard body against mine, my stomach does this little flip. I could fall asleep next to the heat of his body and never want to wake up. His fingers comb the strands of my dark hair.

"I was going to take you to the drive-in in town, but I thought this was better."

Flutters run rapidly in my lower belly, calming the horror I was experiencing back home.

"It's perfect." I smile. "Thank you."

"My pleasure."

We agree on a thriller. He passes me the bucket of popcorn,

and we settle, watching the movie. "Are your parents around often?"

"No. It's me, my brother, and... my dad."

"Where's your mom?"

He swallows. "Dead."

Shit.

"I-I'm sorry."

He shakes his head. "It happened years ago. And you?"

"It's me, my mom and stepdad. My father passed away."

I'm relieved when he doesn't ask how, and I give him the same courtesy. Some things are hard to talk about with others.

"I'm sorry."

I wave him off and take a sip of my Coke. "You said you had a brother. What's he like?"

He leans closer, and I love the smell of him. "He's older and travels a lot."

"So it's just you in this big house?"

He chuckles. "It's not big. It's kind of lonely, but you're here."

I smile. "How come you don't go to regular school?"

It's a question I've been dying to ask him since Jake told me no one knew much about him. Not that I would tell anyone anything he confided in me with. It's none of their business.

"My father is a very private man. My brother is older and was homeschooled. I decided to stay home and try online school. My brother wanted the freedom to travel."

I'm dying to ask what they do, but I hold my tongue. Too many questions asked get many more asked in return.

"How old?"

"We're six years apart. He's twenty-four." That makes him eighteen.

I look up, and our eyes meet. "Do you like online school?"

It's a stupid, lame question, but I've never been on a date. I'm not used to being this close to someone. I've never talked to a boy like this before. I have had so much going on at the house since I was nine. There was never time to do much else.

His eyes caress my face. "It's okay, but I like you better." He leans in, our lips brush, and our breaths meet.

"I like you too," I whisper. My heart hammers away because, deep down, I do. More than I thought I did. The memory of Hades and what he did to my body is a blur. Thoughts of who he might be far away. I want to forget. I want to cut the chains that bind me to Hades Manor with everything and everyone in it.

I want to feel normal.

I want to be set free.

I want to feel love, for someone to kiss me like I'm their last breath in the moment. For it to be real.

He presses his lips against mine. It's soft and hot. Goose bumps coat my skin when his fingers slide in my hair. He's like a breath of fresh air promising me a storm.

He devours me with his tongue. He tastes like salt from the popcorn and sweet from the soda, and I can't get enough. He consumes me. Our breaths are one, breathing the same air, breathing each other. His hand grips the back of my neck. His thumb caresses my cheek, deepening the kiss. I let out a whimper when our foreheads meet, trying to calm the rapid beating of my heart. My hands slide up his torso, stopping on his hard chest.

He holds my face and whispers, "I would love to be inside you right now, Alice. But I didn't ask you to come over so that I could sleep with you."

His words hit me like the storm his touch promised, leaving me stranded in the sea. I pull away, trying to compose myself.

My lips are swollen. I can smell him on my lips, my skin and every time I take a breath. I stare at the TV screen so I won't have to look at him because if I do, he will see how embarrassed I feel. I wouldn't have stopped. I would have let him. I mean, who wouldn't? The guy is gorgeous and a good kisser. I'm sure he is good everywhere else, but it's obvious I will not find out. What if he said that because he lost interest and was trying to be nice? The first time I was here, I ran out the front door like a scared little virgin. Now I want to. He said he didn't ask me to come so he could sleep with me. So why did he ask? It wasn't to play Parcheesi or to watch a movie.

"W-why did you ask me to come over?"

He scoots back on the couch, grabs the remote, and exits the movie. He scrolls through the choices and replies, "So we could watch a movie, and I could get to know you."

I face forward and look down at my hands. "Oh." I doubt that, but okay. He's playing it safe.

I reach to my right and get my phone to check the time, and it gives me something to do. Like tell him I have to head home when I don't. That is the last place I want to go but I can't take his rejection. I wasn't prepared for it to hurt.

I unlock the screen and see that it's almost ten. It's still early, but not early enough that he will think it's obvious I want to leave.

"I have to get going." I move to stand but feel his hand wrap around my wrist, keeping me from turning away.

"It's still early."

I lock my phone and finally face him. His eyes are stormy and filled with something I can't put my finger on. It looks like panic, but it can't be because he was the one who stopped. He's the one who doesn't want more, and I can't sit here and not want to straddle him so he could kiss me and touch me.

It's all Hades's fault. He fucked me in a way I never thought one could be fucked, and now that is all I want. I want sex, but I want the soft kind. I'm not sure if that makes me easy or not, but it makes me feel something, and I don't know what that is. First, it was the house, and now, it's what my body wants. What my body craves. I crave Hades and Lazarus, or what I thought he would give me, but now I'm not so sure.

"It's dark out, and I shouldn't be out too late."

"I'll follow you home."

I shake my head. "That's okay. If I leave now, it won't be so late, and you won't have to go through all the trouble," I rush out.

His eyes meet mine from where he sits, and it's like he can see through my bullshit. It's like he knows I don't need to go home right now, and he's deciding whether he should call me out on it.

But he doesn't.

He tears his gaze away, looks at the TV, and then back at me. "I don't want you to go." He reaches for my hand and tugs me gently so I can sit back down next to him. "Alice?"

I look down at my hands. "Yes."

"Look at me." I look up. "Are you mad that I stopped?"

"No," I reply but look away. "I don't know why you did."

The sound of thunder vibrates through the living room. Then a flash of lightning and more thunder. I can see the trees sway in the wind.

He grabs my hand and leans back on the couch, placing it between his thighs. "It wasn't because I don't want to." His dick is rock-hard. I feel the wide girth of his cock in my hand, sending a signal straight to my wet pussy like a bolt of lightning. He looks at my hand between his legs. "Is this what you want, Alice? My hard dick."

Holy shit. When he talks dirty, it's such a turn-on. There is no way I could say no. There is no way you wouldn't give him what he wants.

He scoots to the edge of the couch and pushes the band of his sweatpants down to free his cock. It's thick, hard, and veiny. The head is swollen and passes his belly button. My eyes flick to his, and he guides my hand so I can touch his cock. It's firm, and smooth, and hot.

I've never touched a man's penis like this before, but his nose flares when I stroke the length with the palm of my hand. The pad of my thumb slides over the tip, and I see him swallow. I want to put my mouth on it, but I'm afraid he'll stop me.

"Can I...?"

"You can do whatever you want as long as you don't leave. Not in this storm."

The flash of lightning illuminates the dark sky from the windows. The rain patters in a rhythm as it hits the floor-to-ceiling windows. After a few seconds, thunder vibrates the windows. The lightning and thunder would scare me if I were alone inside this house. But the fact I'm here with Lazarus makes me feel safe.

I don't want to go home. I want to stay here with him. It's like a higher being was answering my prayers. The sky answered my pleas.

I lick my bottom lip, wondering how he would taste. His fingers slide into my hair at the back of my head, holding me steady. My lips hover over his cock.

My eyes meet his. "This is what I want." Another flash of lightning and peal of thunder pierce through the air.

I take him in my mouth, swirling my tongue over the tip like I've seen in online videos. He tastes salty. The kind of salty you want to keep tasting because it's just right, and you can't stop at one taste. He lets out a hiss. His fingers tighten in my hair, spurring me on. I take him deep. My tongue glides down his thick shaft. I begin to suck his cock like a popsicle. Now every time I eat one, it will remind me of his cock. Of this moment and everything shaped like a cock.

His breathing picks up when I suck faster. The salty taste of him is becoming more prominent, and he's about to come. I can tell with the way his cock jerks in my mouth. The way his hips match the rhythm without hurting me or making me gag. I smile inwardly, loving the fact that I can pleasure him, and he's losing himself with my mouth. I feel in control. I feel beautiful. I want all of him, but this will do... for now.

His cock hits the back of my throat, and I moan after the flash of lightning and the crack of thunder. Drool slides down the corner of my mouth onto his thighs, but he seems not to mind. I bob my head faster, sliding my tongue on the way up, making slurping noises like a popsicle when it begins to melt.

He grunts. "Fuck." He pulls out, causing me to jerk back, feeling like my jaw is unhinged.

It happens so fast. One minute, I'm sucking his cock on his lap, and the next, I'm on my back on the couch, and he's between my legs. One hand is on his wet cock fucking himself. The other tugs on the neckline of my sweater, releasing my breasts from my bra.

"Open your mouth," he demands.

My eyes widen. The first streams of hot cum hit my face, cheeks, breasts, and some lands inside my mouth. The saltiness explodes on my tongue. He grunts and keeps coming. Strings of cum shoot from the tip of his cock followed by his groans.

It's so hot and dirty. Cum lands on my nipples, and I let out a moan. I lick my lips, tasting more. "Mmm..." I moan between swallows, sliding my tongue to get the drops on my chin.

He fists his cock and wipes the last of his cum between my breasts. He puts himself away. Flashes of lightning illuminate his face. He angles his head and holds my gaze, his eyes the color of the dark sky. He leans toward me. He sticks out the flat part of his tongue and licks his cum off my nipples and breasts.

I gasp when the nerve endings from my nipples shoot straight to my lower belly like an electric current. "Oh my God," I say breathlessly. "Yes," I hiss in a plea. "Please...don't..." I pull my shoulders back, thrust my breasts in his face, and beg for more. He continues on one nipple and then the other. Sucking them hard, he then eases the pain by twirling his tongue, and I feel it on my aching clit. I widen my thighs, grinding my hips. His eyes look at his cock, tenting his pants aimed at my pussy. "D-don't stop," I stammer.

He licks his lips, dragging his bottom lip in his mouth and watching him taste himself. He licks the rest of his cum from my chest, collarbone, cheeks, and chin. I never thought a man would not be grossed out by his cum. I don't have much experience with what men like or sex, but from what I've seen online, I have never seen a man lick their cum.

When he reaches my lips, I taste his cum on his tongue when he slips it into my mouth. It's sweet and salty mixed with the taste of his breath. I breathe him in as I slide my fingers in his dark hair, our tongues exploring each other, stealing each other's air. I don't want it to end. I want him to take me apart and tell me what he sees.

He might figure out how to extinguish the flames burning inside me. Maybe he can offer me an escape inside him. A place where I don't hear or see things I'm not sure are not there. A place where I don't fear a man who comes for me at night. The one that takes my innocent thoughts and replaces them with what my body needs.

He holds himself above me with one hand on the armrest—the sounds of our kisses are like crackles in a growing fire. Filling the space between flashes of lightning.

Our lips break apart. Our breaths mingle against one another. His eyes trail to my breast and back to my face. The glow from the TV doesn't hide the way my chest glistens from his wet mouth. My pants are wet between my legs. I can feel my pulse racing between my legs. My heart thuds in my chest.

He thrusts his hips. The tip of his cock rubs over my throbbing pussy, causing a little whimper to escape my throat. I bite my bottom lip, holding back a moan.

"You're so fucking wet," he says with a low growl, grinding his hard cock.

My eyes roll back in my skull because everything fades in and out. I want to come so bad I'll do anything. My hands slide up his hard stomach and the ridge of his muscles. His skin is hot and smooth. I wish it were brighter so I could see the ink on his skin. I want to take off his shirt, but I'm afraid he will stop. I slide the palms of my hands to his lower back, pushing him deeper and meeting his thrusts.

"You want me to fuck you so bad, don't you?" I nod, watching him dry fuck me. He smiles, and it's beautiful. "Like I said, this is not why I asked you to come over, but it's nice." I freeze like I've been hit by tiny little needles all over my body from a bucket of ice water. The bucket snaps me out of it. *Nice?* It's... nice?

Shame hits me for the second time tonight. What am I doing? I'm begging him to fuck me, and he told me it was not what he wanted. It's what I wanted, not what he wanted.

My eyebrows draw together. I push him off me to sit up. I adjust my bra and top, looking out the window. The rain has stopped. I squeeze my thighs together, looking around for my bag and phone. I grab my jacket and stand. "It's late." I grab my phone and purse. "Thanks." But I don't know what I'm thanking him for. He made me feel cheap. Nice is not great. Nice is not amazing. Nice is something you say to someone because it's the only respectable thing to say. In sex, nice is what you call a forgettable sexual encounter. Borderline horrible.

"Are you sure you don't want me to follow you home?" he asks, concern laced in his voice. "It's eleven thirty."

He even knows what time it is. He couldn't wait for it to be over so I would leave. I must have read this all wrong.

He adjusts himself in his pants, and I want to die. I drooled on his pants and wanted nothing more than to take a shower and wash me off him.

"It's fine. I'll make it. It's not like I can get lost with my car."

He rubs the back of his neck. "Right."

I look away and rush toward the front door. I want nothing more than for a bear to pop out of the woods and eat me as soon as I step out.

I open the door, and the blast of cool air ripples through me, blowing my hair and clearing the sexual fog in my head. To cool the heat that was between my legs.

I hastily walk to my car, pulling the driver's door open and replay what I said and then the last thing he said in my mind. He must think I fuck guys on the first date and that I'm bad at it--bad at giving a blow job. I thought he enjoyed it. He came, but technically, he pulled out and finished on me.

He told me he didn't invite me over to have sex, but that's what I wanted. Because stupid me is desperate to have sex with a person I can see. A person who is real.

"Maybe he's not the right person," I mumble.

"Are you alright?"

I look up, about to shut the door. "I'm fine. I need to get home."

"Was it something I said?"

I shake my head. "No, I...lost track of time. I don't want my parents to worry."

"They know where you are?"

If you call this a date.

I lied instead of telling them I was going over to a guy's house. Where I made a fool of myself in all the worst ways. I hate lying, but telling the truth ever since I was nine got me nowhere. Lying was the better option. The road most traveled. Omitting the truth was even better. Not saying anything was best. It was the only way to avoid judgment and frequent visits to the therapist.

"I told them I would be back before midnight," I rushed out.

He didn't pick me up at my house. He didn't take me out or take me somewhere memorable. I showed up to watch a movie, and I sucked his dick and dry humped him on his couch like a dog. Classified as nothing more than a booty call. He'll delete my number when I leave.

He slides one hand in his pocket. "Oh."

Shutting the door, I create a barrier between us and roll the window down. I don't know what else to say to him.

The awkward silence stretches thin for a beat. I'm digging through my shame and embarrassment. *I need to leave. The night is ruined. Again.*

I can't even look at him. Not because I don't find him attractive. I do. I'm embarrassed. I don't want to overthink and say the wrong thing. *Breathe, Alice.*

I could do this. I could play the part.

"I'll see you around. Thanks for inviting me over. It was... nice," I say, throwing the last word right back. He flinches. Good. I could act the same way. It was like we were running too fast, and neither of us knew where we were going.

We weren't on the same page. It happens. Blame it on mixed signals. But deep down, it hurts that he doesn't want me. He wasn't into me and more into himself.

"Bye, Lazarus." I place the car in reverse and move my hand to press the button to roll up the window.

"Bye, Alice," he says before the window closes.

I back out of his driveway as fast as I can without making it obvious. When I place the car in drive, I look up and find him standing in the same spot. I was expecting him to rush back inside the house, glad to get rid of me finally. He has plenty of girls throwing themselves at him, and I am no different. All I wanted was to have sex, and it took little on his part for me to beg for it.

I blame it on not having a normal social life. Maybe I never grieved like I should have, but I was a kid. I was overwhelmed by everything.

My mother moved on. She did not believe me when I said I saw or heard things. Instead, she listened to the doctors when they told her I had a problem and that it could be related to my father's death. Or I could not cope with moving away using the house as a crutch. Or the latest, that I shouldn't be left alone too long or let out of the house. Like I'm some psycho who would hurt myself.

Keeping my mouth shut has also kept me from making the wrong decisions. But I misread everything and have only myself to blame. I want to have friends and go out on a date with a guy and have sex if the mood is right. Tonight made me realize that I need to go out more and stop shutting myself out. The club was a bad idea for obvious reasons. Hades.

Hades is linked to the house. Every thought that isn't normal is linked to that house. If I want normal, I need to find it outside the house. Lazarus is one guy. He may not like me the way I want. I need to find one that does.

CHAPTER 14

Ivy comes back to school tomorrow. At least I'll have someone to talk to. Lunch at school sucks. It would be better if I had Ivy to talk to. Most of the time, I would go to the library and catch up on homework. It's where all the dorks that get picked on go. That includes the freaks.

I shut my math book and reach down to pick up my bag. When I look up, I see Jake sitting across from me.

"I was just leaving," I tell him, grabbing my book.

"I came to see you."

I arch a brow. "How did you know I would be here?"

He grins. "I took a wild guess."

Sure, you did.

I look around to see if his friends are hiding and if I'm part of some lame prank.

He gives me a confused expression. "Are you looking for someone?"

"No, I was looking for your friends. You know, the stupid jocks you hang around with."

His grin deepens. "I deserve that. But I've never made fun of you."

"I didn't ask."

He swallows and slides his hands inside the pockets of his letterman jacket. "I'm sorry if you thought I did."

I zip up my bag. "Doesn't make a difference. It wasn't like you were against them defending my honor."

"I play football with them. That's it."

I stand. "I don't care."

"Go out with me?"

"Excuse me?" I scoff. "Is this some kind of joke?"

"I swear it isn't." He stands. The table between us as we face each other. "I like you, Alice. I've always liked you."

I rub my lips together. "Right. You expect me to believe that."

Jake is good-looking. Smart. Blond hair, green eyes, chiseled jaw. Stockbridge's beloved wide receiver who also runs track. Two serious girlfriends since freshman year. One was a cheerleader, and the other on the debate team. He ended it before school started.

Two class A bitches who gave me shit all four years of high school. We have nothing in common except we go to the same school and have two classes together.

"Will you give me a chance to prove it?"

I snort. "Why should I? Your girlfriends and stupid friends have made my life miserable. Like I said, you did nothing to make me think otherwise. Laughed even."

His face grows serious. "I've never laughed at you, and if my ex-girlfriends laughed or made fun of you, it was because they were jealous of you. Jealous because I said you were pretty. Do you know why guys call you a Freak?"

He's lying.

I pull the strap of my bag over my shoulder. "I don't care."

I move to leave, and he grabs my arm. I look down at his hand and glare. His hand falls. "I'm sorry for touching you. I didn't mean...it's because they know they don't stand a chance with you. You would never go out with them, so it was better to make something up. Even the playing field, but I do like you, Alice. I was hoping we could go to the fair. Something fun. Not the haunted fair, but the regular one. Tonight."

"Tonight?"

"Or... or another night," he stammers. "It's Thursday, and it gets crowded on Fridays and Saturdays. I can have you home by ten."

I look away. I never thought he liked me. Not in a million years. What would his friends think?

"What are you going to tell your friends?"

"I don't care what they think. I don't have to tell them anything."

"Prove it," I challenge.

"I'll kiss you, Alice. Right here. Right now. Don't think I won't. I'll do it in the hallway after school when everyone gets out."

He's serious. I can see the want and determination in his green eyes. He's asking me out on a date. Not to his house or the drive-in but the fair. A friendly, family-oriented place. Tonight.

"Okay."

His eyes drop to my mouth. Shit.

"I'll go with you to the fair," I rush out.

His eyes lift, and he smiles. "Yeah?"

"I'll go."

"I'll pick you up at six thirty."

I pull out my phone. "What's your number so I can send you my address?"

"I know where you live." I look up. "Everyone at school knows where you live, and I have your number from lab class our freshman year." I raise my eyebrows. "I-if it's the same one."

Everyone knows where I live. He's right. It isn't a secret. Everyone knows I live at Hades Manor, but I'm surprised he kept my number all this time.

"It is. I'll see you at six thirty."

"I'll be there."

I walk to the exit.

"Alice."

I turn around. "Is it okay that I call you?"

"Yes."

He smiles with his phone in his hand.

I reach my locker, and my phone vibrates.

Jake: I got a date with the hottest girl in school.

An alert comes through from the school's social media page. It's from Jake posting the same message with a heart emoji. A flood of messages starts to go through, asking who. I open my message app and text Ivy.

Alice: I need your help. I got a date.

Ivy: Lazarus?

Alice: No. Jake.

Ivy: Football player. Cute, Blond with shitty friends.

Alice: That's the one.

Ivy: What happened with Lazarus?

Everything.

Alice: He said our time together was nice.

Ivy: Got it. Forget I asked. When is your date with Jake?

Alice: Tonight. The fair. He's picking me up at my house.

Ivy: Which fair?

Alice: The nice one. What do I wear?"

Ivy: Something hot. Low jeans. Cropped top. Sweater. Docs.

Alice: Lifesaver.

Ivy: It's what I do. :)

I've been meaning to ask her about the circus.

Alice: How was the circus?

Ivy: Crazy. Scary. Weird. I gotta let you go. I'm at work.

Alice: TTYL. Miss you.

Jake: I'm here.

I LOOK OUT MY BEDROOM WINDOW AND SEE A BLACK Maserati pull into the driveway. I wasn't nervous until now. My mom and Nick won't be home until the morning when their flight lands. I texted my mom, but she didn't respond. Nick said it was all right. I grab my small wallet and keys, then look at myself one last time in the mirror.

I jolt when I hear a loud bang come from the wall. I ignore it and walk out of my bedroom. It's the front door. I'm sure Jake used the metal knocker. I hear it again but make it down the steps.

I open the door, and Jake walks up the steps. He smiles when he spots me.

"I was about to knock when I didn't see you come out. I was hoping you didn't change your mind."

"Oh..." I smile, shut the door behind me, and turn to lock it. "Of course not. I said I'd go out with you."

He shuffles his feet. "You look perfect."

"Thank you. You look good."

He does. He's wearing blue jeans and a cream-colored sweater with designer sneakers. He smells nice, too. A woody and amber scent comes off him when I follow him to his car.

He opens the passenger door, and I sit inside. When he gets in, I can tell he is nervous. His finger hovers over the screen like his mind went blank for a second. He powers on the car.

"Nice car."

"Thanks. It's an early graduation present for getting into college. You drive a Tesla, right?"

"You mean the glorified tracking device my mother and step-father don't know how to use?"

He chuckles. "It's nice."

"Until you have to charge and sit in it when you go on trips, you can get to it with a single charge."

"Not easy, huh?"

"It takes getting used to. I keep forgetting to charge it."

"Kind of like us teenagers with our phones."

"Something like that."

We arrive at the fair, but this time, I'm in line on the other side. Moms push their kids in strollers. Moms convince their kids to go because they are the ones who want to go. Who would want to push a kid who cries because they don't understand the meaning of a line? They also have no idea of time or how expensive the fair costs. The highlight for parents is the food because they gave up on dieting and said screw it. I'm fat anyway. One more turkey leg or elephant ear won't hurt.

I offered to pay for my ticket and band, but Jake refused. I didn't expect him to pay. I'm not sure if the guys pay or not. He isn't my boyfriend, but I guess he is being a gentleman.

Once inside, people are dressed up like clowns and different characters. A man in the middle sells balloons. It looks like he is holding a hundred white strands in his hands. I bet you could see the balloons in the air from any side of the park. Kids are every-where. Rides already have lines with kids jumping on their feet, eager for their turn.

I stop in front of a funhouse with the entrance of the mouth of a clown.

"You want to go in?" Jake asks with a grin.

"Why not?"

It's a kiddie ride, but there isn't a line. Clowns are not every kid's favorite. I had no qualms. It's what I couldn't see but hear that gave me the creeps. Jake follows me. We reach the part with mirrors. It alters your reflection in a way no one likes but finds funny at the same time.

We laugh.

When we reach the exit, there is a large cylinder you have to walk through. I almost stumble.

Jake grips my waist. "Whoa."

I freeze. It was innocent. Our eyes meet for a second. "You okay? If I let go, can you make it?"

"I think so."

I make it and wait for him. "Thank you," I say.

"I enjoyed it."

I ignore his heated gaze and walk to the next ride. This time, it's a horror house. "You might get separated inside," the ride operator says in a scratchy voice like he's been smoking too many cigarettes. "If you do, don't go looking for each other inside. Come out the exit and wait."

"Got it," Jake says. He leans close. "Stay close to me, and we should be fine."

That plan was short-lived. Like the haunted fair, this house is similar. Dark hallways and props come out of nowhere, but the difference is that it's dark. You can see nothing until a light turns on, and a monster pops out to scare you.

We get separated. It's too dark to see in front of me. An actor in a bloody mask comes at me from behind a corner, and I run. When I look back, I stop. He's gone.

"Jake," I call out.

I'm shoved into a dark alcove. "Hey," I cry.

"Shh..."

Fear curls inside my stomach. A hand covers my mouth, and I'm pressed against a wall--a light flicks on. A man with a black Venice carnival mask is in front of me. "Welcome to door number two."

Hades.

I try to wriggle free but can't break free from his hold. He hasn't come back since the night in the woods. It's like he disappeared, leaving my phone with a note. His hand slides off my mouth.

"What do you want?"

He cups my pussy. "You have two minutes, or lover boy will send a search party for you. If he touches this, he dies. The choice is yours," he says in a deep robotic voice. "You've seen my work."

Imagining that happening to Jake has my stomach in knots. He can't kill every guy I go out with.

"What are you going to do, huh? Kill every guy I go out with?"

"That depends."

"On what?"

"How many guys do you go out with?"

"You're sick," I spit.

"You like it."

He shoves his hand inside the front of my jeans, finds my clit, and pinches it.

"Hades..."

"One minute and thirty seconds. How fast can Alice come?"

He plays with my clit, fast and rough. It's almost painful but feels good. My knees buckle, but he keeps me from falling. "Fuck." I grip the fabric of his cloak in a tight fist. "Hades..."

"Come like it's the last time, Alice. It's what you crave... it's why you let me."

"I hate you." My orgasm crests. I'm coming. My hands tighten.

He chuckles. "Let go, Alice. We both know he could never make you come."

I come. "Ahh... yes." He dips his finger inside, and my walls clench around it. My ears ring. Screams and slamming of doors from the house fade in the background.

"Don't forget, Alice. I see everything." He pulls his hand out and walks away.

CHAPTER 15

I walk out of the horror house. Jake spots me with concern in his voice. "Are you alright?"

"I'm fine. Got lost and couldn't find my way out," I lie.

Jake eyes me warily but then smiles. "Want something light to eat before we head to the rides."

"Sure."

We stop by the elephant ear and lemonade stand. It isn't light, but it will do. He buys us both an elephant ear and two lemonades. We take a seat on the bench.

"Are you having fun?"

I take a big bite to avoid answering him and nod. Am I having fun? I was finger fucked inside a horror house at the fair while my date waited outside for me to come out. Real fun. Unforgettable.

I think about what Hades did to Lance and imagine him doing the same to Jake. Panic sets in, and I drop the greasy, sugary elephant ear on the plate. I swallow and wipe my mouth.

"Are you?" I ask to break the awkward silence.

His eyes shift to mine. "Huh?"

"Having a good time?"

He nods, but I don't miss the guarded look in his eyes. Something is wrong. His eyes shift behind me. "Hey," Jake says.

The metal bench vibrates, and someone takes a seat next to me. I recognize the scent of cologne that drifts with the breeze.

Blue eyes meet mine, and my stomach somersaults. "Hey," he replies. His head swings to Jake. "What are you two doing here?"

Jake straightens, taking a sip of his lemonade. "We are on a date."

Lazarus clears his throat. "A date?"

Jake nods, placing his cup back on the table. "Yeah."

"I didn't think Alice was your type."

"Yeah, well...she is," Jake says, watching me.

Lazarus turns his body to face me. I take another bite, but I ignore him and look straight ahead. The tension is palpable. Lazarus seems bothered, but I couldn't care less. He had his chance both times he blew it, and I made a fool of myself. I don't owe him an explanation, but I feel guilty.

"Are you here alone?" Jake asks.

The thought didn't cross my mind. He's probably...

"I came with a friend of mine while he's in town. He never gets to go to this stuff," he says. *He*. I expected a girl.

I look to my left and stiffen. His friend is sitting on the corner of the bench, watching me with Guyliner and is wearing a band T-shirt-shirt. He has piercings on his lips, black fingernail polish, and long black hair tied in a bun. He nods in acknowledgment and says, "My name is Keir."

"My name..."

"Alice." He smiles and glances at Lazarus. "I've heard a lot about you, Alice."

My cheeks heat. "Good things, I hope," I reply.

Keir smiles. "Why wouldn't they be."

"Keir is a good friend of mine. He travels with my brother. We've known each other since I was little," Lazarus adds.

"Is your brother here?" I know it's rude to ask in front of Jake, but I'm curious.

Jake balls up his napkin and tosses it on his uneaten plate. He looks annoyed. Mad even.

"He came but had to leave. Work."

"Oh."

"Don't worry, you'll get to meet him soon," Lazarus says, his voice dripping with promise like he's sure of it.

Jake stands, leaning slightly forward. "Ready?" he asks.

I look down at my food and barely touch my lemonade.

"She isn't finished," Lazarus tells him, but I don't miss the warning in his tone.

Keir chuckles mindlessly, but there is nothing funny.

I went from being called a Freak to two hot guys having a pissing contest over me.

"That's alright." I move to stand.

"You'll get thirsty. You haven't finished your lemonade," Lazarus argues.

"I'll buy her water," Jake adds.

"I said it was alright," I say, sternly.

Lazarus nods and stands. "I'll call you later." He kisses me on my cheek and walks away with Keir following him. But I never gave Lazarus my phone number.

JAKE HAS ME HOME BY NINE O'CLOCK. HE'S BEEN QUIET since Lazarus showed up, giving me curt answers and short nods.

"Thank you," I say and open the door.

Another night ruined by bad decisions, laced with guilt and shame. I tried to give Jake a shot, but I didn't see what I did wrong in his eyes.

He stares straight ahead with a disapproving look on his face. I feel horrible but mad at the same time. Mad at Jake for shutting me out. We aren't even a thing. I'm more pissed at Lazarus and Hades.

I open my wallet and pull out two twenties to cover the fair ticket and food he bought for me. I place them by the cup holder and step out, ignoring him when he calls out my name.

"Alice! Alice…"

I shut the heavy wooden door, hearing the metal knocker clank behind me. I peek through the curtains, careful he can't see me from the large window. I watch as he reluctantly gets back in his car and drives off. I sigh in relief, but it is short-lived.

The piano starts playing loud, imposing, and haunting like it's a calling. Hades. I walk over but pause. I expected the piano to stop playing like it usually does. It keeps playing the haunting melody like a summons.

I walk in the living room, and there he is. Black mask. Long cloak. Black boots. Fingerless gloves. Like a phantom in the night. The beautiful music floats like a caress. Goose bumps coat my skin. He pauses and then picks up again, lost in playing music.

When he's done, he turns around on the bench. "Kneel," he demands.

"No."

"You chose. He lives."

"He was upset. It didn't have anything to do with you."

He widens his legs. "Oh, and why was that? Did he hurt you?"

I shake my head. "No."

"Are you sure? Because if he did, Alice…"

"He didn't. He was mad because…"

"He was jealous of…" He pauses. "A certain someone."

"I don't know what you're talking about."

"Lying has been a natural thing for you. I blame myself, but there is no reason to lie. He was jealous. An insecure little prick."

"At least I can see what he looks like," I fire back.

"If you were blind, would it matter, Alice?"

"I don't suppose it would, but I'm not blind. You're not blind."

"You like the fact that you can't see me. It's why you can't say no when I fuck you. When I tie you up. When I take you in the dark, there is no judgment. There is no wrong. There is no right. It is whatever you want it to be—freedom to express. To appease what you crave. You don't have to worry about what anyone thinks. Because...I only exist to you. I only exist in your mind."

"What if I don't want you to exist?"

"Is that what you want, Alice?"

I want to feel normal. I don't want to feel like I'm trapped. I don't want to think of him when I'm with someone else. He can't ever be real, and I don't want anyone else to get hurt. It's not that I'm ungrateful, but he shouldn't have happened.

"Yes," I reply, even though I'm not entirely convinced, and walk away. I pause, but when I turn, he's gone.

"Hades? Hades?"

Nothing.

I walk back. Check the back door. The kitchen. The front door. The bedroom. Nothing. He's gone.

Some people suffer from depression; they cut to feel, and they're suicidal to end the pain. But not knowing what is real or not real is worse. When your mind is in a dark room, and you're unsure if you're alone. If you see or hear the truth. Or everything is a lie, and you don't want to admit it.

CHAPTER
16

It has been a week and no Hades. My mother insisted I still go to my quarterly appointments with the therapist. I didn't protest. For the first time, I wanted to go. I had questions to ask. Questions about my sanity. If my mother found it odd, she said nothing.

I walk inside the three-story building and press for the elevator. Dr. Namsen's office was on the third floor at the end of the hall. I could never forget the smell of the third floor. It smelled of stale coffee and old books compared to the smell of the cheap air freshener. The one that makes a whooshing noise every time you walk inside the lobby.

The old brown carpet had seen better days. Brown spots in the corners and some areas where you knew most people visited on the floor. The building rented office spaces. The first-floor dentist's offices. The second CPA and struggling attorneys. Everyone knew the successful ones were located downtown. The third floor was empty except for Dr. Namsen's office, a chiropractor, and a massage therapist. My mother found Dr. Namsen on Google when I was ten, and it all started. Nine, to be exact.

I open the door and walk to the clipboard with only three names and sign mine underneath the third line. It was obvious Dr. Namsen saw a few patients a day. I tap the glass and walk away to take a seat in one of the mismatched chairs in the small waiting area. I pick up a six-year-old magazine someone left on the center table. The table had different words carved on it by the patients that came through. My favorite read, I AM NOT CRAZY carved in big capital letters.

After ten minutes, the door to my left opens, and Dr. Namsen appears in the doorway. He reaches over and grabs the clipboard. "Miss Grayson," he says like he doesn't know who I am and places a line through my name.

I drop the magazine on the table and stand. "Ready when you are."

"Right this way," he says, waving his hand so I can walk inside his office.

Dr. Namsen is in his mid-forties with waves of gray at his temples and dresses like Mr. Rogers. This time, a dress shirt, light blue tie, and dark blue vest sweater. Brown pants and white laced sneakers he purchased from Walmart. I know this because I saw the same ones when I went to buy my first box of period pads with my mother.

"How have you been?" he asks, taking a seat.

I sit on the small brown loveseat that reminded me of the carpet after I stepped off the elevator. It looks like it came from the side of the road, or he bought it from a garage sale.

"I've been good," I lie.

If I were good, I wouldn't be here, but I don't want to say that and seem rude. He's seen my toxicity when pressed.

"How have you been?"

"Good."

I know he's not *good*. Look at his office. I've been sitting on this same couch since I was ten.

He crosses one leg over the other. "How's school? Any issues there?"

Yeah, bullying. Name-calling. The usual.

"No."

"Boyfriend?"

I sigh. "No. I went on a couple of dates. Nothing to write about."

"How did that go?"

"Huh?"

I know my mother is behind the question, but why lie? It is what I wanted. To go out on dates.

"How did the dates go?"

Horrible.

"They were okay, I guess."

"No repeats."

"I wasn't interested in a repeat."

"How come."

"I haven't found the *one*."

He smiles. "I suppose high school can be challenging."

"How so?"

"It's a confusing time. Everything is––magnified. Relationships. Friends. It's a crossroad from being a minor into an adult."

"I can agree with that. You should tell my mother. She has a hard time letting go. She thinks I'm still a child and not an adult."

"I see. How's the house?"

"If you want to ask me if I still see and hear shit, you should say so."

He uncrosses his leg and rests his chin on his hand, observing me. "Do you?"

"No. I guess I outgrew whatever it is you said I had."

"Why do you think that?"

I grin. "I had sex. I'm not a virgin anymore, Dr. Namsen." He blinks like he has a twitch and clears his throat. "I'm cured. Sex cured my mental instability."

It fucked me up more, but he need not know that. I need him to tell my mother nothing is wrong so she can back off. No symptoms to address.

I made it to school, not wanting to go home after I left Dr.

Namsen's office. It's after the third period, right before lunch, when the bell rings. The doors on each side of the hallway open, and students start piling out.

When I reach my locker, I notice Jake talking to Summer from the cheer squad. His arm is leaning above her head near her locker, smiling at something she said. I've ignored his attempts to talk. I didn't answer his texts and dismissed him in class. He never admitted who the lucky girl was, and everyone assumed it was Summer he was talking about. Popular, pretty, and stuck up. His type. Lazarus was right. I'm not his type.

I shut my locker. "Hey." I look up and see Ivy leaning against the wall.

She looks different. Confident. Her clothes are different—emo-goth. We haven't hung out because I have been dealing with my inner thoughts and what I want to do after graduation.

I smile. "Hey."

"Are you doing anything tonight?"

"No. Why?"

She pushes off the wall. "I thought we could hang out. Go somewhere."

"What do you have in mind?"

She angles her head and looks behind me. I follow her gaze. Jake is making out with Summer. His tongue is almost down her throat.

I face her. "That didn't take long."

"He isn't into her. He's trying to make you jealous."

I snort. "All he did is prove to me he is no different from the idiots he hangs around with and a liar."

"What's up, ladies?" Mich says, walking toward us along with Tommy. Jake pulls away from Summer, making a sucking noise from their kiss and looks over.

"What do you want?" Ivy asks.

Mich grins. "I want to know if you ladies want to go to a party tonight. Everyone's invited, and I thought you two should go."

I grab Ivy's hand. "We'll think about it."

He nods. "Sure, sure." Tommy winks at Ivy while I pull her down the hallway.

We make it outside, out of earshot near a tree by the bleachers. The sky is overcast, and the temperature is cool. The wind picks up leaves, dragging them to the grass.

"What was that all about?" I ask.

"I don't know. Why would they invite us?"

"Because they want to do something they shouldn't, like fuck with us."

"We're not going," Ivy says in a cold voice.

She didn't want to go, and I didn't either.

"Of course not."

"Nothing good can come out of it."

"So where do you want to go?" I ask, changing the subject.

I didn't want anyone to overhear where we planned to go tonight. You can't trust anyone at this school.

"I know a spot on the other side of town. I heard my mother talk about it on the phone the other night to one of the ladies she works with. It's a bar."

"How are we going to get in?"

"They don't ID if you dress the part." She grins. "So we dress the part."

"Are you sure it's a good idea to try?"

"You have a better idea?"

"No."

"There haven't been any more cases of girls missing."

I take a seat on the lowest bench. "They haven't caught the guys responsible either."

The clouds are rolling in, covering the blue sky. The wind picks up again, causing a chill to spread down my legs.

"It's getting colder."

"It looks like boots are the choice to wear tonight." I lean back on the bleachers. "Do you have any fashion tips?"

She takes a seat. "I don't know what you have in your closet."

I smile. "Do you work after school?"

"Until six," she says.

"I can pick you up, and we can get dressed at my house. You can raid my closet," I offer.

She gives me a mischievous look like a kid about to steal her mother's car to sneak out. "Sounds like a plan."

CHAPTER 17

I arrive at the Big H ten minutes before six and walk toward Ivy's register, excited about tonight. I told my mother I was having a friend over, and she was...amused. I guess going to see Dr. Namsen worked, and she got the memo to back off. She doesn't know what we have planned. We will wear a coat to cover up our outfits and tell them I'm dropping her off back home and say I fell asleep at her house. If I'm lucky, she'll fall asleep and not care.

She finishes with a customer and wipes the conveyor belt down. It's store policy. There is a sign in front of the register for the cashiers telling them to wipe the belt down after every customer.

"Ready for tonight?" I ask with a smile.

She smiles. "Yep."

"Ready for what?" I freeze and watch a Gatorade and a pack of gum activate the belt sensor.

My gaze meets blue. My heart is pounding. "We're going out," I tell him.

Ivy looks between Lazarus and me as she scans––the two beeps like a countdown in the awkward silence.

He walks up to pay, making me step back. "Where to?"

"It's kind of a girls' night out."

"Hmm... you think that is a good idea?"

He means because they haven't caught the serial killer. According to the news, the trail has gone cold. There are no leads or witnesses. Only the dead bodies of the girls they found raped and mutilated.

He hands Ivy a ten-dollar bill. "You have a better idea?" Ivy asks with a raised brow.

I give her the *what the fuck are you doing* look, standing behind him.

"I don't know. What are you girls into?"

He faces me, and I try not to look. I try but can't help myself. My gaze sweeps him from head to toe. He's cocky and sexy as hell, wearing a cream-fitted sweater, jeans, and sneakers. Simple, but on him, it's hot. He could wear a dirty shirt with holes, and I still would find him attractive.

"Dancing. A couple of drinks at a bar Ivy knows about."

He turns to Ivy. "Bar?"

He means, how are you going to get in?

"You can come if you can get in. It's called the Moon Bar on Spencer Street off the main highway."

He nods and picks up his Gatorade and gum. He turns to face me before he leaves and says, "I'll see you there." He smiles and walks away.

The automatic doors open. "Doors open at nine," Ivy calls out, and he disappears. The doors close behind him.

I'm standing in front of the floor-length mirror. "You think he'll show up?" I ask Ivy.

SHE IS RUMMAGING THROUGH MY CLOSET. SHE TURNS when she finds what she thinks would work and walks out with a thin red camisole top. The kind that comes attached to a shirt so your tits won't show. I detached it so I could use it for something else.

"Here." She holds it out to me. "Wear this under the sweater. It gets hot in bars. If he doesn't show, it's his loss."

I take the thin red shirt. "Are you sure?" I ask, holding it up. It looks like a bra.

"No bra," she says with a smile.

I remove my sweater and take off my bra, not caring that I'm standing in front of Ivy topless. Her eyes find mine through the mirror, but I don't miss the way they dip lower.

"Has anyone ever told you have pretty breasts?" I shake my head, dropping my gaze at the way my breasts sit high on my chest. The way my nipples pebble from the cold. Ivy steps close behind me. "Well... they are." She smiles, resting her chin on my shoulder. "Have you ever had sex?"

I have unless I imagined the whole thing. It felt real, but I'm not sure of anything anymore because he's gone.

"Yes."

"And he never told you that you're beautiful?"

"No."

"You're gorgeous, Alice. Don't let someone take advantage of that or make you feel different. Don't be afraid."

"I'm scared of everything."

I have never admitted that to anyone. It wasn't like I had anyone to tell.

"We are all scared of something. It's if we let that fear win and destroy what we want."

I turn to face her, and something is haunting in her eyes. Things she has seen. Things she has accepted.

Her eyes fall to my lips.

I gasp when our tongues meet. She tastes sweet. Her mouth is soft. Her hands find my breasts. They tease my nipples, and I'm wet. My clit throbs. I cup her face, deepening the kiss. I like the way she feels on my tongue.

She explores my mouth like she's tasting a piece of fruit for the first time. Her tongue slides down my neck. She stops when she reaches my breast, takes my nipple in her mouth, flicks her tongue, and then sucks.

A moan escapes my throat. It feels so good.

She moves to the other breast and does the same. Her blond hair slides away from her face. I watch her and imagine her mouth between my legs and how it would feel. Soft. Wet.

I never thought of being with a woman or looked at one in a sexual way. I would never let another woman touch me, but Ivy is different. Safe.

She looks up with a smile, and I bite my bottom lip. Her hazel eyes ask me permission.

Permission to explore.

And all I want to do is feel.

IT SEEMS LIKE HOURS HAVE PASSED WHEN I WAKE UP, but it's only been two hours, and it's almost nine o'clock. We dozed off... after.

My clothes are on the edge of the bed.

"You still take these?" Ivy asks, picking up the pill bottle on my nightstand.

"Only when I can't sleep."

"Have you?"

I grab the red camisole and sweater, feeling weird that I'm naked. She let me sleep because she's dressed.

"I do now."

"How come?"

"I have trouble sleeping."

She nods and places them back on the table. "Don't we all."

"I'm gonna head to the bathroom before we take off."

"I'll wait downstairs. Hopefully, I'll run into your mom," she says mischievously.

I snort. "I'll meet you downstairs."

I open my bedroom door and run into a hard wall.

"Whoa." Strong hands steady me. I look up. It's Nick. "Are you alright?"

I nod but don't miss how his eyes land on my mouth. I step to the side to create space.

"I came to check on you. I heard..."

"What did you hear?"

We were quiet. Weren't we?

His eyes fall to my chest and then back to my mouth. "Nothing. That's why I came up."

"I'm going to freshen up and then take Ivy home."

"Hello," Ivy says from the doorway.

Nick slides his gaze to Ivy. "You must be Ivy," he says, but he knows that.

She smirks. "In the flesh."

He smiles. "I'm Nick. It's a pleasure meeting one of Alice's friends."

Ivy's gaze shifts to mine and back to Nick. "It's good to meet you, Nick. We were catching up on some homework." She looks at me with a grin. "We finished it all."

"I see."

"Well... I have to take Ivy back home. I want to meet her mom when she gets back from work before she heads to bed."

"I'll wait for you downstairs," Ivy says.

"I'm going to head to bed. Your mom is already fast asleep."

I'm not surprised. She is always asleep or out of town or somewhere that isn't where I am. She's embarrassed to be around me. She is afraid I'll say something.

"YOUR STEPFATHER IS A CREEP."

"Huh?"

My gaze swings to her after I place the car in park in front of the bar.

"You heard me. He knows and is not stupid. I also don't like the way he looks at you. Be careful."

"Nick?" I ask, but she isn't wrong.

I've never liked the way he looked at me sometimes. I've never said anything because he did nothing.

"Yeah, Nick. He's a creep, and you should stay away from him and make sure you lock your door."

"Are you sure?"

I keep asking because it is something I have been dealing with for a long time in the back of my mind. I had no one I could trust to talk to about it, but I trust Ivy. My thoughts go to Hades.

Is Nick Hades?

Or is Hades all in my mind?

No one knows he exists except me. Like a child creating an imaginary friend no one else can see or talk to. I don't believe in ghosts. Not the white kind that floats. I believe in shit that people can't explain. People who have seen or heard things no one else has.

She turns in the passenger seat. "I see it in your eyes. You know, but he hasn't done anything, so you dismiss it. You blame it on other stuff. But I'm the first person to tell you that whatever you think of him is correct. Don't trust him, Alice. He knows we weren't doing homework. He came to check, or he came to hear while your mom was asleep." I swallow. She's right. "Like I said, lock your door, and if he's home alone, make sure you wait until your mother gets back."

"You think he'll do something, Ivy?"

She looks out the windshield. People are walking to the entrance of the bar laughing. Headlights from cars pulling in flash across her features. "It's not if he will, Alice. It's when."

Fear curls around my stomach. Chills snake up my arms. What if he has already?

She opens the door, snapping me out of my thoughts. "Come

on? Let's go have fun and forget about it." I lock the car when we both shut the door. "Let's see if your man shows up."

"He's not my man."

"Keep telling yourself that."

"Trust me, I know."

"We'll see, tonight," she says like she knows something I don't.

Ivy knows a lot. You can tell by her facial expressions when she talks about things. Like Nick.

Sometimes I want to know how. Other times I don't because I know the reason is not something I would like to hear. I'm sure she doesn't want to share either. Talking about things is like reliving them, reminding yourself that they happened. In the back of your mind, like a file in the back of a cabinet, you can't throw away.

Ivy convinced me to leave my sweater in the car. It's a sure way without getting carded at the door. She was right. The guy manning the door was too busy staring at my tits and at Ivy's ass to give a shit.

The bar is at half capacity and opened an hour ago. It smells like alcohol and cologne. In another hour, it will be sweat, musk, and cigarettes. My experience at the last place reminds me how it gets. I hope the rest of that night doesn't end like that.

Ivy finds a spot at the bar and wedges herself between two guys.

She gets the bartender's attention. "Two blow jobs," she orders.

I've never had a drink called a blow job, but there's a first time for everything, and if Ivy ordered it, they must be good.

"If you're offering," the guy to her right says.

"It's a drink, genius," she replies with a sarcastic smile.

He gives her a once-over, liking what he sees. "How about I buy you two ladies a drink, and we can talk about what makes a good drink."

Nasty. I take in his jeans and red shirt. His beard looks like he forgot to shave because he's dirty and lazy. He looks around Nick's age.

"Pass," I reply.

The bartender hands her two shots, and when she pulls out money to pay, he shakes his head. "You're good."

"How?" she asks.

The bartender with light green eyes smiles. "I'm not at liberty to say, but you two ladies have an open tab."

"Cool." Ivy grabs our drinks, and I look around to see how that is possible but see no one giving us a knowing stare. Everyone is engrossed in their conversations or looking toward the dance floor.

I will not pass on free drinks, but still. Nothing is for free. If it's a guy thinking he will get lucky by opening a tab for us, I'll throw up the blow job right in his face.

"Here," Ivy says, handing me the shot glass. "And don't act like it's your first time."

I smile, taking it. "But it is."

She shrugs and takes the shot. I follow and wince, trying not to cough. Sweet but strong. Like fire candy. I clear my throat, hoping my mascara doesn't run from the tears that sprang.

"Shit."

"Too strong?" she asks. "It's lighter compared to the other stuff."

"If this is lighter, I'll deal."

The song changes, and I notice a man with a laptop in the corner. It must be the DJ controlling the music. I never thought bars had a DJ. I figured they all had a jukebox, and that was how they played music, but I guess this place is different. They have both.

After one song bleeds into another, there is no sign of Lazarus. I guess he couldn't get in. Ivy pulls me close to give everyone around the illusion that we are together. It works. No guys are coming up to us from behind. We dance for what seems like hours. I'm hot and sweaty. Ivy's neck is gleaming. A trickle of sweat slides between my breasts. We sway and dance to the rhythm of the music, having a good time.

After the second shot and a few hours, I leave Ivy at the bar and head to the restroom. I make the line, thankful there are only two people up front. When I make it out, the guy with the red shirt is leaning against the wall.

"Say, how about that blow job? You dykes love to suck."

"Fuck off," I spit. "Why don't you ask your friend since you're so desperate? I'm sure he can break you off real nice."

I hear a throaty, deep laugh from my left. Lazarus leans with his shoulder on the wall. His arms crossed, dressed in black jeans, black boots, and a fitted black sweater. He looks delicious, as always.

He came.

"What are you laughing at, faggot?"

"You. You're upset that she called you out. And don't use those terms to describe people who enjoy others of the same sex. It's impolite. Wrong. Offensive."

He pushes off the wall. "Oh yeah, faggot. What are you going to do about it? How about I let you watch her suck my cock. I'll show her what a real man looks like."

"Lazarus, let's go. He's drunk."

I'm not sure if he is, but the look in his eyes says he will not let this go.

The man snickers. "Yeah, Lazarus. Go. Run away like a pussy."

Lazarus's face hardens. "Let's go, Alice."

I walk up to him and take him by the hand, but his gaze never wavers on the man. Unease tugs but before he takes hold, Lazarus guides me to the main bar.

"What's going on?" Ivy asks once we are outside.

"The guy in the red shirt was waiting for me outside the bathroom. Thank God Lazarus showed up."

"Oh..." she says with a smile. "Let me guess. You're doing the right thing by leaving and not kicking his ass."

We reach my car. Lazarus opens the driver's side door once the sensor recognizes I have the key. "Something like that." He turns to Ivy. "Do you have a driver's license?"

"Yeah, why," she asks with a frown.

"When was your last drink?"

"Hours ago, and I only had two."

"Good, take Alice's car home. She'll pick it up in the morning."

"What?" I ask. Is he crazy? "I'm not going anywhere with you alone."

"It's not like you haven't been alone with me before." He grins when I shift on my feet. "Come on. You know I wouldn't hurt you. It will be our third date."

"I didn't realize we were dating."

"Go." I glare at Ivy. "Stop being a chickenshit and go with him, Alice. You have an alibi for your parents. It's perfect. I can't get lost with this electrical thing anyway."

No. This is a bad idea. What if he doesn't take me back, or Lazarus turns out to be the serial killer? Unlikely. He would have done something to me by now, but still...

"Give me the key fob. It's getting late," she says, holding her hand out.

I hand her the key.

"I'm parked over here," Lazarus says, pointing behind me.

"Where are we going?" I ask him.

"Somewhere."

CHAPTER 18

Lazarus's car is loud. The windows are limo-tinted black. The streetlights glow orange as we zoom through the dark streets. The car's interior is restored with a modern touch by adding a screen with GPS and apps to stream music.

"So where is this somewhere you're taking me?"

"Somewhere quiet and a place you can't run out on me."

"I didn't run out on you."

He gives me a side glance. "You did. Twice."

"I didn't see you run after me."

"Is that what you wanted?"

"Huh?" I play dumb.

I do. Who wouldn't?

"For me to chase you and bring you back."

"You don't strike me as the chasing type."

"I didn't ask what you thought. Is that what you want?"

"I don't want a reason to leave."

"Did I give you one?"

Several. I lost count.

I look down at my shirt, cursing myself for not grabbing my sweater. I can see my nipples. Who knows what I showed everyone else? It's not like I could get out of my body and stand in front of me to notice. I'm grateful he didn't turn the air conditioner too cold.

"I'm not sure. I felt it was time for me to go."

"I didn't want you to leave."

"Why?" I ask.

I thought he couldn't get rid of me fast enough. He didn't call me or show up. We ran into each other at the store by coincidence.

"Because I wasn't finished."

"It looked to me that you did."

"But *you* didn't."

He's right. I didn't, and I wanted to.

"It doesn't matter now, does it?"

He turns on a dirt road leading deeper into the woods. It's dark. The headlights from his car are the only light guiding him deeper. The tires go over rocks on the rough terrain. The car sways like we are out at sea.

The trail widens, and he stops at a lake. The half-moon gleams off the water like a mirror. Pieces of clothes hang off trees from people who have come here. I've heard of this place. They call it Lovers Lake at school. A place guys take their dates to fuck.

"You didn't have to bring me here if that is all you wanted."

He shifts in his seat. "I brought you here because it's quiet. And you can't run unless you want to get lost in the woods and be eaten by whatever is out there."

"Doesn't mean whatever *is* out there can't get us."

"Not while you're with me."

"Cocky much?"

He smiles. "No. I'm sure of myself. If I say something, I mean it. It's quite simple."

"So why me?" I ask, shrugging my shoulders.

"I'm not following."

"Why did you bring me here and not some other girl from school? I'm sure there are plenty who will do whatever you want."

"I don't want them. I want you."

I scoff. "I find that hard to believe."

"Like I said, if I say something..."

"You mean it. I got that part."

He sighs. "Look… I'm not good at relationships." I roll my eyes. Typical. "I didn't mean it like that. I'm serious. I'm not good at being charming or soft. I don't know what…" He pauses. "What I'm trying to say is… I like you. I'm not good at asking a girl out or being a boyfriend. Not the kind that does the flowers or the soft sex."

"What are you saying?"

"I want to fuck you, Alice. I want to drag you out of my car and fuck you on the hood until you lose your voice from screaming." Okay, I misread him. "I tried to do soft, but I suck at it. I don't know how to go slow, but I want you, Alice."

"Show me."

He does a double take. "What?"

"I said. Show me." His eyes dip to my chest. "Stop looking at them and do something about it."

I don't know why I said that. Some think girls are incapable of understanding men because of how emotional we get regarding sex. We can shut that part of our psyche off and become carnal like they are. Some men don't know what to do about it when we do. It's why they call us sluts. Whores. I call it freethinking or rather––free feeling. Satisfying our own needs. Some of us do it in private. Like right now.

Lazarus rushes toward me. His mouth is on mine. Rough and possessive. *Fuck, yes.* His hands shove my red shirt under my breasts. My nipples tingle with nerves with every stroke of his tongue. My fingers grip his hair and tug.

He rips his mouth away, and I'm stunned. Confused. He opens the door and walks around the car. He drags me out. Lifts me and sits me on the hood of his car. "I said I wanted to fuck you on the hood of my car."

In a flash, he's between my legs, pushing them wide. My skirt is pushed roughly to my waist. I'm glad I'm wearing thigh-high pantyhose under my boots. A finger curls around the scrap of lace of my panties and pulls, tearing them free. He tosses them over his head. It catches on a leafless branch of a tree near the shore of the lake.

It's cold, but the fire from his gaze tells me not much longer. He undoes the button of his jeans and takes himself out. One hand grips my thigh. My hands wrap around his neck.

"Scoot your ass to the edge," he rasps. I do, and he removes his shirt.

The moonlight glimmers over his skin. He's inked everywhere. Skeleton faces. Doll faces crying black tears. Silhouettes of girls on a swing. Swirls of clouds create a sky on his chest. Evil clown faces with a jester hat cover his left and right pecs. Another with an evil smile. The other one was crying. I'm captivated by the fire drawn under them like they are in hell. He's pure muscle like he spends hours in a gym or a man who trains in gymnastics. Fit. Hard. Beautiful. There isn't an ounce of fat on him.

I look up. "It gets better the lower you go."

"That's a bold statement."

His hand shoots out and grabs my neck. "Let me show you."

My hands grip his biceps, and he shoves his cock into me in one go. "Oh... fuck," I cry out.

It burns so good.

"Told you."

Shadows cover his face as he begins to move inside me. I lean back, meeting his thrusts. My hands are flat on the hood of the car. Grinding my hips. My nipples are hard from the cold air. He leans forward, his dark blue gaze like the Red Sea, offering me salvation from the fire he's causing between my legs.

He grunts. "Let me break you, Alice."

His thrusts are measured. His grunts are strained like he's holding back something powerful. I want it. I want him to break me.

"Break me," I plead.

His eyes lift. His nostrils flare. In one deft movement, I'm on my stomach, and my ass is in the air. My hair pulled tight in a menacing grip, causing my neck to arch. He rams his cock into me from behind.

"Ahh."

My vision goes in and out, but it gets clearer as he swells inside me, and my body accepts.

"There is an agreement between a man and woman when she allows him inside her. It doesn't matter if she's his wife or not. Girlfriend. Mistress. Lover. Pet. There's an agreement when he first sticks his cock inside her." He licks the side of my face. "This is ours, Alice."

He fucks me like an animal. Like a fucking savage out for blood. *My blood*. I grip the edge of the hood. My feet lift off the ground with each thrust.

He growls in my ear. He bites my neck and licks the sting.

I yelp when he slaps my ass hard. "Lazarus!"

The heat of the sting spreads like wildfire to my clit as he violently thrusts inside me. He's right, there is nowhere to run. How could I when all I wanted to do was burn for him? Make him mine. The way he was making me his. Hard. Deep. Explosive like a cork shooting from a wine bottle. I want to come but want to feel him come first. I don't want to miss it if I'm flying high, lost in my own mind. I wait.

He tenses. He roars when he comes. "Alice!"

I come right after like a dam breaking, and the water rushes in. My breaths come short. "Mmm... I'm coming."

I can feel him inside me. Sweat drips down my neck. The cool air welcomed on my chest. The palms of his hands cup my breasts, holding me when he pulls out. I wince from the sting. It's hot and sticky between my thighs.

"Sit on the hood of the car." He sees me struggle and helps me up. "Open your legs," he demands. "Scoot up to the middle of the hood."

I do. His head dips, and the touch of his tongue on my pussy has me moaning again. "Mmm..."

I look up at gray clouds like a mist in the dark sky. It feels like

I'm floating in pure bliss. He cleans me with his tongue. His lips are soft. The breeze cools the fire on my heated skin. There is no way he could make me come again, but he does. I cry out his name to the dark sky. My back arched. My hand on his head pushes him deeper between my legs, igniting me with his tongue. This is the best sex I've ever had. His cock is like heroin. His tongue is like a new drug I know I would never get enough of.

Snapping twigs grab my attention. He pulls away, and I whimper from the loss.

He frowns. "Come on. Someone is coming."

Waves of panic flow through my veins. I fix my top and push my skirt down. He buttons his jeans and slides his shirt over his head. He helps me down. Headlights blind us both. It's a black car, and laughter blankets the silence. It sounds like a yodel.

The black car stops a few feet away, and four guys get out of the car. It's Mich, and three older guys I don't recognize.

"So you are fucking her." His eyes swing, and he licks his lips. They're red like he's on something. "You're full of surprises, Freak. I should have beat him to it. Tell me, Laz, how's the pussy? Tight?"

Two guys step forward, and the other goes to the driver's side of Lazarus's car.

"What the fuck are you doing here?"

"What we come to do. You know... fuck. Smoke. Find pussy. Snort. But I'm interested in pussy right now. Isn't that right, guys?"

"Pussy sounds good," the one by the driver's side says. He's wearing a leather jacket and a black shirt. He's big, and so are the other two who came with Mich. I suspect they used to go to Stockbridge and now play college football.

The blond one closest to Mich keeps watching me like he will pounce. Nausea pokes my stomach. They'll rape me.

"Get back in the car and leave," Lazarus warns.

I know Lazarus is strong, but there are four to one, and the odds that they don't knock him out and get to me are slim.

"Nah. Everyone has wanted a piece of that ass since freshman year, but she's too crazy to give anyone the time of day. Poor Jake lucked out, and it was because of you. I'll take my chances now. No one would believe her crazy ass anyway, and my boys know how to keep quiet. Besides, you didn't think I let you get away with hitting me, did you?"

"Fuck off, Mich," I snarl.

He chuckles. "No can do. I bet; your pussy is already wet. It can take four more cocks."

Bile rises in my throat.

"You'll have to get through me first," Lazarus says in a hard tone.

"I'll take my chances. I never liked you. Everyone kisses your ass like your shit doesn't stink. Every girl in school wants to fuck you, but you give her the time of day. I'm curious as to why." He licks his lips. "It must be her pussy."

I step toward the car, knowing Lazarus left the keys in the ignition. "Move again, and you'll be sorry," the guy with the leather jacket warns.

"How about we make a deal," Lazarus offers. "You get through me first."

Mich chuckles. "I'll toss your pretty ass in the lake, or I'll let you watch while we defile her over your car."

"Then I guess you have it all figured out."

Lazarus is calm, but I'm panicking. He cannot take them all out without them getting to me.

"Lazarus," I beg. "Don't."

He turns. "Come here." I walk up to him. My hands are shaking. "Look at me." My eyes lift but I don't see fear. "I need you to listen to me." He kisses my temple. "Run," he whispers. "Run and don't look back."

His eyes turn down to mine. He's giving me a chance. What if he gets hurt or worse?

But I don't have a choice.

My lip trembles, not wanting to leave him, but I give in.

"Okay."

He steps away and turns to Mich and his cronies. "Alright, Mich. Four to one. Only pussies fight four to one but...that is what we're fighting for right? My girl's pussy."

He called me his girl.

"She won't be yours for long, bitch." Mich gains on him-- the other three flanking Lazarus. I don't have time to ponder. Lazarus takes off in one direction. I take off the way we came down the dirt road.

"Get him!" Mich yells. "Jimmy, get her!"

I hear footsteps behind me, but I run. I run down the dirt road, careful not to twist my ankle on a rock. I can't see it's so dark. I can hear yelling. Footsteps. I veer through the brush of trees, trying to find a hiding place.

The deeper I go, the colder it gets. I stop. The only thing I can hear is my breathing. A branch snaps, and I know he isn't far.

I hear a loud wail. A man's cry in agony. My heart beats fast, and my hands won't stop shaking. Tears run down my cheeks and my nose. I'm afraid to sniff, or he will find me. I look between a row of trees, hoping it's the right way to escape. I can hear Lazarus's voice in my ear. *Run.*

I run. My lungs burn. My legs are on fire. My eyes blur, but I blink back my tears and wipe my face. Running wards off the cold, but my skin is like ice.

"Come on, baby. I can smell you." He laughs. "Running is pointless," Jimmy says.

Goose bumps coat my skin like a rash. I pause. He's close, but I can't see him. I turn my head left and right, careful not to move my feet until I find another clear path.

Another piercing scream assaults my ears, and I run. He'll be too busy listening to notice me running through the trees. I run and run until I trip and fall to my knees, hitting the root of a tree poking up from the ground. I bite my tongue, holding back the scream in my throat from the burning sting. I look at my knees, and they're bloody. The moon gives me enough light to see that my boots and thigh-highs are torn. I stand, and my knees almost buckle. I can feel the trickle of blood down my shins.

I hear shuffling, then silence. My whole body shakes. I'm so cold. I open and close my hands to get a feeling in my fingertips since they've gone numb. I hope they didn't kill Lazarus. I hope he's okay, but I'm alone, and everywhere I look, there are more trees and no light.

Every rustle of leaves or snap of a twig behind me sends a jolt of terror through my veins, and I dare not look back. There is a thick underbrush to my right, and I'm afraid I won't see a creek and fall in.

I try to listen to see if I can hear cars, but it's late. It must be past midnight, so no one will be on the road. It's funny how you want to find a secluded place, and then you want to find people when something bad happens. It's cliché like a scary movie.

"Where are you?" Jimmy singsongs. "You know I'm going to find you. You can run, but I can smell you. I can smell your wet cunt, and it's only a matter of time."

The clouds move. The moonlight filters through a lattice of leaves, helping me see through the shadows.

The hairs on my neck stand on end, and I strain to listen. A third scream pierces through the air. Closer now. Fear grips my stomach. My teeth clatter. I hear footsteps. Twigs snap, and then I hear Jimmy scream, "Nooooo! Ahhhhhh!"

I run through the brush, and trees cut my arm, but I keep running. I won't stop until I reach the road. I gasp. My lungs, screaming for air as I look left and right. It's dark, and the road is empty. My ears ring.

I walk the way we came on the main road. The air turned frigid, and I could feel an invisible malevolence closing in. My chest is tight from running. The forest seems to pulse with sinister energy, but I push myself harder. The urgency of escape burns in my chest.

A car approaches from behind. I look over my shoulder, but

there are no headlights. A guttural growl reverberates through the night, freezing me in my tracks.

I stumble, trying to get away. I move to the patch of grass, the car stops and the driver's side door opens. I fall to my knees, exhausted. Sobs wrack through me. I will die.

"Alice!"

He's alive!

"Lazarus," I croak through chapped lips.

He reaches me and picks me up like I weigh nothing. "Oh, baby. I got you." He places me inside his car like I'm a small child. He cranks up the heat and shuts the door.

I watch him drive, and the only thing that escapes my lips before my eyes close is, "How?"

CHAPTER 19

My eyes flutter open. The sound of a door closes. It smells different, like stale cigarettes. I'm not home, and this is not my bed.

"Hey." I turn to my side, and Ivy stands dressed, ready for school. "Are you okay?"

"I have some breakfast for you. Lazarus left it for us." Everything from last night comes flooding back, and I sit up. "Whoa. It's okay, Alice. When he brought you here, you were knocked out. What happened?"

The best and the worst night of my life happened. I look at my knees, and they are bandaged. My arm too. I have a black hoodie and sweat shorts on. I bury my nose in his collar, and it smells like him. Like Lazarus.

"He took me to Lover's Lake and… I fell." I leave the worst parts out.

"He didn't say, but he did say to make sure you ate breakfast and he told me to call your mom this morning. I did and told her you fell asleep. She said it was okay but to make sure we made it to school on time."

Mich. What did he do to Mich?

"How much time do I have to get ready?"

She tosses me a shopping bag. "Twenty minutes."

When I pull into the slot in the student parking lot, news

crews are everywhere. What the hell? Kids crane their necks at journalists reporting with their cameramen recording live.

"What the hell is going on?"

"Didn't you hear? It's all over the news. Mich and a couple of his friends were found dead last night. They were found in Mich's car on the side of the road."

"Where?"

"Main highway, I think. No one knows who did it, but it was hard to identify them. They had no eyes. No tongue and no"--she makes a gesture to her groin area--"dicks."

Holy shit. "No eyes."

"Funny that you mentioned that part and not the fact that they had their dicks cut off but yeah, no eyeballs."

He cut their eyeballs out so they couldn't see. Tongues so they couldn't speak, and dicks so they couldn't...

School is a madhouse. People crying. No clues were left at the scene, and the police have questioned people at school about Mich.

"I have to tell you something," I tell her once we sit in class.

She smirks. "There is nothing to tell, Alice." But I don't miss the look in her eye.

She knows.

Did he tell her? That's impossible. But she knows something. Something I missed.

"Ivy?"

Her red-colored lips curl in a smile. "Did anyone tell you that you look beautiful this morning? If they didn't, that would sound crazy, right?"

I skip school around lunch and make it home. I walk into my bedroom, ignoring the nagging feeling crawling over my skin. I close my door and flip the lock. I sit on my bed, pull out my phone, and call Lazarus's number.

It rings, and his voicemail picks up.

"Hey, it's me. Call me when you get this."

I sent him a text to call me. I look at the screen to see the three little bubbles, but they never come.

Fuck.

I remove the leggings he must have bought me and check the bandages on my knees. It looks like someone who knows first aid applied and dressed my wounds. There is ointment on my cuts when I lift the tape. The cut on my arm also has a white gauze taped.

I look around my room and then under my bed, but there is nothing. It wasn't a dream, Alice. Last night wasn't, but what about Hades? Ivy is acting weird. I left school because I couldn't take the news and the questioning of who could have done it when I knew who did. Some feel bad for Mich. People talk nonsense like they were this great person who left the earth, when Mich was a son of a bitch who deserved what he got. He was a horrible human. He wasn't good. None of those guys were.

I would never tell the police what happened. Lazarus saved me. He protected me.

I hear a rattling from the doorknob, and a sense of unease grips me. My heart leaped in my chest. I close my eyes and open them, trying to see if it's my mind playing tricks on me. The doorknob rattles like someone is trying to get in.

"Hello?" I call out. The rattling stops. I sigh in relief, but then it starts again. "Stop it," I whisper more to myself. "Stop it," I repeat.

Pissed off, I unlock the door and open it, but there's no one when I peer out, and strong arms grip me.

"It's about time." A scream escapes my throat in panic, but it's muffled when his hand covers my mouth. He drags me back into my room and slams the door. "I've been waiting a long time for this."

Nick slams me on the bed and shoves my legs open. "No!" He slaps me hard across the face. Pain explodes across my cheek. A metallic taste lands on my tongue.

I spit blood in his face, and he rewards me with another slap.

"Stop it, Alice." He undoes his belt. The sound causes sobs to escape. Ivy's words. *"Your stepfather is a creep."*

"Please, Nick. Don't," I beg through tears.

"I can't take it anymore, Alice. I've wanted you since the first time I laid eyes on you. You were so beautiful, and there was only one way to have you. I had to marry your cunt of a mother and watch you. Wait until the day you let me in so I can fuck that sweet cunt. It's time. I've gotten you a house. A pretty house so I can fill it up with our children. A beautiful car. All for you, baby. I'll give you anything, and don't worry about Mommy. She'll be going away soon."

"No!" I scream, gasping for air. I writhe and flail my arms.

He grabs me by the neck hard. I can't speak. I can't scream. "Stop it, Alice. I switched your pills. You're not on birth control anymore, and it's time."

No! He... I feel his penis near my thigh, and I want to gag. There's a loud bag from the wall. He looks up with a look of confusion. He puts his cock away, and I sigh in relief.

He looks down between my legs and cups my pussy with his hand. "This is mine. Let's see who's making that noise, shall we?"

"Fuck you!"

He smiles malevolently and presses his lips to my cheek, and I want to gag.

"It's a promise. I've been watching you for so long, Alice. I love stroking my cock to the thought of you. Watching you when you think it's all in your mind. Thinking you are crazy the whole time when I've been the one crazy... crazy for you."

"You're sick."

He smiles. "For you."

I try to push his hands away, but he pinches my clit over my panties. "Stop being a bad girl. I'll pound that cunt the way you like." He lowers his voice. "Suck your pussy like Ivy did the other night." I slap him, and he slaps me right back. "I don't like striking you. Stop making me do it. It's not my style."

Another loud thud and a bang. Footsteps cause the wood to

creak from the stairs. Nick releases me, and I sit up and pull my leggings on. I wipe the blood from the corner of my mouth, grimacing at the sting from the cut on my cheek. I never wanted the ghost to be so real until this moment. Ghost that will scare Nick to death, literally. I scan my room for a possible weapon but come up empty. The best I have is my lamp. I found my phone to call the police but saw a message.

> Unknown: Don't call the police.

I hear a struggle and a bunch of thuds in rapid succession. The door is open halfway. I hear the floorboards creak. I hold my breath, but I see no one.

I walk toward the door, taking slow steps. One then another. My phone is in my hand, and when I reach the door, I scream, "Noooo!"

It's Hades. I back away from the door until I reach the bedroom window. He stands imposing with his black mask on and the leather one with spikes in his hands. "Put it on."

"No."

"Suit yourself." He tosses it by the mirror, hearing the metal spikes hit the wood floor, and walks out.

What the fuck? I unlock my phone, and when I try to dial, the call doesn't go through, and an exclamation point is over the signal icon. Fuck!

I look out the window to find Wilfred. I freeze. He's looking up at me, shaking his head slowly. His face was white like cheese and wrinkled. I bang my hand on the window. "Wilfred! Help me. Call for help!" He shakes his head and walks away.

"He won't do it." I turn around. Hades sits on the edge of my bed. I calculate the distance to the door from my bedroom window, accepting that I won't make it out if I run.

"Where's Nick?"

"He's indisposed at the moment."

Is he Nick, and he's messing with me?

"Take off the mask." His head turns robotically. The mask obscures his face. "I told you never to come back."

"Kind of good that I didn't listen."

"Take it off," I demand.

"Are you sure?"

"Yes."

"I want to tell you a story first. There were two boys. The older one wanted to be a performer, and the younger one wanted to create the greatest place on earth to have fun. Together, they lived and breathed the family business. It was in their DNA, you see. It was passed down from generations. It so happened that one wanted to do the unthinkable. He wanted to perform, but he had to prove himself, so he needed the help of his younger brother. He had to convince his father to allow him to join the circus, but not just any circus--a special one. The younger brother felt left out when their father agreed. He felt abandoned, but his father prepared. He built him a mini-fair before he was born like the one you saw. His sons were his pride and joy. It wasn't the money. He has plenty. It wasn't the legacy of the fair. It was his wife, and it was his sons. That was his greatest achievement in life. But one day, his parents wanted to surprise their older son by watching him perform--"

"What happened?"

He's talking about the family who lived here before. He knows the story.

"They died in a car accident. The older son never saw his parents watch him perform, and their youngest son was left orphaned."

"I thought they all died."

He chuckles. "It's what they wanted everyone to think, but I guarantee you that they didn't die."

"Where are they? Why would they let someone rent their house?"

"They were kids. One decided to stay behind, and the other left to continue his dream as a performer."

"Why did he stay behind? Why didn't he leave?"

"He fell in love with a girl. A girl he has waited for. "

"He was a child. How--"

"There is no rule at what age one can fall in love, I assure you. The boy fell in love and never left her side. She didn't know it, though, but he needed to protect her. This house holds secrets."

"From what? Who is she?"

He removes the hood from his cloak. Then his black mask and my voice stops in my throat.

"It's me, Alice. It's always been me. Since we were little, in these walls keeping that man out of your room."

My mind goes back to when I sat in the Ferris wheel behind the house. The initials L.H. Hades. Lazarus Hades.

"You're Lazarus Hades."

"In the flesh, my love," he says in a thick British accent.

"Did you—"

"I killed him."

"And my mother?"

"She was drugged every night since you were nine, Alice. I couldn't do much for her, but she's alive. She's been handling his work. She's been running his business while he comes here to watch you. Wilfred and I have made it very difficult for him. The worst thing a person wants is to get caught."

I look out the window and see him drag a large bag. He looks up at the window, nods, and picks up the shovel.

Lazarus stands next to me, watching Wilfred dispose of Nick's body. "I'm sorry. I've tormented you all these years, but you have to understand... I was raised with a circus, and they protect this town."

"How so?"

"My brother--"

"The man at the haunted fair. The one with the white mask who rode with Ivy. It was you. You rode with me on the roller coaster."

"I've always been with you. I was tormenting you... loving you the only way I knew how. I'm not normal, Alice. Forgive me. Forgive me for making you think you were crazy. That you heard things, but that was better than--"

"Him finding me alone."

"Precisely."

"And Ivy?"

He smiles. "She met Draco. I think he's taken with her. There is much you don't know, but Ivy can fill you in. I think it should come from her."

"What happens now?"

He faces me. His blue eyes caressed my lips. "I made it look like Nick disappeared. And... I introduced myself to your mother as Lazarus Hades and... as your boyfriend." He leans close and whispers, "I don't want to seem forward, but you might be pregnant with a little Hades."

The pills. He switched him. It's possible.

"I'm scared."

"You have nothing to be scared of, Alice. Wilfred is taking care of things, and I've been taking care of the parks."

I smile, loving his British accent.

"What are you smiling about?"

"I love your accent. You hide it so well."

"I had a lot of practice," he says without it. "I'll keep it, then."

I angle my head. "What do you mean parks?" I ask.

"I own all the fairgrounds in North America and in England. My brother owns the circus in our parks. Remember, he travels."

"What happens inside the circus?"

"Ivy can answer that, or I'll show you. Halloween is coming. Every year, we perform on Devil's Night. It's a special night for purging."

"Purging?"

Something in his eyes flickered...for a moment. "Yes." His eyes soften. "I love you, Alice. I'm always with you, and I'll always love you in this life and in the next. Forever."

"I love you, Lazarus Hades."

CHAPTER 20

My eyes fly open, and it's pitch black. I can't see. Not even a flicker of light. I move to sit up, but my hands are bound. I hear the chains scraping against the wood. I relax and take a deep breath, trying to get the cool air to filter through the mask. This isn't real. It's a dream. Like last time. I feel a hot breath between my legs. A tongue is between my thighs.

I'm not crazy. *It's a dream*, I tell myself repeatedly.

"Mmm…" I moan as I feel his tongue inside me.

It's him. There was one time it was her, or was it?

"It's me, Alice. It has always been me inside you. Inside your head. Inside your body. Now…wake up."

My eyes fly open. My hand touches my face, but there is no mask. The sun streams through my bedroom window. The rays brighten the mint-green walls. I look beside me and smile. A single red rose is on my pillow with a note that reads Mrs. Hades. My hand flies to my stomach, and I feel the small swell of my belly.

A woman walks into the bedroom in a gray and white maid uniform. She's wearing a white hat. Her hair is up in a French twist with a tray of breakfast. "Good morning, Mrs. Hades. I brought you breakfast. Mr. Hades is waiting for you. He says he's finished."

I pinch my brows in confusion. "Finished with what?"

"Why the small fair, my dear. Don't you remember? He's spent all summer making it perfect so it will be ready for children." She gives me a knowing smile. "He kept you awake again, didn't he? You were dreaming. I came to check on you, and you were tossing and turning. I couldn't find it in me to wake you."

I place my hand over my head. It feels foggy. "I was dreaming?"

"Mr. Hades says you have dreams or visions all the time. So what did you dream about this time?"

A man walks inside the room that looks like Lazarus but an older version of him. "What was it this time?" he asks. "Your visions or the gift of *the sight* as we like to call it."

"Lazarus?"

"Yes, my love. I have been waiting all morning so I can show you the swings and the Ferris wheel. It has been tested out. I wanted you to experience it before you got bigger, but I'm sure Lazarus will love it."

"Lazarus?" I question-tested the name again on my lips.

His gaze lands on my belly. "Yes, it's what we will name our son. L.H. will go on for generations. We let you name our first, but you know how articulate he is."

Draco...

CIRCLE
OF FREAKS

Ivy Sloan

Since I was a little girl, I fell in love with the circus. It's all I ever wanted to see up close or be a part of. There was no room for things like that where I grew up. There was no room for anything except bad memories and bad expectations.

Every year around Devil's Night, since we moved to Stockbridge, the Circle of Freaks paranormal circus comes to town. It's an eighteen-and-over horror show in which no one talks about what goes on inside because they can't.

But this year is different. This year, my prayers have been answered by gifting me a ticket. Despite what people think of me at school. Despite the girls gone missing––– Found dead. I wasn't prepared for what I would see.
I wasn't prepared for...him.

CHAPTER

1

I stare at the wall with all the scuffs of dirt that needed paint. The kind you wonder how they got there or if the wall is even worth painting over because it will look the same a few weeks later. I wonder how much longer. How much longer will it be before I get out of this shithole.

When you have money, that wouldn't matter. You would paint it. Except for those who earn a paycheck above poverty—for people like us, that isn't an option. And if you live at the Meadow River apartment complex in Stockbridge, Massachusetts. The ones who couldn't pay their light and rent in the same month.

The Meadow River apartment building is old. It still has the box air conditioners that hung out the windows. Some have duct tape to make sure it wouldn't fall out.

According to state law, a landlord is not required to provide air-conditioning. When the summer heat came, I had to walk around half naked. We didn't have enough for the electric bill. Like most tenants living in Meadow River, they had to choose the rent or the air conditioner in the summer.

I pour the last few drops of milk into my cereal bowl. A sheen of sweat coats my forehead. I look at the dry cereal, debating whether to throw it out or eat it dry. I walk over to the sink and turn on the faucet, adding some water into the bowl. Placing it down, I check the time. Ten minutes before the bus pulls out front.

I mix the cereal with water and milk with my spoon, close my eyes, and take a bite. It's not the worst I've tasted, but it sucks to eat cereal with water.

I take a deep breath, checking the time again, bracing myself for my last year of high school. Three minutes.

If it were up to my mother, she would have told me to hell with it and ask for my hours back at the grocery store. I repeated the eleventh grade because I had so many absences and failed all my classes. I had no choice but to skip school that year and get a job or risk getting evicted. My mother doesn't make enough at the diner she works at, so it's up to me to help with rent.

The kitchen light goes out. I drop my spoon with a clank and open the front door to see if the yellow light in the hallway is still on. If we were a couple of days late paying the electric bill, the first thing I did was look outside to see if anyone else's light was still on. If it's not, it's a blackout. If it is, our light was shut off for non-payment.

Looking up, I let out a relieved breath. It's a blackout. I have to ask my mother if she paid the bill before the shut-off date. If not, we wait until I get paid from work or when my side hustle comes through.

Grabbing my bag and dropping the bowl in the sink, I head out, locking the door behind me. The Meadow apartments aren't bad compared to where I lived my freshman year in South Carolina. This place beats the trailer park filled with meth addicts. This was the best my mother could do, coming from a background of jobless addicts and prostitutes.

I walk down the stairs because the elevators are out of order, which is no surprise. They smell like piss anyway.

The obscene graffiti was something that always stood out. It was on the neighbor's doors and the walls in the hallway in big black letters sprayed over the peeling paint. Some were on the elevator doors. No one complained that the building hadn't been painted. It looks like it's been that way since the early seventies. No one wanted the place to look too nice for fear they would raise the rent, and we would all get screwed.

I look at the thoughtful message, SUCK COCK. It has a picture of two big testicles with a gigantic penis drawn above it and, SMOKE AND FUCK. The messages changed every so often. No one knew who did it, and the security guard was too busy sleeping on the night shift to give a shit about it. There were no cameras or daytime security. Anyone could come inside the building, which was disconcerting.

The yellow public school bus arrives on cue with FUCK SCHOOL spray painted on the side. The apartment complex is behind the Stockbridge Mall. The drive-in theater behind the mall is called the Coyote Drive-In. The drive-in plays one new release and three classic movies every week.

Stockbridge was founded in the seventeen hundreds. A forest surrounds the whole town. It has old architecture and historic homes on the west side of the school. A fair also opens when it is above thirty-eight degrees in the colder months. Stockbridge High is the middle ground. The center of it all. Where the teenagers meet, graduate, and go their separate ways.

I hop on the bus, ignoring the smirks and stares aimed my way. The bus gets on the highway from the parking lot that separates the plaza from the apartment complex. The only way to reach this side of Stockbridge is the main highway. It's old, and no one comes to this side unless you live here or want to park to watch a movie or the mall. No one goes to the plaza. Everyone knows that is the last thing people do at drive-ins. It's an excuse to park your car with dark-tinted windows so you can fuck in the back seat.

I should know. It's how I lost my virginity my sophomore year in the back seat of the star quarterback's Mustang. He said the right things to get me to go out with him.

It didn't even hurt the first time, and every time I think about it, I hate myself for being so stupid. I didn't care about losing my virginity. I had to lose it to someone, but I should have done it with someone else. Not a six-foot-two, tanned skin, ash-blond hair, blue-eyed asshole like Tommy Hill.

After reading about how perfect and magical sex and love were supposed to be, I realized how bad at sex he was. A girl like me didn't expect love. Not where I came from or how I was raised. When we moved to Stockbridge, I wanted to fit in. I wanted to experience what I read about, and no one knew where I came from. I thought Tommy was different, and he knew what he was doing since he was so good on the football field. I wasn't prepared for how bad it would be.

I can feel Tommy's hot breath on my neck. He rubs his fingers over my clit to get me wet. His fingers are rough and uncoordinated. I watched enough porn on my piece of shit cell phone in my bedroom to see how it was done. He shoves into me, and I expect a burn from him penetrating my barrier, but nothing—a lot of rubbing and no sparks.

He looks up, and I make the same face I saw the girl getting fucked on my phone. It works. He ate it up.

"Oh fuck. Ivy. You feel so good and tight, baby. Oh... fuck."

But it was over before it began. I could feel nothing, but he couldn't tell by the fake noises I made.

He grips my legs on the uncomfortable back seat of his Mustang and trembles like he has the chills.

When he's done, he lies on top of me, out of breath, the seat belt buckle digging into my lower back. I feel hot and sweaty. I wince when he goes soft, sliding out of me like a tampon.

"You were amazing. Did it feel good, Ivy?"

I paste a fake smile when he looks up. "You were perfect."

I want to cry. I hate it. He plants a wet kiss on my mouth, finally getting off me.

The next day at school, I found out we were both liars, but for very different reasons.

CHAPTER

2

Walking through the doors of Stockbridge High on the first day of school, I ignore the stares. Most of the popular guys at Stockbridge are jocks hoping to get into a D1 school to escape their parents. Girls from rich families have nothing to worry about when they graduate. The rest of them are rich kids who smoke weed and snort coke and live for the weekend. Like every school, there are the students who get picked on for fun because they are broke or didn't fit in popular society.

Every school had a group of kids like that. The nerd or the emo kid who didn't wear the right clothes and wasn't good enough to get the attention.

The halls echo with people walking, door lockers slamming open and closed. Guys lean against the wall making out, while feeling up their girlfriends.

I make it to my locker, ignoring Jason smirking at me with his shoulder against the wall. My eyes roll when I see what they wrote over my locker in huge black letters when I spin the dial.

IVY SLOAN IS A SLUT

Five guys from the football team show up next to Jason, including Tommy.

"Hey, Ivy," Jason mocks. He clears his throat like he's getting ready for a speech. "I had a hard-on this morning. You should have seen it. I thought of three letters and remembered your name when I had my hand around my dick."

I grab the two textbooks I need for my next two classes, slam the locker closed, and turn my head. "I guess there wasn't much to grab, being that my name has only three letters."

"Damn, Jason. You got a small dick," one of them says, laughing behind me as I walk away.

"That is exactly what a slut would say!" Jason yells over the noise in the hallway.

Walking into my US history class, I take a seat in the back. After a few minutes, a girl with straight black hair walks in. Her name is Alice. I heard she grew up here in Stockbridge and lives in an old estate on the west side.

"Watch it, Freak," the guy blocking the aisle says when Alice tries to step over his shoes.

She sits beside me, and I give her a tight-lipped smile. She looks like she hasn't slept. The dark circles under her eyes don't hide how gorgeous she is. I wonder why they call her a freak, but she must wonder why they call me a slut.

School drones on. When it's the end of the day and I open my locker, a flyer slides out. The flyer has a black-and-white circus tent with red letters on the top that read,

CIRCLE OF FREAKS PARANORMAL CIRCUS OF HORROR IS COMING BACK TO STOCKBRIDGE. COME IF YOU DARE. 18 AND OVER TO PLAY.

I smile to myself because I tried to go last year when I turned eighteen but didn't have the money. A paranormal circus fascinates me, but you had to be an adult to go. I heard they travel to warmer states when it gets cold up north. The bottom of the flyer reads in fine print that the show is for adults only. You have to sign a waiver, and you cannot bring your phones inside the show.

The fair in town is from August through November. Two sides mirror each other at the entrance. One side is a traditional fair with carnival rides and games. The other is the Carnevil of Horror filled with haunted houses and themed for Halloween. A side entrance is for adults only, where the Circle of Freaks paranormal circus is set up. I've never been to either fair, but I've seen pictures online.

I pocket the flyer, hoping I could go this year, wondering how I will come up with the money. I scoured the internet to see if I could find anything on YouTube to see what goes on inside the tent, but I came up empty.

A blaring sound goes off, echoing through the hallway. I look at my phone and notice an amber alert for another missing girl. That's the fifth one this year. The Stockbridge police assumed the first incident was a runaway teenager. That was until they found her body beaten and raped. Then the second, third, and fourth girls went missing.

After a couple of months, they found their bodies. They were all tortured and raped and found in different parts of the state. The first one was Mandy Walsh. They found her body floating in a lake five miles from the edge of town. The second was Emily Bowden. They found her body near the tree line in a black garbage bag near the main highway. It made headlines across the news channels. More girls came up missing in different states, all found in the same condition. Some are still missing from other states. Experts say that it's part of a human trafficking ring targeting teenage girls. They've warned everyone to stay vigilant and for parents to talk to their kids about reporting someone suspicious and not walk home alone. But some of us don't have a choice.

The bus lets me off at the stop near the Big H grocery mart. It is the only grocery store in town and the only place hiring my junior year. Kevin, the manager, is a middle-aged asshole who hates his wife and works open to close to avoid having to go home.

The parking lot is not as full in the afternoon on Mondays as I make my way across it. A plumbing store called Down to Flush is next to the grocery store. The employees wear shirts with DTF written in big gold letters on the back. When I first saw an employee with the shirt, I couldn't get over the owner using DTF as its logo. DTF to us teenagers means Down To Fuck. It hasn't hindered their business when they go out to service their customers.

I walk inside and head to the employee locker room to change out of my school uniform.

"Hey, Ivy." Kevin greets me with a smile. His eyes linger on the hem of my skirt where it ends mid-thigh.

"Hi Kevin, how's the wife?"

His eyes scroll up my thighs, licking his lips, making me cringe. Kevin has a belly that hangs slightly over his belt. I wonder if he can still see his dick. He's balding and has beady eyes, but in his mind, he thinks he's good-looking.

"She's...home," he answers finally when his eyes land on my face.

"Say hi to her for me."

His eyes harden because we both know he will do no such thing. I'm also not stupid enough to believe that I got this job for any other reason than for his personal sick fantasy. But beggars can't be choosers, and as much as I want to tell him to stick the cashier position up his ass, I can't.

After changing into the cashier uniform, which is a white dress shirt Kevin ordered a size too small, I try to pull the vest to hide my cleavage the best I can and fix my name tag. I flick the light to my register and wait until Barbara places her items on the conveyor belt. Barbara is an old lady who comes in every Monday around the same time to go grocery shopping.

"How are you, Barbara?"

"I'm fine." Her hands shake when she places the jars of pickles on the belt.

"Do you need help?"

"Oh, no. I got it," she says, waving me off.

Last time, she dropped the jar of pickles, and I couldn't get the smell of pickle juice off my hands for a week.

"How about to your car?" I ask, double-bagging the jars.

I wonder what she does with all the jars of pickles. I have scanned six this time. She usually buys three every week.

When she swipes her card, it doesn't go through. I cleared the payment so she could try again.

"I'm sorry, Ivy. I can't remember which card I used last time."

"It was a blue one."

"Is everything alright?" Kevin asks, standing way too close behind me. If I step back, I'll run into his stomach.

I smile at Barbara when she looks behind me. "Everything is fine," she replies, waving her crinkly hand. "Ivy was being a peach, helping me remember what card I used last time."

After a minute of watching her rummaging in her big bag, she finally pulls it out. Kevin reaches over to help her swipe her card instead of going around. His stomach presses into my side in the small space between the register and the scanner. His face is inches from my cheek. I try holding my breath so I don't smell the Old Spice mixed with the smell of an ashtray coming from his skin. His smell makes me want to puke.

I'm relieved when she swats his hand away with a huff. "I got it, Kevin. I'm old, but I still work." She swipes her card, and it goes through.

"You're all set, Barbara."

Kevin helps me bag the last of her items, prolonging the fact that he shouldn't be this close.

When she leaves, pushing the cart out of the exit, I can feel his cigarette breath on my neck. "You could ask me for help. I'll gladly give it to you, Ivy," he says, but I don't miss the innuendo on the last part. My creep-o-meter rises in warning.

"I didn't need any help," I counter. He grips both my arms, and I give a little shrug, hoping he takes the hint to back off.

"Like I said, anytime," he says, sliding his hands down my

arms while I breathe through my mouth. I sigh when he walks away.

I clear the register and mutter, "Creep."

After four hours of scanning customers' groceries, the last one walks through my lane. I press the button on the belt so the three items he usually gets reach the sensor. My shift is over in three minutes. I shut off the light, indicating that my lane is closed.

"You need a ride home?"

I look up at what I call my side hustle, scanning the energy drink and box of condoms with a pack of gum.

Dean Foster, the owner of Down to Flush, from next door. He is thirty-eight, not bad-looking, has no children, is not married, and fixes toilets for a living.

"Yeah," I mumble.

Girls like me don't have a choice. We have to survive somehow.

CHAPTER

3

"Arch your back," Dean says, wrapping his fist around my blond hair.

I place my hands flat on the island in his kitchen, bent over the edge. My skirt is crudely shoved up my waist. I can feel the tip of his cock wrapped in the condom nudging my entrance. I close my eyes when he shoves his cock inside me, feeling his fingers gripping my hips with each thrust. I press my teeth on my bottom lip to keep it from trembling, trying to think of something else. Anything that will help me escape. I hate the burning sensation when he penetrates me because I can't get wet.

"There you go, baby. That's it. Give me that tight pussy," he says, followed by a grunt. His hot breath is on the back of my neck. He fucks me in rapid, measured thrusts for about a minute until he comes shuddering, gasping for air.

I ran into Dean at the grocery store when I argued with my mother about money on the phone. It was the summer before repeating my junior year. I had to tell Kevin I needed my hours cut short to finish school. I got a glimpse of my life working at the grocery store and figured without a high school diploma; my options were slim in getting out of Stockbridge. Dropping out wasn't an option.

Dean saw me walking across the parking lot and offered to give me a ride home. The sun was setting. It was getting dark, so I agreed. I agreed to more than that. A hundred bucks every time he would give me a ride home, and I would return the favor. I cried the first time when I got home after he fucked me, but I was relieved when I could pay the light bill.

Then it became a routine. He would come into the grocery store, buy a couple of things, never forgetting the condoms, and ask if I needed a ride home. He would bring me to his house four blocks away and fuck me on his kitchen island. With my school uniform on, always on weekdays, and always after my shift at the grocery store.

"Turn around."

He slides his cock out, and I wince from the sting. He disposes of the condom and watches me while he strokes himself. He slides on another condom. His brown hair is sticking up like he was running his fingers through it, standing naked in his kitchen.

Dean is six feet tall, lean with a flat stomach, a patch of hair on his chest, and brown eyes and hair. An average guy without a romantic bone in his body. He's rough like every man I have ever met. He makes me feel cheap and wants only one thing. To fuck me.

"Do you know how many guys who work for me want to fuck you?" He jerks his dick faster. I can see the red tip through the condom every time his hand goes up and down, trying to get it hard.

"Let me guess, all of them," I answer sarcastically.

He chuckles. "If they only knew I'm the one fucking that tight pussy."

How charming. He forgot to mention the one-minute warning.

"Lucky you."

"Let me see those pretty tits, Ivy."

I harden my jaw, looking at the cabinet behind him. I cup my tits, playing with my nipples so he can finish, and I can go home, take a shower, and find something to eat.

"Tell me you want me to fuck you, Ivy."

I found out why he's single. He comes before he even starts. He does this every time, trying to get his dick hard, stroking it like a fourteen-year-old. His skin is already clammy from the effort. The veins on his neck are sticking out. His face flushed red.

"I want you to fuck me," I say in a flat tone.

He licks his greedy lips. "Fuck, baby." He steps closer, but his dick is flaccid inside the condom, and it's about to slide off. Dean's cock is on the below-average side, but when it's soft, it's small.

My eyes slide up, his face beet red, and then he lets out a ragged breath. "Fuck!" he yells, causing me to jolt. I quickly shove my skirt down and button my shirt when he turns around, throwing the condom in the trash.

When he walks back, I'm ready to leave.

"I'm sorry." He shuffles on his feet. "I didn't mean to yell." He slides a sweater over his head. "It's not your fault. I'm stressed with work... you understand, right?"

I smooth my hair so I don't look like he fucked me in the back seat of a car when I get home. "It's fine."

He says the same thing all the time. It is always stress, work, or whatever excuse he comes up with. He is single. His outbursts are also a little scary. I couldn't imagine what woman could deal with that if she dated him on top of his rough hands.

He pulls off the main highway in his white late model Dodge Ram pickup truck, stopping by the side stairwell. Checking the time on the big screen in the center console, it's nine-thirty.

"Here." He hands me a crisp one-hundred-dollar bill. "I won't be able to do this next week." My stomach bottoms out because I need the money. "I-I have a date with someone. I'm dating someone," he admits.

I turn my head, taking the money. "Okay." I jump out of his truck, shutting the door, dying to leave. He doesn't wait until I get up the stairs before he drives off. Asshole.

I stomp my way up the stairs, trying to figure out how to make up the money. I was making a hundred bucks about twice a week with Dean on top of the three hundred and eighty a month part-time at the grocery store after taxes. It gave me enough to help pay the utilities because I knew my mother wouldn't have it, plus the other half of the rent. We could barely afford groceries to last us until the next paycheck. Money for gas was another issue living in a small town where public transportation was limited. Compared to the city, gas in Stockbridge is expensive on top of the car insurance for the old piece of shit Oldsmobile my mother drives that's on its last leg. But she has money for cigarettes and who knows what else.

The apartment door to my right opens when I reach the second floor. The stench of marijuana causes me to crinkle my nose.

"Hey, Ivy."

I look over at Scott—the Meadow apartment's pothead and drug dealer—leaning on the doorjamb. He's lighting a joint with a lighter that doesn't work every time he tries to turn it with his thumb.

"Getting the last hit for the night, Scott?"

"Want to take a hit?" he asks with a grin.

"I don't smoke. I gotta go. I have school in the morning."

Scott mostly deals with marijuana and cocaine. He sometimes sells Adderall and X, but he isn't a successful drug dealer. He always offers me something that is related to drugs, trying to lure me in. The phrase "don't get high on your own supply" doesn't apply to Scott. If he still lives here.

He finally gets the lighter to work and lights the joint, taking a drag. "When are you going to hang out with me? Every time I ask, you got an excuse."

"I'm busy," I reply, walking toward my front door and fishing out the key.

He wants me to get high with him, hoping we can hook up, and who knows what else he has in mind. I have enough problems.

"You're not busy right now," he says, echoing down the hall.

I turn the lock. "Good night, Scott." I shut the door, leaning against it. Why do guys have to be such creeps? It's not like I have a sign on my forehead that screams I'M A TARGET FOR ASSHOLES. TAKE ADVANTAGE OF ME.

CHAPTER

4

"I don't know why you just don't ask for your hours back at the grocery store, Ivy."

I slam the refrigerator door closed. It doesn't rattle because nothing is inside except a tap water container, a ketchup bottle, and an empty juice carton.

"If I want to graduate this year and get my diploma, I can't do that working at the grocery store during school hours, Mom. I can't be at two places at the same time."

"Well, school isn't paying the bills. Is it?"

Her voice is getting worse with all the cigarettes she smokes. I have to air out the house and buy the bootleg Pine-Sol they sell at Dollar General so the house doesn't smell like a month-old ashtray.

"It will, once I graduate and can get a decent job. Not some minimum wage cashier position where the manager looks at me like he wants to take my clothes off and screw me on the register."

She laughs. Her teeth are a yellow shade like the ones you see in an eighties movie. All the actors in that era had stained yellow teeth, not the pearly whites you see on social media or the latest blockbuster when it hits theaters. It's a shame to see my mother like this. Her face is already showing signs of age, and she is only forty-four. She has jowls, sagging skin on her jawline, and wrinkles over her top lip, made worse by smoking. Her hoarse voice doesn't help, and neither does the smell of cigarettes that clings to her skin. I remember her being pretty.

"You should fuck him. You're nineteen, you know," she says, with an unlit cigarette between her lips. She lights it and takes a drag. "He'll give you a raise."

I lean back on the Formica counter, bile rising in my throat when I imagine what Kevin would look like naked.

"That's gross. I can't believe you would say that."

"I did it. Your grandma did it," she admits. "You should be grateful I blessed you with platinum blond hair and a pair of nice tits to go with a nice perky round ass. You would be stupid not to use that to your advantage."

I have, and there is nothing useful about it. All it gets you is a hundred bucks, a load of shame, and a bag of self-esteem issues. I'll never tell her about Dean because that would make me like her. The last thing you want to do is become the thing you hate the most. A woman who has sex for money because she isn't good to be anything else. My mother dabbled in drugs, and all the smoking made her look older, and then, men stopped looking at her. She got a job wherever she could or whoever would hire her.

"That is not what I want, Mom. You would have never had to do that if you stayed in school and tried to do something with your life."

She snorts. "Sooner or later, you'll have no choice." Not wanting to hear more of this shit, I walk toward my room. "Walk away!" She raises her voice. "That's what you do best. Just like your father did when I told him I was pregnant with you. I had no choice but to do what I had to do to survive." I slam my bedroom door. "And neither will you!"

Why do parents expect their kids to follow in their footsteps? It's because their life is so shitty, they think that you can't do better. They expect you to follow the same narrative. In my case, white trash, raised in the trailer park with a dead-beat parent and an absent meth dealer for a father. Now my mother works as a server who fucks whoever for a price if given the opportunity. She has no education and no aspirations to do shit with her life.

After a cold shower, I lie naked on my bed. It's still hot the last week of August and running the air conditioner is not an option right now. I look at my phone, pulling up the Circle of Freaks paranormal circus website. Tickets are available every weekend until the first week of November. Then they head off to other states across the country. Tickets are for both Saturday and Sunday. Two shows that include access to all the rides at the Stockbridge fair. Price. Three hundred bucks a ticket plus tax. There is a pop-up that comes up.

ENTER TO WIN A FREE TICKET.

I read the fine print. No purchase is necessary. I click on it and enter my phone number, email, and address. What are the chances? Probably a million to one, but a girl could hope. The tickets sell out almost every weekend.

I've been fascinated with clowns and the circus since the age of eight. I thought it was cool and still do.

Some kids fear clowns and creepy masks, but I never did. I love the makeup, the acrobats, the illusionists, and the breath-taking acts. When the paranormal circus became popular, it was a twist that took the audience into a darker world.

When I was in middle school, I imagined being part of a circus. I wanted to dress up like a clown for Halloween every year. When Stephen King's *It* came out, I checked it out of the library and read it. It was good, and I couldn't put it down. When the movie came out, I couldn't watch it because my mother said she would not pay for me to watch a bunch of kids afraid of a stupid clown. If I wanted to see it that bad, I should wait until I could get it for free.

I had to kiss Brandon Smith in seventh grade to get a copy. It was like kissing a wet fish.

Sometimes, the drive-in theater, around Halloween, plays *It* on the screen. I climb up on the roof of the apartment building to see it from the north side. The trees on that side haven't grown high enough to block the view.

I scroll through my photos of screenshots of different acts and clowns I found online. The women look spectacular and sexy in their outfits, and the men in their costumes with face paint. The paranormal cirque is like an R-rated movie. The traditional circus in the US began in Philadelphia and was first introduced in the eighteen hundreds by the Ringling Brothers. I heard in Stockbridge that a fair started around the same time and is still here. Then, the circus was added, and it was called the Circle of Freaks.

When the paranormal circus became popular around Halloween, it became the year's event for the last twenty years. Every weekend, late August through the first week of November, the circus comes to where it all began. Two years ago, they introduced the haunted carnival that surrounds the circus to attract more visitors. But no one talks about what goes on inside the tent. No one.

In my sophomore year, I was obsessed with finding everything there was to know about the Circle of Freaks. I asked around, searched online, but found nothing except a review that said it was scary as fuck and awesome. All that did was make me want to see it even more.

After locking up and eating what was left of the dry cereal, I make my way past Scott's apartment with GOT WEED? spray-painted next to his front door, each letter in the colors of the rainbow. Whoever did it must think Scott is gay because right at the bottom, it reads FAGGOT offensively. He probably pissed off someone last night. It's quiet coming from his apartment. He must be passed out from all the drugs and weed he consumes. On the weekends, beginning on Fridays, he gets more visitors than a public bathroom at all hours of the night.

When I make it to school, I notice more flyers for the fair. These are geared more toward the circus and the haunted carnival.

CARNEVIL in big black and red letters with the Circle of Freaks logo and a circus tent on the bottom.

"Hey, Freak?"

Turning around, I watch Alice walk from the student parking lot, ignoring Jason. He's sitting with a bunch of cheerleaders and most of the football team.

His gaze follows her until she is almost about to pass me. Then he spots me. *Great.* Better me than her, I guess.

"Hey, Ivy. Do you and the freak want to suck me off after school?" I roll my eyes and tilt my head. "I thought we talked about this, Jason. It's too small." The stupid smile on his face drops when everyone around him begins to laugh.

"That's because a slut like you needs to have a huge cock to stuff inside that loose pussy. We've been over this."

To my surprise, Alice flips him off before heading into the main building. Her long straight dark hair covers the side of her face like a curtain.

"Anytime, Freak." He gets up from the bench. "I'll even throw in a pity fuck while you watch your whore of a friend Ivy when she takes my cock."

Jason is an insufferable pig who loves to treat girls like shit. He thinks because his father owns a Mercedes Benz dealership that he's hot shit. Some girls might find him funny or get turned on. Or that he drives a Mercedes GT and has Daddy's money, but not me and Alice.

"Hey, Jason?" He looks up. "Good luck finding your dick." I turn around, ignoring his last jab.

"It's right here, you desperate slut. Tommy told us what a greedy little whore you are."

He left out the part where he came in less than two minutes but whatever. I've had enough of Jason for the day.

I catch up to Alice walking down the hall through the throng of bodies. "Hey, thanks." She keeps walking until she stops at her locker and turns her head to look at me. "For what you did back there. I'm not what they say I am."

Not intentionally.

She nods. "I know."

I raise my brows in surprise. "You do?"

She slides the textbook for the class we have together out of her locker. "You went out with Tommy on a date after he kept asking you your sophomore year. I was a freshman, but everyone knew you went out with him that one time. He made sure everyone knew you slept with him and made-up crap slut shaming you. That's what guys do when they see a girl, and they know she doesn't feel the same. You found him lame, and it's obvious you don't like him." She shuts her locker and spins the dial. "That doesn't make you a slut. Besides, I have never seen you with another guy since my freshman year. Not one."

I wish I could tell her she is right. In the traditional sense, I haven't. But I'm not sure anymore, not after my thing with Dean.

"I don't think you're a freak."

She grins. "Thanks, I guess."

I heard Alice lives in an abandoned estate on Avirce St. surrounded by miles of trees. Her mother talked to the school counselor, and word got around that she takes medication to help her cope. Some crap about her seeing and hearing things that aren't there. I have never seen her act weird at school. In the same way, I've never seen her around any friends. Alice keeps to herself and avoids everyone like I do. We both have that in common.

"I guess we both have something in common," I say, walking alongside her toward class.

She pinches her brows. "What's that?"

"We both have people saying things about us that are untrue."

We walk in class, and she actually smiles. She takes her usual seat in the back of the class. When she smiles, it makes her even more beautiful. She has dark lashes that frame her pretty brown eyes with a natural arch to her brows. She has a small, straight nose and full-shaped lips.

"I agree," she says, "It's when we believe what they say that it becomes a problem."

I stare at the old wooden desk in my seat with IVY IS A SLUT carved on the surface. She's right. That's when you begin to lose yourself. When you believe what people assume they know about you.

CHAPTER
5

The bus drops me off, and I head toward the Big H for my shift. I ignore Kevin when I walk in to change and his eyes remain stuck below the hem of my skirt. My mother's words last night mess with my head, making me feel worse than I already do. At least she said she paid the light. That means I can help with the other half of the rent, and I need not worry about Dean.

Since repeating my junior year in high school, forty times I let him fuck me on his kitchen island before he took me home. Last night had been the first time he told me he couldn't take me home because he had a date or was dating someone. I hadn't given it much thought if it was dating or not. In those moments before I shut down, all I could think about was if he was wearing a condom. Like my past, he's a secret I want no one to know about. Because that would make what the kids called me at school true and prove my mother right.

It's not that I'm hung up about it. I used to be, but you can only cry so many tears. Soon enough, they dry up. I couldn't do anything about it. I had no one except my mother and nowhere to go. It was the only way I could stay in school. Some kids hate having to go to school and take living in a stable home for granted. They always complain, preferring to skip class for the mall or the lake to screw around, get high, and fuck. I was groomed to sleep with men for money. I had to fuck for a buck to stay in school. It was a transaction. I always told myself it could be worse. Dean could expect more from me.

When I was thirteen, I didn't understand why men looked at me funny. I understood the day my mother brought a man to the house. He made me go down on him when my mother left for the store. I threw up, and he hit me across the face. He made me clean it up and shoved his dick in my mouth. He told me he couldn't wait until I was older. The school saw the cut and bruise on my face and called social services. My mother said I fell off my bike, and they bought it. When it happened a second time, she pulled me out of school, and we moved here.

I watch the belt run with two bags of chips, two cans of Coke, and a Hershey bar.

"Oh my God, she works here?" I look up to see Emma, captain of the cheerleading team, and Tommy Hill. She stifles a laugh when I scan the items and place them in a grocery bag.

"Did you know she worked here? Is that why you brought me here instead of the gas station down the road?"

I ignore them, smacking my stale bubble gum, blowing a small bubble, and scanning the cans of soda.

"I didn't know she worked here," Tommy replies.

Liar. He knows I work here. He came in a bunch of times in the summer on Sundays with his mother. He knows where I live too. He knows more than he should.

When I look up, Tommy is standing behind Emma. Since he's above six feet, he takes advantage. His eyes focus on my shirt, where the button causes a small hole, and you can see my bra.

I pop the bubble and twirl my tongue around, dragging it in my mouth. "Will that be all?" I ask.

He tears his eyes away. "Wait," he says, rushing to the pharmacy aisle and coming back with a pack of condoms.

Emma smirks at me, sliding her arm around Tommy's waist. If she only knew I don't give a shit. If she only knew she was doing me a favor.

I scan the box of condoms, dropping it into the bag with the potato chips. "Will that be all for you both today?" I ask with a smile.

"Yes," Tommy says stiffly.

"That will be... eighteen dollars and fifty-five cents."

I can't say I'm surprised when Emma pulls out a twenty and pays. I give her the change, sliding the bags over to her. "You both have a nice rest of your day."

She takes the bags. "Have fun bagging groceries," she quips.

"Make sure you get your three condoms worth," I shoot back. More like three minutes' worth since she paid for the guy's snacks and condoms. He didn't offer to chip in at least.

Her face falls, and Tommy stands there without a word instead of defending her. She glances at him, his light green eyes staring at me for a second too long. "I knew it!" She screeches and storms off with the bags in her hands.

"You should go after your girlfriend."

"She's not my girlfriend."

I pick up the cleaning spray bottle and paper towel and clean the scanner, hoping he can see the disgust on my face. "Will people slut-shame her tomorrow as they did me since she isn't your girlfriend?" He turns around and walks out.

Bastard.

The next day at school, I had my answer. No one mentioned Tommy and Emma ever going out. They didn't call her an easy lay or a slut. He didn't spread rumors about her. He also didn't stop the one he created about me, either.

Sometimes, I wonder what I did to deserve it. I would ask myself if that was what people saw in me, especially men. Did they know my mother had loose morals, and by default, it made me like her? I gave no reason for anyone to think that about me when I moved here. Unless they found out about Dean. But that would make him an asshole for paying for it, and it was never something I wanted to do. I knew I had no choice, but I had a goal.

I'm bagging the last of the customer's groceries. Clear the register and mindlessly begin scanning the next items without looking up. But when I hear a familiar name coming from a woman, I pause.

"I don't like those, Dean. The almond ones are better," the woman whines, placing a bag of chocolate almonds on the belt. She isn't wrong; they are better.

But what has me angry when I look up is Dean's smug face. It's not that he's dating someone, but that he brought her here out of all places. First Tommy yesterday, and now him. What the hell? And with Sarah? I know her because she works at the only insurance office by the mall. She's in her late twenties. Brown hair, and eyes, and is skinny. Not what you would consider pretty because her nose is too big for her face and her clothes sag on her frame. Her yellow sundress reminds me of a mannequin when you try to fit it into a dress that is too big.

It's not that I'm bothered he's dating her, but it's a dick move knowing I work here and to come into my lane—selfish prick. Why do guys get a kick out of doing that? Is it because they lack where it matters? They treat women like shit but love to call themselves a man.

I can feel Dean staring, but I do my job as a cashier, scanning and bagging the items. I smile at Sarah when she walks down the lane past the payment system.

"How are you, Sarah? You probably don't remember me," I say, watching Dean shift uncomfortably with his feet.

"You're Maggy Sloan's daughter, right?"

"Yep."

"I remember now. I sold your mom the policy for her car, and you came in with her."

"That's right."

"Isn't a small world?"

I glance at Dean. "It is. You never know who you might run into these days."

"You must run into Dean all the time since his business is right next door."

I glance back at her, ignoring the way his fists clench, and reply, "Once a week at least."

"We ran into each other the same way you and your mom did," she gushes. "We've been dating for about two weeks now."

What a lying sack of shit.

I plant a fake smile after ringing them up. He slides his card harder than necessary and waits for the machine to approve the transaction. It spits the receipt. I don't miss the anger he is trying to hide, but I'm relieved. My idea of sex was never to get paid for it, and if my circumstances were different, I would have told Dean to fuck off.

I hand him the receipt with a grin. "I wish you both the best."

Her cheeks bloom. "Thank you."

The way Dean is quiet and looking straight ahead, I doubt he feels the same way.

CHAPTER
6

By the time my shift ended, it was late. I had to help stock different grocery items in my lane. When Dean didn't take me home the rest of the week, I took the shuttle to the mall. It was better than walking the three miles on the main highway to get home. The shuttle bus at least had air-conditioning and so did the mall, which made the trip easier.

Instead of walking across the parking lot to get to my building, I would walk inside and out of the back exit. I also got to window shop. I have always loved the smell that comes from the different spaces compared to the apartment. It smells like new clothes and different fragrances. Like the perfume samples from the magazines you find in the mail. I couldn't afford anything, but it was still nice to look at what was trending.

I make my way to the stop where the shuttle picks up people trying to get to the mall and check the time on my phone. It's already eight thirty, so I missed the last shuttle for the day. The mall would be closed and the last movie at the drive-in theater during the weekday would have started.

My mother doesn't get off for another four hours, and she can't afford to step out of work to take me home. I have no other choice but to walk the three miles home. It's dark, the sun has set, and I have fifty percent battery life on my cell phone.

The clouds move heavily across the moon. The main highway is a two-way street with no sidewalk and woods surrounding the side. Every so often, the smell of roadkill would hit me.

Occasionally, you would see cars speed by, and some would slow down. My heart would beat fast inside my chest, fear gripping me in its fist. All I could think about was to run into the woods and hide if it stopped.

The grass reaches my ankles, brushing my sweaty skin. It was hot today when the sun was out, but as the night settled in, I could feel the slight breeze from the wind cooling my skin. The trees sway, causing the leaves to float to the ground. The smell of fall floats in the air.

I look to my left and my right when I hear a noise coming from deep in the woods. I drag my finger across the screen of my phone, pressing my thumb on the flashlight and hoping it's not a bear.

Bears in Stockbridge are a problem. They can come out of the woods when looking for food, and right now, I look like their next meal.

"Hey, you need a ride?"

A gray minivan with fingerprint smudges on the window pulls up and reminds me of the moms who come to the Big H with their kids screaming because they won't share the bag of snacks they opened before they were paid for.

A couple about the same age as my mother pulls up beside me, giving me a warm smile. There is a collection of items hanging from their rearview mirror—graduation tassels, a collection of air fresheners, beaded necklaces, and a rosary.

The man reaches over the woman in the passenger seat with a Boston Celtics hat that obscures most of his face.

"It's dangerous to be walking on a road like this. The cars drive by fast, and bears come out of the woods around this time of year. Do you live nearby?"

My unease blankets my chest, cursing myself for staying later than I needed to. "Thanks... but...my boyfriend is picking me up." I check my phone. "He should be here any minute.

"Alright, you be careful now," the woman says with a baleful grin.

The window rolls up, and the van pulls away, leaving me with a sense of dread.

When the taillights are like red beacons in the distance, I run toward the tree line, but a loud horn blaring behind me causes me to turn. I let out a sigh of relief when I recognized Alice's car.

She rolls her window down. "You need a ride?"

I nod. "Yes, Alice. Thank God." I run up to her Tesla and get in.

"Is everything alright? You look like you've been running from Jason Voorhees."

"Close. This couple stopped to offer me a ride, and something was off. I told her my boyfriend was going to pick me up, and the way she smiled before they pulled away gave me the creeps. All the talk about teenage girls missing has me thinking everyone is a body snatcher."

"That must have been really scary. It's dark out." She looks up through the moon roof. "The moon is full. You know what they say, weird people come crawling out when the moon is full."

I look around at the simple but high-tech car. "Thank you for stopping. Nice car, by the way. The handles are bitch to figure out, though."

"Trust me, it's not nice when you have to wait inside to charge it when the battery runs low after driving in it all day. I'm lucky it's charged every morning because I forget. I think it's my mother or stepfather who remembers or I wouldn't make it to school. They keep giving me shit all the time."

"Mine can't make rent." I point at my uniform shirt with the Big H and name tag. "It's why I'm walking home. I had to stay late and missed the shuttle."

She pulls out onto the road. A bell chimes from the screen, flashing that she is going the wrong way, but she continues in the opposite direction.

"I had to get out of my house. My parents don't want me out, but I couldn't take it any more so I snuck out."

"Have you been to the haunted fair?"

"I'm not allowed to go. My mother and my therapist don't think it's a good idea. Too much stimulation."

I snort. "What do they say about sex? That's stimulation."

Alice laughs. "I asked if I could have a boyfriend, and they said they didn't think that was a good idea either."

"What? Are they going to send you to a convent or something?"

"Doubt it. They might think I'll come out like that diabolical nun in the movie."

I don't want to ask what they say she has because Alice looks normal. I see no signs of crazy. Unlocking my phone and scrolled to the last website I was browsing to see if they've announced the winner for the ticket giveaway.

"Are you going?" she asks, glancing at the Circle of Freaks page.

"I want to, but it costs three hundred bucks. I make that in a month working at the grocery store, but I need it to help my mother with rent. I signed up to see if I could win a free ticket on the website." I'm short even with what I make in the grocery store, but I don't tell her that.

"I heard if you go to the haunted fair during the week and you're wearing an eighteen and over orange band, they hand out free tickets."

"Really?" I ask excitedly. "How do you know that?"

"I heard Mich from the football team tell Jason. I think they were going since they turned eighteen."

I search for free tickets for the Circle of Freaks circus and bingo. "He's right. There's a blog. It says the Circle of Freaks will hand out a few tickets to fairgoers if they enter the haunted carnival during the week."

"You want to go that bad?"

I glance at her. "Yeah, I've loved the circus since I was a kid and figured I was too old to go, but this one... this one I really want to check out."

She drums her black-painted fingernails on the steering wheel like she's contemplating. She slows down, turns the wheel, and drives in the opposite direction right before she reaches the apartment complex.

I point with my thumb over my shoulder. "That was my stop?"

She grins and says, "I know." She presses the search icon on the gigantic screen that looks like an iPad and types in Carnevil. The address pops up, routing the car to the destination and letting her know how much battery she has left.

"The ticket to the haunted fair is twenty-eight dollars, and it includes all the rides. I could loan you the money."

I have the hundred I got from Dean.

"Thank you, but I have enough." I look down at the vest, take it off, stuff it into my bag, and fix my hair.

"You never know. Maybe you'll get lucky. Even if you don't, you'll have fun trying. The circus tent shouldn't be far. No one knows what goes on inside unless you pay to go."

"Tell me about. I think it's why I want to go so bad."

"You like the dark paranormal circus stuff?"

I shrug. "Yeah, why not? Beats the hell out of work, school, and where I live."

"Trust me, I know the feeling."

I wonder what she means by that, but I don't ask.

CHAPTER 7

The moon is drooped low in the pitch-black sky, and a quiet, cool breeze blows through the amusement park. The haunted side of the carnival looks abandoned compared to the traditional one. A yin to the yang. There are screams on one side and laughter on the other. Like two dimensions.

We walk up to the dilapidated entryway, the lights flick to life, throwing shadows over the rusted ticket booths. An old, tattered sign reads "Welcome to Carnevil: Where Fear Meets Fun."

A chill mixed with fear and excitement grips me at the thought of promise. I spot people from school and a bunch of kids who looked like they were in middle school.

We make the line far enough to the left to avoid being spotted by anyone from school.

"Are you sure you won't get in trouble for bringing me here?" I ask.

"I don't think my parents will notice me gone. I closed the garage so they thought my car was inside. My stepfather is usually away on business, and my mother is fast asleep. How about you?"

"My mom couldn't give a shit as long as I come up with the other half of the rent."

We step forward to the front of the line. "That bad, huh?"

I scoff. "You have no idea."

The Ferris wheel is the focal point in the center when we hand our tickets to the guy at the ticket booth. Skeletal figures are seated in the creaking gondolas with bony fingers. The wheels spin with unnatural speed. The riders' laughter turns to terrified screams. It is obvious they made the Ferris wheel look haunted for added effect.

We both jolt when a sinister clown pops out of nowhere through the fog. His grin wide, and his teeth gleam with malevolence.

"Come, play with me," he hisses, beckoning us to come over.

We keep walking. Masked characters pop out from hidden spaces.

The cotton candy vendor holds up what looks like blood-red wisps and hisses, "Hungry."

The cotton candy he held dripped dark red to look like fresh blood. The popcorn in the cart looked flavored with a hint of something unsettling. Vendors with face paint are on each side in decorated sinister-looking carts.

I glance at Alice, her body tense and eyes wide as she takes it all in. The makeup on each of the actor's faces looks like they spent hours applying it. I wonder how they can keep up with it every night.

We reach the ride section of the fair. The rides are designed to fit the theme. The Roller Coaster of Evil is a rickety, rust-covered monstrosity that appears on the verge of collapse. It races through dark tunnels with flickering lights. There is a sudden drop that plunges into total darkness. Sinister laughter echoes throughout the air, leaving you with a sense of upcoming dread. Then comes the laughter. People get off with smiles on their faces from the thrill.

"Do you want to ride, Alice?" I hold up my left hand, flashing her my orange band we got from the ticket booth. "We can ride everything," I say with a smile. "Let's have fun."

We stand in line after dodging a couple of creepy nuns popping out to scare us with upside-down crosses hanging from their necks. My stomach hardens, and my palms sweat, anticipating the roller coaster and how fast it dips on the track.

"Alright, fuck it. How bad could it be?" she says and looks over. "Are they letting the people in costumes ride with random people?"

I follow her line of sight. A bunch of actors from the scare zones are getting on the ride. Some wear masks, and some wear makeup. They are walking like a group of killers in the movie *The Purge*. Only actors who work for the fair are allowed to wear masks and costumes. I didn't miss the big red sign with a line across that read,

NO MASKS ALLOWED

"Yeah."

"That's...crazy."

I turn when I hear a scream. " This place is crazy," I mutter.

A tall figure in the center of the group with a black cross painted on his white mask grabs my attention. He jumps over the railing like he does it all the time. As we walk closer to get in line, he's even taller. His shoulders are broad, and his back is massive. You can tell by the way his muscles move under the black fabric.

"Whoa." Alice leans close when she notices him. "Where did he come from?"

I look over my shoulder and see where the rest of the group is walking away from a blocked area that reads, MORE BLOOD THIS WAY and CIRCLE OF FREAKS PARANORMAL CIRCUS.

I grin. "They're part of the circus." I point behind her. "They came from over there."

Alice cranes her neck. "You're right."

The line moves, and we're next to ride. I tug Alice forward. My pulse pounds when I see the masked actors slide inside random carts.

"Have fun dying," one of them jeers.

A woman dressed like an erotic circus performer wears fishnets under a short skirt and boots stopping mid-thigh. She has fake blood dripping over the swell of her breasts.

"I'm hungry," she says, baring her teeth. "Women are my favorite. So soft." She tilts her head and says absentmindedly, "So pretty." She licks her blood-painted lips.

She jerks her head and straightens when the guy in front of us sits inside the cart. "He'll do," she says, sliding next to him. The poor guy's eyes widen in terror. She tilts her head back and laughs when the ride attendant secures the lap bar.

I smile. "She's awesome," I say, mindlessly sliding inside the next cart.

I'm startled when a dark hooded figure slides in next to me instead of Alice. It's the man with the white mask and an upside-down cross painted in the center. He angles his head slowly and places a gloved finger over his masked lips, silently telling me not to scream. He's so tall, his knees are bent uncomfortably, making it difficult for the lap bar to close.

I try to keep calm.

I crane my neck to see Alice seated with another man wearing a hooded cloak with a black mask that looks like it's made of carbon fiber. Alice stares straight ahead, her shoulders tense. Her knuckles are white from gripping the bar. The ride operator checks each lap bar beginning with the back carts.

When I face forward, I let out a yelp. The man is looking straight at me. I can't see his eyes, but I can hear his muffled breathing.

The ride attendant gets to our cart and reaches over to pull the bar near my hand. I pull my skirt down the tops of my thighs for modesty, wishing I'd worn pants. A gloved hand shoots out, snatching the operator's hand in a tight grip and shoving it off.

"Just checking it," the ride operator says nervously with both hands raised. He glances at me. "Making sure you're safe."

He walks away toward the operator booth. He flicks a couple of switches.

When the ride lurches forward, people scream prematurely in

excitement. The tension builds as the coaster moves higher with every *clank-clank-clank* from the chain mixed with the rush of fear and exhilaration.

A surge of electricity shoots up my arm when his gloved hand laces his fingers through mine.

People continue to scream behind us, but it fades as we reach the crest. Everything becomes clear for a few seconds. The lights, the crisp air, screaming, people running through the scare zones, and the smell of fair food.

Then, one by one, the cars fall down the track, eliciting bone-shilling screams.

The coaster stops right before the drop. I grip his hand tighter, thankful that it's there.

"Shit," I mumble.

My heart continues to beat hard in my chest, waiting for my stomach to drop. I can feel his gaze on me like fire over my skin.

A shrill laugh comes from the giant clown mask on top with flashing red eyes. The sound of screams pierces through the air. My hair blows from the wind. I look over, and my eyes widen when the first cart drops. I scream, and my body slams against his. He slides his arm around my shoulders, holding me close. I breathe in his rich scent of citrus and cedar, close my eyes, and feel how hard his muscles are underneath his costume. The man is solid. He must be one of the main circus performers. From what I've seen online, they have amazing physiques.

The coaster jerks with each turn, but he holds me against him. I squeeze my thighs together, arousal blooming between my thighs, not wanting him to let go. I've never had a man hold me like this—like I was his.

The coaster comes to a stop. He lets me go, the lap bar pulls up automatically, and he slides out of the cart. The loss of his heat causes me to shiver.

I follow everyone out the exit, looking for Alice, a little dazed. I finally spot her.

"Alice." I wave over.

She turns around. "That was insane," she says, but I don't miss the worried look crossing her features.

"Are you okay?"

She nods. "Yeah," she says, looking around.

I bet she's looking for the guy who rode with her because I can't find the one who sat next to me. They disappeared into thin air once we got off the ride.

"Did that guy say anything to you?" I ask.

"Not a word. He... sat there. He made sure I didn't jerk around, so that was a relief. I'm not sure, but if we rode together, we would have flown out of the cart. It was so fast."

I laugh. "I thought my heart was going to pop out of my chest when the ride stopped, and the clown started laughing."

We walk over to a guy wearing a costume with his face painted like a jester holding a red drink with smoke floating around the rim.

"Want some blood?" he asks with a sinister smile.

"How much is the blood?" I ask with a grin.

He looks behind us, his sinister grin falling off. Alice and I turn around, but all we see are people rushing by, screaming.

When we look back, the guy hands us two drinks. "Have a bloody night and be careful... you never know what can follow you."

"Funny." Alice grabs a drink and takes a sip.

I watch her face light up. "It's good." And she takes a bigger sip.

I try mine, and she is not wrong. It tastes like red fizzy soda. I hand him a ten-dollar bill, but he shakes his head and looks away. "How much for the drinks?"

His eyes are black from his contacts, but he doesn't respond and ignores us.

"Fine." I'm not going to turn down a free soda.

I look around for my masked guy but can't find him.

"Funny finding you here?" I whirl around, almost spilling my drink, to see Jason, Matt, Tommy from the football team, and

Emma with a couple of girls from school. "You two a thing now? You know, we don't mind a little lesbian action."

"Fuck off."

"Fuck I can do, baby. You name the time and place, and I'll slide right in," Jason says, stepping closer.

"Oh, you finally found your dick?"

"You want me to show you, Ivy?" His eyes fall to my chest. "Do you want to see how big my dick is so you can ride it? I promise to make you scream louder than any ride here."

I don't miss the lust in his eyes.

"Let it go, Jason. Stop fucking around," Tommy scolds.

But he isn't. All he needs is the right push, and I have a strong feeling Jason is the type who wouldn't accept the word no.

In his mind, I'm easy and considered a slut. No one would believe me if he touched me without my consent, and he's preying on it.

I'm so sick of these assholes.

"I don't do kiddie rides, Jason. I like real men." I glance at Tommy. "The kind who finish the job."

"Spoken like the true slut that you are," Tommy sneers.

Emma sniggers. "You're such a ho."

"At least I don't pay for a guy's condoms so he can fuck me. Tell me, Emma. How was your three minutes in hell?" Her mouth falls open like a fish.

Emma thought she got a winner in Tommy, only to find out that he's a three-minute hit and quit.

Jason's lips twitch. "I can go all night."

"Pfft. Yeah, annoying everyone." I walk away with Alice in tow and mutter, "Prick."

"They're insufferable. All those guys do is think with their dicks. It's all that asshole Jason talks about."

"That's because he can't get laid."

"Is it true?" she asks. I pause in front of the trail leading to the haunted houses. "What you said about Tommy?"

"Yep." I sigh. "Awful. I didn't feel it, and it was my first time.

He lasted three minutes. I counted." We step closer and get into the line to the first haunted house. "I faked it," I say with a laugh. "Then he called me a slut."

I'm relieved she doesn't ask if I've gone out with anyone else— if I had sex with anyone else. I prefer to omit than deny. I've never seen Alice with a boyfriend, but she mentioned her parents didn't think it was a good idea.

CHAPTER 8

We toss our drinks in the trash before we enter the haunted house. My eyes try to adjust to the darkness inside. Noises of doors opening and closing in the distance. Screams floating from deep inside.

Footsteps shuffle in the next room, followed by screams and then the sound of a chainsaw. Chills snake down my legs. There are beds with props of human bodies cut open with their insides hanging out.

We take small steps through the maze of the hallway. Alice screams when a guy with a deformed mask jumps out, and bumps into the wall. He looks grotesque and is making inhuman noises.

Doors slam ahead.

We laugh after we scream when another one pops out, making a weird animal noise.

We continue the labyrinth through the hallway, trying to find the exit when the floor gives way. I try to hold on to Alice when she shrieks before we plunge into a dark underground space.

"Alice!" I shout, looking around, but it's pitch black with minimal light coming from the wooden slats of the walls.

"Alice!" I call out, but nothing.

Anxiety sets in when I cannot find an exit. "*Aaaaaaalice.... Aaaaalice. Are you there?*" Someone calls in an unnerving voice, reminding me of a horror movie.

"Who's there?" I ask.

I move to the left, trying to find the exit, when a mechanical monster rises from the ground with glowing red eyes, startling me. I run the other way when mechanical hands pop out followed by an ominous laugh. I try to scream, but I don't have enough air in my lungs and run into something hard. I look up, trying to focus, and notice someone tall in the dim light.

When it steps forward, I recognize the same guy who sat next to me on the roller coaster wearing the white mask.

I step back and sigh in relief. "It's you." He angles his head like a masked murderer. "Real funny. Can you help me get out of here and find my friend? We got separated when the trapdoor gave way, and I can't find the exit."

He shakes his head and slides a finger down the center of my neck, causing a ripple of fear to curl around my gut. There is no reason to be scared. People who work for the carnival don't harm the guests, but they don't usually touch them either.

I take another step back and hit a wall. He steps forward, closing the distance.

"What are you doing? I ask in a shaky voice.

He leans close. His mask touches my cheek.

"Shh..." His finger descends from the center of my neck to my collarbone, then lower, fingering the button on my white blouse in circles. "Mm..." I close my eyes.

I should scream, but I can't do it.

His finger glides to the swell of my breast, then back up to my neck. My eyes fly open. Something warm is on my thigh, but I can't see clearly. I can feel him towering over me, swallowing me whole.

I'm frozen in place when his hand slides up my thigh.

"Please," I plead, but I don't know if I want him to stop or keep going.

I'm fucked up. That must be it. I'm not normal. A sane person screams. A sane person would push him away and fight him off. But I'm not sane. I'm fucking crazy and desperate for him to keep going. To keep touching me in the way I craved to be touched.

The friction builds between my legs, wanting him there. He slides his gloved hand higher on my thigh. Close, but not close enough to give me what I want. I grip his hard shoulders. A tingles slither through my fingers.

Logic rattles my brain, and I push him away. "Let me out!"

He drops his hands and steps away toward the other side of the room, then pushes the door open like it appeared from thin air.

I checked everywhere, and there wasn't a way out. The light from the carnival rides guides me out, and I run. I look left and right, following the way out. The smell of popcorn hits me with the sound of a bell ringing from a game. I glance behind me to see if he followed me.

"Ivy?" I turn and sigh in relief when Alice runs up to me. "I've been trying to find you. I looked everywhere. Are you okay? You look flushed."

It's not from fear. I'm turned on by the man wearing a white mask and black costume.

"I was trying to find a way out. I called out for you, but you didn't respond. It was dark, and it took me a bit to find a way out."

"Did a guy in a mask show up and freak you out?" she asks.

"Yeah. You?"

She has an uncertain look in her eyes. "The same one from the roller-coaster ride?"

"I think we better call it a night."

"Yeah," she agrees. "This place is crazy."

"Now I know why they're strict about the age limit." I slide my hand through her elbow and walk toward the exit. "Come on, I need to get home. I've had enough for one night."

The fog is thick. The machines on each side shoot more like thick clouds. I can't see the ticket booths by the exit. The smoke makes it hard to see the deeper you walk. I can feel Alice tense, her arm pressed around mine, expecting something to pop out and scare us.

We're about to reach the exit when the man wearing the white mask appears again. I ignore him this time and walk out of the way.

He steps in front of me at a safe distance and gives me a theatrical bow. You can tell he's mastered it and has done it a million times. He's holding a ticket in his outstretched hand. Butterflies swarm in my stomach, and I remember his fingers on my skin.

"Oh my God," I whisper softly when I see it.

I look at Alice.

"Take it, Ivy. He chose you," she says, urging me on. "Don't think about it and just...take it."

I've been waiting years to see a live circus and almost two to see the Circle of Freaks.

I grip the ticket. He raises his head for a second and kisses the top of my hand. The ticket is the only thing keeping our fingers from touching. It's not a kiss from his lips because of the mask, but it's hot.

When he finally releases the ticket, I say softly, "Thank you."

A clown hobbles over with big red shoes and fake blood dripping down his multicolored outfit. His clown makeup has a deadly twist. The corners of his mouth are painted upward in a grotesque parody of mirth, revealing yellow teeth that are jagged and irregular. It creates a nightmarish contrast to a clown's pleasant appearance. The teeth seem more like a predator's, ready to sink into prey. His smile is wide, stretching from ear to ear. It seems to defy the limits of human facial anatomy with lips that are a sickly shade of crimson.

"Thank you... for playing with us tonight," the clown says in a screechy voice. "We're DYING to have you come back." His cold and calculating eyes slide over me. "We can play a game... if you want. Do you like games?"

I step back. "T-that depends," I stammer.

Malevolent intent emanates from his eyes. They seem to

pierce into my soul like he knows my deepest fears and darkest secrets.

"On what?"

I'm annoyed with myself for stammering like a nervous idiot. He's a man in a costume.

"How it ends."

"Come back and find out," he quips.

My masked performer straightens to his full height. Tall and commanding. Compared to the clown's average height, he seems taller than six foot three at least. The clown cowers dramatically, but I could see genuine fear in the clown's eyes.

"Come on," Alice says, tugging me toward the exit. "They're just messing "

But I'm not convinced. Right before we exit, I look over my shoulder, and the man with the white mask watches me while the fog whirls behind him. Behind the facade of fun, a darkness radiates within him that is terrifying.

CHAPTER
9

DRACO

"I-I didn't mean to frighten her, but she came to a haunted carnival," Levi says, pulling off his wig and clown shoes.

I tear my mask off my head and follow him inside the tent we use to change between shows. When he turns around, I wrap my hand around his throat, watching his eyes bulge—pure fear washing over his features.

"It's not that you frightened her, it's what you said and how you said it," I snarl. "The only one who can frighten her is me." I squeeze harder, watching his makeup crack. The skin around his pathetic smile is almost corpse-like. A contrast to the splatter of blood on my skin from my last victim. "The only game she plays is mine."

His hand tries to free the grip I have around his throat, but I'm taller and stronger than him. I find his attempt amusing. Levi has a problem switching off when he's in character. In this case, with her.

My phone vibrates in my pocket.

I broaden my smile. "You're lucky I'm expecting a phone call. If what you said causes her not to come back, start thinking about how you want to die." I release him, watching him fall on his ass while clutching his neck and gasping for air. I'm not sentimental, but she's different. I don't know why, but she is.

L: Thank you. She's home.

Draco: Who's the blonde?

L: Friend from school.

Draco: I want her.

L: It's not that simple.

Draco: Then I'll see how simple I can make it.

L: She's not what you're used to.

Draco: No one is, but that is beside the point. I want her.

L: Don't cause problems for me.

Draco: Is she yours? How old?

L: You know better than to ask me stupid questions. Nineteen.

Draco: Then what's the problem? I want to play.

L: Catching feelings?

Draco: Not my style, but I'll keep out of your way.

L: You're not the only one.

Draco: I'm not following.

L: Who is interested in her.

Draco: I'll make her choose, but I have a feeling she'll like it when I make her scream.

CHAPTER
10

The ticket he gave me is different from the one sold online. It allows me free entry to the haunted carnival and circus. It also includes VIP seating at the show. It's even better than buying a ticket. This one is unique because I can choose to go on any weekend until they leave. Buying a ticket online is for a specific weekend, and there are no refunds or date changes.

Every time I look at the ticket tucked away inside the drawer in my room, it reminds me of him. The man who gifted me what I wanted, only to terrify me when I finally received it.

Since last week, all I have thought about is if I should go or when I *should* go. My mind plays different scenarios, like a first date, imagining how it would go or what you would say. What you would wear.

What if he tricks me into a dark room at one of the haunted houses? I swear I can still feel the burn of his touch on my skin since that night. That's all I could think about when I got home and have thought about every day since. After Alice dropped me off, I stared at myself in front of my bathroom mirror naked after a shower. My skin flushed from the hot water. My nipples hard with need. The ache between my thighs. I closed my eyes in front of the bathroom mirror, imagining him touching me with every stroke of my fingers until I came. My eyes opened when I felt the first wave of pleasure, memorizing the way I looked. The way my mouth parted, and my expression when my pussy clenched my fingers, wishing it was his cock. It was all I could think about since that night in the dark room of the haunted house.

Like right now, it's the same expression I see in the mirror's reflection. After I come, I bring my fingers to my mouth and suck. My cum tastes sweet, and I wonder what his tastes like. I place my fingers between my thighs, slide three fingers in my cunt and rub my clit with my thumb, fucking myself again.

Pressing the button on the scale and place the bananas to charge a customer, I hear a familiar voice. "Hey, Ivy."I see Dean place a couple of TV dinners on the black belt behind the yellow plastic grocery store separator bar.

"Hello," I say dryly.

He is the last person I want to see. When I scan the last item, the older gentleman swipes his card, the machine spits out the receipt, and I hand it off.

After I bag the last of the gentleman's groceries, the belt runs forward. "How are you?"he asks as I scan the first TV dinner.

Beep... Beep.

"Are you okay?"he asks again.

"Yep," I quip.

I turn and bag up his food so he can be on his way. I have fifteen minutes left of my shift and want to make it home before dark.

I ring him up. There is an awkward silence while I wait for him to use the pin pad.

The machine accepts his card.

The receipt slides out.

"D-do you need a ride?" he asks with a hopeful expression.

I hand him the receipt. "No, thanks."

I watch him frown in dismay, taking the receipt. "I ended it with Sarah."

He thought he would come in here, and we would pick up where he left off? I won't come up with the money to make rent this month. My mother will go on a rant, but I'm not fucking Dean for it. Not anymore.

I cross my arms over my chest. "I'm sorry to hear that, Dean. You have a nice evening."

He grabs the bags harder than necessary, almost tearing the plastic handles off.

When he's about to walk out of the exit, he turns back around. "You should reconsider. It is dangerous out there. Did you hear about the teenage girl missing one town over?"

I've heard. Christina Marsh was reported missing when she did not return home after school. I saw the picture posted on the news alert online. She's a senior, eighteen, with strawberry-blond hair. Popular girl. Straight-A student in charge of the school newspaper with a bright future. Her mother said she wanted to be a veterinarian. She was last seen leaving school on her way home around four o'clock on September 12th. That was three days ago.

According to the news, every month, another teenage girl goes missing. The news has spread like wildfire, but no one has found out who's behind it. Rumors are there is a suspected serial killer and a bunch of theories. They make theories when they don't have facts. The authorities come up with the what-ifs, but there is no solution to stop it from happening again.

"I have."

"I can give you a ride home."

He wants to give me more than a ride, and I'm not interested. Even if he would tell me it was just for a ride, I wouldn't do it. Accepting a ride from him will give him hope. He will come back and ask again, hoping one day I'll give in.

"I told you, I don't need a ride, Dean."

I see him tense. He has a white-knuckle grip on the plastic bag. His eyes go vacant for a split second, then a shadowy grin crosses his face. "I'll keep asking, every day...until you say yes."

Pathetic.

"And I'll say no. Every day... until you stop."

"I'll never stop, Ivy."

I roll my eyes and suck my teeth. "You never fucking began, Dean."

His eyes harden when I point out what he is trying to hide. What excuse did he give Sarah? Most likely the one where he says he's stressed when he snaps.

I'm relieved when a customer pushes a grocery cart in my lane. I turn around and smile at the middle-aged woman.

"Did you find everything you were looking for today?"

"Yes, I did," she replies.

I hear the automatic doors open.

When I turn, they're sliding closed, and he's gone.

After I clear the register and clock out, I walk across the parking lot to catch the shuttle. It's still light out. The sun casts a soft golden glow across the landscape. The sky above transitions from a brilliant blue to shades of orange, pink, and purple as the sun sets. Not wanting to be caught walking home along the main highway, I hurry to the bus stop and sit on the warm bench.

I can't stop thinking of Dean's reaction when I turned him down, or what he said before he left, or the feral intensity in his eyes. I don't think he ever thought I would turn him down, but I did, and I'm proud of myself. It felt like I could finally breathe above water after removing the brick slowly weighing me down.

When the shuttle bus arrives, I hop on and walk toward the back. One man has his head leaning on the window with his eyes closed and headphones on. Another woman with fire-engine-red hair sits across from him, busy looking at her phone.

The sun has almost set when the bus drops everyone off in front of the mall. I walk inside, feel the cold air from the AC system hit my skin. Mall shoppers stop to look at the window fronts. Some walk out after they make their purchase, and some head out the front exit.

When I push the exit door to leave out the back, it's already dark. A chill slithers over my skin when a sense of unease washes over me after I round the corner.

I freeze.

In the dimly lit parking lot is a stark silhouette against the backdrop of the asphalt. It rises, casting a long and slender shadow that stretches out like a solitary sentinel.

I run back to go inside and tug on the door handle, but it doesn't budge. My hands shake.

Dread sinks in.

The door locks when you exit and can't be opened from the outside.

I look over my shoulder, and it's gone. I wipe my eyes to make sure I'm not seeing shit. Nothing. The lot is empty. I look left and right, but there is no one. I can see cars in the distance heading toward the front exit of the parking lot. There is not a single vehicle on this side.

The glow of the lights from the drive-in theater to the far right gives me a clear view of the apartment building. The light pole flickering by the general waste bin grabs my attention.

A yellow light reflects off the back of the complex by the stairwell, and I run. My bag shuffles behind me with the weight of my books. My lungs burn with the effort. The voice inside my head tells me, *Keep running. Don't stop.*

CHAPTER
11

I'm startled awake by a constant ringing. I reach for my phone but can't shut off the sound.

It's another Amber alert.

Another girl went missing. Brooke Jensen. I search for her name, and she's a junior from Fenmore High School. It's located one town over and is the same school Christina Marsh attends.

News alert says Brooke Jensen was last seen walking to her car after cheerleading practice and never made it home. No one has seen her since yesterday. Her car was towed from the parking lot at school this morning. There are no witnesses. The alert notification reads if you see something, you should say something.

I snort. "It's too late after they snatch your ass," I say aloud.

When I head out to the school bus after locking my front door, unease sets in when I see what is written on the walls by the stairwell. THEY ARE WATCHING. The next one beside it isn't any better. TO FUCK YOU.

Everyone is trying to fuck someone, I tell myself.

After last night, I have been trying to piece together what I saw or thought I saw. Was the man standing in the parking lot real? Is it because I'm paranoid?

Every month, they find another body of a missing girl, but they haven't found the person responsible.

I have to remain vigilant and keep in mind there is a killer or killers out there. One thing those girls have in common when they come up missing is that they were all alone when it happened. It means I can't walk home, or I could be their next target. My thought flies to Dean and his incessant behavior about taking me home.

WHEN THE BELL RINGS, I SHUT MY LOCKER AND TURN the lock. It's my last class, but I need to use the restroom. I don't care about science. I already did all the work and turned it in. I'm about to make a quick left to the women's bathroom when I see Jason walking with one of his teammates Paul Carson. Paul gives me a once-over. Jason murmurs something to Paul, but from where he's standing, I can't make out what he says.

Jason walks closer. "Hey, Ivy," he says, gripping his crotch. "Are you ready for this big cock?"

Paul smirks, but it quickly fades when I shoot back with, "Looks like Paul is getting you off nicely. As soon as you grabbed your junk, his face lit up."

Jason's eyes narrow, and his jaw hardens. "Are you calling me a faggot?"

"I think the correct term is gay, and there is nothing wrong with it. You two look good together. I think it's cute he walks you to class"—I smile—"whispering to each other."

"Come here, and I'll show you how gay I am. Paul can watch."

Fear claws my gut because I know he would show me, and it doesn't involve Paul participating. The look in his eyes is feral.

The hallway is empty. The silence begins to stretch with every second. His mouth widens with a malevolent smile. He charges forward, and I bolt inside the women's restroom.

I run inside the last stall, sliding the lock shut and hearing the groan of the bathroom close. My chest is rising and falling. A scream is lodged in my throat.

My ears strain to hear the groan of the bathroom door,

looking through the tiny crack in the stall door. Hoping they didn't follow me. All I hear is the sound of my rapid breathing, and I feel the burn in my lungs.

I hear footsteps outside.

"Oh God," I whisper.

I step back, hoping it's a girl who needs to pee. I take another step back and feel something hard behind me. When I turn, my scream is muffled when a large hand covers my mouth and a body pins me against the stall.

It's him.

"Shh...."

My eyes widen, taking in the white-and-black face paint like a jester. He is wearing a black hooded sweater.

I'm trying to make out his face, but all I can make out are his full lips, a sharp jaw, and a straight nose. What has me mesmerized is how dark his eyes are. They are dark, like a bottomless pool of ink holding secrets in their depths.

I try to move, but he shakes his head. The door groans when it opens, and a sense of overwhelming terror washes over me like a suffocating tide.

"We know you're in here, Ivy. We just want to talk to you for a minute. I need to handle this thing we have between us." *Slam!* They begin pushing each door with a force that rattles the stalls. "I promised to show you what you're missing." *Slam!* The next stall door opens with force.

My eyes refocus on the man in front of me with his head canted to the side. How did he get in here? How did he know?

They know I'm in here, but don't know he's here with me. He raises his finger over my lips, and I notice the ink on his hands, but I can't determine what they are. He pushes me slowly behind him and motions for me to sit on the toilet.

Another door slams open. "I know you're here, Ivy. Don't be shy. I just want to show you, baby. I promise I can fuck you harder than Tommy."

My masked performer's cavernous eyes flick down to mine. A

thunderous drumbeat pulses in my ears. The tension builds like a bomb ready to go off. He rolls his neck like he's getting ready to do something strenuous.

He gives me his back, and I let out a shallow breath.

Everything goes quiet.

I hear the lock open with a click.

"That's it, baby. Come out," Jason coos.

"We want to play, Ivy," Paul says darkly. "We want to hear you scream like you did for Tommy."

Oh my God. They want to rape me.

My masked hero pushes the door open. My chest tightens when the door swings back.

"What the fuck?" Paul and Jason say in tandem.

Then a cacophony of noises. The sound of violence being unleashed—skin meeting flesh in rapid succession. A loud thud followed by groans, and metal. The ground trembles when flesh and bone hits the floor.

I stand on the toilet and hunch over. My gut is churning. I try to see what is happening through the open door, but then I hear a loud crunch and then...nothing.

After a few seconds, I hear footsteps.

The bathroom door squeaks.

I hold my breath, slide one foot and the other from the toilet seat. I lean to look between the crack from the stall door. Paul and Jason are out cold on the bathroom floor. Paul's arm lies at an awkward angle. My masked hero is gone.

"What happened?" Principal Miller asks.

"I told you. I didn't see anything. I was in the stall and heard the bathroom door open. There was a scuffle—"

"You didn't come out to see what was going on?"

"I was using the toilet. I wasn't going to walk out with my pants down—"

"You expect me to believe that, Ivy."

Principal Miller has been working at this school for the past twenty-five years. He is bald at the top of his head with hair on the sides like he refuses to cut off the rest so it's even. He has a round belly as if he just swallowed a whole watermelon because the rest of him is skinny. His throat is irritated with bumps from shaving.

He drives an old station wagon and likes to drill students he thinks are trouble. Basically, the ones who don't play sports or have parents with deep pockets. I don't fit any of his requirements except the one that requires a private room and his right hand. He thinks I didn't notice him adjusting his brown slacks when the lady at the front desk showed me in. He wears flannels every day to school and golf pants. Who the fuck wears flannels with golf pants? And don't get me started on his glasses. He looks like he kills fire ants in his spare time with how thick they are.

I slouch in the chair and look at the picture of his family on his desk. Two girls, and they look bored just like his wife. All three brunettes.The frame reminds me of the ones you find at the dollar store. Nothing I say is good enough. He wants someone to blame because his precious football team is out of two of their starting players. How is that my fault?

"It's not my fault they chose the bathroom to fight whoever it was, and I was in the stall taking a piss, if you must know."

"That's enough, young lady. I don't know if your mother allows you to be disrespectful, but I won't tolerate it."

"It's hard when you're trying to blame me for something I didn't do. There is no way it was me."

"You're covering up for someone, and I don't know why."

"I didn't see anything, so how is that possible?"

He looks at me steadily. "You're suspended for two weeks."

I sit up. "What? Why? I didn't do it. You're acting like I did."

"Two students on the starting football team are out for the season because they were beaten up in the girl's bathroom during school. And...you were there and didn't do anything. You also happened not to see anything either. Which means... you are hiding who did it."

I overheard him on the phone talking to their parents. Paul has a broken arm, and Jason has a few cuts and bruises on his face and body. His ankle and hand are questionable. The doctors said they couldn't play the rest of the season if they planned on making it to college.

I scoff. "Are you hearing yourself right now? What was I supposed to do? Go after whoever did it? Fight? This is stupid. Whatever happened has nothing to do with me. You haven't asked if anything happened to me."

He blinks like a reptile. "That's it..." He walks over to the door and opens it with more force than necessary. "Out!" he shouts. "Come back to school two Mondays from now. I'll inform your teachers, and I suggest you pick up any work you need to turn in while you are suspended. You wouldn't want to repeat your senior year a third time, Miss Sloan."

What an asshole.

"Whatever."

I stand, and right before I leave, he says, "The police will be in touch if they require anything. It would behoove you, Miss Sloan, to cooperate. Your senior year is on the line."

I smile sarcastically. "I hope you catch whoever did it because we both know it wasn't me. And"—I point at the bulge in his crotch—" you should take care of that, or you might not make it to retirement, Mr. Miller." His face turns red.

I hope they don't catch him because those two idiots deserved to get their asses kicked. It would be pointless to tell Mr. Miller the truth because he wouldn't believe me anyway. Even if he did, I wouldn't say shit.

"Be careful what you say, Miss Sloan...your reputation around school isn't the best."

I shake my head. Unbelievable.

"Your reputation to find the truth isn't either, Mr. Miller," I shot back and walk out and continue, "Thank you for the chat. I'm sure you will have the report of our conversation sent to the counselor." I turn around, I look at the huge bulge in his pants and smile. "Don't leave anything out." And walk out.

He shuts the door with a slam.

On the positive side, I could pick up shifts at the Big H and earn money I need for the rent. I could also pay my masked hero a visit at the circus to thank him.

CHAPTER 12

"Here." I hand my mother one hundred and fifty dollars. She looks up after taking a drag from her morning cigarette, takes the money, and stuffs it in her bra.

"Why aren't you at school?" she asks after blowing smoke from her lips. "Took my advice and dropped out."

"No. I got suspended."

She chuckles and takes another drag. Her upper lip wrinkles, reminding me of beef jerky when she sucks on her cancer stick. I try to hold my breath when she does it. It will take me twenty-five minutes to air out the apartment followed by another shower.

"What did you do?"

"Nothing. I was in the bathroom when two guys came in fighting, and the principal suspended me because I didn't know who kicked their ass. I was in the bathroom stall taking a piss."

This is the version I'm going with, not like my mother cares. Her focus is on me coming up with the rent money, and her advice is to use my body to get it.

"What does that have to do with you?"

"Exactly. It's none of my business who fights and who gets beat up. I didn't see anything, and I'm no snitch."

"How long?"

"Two weeks."

"You got the other half of the rent?"

"I got the light."

She snuffs out the cigarette in her coffee. "I didn't ask you that, Ivy. I asked if you have the other half of the rent. The diner is slow, and I'm not making enough in tips."

Not for cigarettes. She smokes a pack a day. There is always enough for those.

"I'll ask for more hours during my suspension. It's all I can do."

"Well...if you don't, you will have to find somewhere else to live."

"But Mom—"

"I'm sick and tired of telling you, Ivy. I've told you to quit school—"

"If I finish, I can get a better job."

"We moved because you threw a fit about Hank, and I told you what you had to do. You think you're better than me. That you are going to make a ton of money. The only job you'll get is spreading your legs, and you might as well get a head start. You won't be young forever, which is why Hank wanted you. If you would have agreed, we wouldn't have had to move here."

I flinch. Hank shoved his cock in my throat and forced me to do other things I didn't want. My mother didn't care that he did. She cared more about her not being pretty enough to keep his attention. Hank is a meth dealer. He paid attention to my mother because he wanted to take advantage of me, and she hates me for it. She knows I would never have agreed to do it. This is her way to blame me.

"Why are you like this?"

She gets up and digs in her front uniform pocket for another cigarette. "Because it's how we pay rent. It's how we eat. It is reality." She lights the cigarette until the tip glows red. "Come up with the money or get out, Ivy. Either way, you will be under someone. Hank, the married asshole from the Big H, another asshole that doesn't like his wife's cunt because she's a nag"--she takes a drag—"he will do anything for a young cunt."

"Like rape and kill them. Haven't you seen the news?"

"I have, and you know what, those are the dumb ones who get snatched up unawares. Because they think men aren't monsters. Those little pricks at your school think with their dicks at a young age, and it doesn't get better as they get older. Don't think for one second there is a special prince who will come save you on his white horse. The white horse is a van to take advantage of you, and when they're done, they get rid of you. That's the truth. It's sad for those girls." She nods like she needs to convince herself of the bullshit she's spewing. She takes a drag, then another, and continues, "If they had a mother or a parent to tell them the way of the world, they would be better prepared. I'm doing you a favor, Ivy. I'm telling you what men see when they look at you. A short skirt, pretty face, and pair of tits. Use it to your advantage while you can. You'll thank me later."And with that, she grabs her keys and walks out the door.

I wish I could yell at her and tell her she's lying. I wish I could tell her she is bitter because she didn't do more with her life and blames me. But the truth is I can't because everything she said about men is true. Not the girls—it's not their fault. It's not their fault vile people exist.

But guys like Dean, guys at school, Kevin at the Big H, Hank, and Scott, the drug dealer. They all prove my mother right. Only one so far has proved her wrong. The one who saved me. The one I don't know but know where to find. The man who stopped the minute I said no. The man I can't stop thinking about and need to see.

I SHOVE MY SMALL DUFFEL INSIDE MY EMPLOYEE LOCKER and shut the door.

"You said you needed to see me?" Kevin says from the doorway.

I grab my name tag and walk out of the employee's lounge.

"I wanted to ask if I could pick up any full-time shifts this week and next week."

He smirks. "Dropping out of school?"

"No. I have some time off. Can you give me the shifts or not?"

I'm not going to beg him. He can kiss my ass.

His eyes land on my chest. "I can work something out."

"I also need to leave in time to catch the last shuttle after every shift from now on."

"I can't make any promises about that."

"Haven't you heard the news?"

"I have, but I don't see what that has to do with you receiving special treatment. Hanna doesn't. Trisha doesn't."

Hanna is sixty-three and has a husband who picks her up. Trisha is twenty-eight, pimpled-faced, weighs about three hundred pounds, and blames it on having four kids. She lives with her grandmother and drives a minivan. I'm not judging, but neither of them is a teenager going to high school. The girls that have been found dead are all juniors and seniors in high school. Trisha and Hanna both have a way to get home, but I don't tell him that.

"I don't want to walk home after the sun sets."

"What happened to your ride?"

He means Dean. I'm sure he thinks the worst, and he's right.

"He has a girlfriend."

"Oh." His eyes lift. "I could give you a ride," he offers. "It's no trouble."

"That's okay. I'm fine taking the shuttle."

"I can't make any promises, Ivy. I can't let you leave early every day. It's not fair to the other employees, but I can give you a ride home," he offers.

I don't miss the intent behind it or the way his eyes undress me as he says it.

"Don't worry about it. I'll try to make it work."

"Offer still stands, Ivy. I don't mind."

I'm sure you don't.

"Do you need me at register five today, Kevin,"Trisha asks, looking between me and Kevin.

Trisha is nice but is overwhelmed by being a single mom. You can tell she had a rough night with the bags under her eyes. She works hard, but Kevin treats her like shit.

"No. I need you to stock the shelves."

"Why can't Ricky do it?" I ask.

"Because I said so, Ivy. Now get to your lane."

Stocking shelves sucks, and he makes her do it all the time.

"I'll switch with her," I offer.

Trisha looks relieved. I bet her back and feet are killing her. I stocked shelves my first day working here, and my feet killed me for two days straight. My back felt like it was trampled on.

"Are you the manager of this store now, Ivy? "

"No, Kevin. I'm not, but I've stocked shelves, and it's a lot of work when you do it every day. It also helps to work in other areas in the store in case someone calls out."

Trisha smiles at me like I'm her savior. I'm not, but someone needs to help her out. Her feet look like they got stung by bees. They are red and puffy, and the flats she is wearing are warped.

"Is that what you want, Ivy?" he asks, making my skin crawl.

"We could rotate. She can handle the register, and I'll stock in the morning, and then we can switch in the afternoon."

"Fine," he agrees, "if you need a ride after, let me know."

When he walks away, I swallow the nausea pricking my throat.

Trisha passes by me and says softly, "Thanks, Ivy. He can be a prick sometimes."

"More like all the time,"I tell her, watching him walk into the management office.

"If you need a ride today, I can take you. My mom can watch the kids for ten more minutes."

A thought crosses my mind.

"I normally wouldn't say yes, knowing you need to get home

to your babies after working all day, but could you drop me off at the fair?"

"The fair?"

I smile. "Yeah."

CHAPTER 13

After Trisha drops me off, I walk to the closest booth at the entrance of the haunted Carnival. I hand the man dressed in a clown costume my ticket.

He takes it, shines a light on it, and looks up. "Hold out your left hand, please." He fastens a red band around my left wrist. "That's a special band, do not take it off." He secures a black band. "This band is for unlimited rides. The red is for the VIP area at the Circle of Freaks Show. They will scan your ID at the entrance to verify your age. Then leave your bag and phone with security."

My heart pounds in excitement.

"Thank you."

He hands me my special ticket for tonight's show at the Circle of Freaks tent and a carnival map. "Thank you for coming. We've been DYING to have you," he says in a deep, slow cadence.

I walk in and head through the fog. It's different from the first time. A bit scarier because I'm alone. There is no one I can hold on to if I'm scared.

My heart beats so fast I can feel my blood pumping in my ears like a drum. The fog around me is thick. A couple walks ahead of me through the mist and disappear. I look to my left and right, waiting for something to appear. But nothing. I pass the signs that read, ABANDON ALL HOPE, KILLING BOOTH, and I CAN SMELL YOUR FEARS.

The couple walking ahead scream. The fog clears. The actor

with the bloody mask glances at me and walks away. Why didn't he scare me? I look down at my wrist. Is it the band? Are they not allowed to frighten me because of it?

I spot a palm concession booth.

A woman walks out, planting herself in front of me, and asks, "Would you like a reading?"

She has a British accent. It sounds nice. Different from the Southern twang I learned to hide when we moved here. I always pictured a fortune teller as having a Romany accent when in character. She wears a long, gauzy skirt, big hoop earrings, and a shawl with different occult symbols. Her hair was black with gray streaks beginning from her temples.

"I'm not sure?" I tell her.

I'm curious but don't want to seem eager. I know whatever she is going to say is a lie, but it looks fun.

"You doubt me," she announces. "I assure you, I'm not."

"Oh, I..."

She grabs my hand and looks at my palm. "Come with me." She looks up. "I won't charge you."

"Why not?'

"You're special." She leans close. "He would be so disappointed in me if I did."

I pinch my brows in confusion. "Who?"

"Come," she says and pulls me to her booth. "I don't have much time before the show starts, and he's waiting."

How did she... and then I look at my wrist. It's no secret she is talking about the show. I'm wearing the band. Anyone could have guessed where I was headed. But what did she mean when she said *he*?

"Who is...? "

She tugs me inside. "Have a seat," she says.

She sits on the opposite side of the table, covered with a dark purple cloth adorned with golden motifs that shimmer subtly under the low light of flickering candles. A medium-sized crystal ball rests on the table, emitting a shimmering radiance from its surface. Scattered throughout are many old items, such as polished stones, tarnished coins, and intricate metal charms, each carrying a mysterious and magical aura.

Her chair has luxurious velvet upholstery and a finely embroidered tapestry portraying whirling galaxies and magical sigils hanging on the wall, contrasting the horror theme outside.

She holds out her hand, motioning for mine. She takes my hand and leans close, closing her eyes and moving her lips in a silent prayer.

When she's done, she opens her eyes and begins, "You are his chosen one. The one he has been waiting for."

"Chosen one?"

"Shh...I'm not finished. I will give you a reading. Believe me or not. You can do with it as you wish."

"Okay, my name is Ivy. What is your name?"

"Madam Seraphina," she says and continues, "You were chosen since before your time. Fate has brought you here, and you have a gift." Her eyes stare at me intently. "You draw people. Men of the opposite sex are entranced. Women mesmerized. This is your power, but it's to be shown and only given to one. You were his, and he was yours before you took your first breath." She traces the line on the palm of my hand, tickling my skin. "The house chose you. It holds secrets. Secrets that continue the circle of life for generations. Anyone who tries to break the circle dies." She looks up. "You will have a family and bear another son. One woman in their lineage bears two sons, and one day, you will have a vision of the future to pass down to your son. Don't doubt your dreams, Ivy. All your wishes will come true, but with the good, you need to accept the bad. Bad people exist, and some must die. It is all that I'm allowed to tell you. It will all make sense."

"Who's he?"

I ask, not believing a word she's saying. A house. A family. All my dreams coming true. It's fun and nice to hear. Also, very generic. How many people does she spin this bizarre tale to? But nonetheless, I'm curious.

She releases my hand and caresses the crystal ball. "He will be the one who makes you feel what no other has made you feel. He is...everything in your world. He will scare you. He will make you scream in rapture. *He* will do anything for you. You are the air he needs to breathe. You will know who *he* is because he will captivate you the same way you captivate him."

AFTER THE FUN READING WITH MADAM SERAPHINA, I make it to the entrance of the Circus of Freaks—the red-and-white tent with lights shooting up toward the sky. Red lights run parallel on each side. I noticed four tents connected in the back and two late-model luxury RVs. It's amazing. You feel the excitement before you step inside.

There is a red carpet and a man with a scanner wearing a black cloth mask covering his entire head. He swipes an ID and looks up to check if it matches the same person before waving them through the metal detectors. Three more men in suits with similar masks take cell phones and bags, placing them in bins. He hands each person a ticket to claim their belongings.

I give the man my ID. He scans it and hesitates before handing it to a man behind him.

"Is there a problem?" I ask, but they both ignore me.

The second man scans my ID on a reader and returns it.

"Go ahead," he says, gesturing me forward.

"Is everything alright?"

He turns to the next person, dismissing me.

Dick.

I turn in my phone and small duffel bag before passing through the metal detectors. When the curtain pulls up to let me through, I stop. The tent is dimly lit. I expected bleachers and heat. The smell of plastic, like the tents schools set up for outdoor events.

Instead, I find air blowers. Comfortable seating. Rich decor. It looks like the interior of a Las Vegas hotel I've seen on TV, but what has me fascinated is the stage. There is a catwalk with lights coming out of a huge mouth of a clown with red lights for the eyes.

To my right and left are pictures of clowns painted on canvas resting on easels. Grotesque creatures and performers. A sign to my right says:

ENTER IF YOU DARE TO GET FUCKED

To my left it reads:

THE WICKED SUFFER HERE.

Only five people are seated at the front closest to the stage, sanctioned off with a sign that says: RESERVED RED BANDS ONLY.

I look at my wrist, impressed at the choice of seating. Women walk down the aisles with trays of food and drinks, wearing top hats, corsets, short skirts, and fishnets.

I have ten minutes before the show, so I turn left to see the exhibits.

I walk deeper into a makeshift hallway with props of headless men on gurneys with bloody sheets. There are pickle jars sealed with what looks like fake body parts. Eyes, fingers, and...cocks on a display shelf.

It smells like the fog machines outside mixed with a weird scent. It smells like the lab at school when I dissected a frog in middle school. The teacher said it was formaldehyde, a fluid used to preserve tissue. My stomach turns when I see eyeballs staring back at me.

I walk deeper and see a body whose head has no eyes, and his fingers and cock were cut off. He's tied like Jesus on a cross with rope on his wrists and ankles. A wooden stake is in the ground behind him, holding his torso and neck.

I get close, curiosity eating me. It's fake. It has to be.

There is no way they can have real bodies tied up like this for a circus show. The skin has a sheen from the red light above. It looks like a man. There is no blood and looks embalmed. The center of his torso has been sewn with a thick string like the insides were scraped out.

I've never seen a dead body up close before, but this looks as close as you can get without killing someone. I'm dying to see what the performers look like.

Heading back, I watch as people begin to take their seats. The tent is full. People you would never guess who would like the circus. Couples of all ages. Old, young, and middle-aged ready to watch the show.

Metal gates lead to the center aisle. A flashing red sign says the BUTCHER. A man walks out, and it's disturbing. He's shirtless with two pieces of human leg props with blood dripping in each hand. His face is painted white. Eyes red. He licks one of the legs. His teeth glow. Blood drops out of his mouth.

Security lets me through after I show my band, and I sit on a black leather seat.

The light dims. The red light shines bright from the open mouth in the center of the stage.

The tent grows quiet.

The audience waits anxiously for the show to begin. Music starts as clowns run out of the mouth onto the stage. They move through the audience with mischievous energy. People laugh nervously between humor and horror. The clowns turn their heads in awkward angles, waving knives in the air. One throws one up and catches it with his mouth before hitting a woman.

My lips lift in a smile, feeling the excitement and adrenaline in the room.

An illusionist takes the stage. Eliciting awes from the crowd and then a scream when a clown startles another with a knife.

The music shifts to "Kore" by DEADONTHE-CAROUSEL.

Knives from the clowns levitate. The illusionist gestures toward them with his hands floating through the air. The Butcher interferes. Drops the leg and grabs the knife, slicing the leg repeatedly. He removes his shirt. Fire shoots out behind him, and the Butcher levitates his body, ripped with muscle.

A tube with smoke is shoved in front of me. I look to my left. It's the woman from the roller coaster.

She licks her lips with a smile like we share a secret. "Here. Drink it."

I look at the tube. It seems like a shot of something.

"I don't have any money."

She leans close. Her face was painted ghostly white. Her lips blood red. She smells like something fruity I want to lick.

"I don't want your money. I want you to drink." Her lips ghost my ear. "He wouldn't want you to be thirsty."

I turn so that our lips are almost touching. "Who?"

Her eyes fall to my lips. "Be careful, I like pussy."

"Well...I don't lick."

"Good. He prefers sucking."

"Who are you talking about?" I ask.

She's beautiful. Her makeup is flawless. Her eyes are lined with thick black eyeliner and red eye shadow.

"You'll see." Her eyes drop to the tube she's holding between us. "Drink. I want to see you swallow." I take it from her hands and wrap my lips around the top. The swell of her breasts lift as she watches me tilt my head back and drink. It's fruity and burns down my throat. I hand her the empty tube. She angles her head robotically. "Was it good, Ivy?"

I furrow my brows. "How—"

She takes the tube and walks away, swaying her hips.

How did she know my name?

Darkness blankets the tent, and the music stops. People cheer and scream in the dark. Electronic music begins to play a haunting beat. The stage is empty. Fire shoots out. Heat fills the air for a beat.

A man in a top hat appears dressed in an impeccably tailored coat. The music shifts to "The Clock Strikes Midnight" by Icky Ichabod. Bells go off in a haunting melody as the man reveals himself.

His coat is a rich burgundy, catching a glint of the red spotlight. The coat flows gracefully over his ripped, muscled frame. He has tattoos all over his chest and stomach. Intricate designs dipped in his muscles over his skin. The man is pure strength with an athletic physique. When he walks upstage, his high collar gives off Victorian elegance.

His face is painted white like a skull—black around his eyes, nose, and lips.

"Welcome to the Circle of Freaks. My name is Draco, and..." He pauses. My eyes lift, mesmerized. It's him. There's no mistake. It's my masked hero. His eyes land on mine, and he announces, "I'm the ringmaster."

My hands are sweating. My stomach does a little flip. He's gorgeous. Chiseled jaw, dark eyes, straight nose, and cheekbones so defined it would make a *Vogue* model jealous.

His top hat tilts to the side. His piercing eyes command the stage. It's like he holds the power of everyone's attention in his hands.

The audience claps and cheers.

"First, we bring you the wicked. The ones who don't deserve to live among you. If you feel that you will not be able to handle the show...please leave. Now is the time. Once the gate closes...you belong to the Circle of Freaks," he warns in a deep tone.

Everyone looks around, and a few get up and leave. He waits until they are gone, then the gate locks. Three security guards with suits and black masks stand in front.

"Now," Draco's voice echoes. "We can begin." The Butcher and another man with grotesque makeup push three men tied to chairs with wheels. They have a gag in each of their mouths.

"Here we are," Draco says with a menacing smile. "I've been waiting for you."

You could hear the muffled screams from the men. The red lights glow over the three of their faces. Their eyes bulging out of their sockets. *It's fake. They're actors.*

"Ringmaster's Show" by DEADONTHECAROUSEL blares from the speakers. Three women walk up behind the men and pull their hair back roughly like they're drinking blood.

The knives from the illusionists fly in the air, gesturing with his hands. The knives land, slicing their necks. Blood squirts, and the knives drop.

"Oh..." one guy says behind me.

"It looks real," his girlfriend says.

"It isn't," he replies.

I'm sitting on the edge of my seat because I'm not so sure. It does look real. Like the three men are being murdered. The air is tinged with a metallic smell.

The three women levitate from the suspension wire. They twirl in the air, defying the laws of gravity by their long hair.

I recognize one of them being the one from the roller coaster as she lands on her feet. A wicked laugh bubbles from her throat. She swipes her hands over her white hair. Her neck tilts back, and she's suspended by her hair, this time floating above the audience.

My hand flies over my mouth. Her neck could snap, but it doesn't. She's in total control. She's spectacular. A true talent.

When she lands safely, the crowd goes wild. Draco looks up, and jealousy grips me from the admiration in his gaze. I would do anything to have a man look at me like that.

CHAPTER 14

When the show is over, I turn right to the area I didn't get to explore. It's blocked off about three feet inside. The show was everything—the ringmaster was everything. If I had paid, it would have been worth every penny.

I'm about to walk back out when security blocks my path. He motions for my band.

"Oh...I only have a black and red one. I'm sorry, I didn't know I wasn't allowed here."

He points behind me. I look over, and his partner gestures for me to go in. It would have been simpler to tell me that part, but not speaking is part of the show.

I'm let through, and the atmosphere changes. It smells sweet. It feels colder than the main stage. I look behind me, but security doesn't follow. The lighting glows red. I'm in one of the back tents I saw from the outside. Metal skeletons line the walls like soldiers in a palace.

The area opens to a stage in the center. It's much smaller than the main one, but this stage has mirrors on the floor. A throne in the center like it's waiting for its king. There is a walkway that leads to a glass enclosure. The glass is a bit fogged, but as I get closer, I notice props and chains on a St. Andrews cross and...sex furniture.

I know what they are called because I researched it when I was watching porn and wanted to know what the special chairs and beds were used for.

To the left of the room, there is a red and black sex chair. In the center is a bondage table and a fun stool to the right. I look up, and it's completely enclosed and can only be accessed from the back. Is this where they...

A man in a leather mask walks inside, and my breath catches in my throat. He's wearing a hooded cloak and black leather pants. He pushes the cloak over each shoulder. His body is chiseled. He is ripped with muscle and tattoos. He's perfect.

A woman walks in, and I recognize her from the show, dressed in a corset with no bra. Her nipples stand proud pink and hard. Her hair is white, and I can tell she's wearing a wig. She is wearing black-and-white clown makeup. She walks in her sky-high, shiny black stilettos and bends at the waist over the bondage table. Her ass is in the air. The netted tights she is wearing are attached to a garter, giving the man a full view of her shaved pussy.

I clench my legs together when he stands behind her spreading her ass cheeks open. My clit tingles. He dips his head and licks her slit. My heart begins to beat like a jackhammer. The illusionist walks in dressed the same way without the cloak. His eyes are lined with Guyliner.

He's good-looking—they all are.

Gorgeous bodies and pretty faces.

He walks close to the glass and blows hot air, fogging up the glass. He writes KEIR.

"Keir," I say out loud. He nods. "Your name?"

He nods again.

More performers walk in. Three females and eight men dressed the same way. I even recognized the clown the night I came with Alice. His eyes sweep over me, but what has my attention since the first time I saw them is the ringmaster. He walks tall and commanding toward the woman who gave me the shot. The one he looks at like she's everything.

The familiar pang of jealousy grips me again, squeezing my throat. He approaches her and grabs her delicate neck in his big hand. She looks up at him with a salacious smile. Her red lips are glossy under the lights.

Keir turns, giving me his back. Draco doesn't notice I'm watching, and I am not sure if I'm happy or disappointed. My mind wanders to the day in the bathroom and why he was there, but that thought quickly evaporates. The first couple starts fucking. He slides his cock inside her ass after squeezing a bottle of lube over her ass and pussy. Her forehead wrinkles, followed by a moan. I can see the pure lust in her eyes when he thrusts inside her. Another man in a clown outfit shoves his cock in her mouth. She makes a choking sound as she takes him deep.

I place the palm of my hand over the glass and notice the little holes. I can hear them. The slapping of skin as the Butcher takes her hard, grunting with each thrust.

My eyes swing to Draco, but Keir never moves like he is a shield. I don't know why. I step to the side and my eyes are transfixed on Draco and the beautiful woman. Was he blocking me from seeing them?

She drops to her knees like a servant. She undoes his pants, licking her lips like he's a delicious meal she can't do without. I don't want to watch, but my feet don't cooperate because curious I want to see his cock. I've imagined him fucking me since that night in the haunted house. I remind myself that he's a man. Not some bullshit hero I made up in my mind or some guy a fake fortune teller told me about.

He takes.

He uses.

The way my mother warned me about. This man is no prince, and I'm no one in his eyes.

In my fantasy, he was a demigod. The one who would save and want me, but it is all a lie. A stupid crush I made because my life is so shitty. For a second, he had the power. The power to make me feel like I was important somehow. But now, he's going to fuck her. He's going to pleasure her while she pleasures him. They're perfect for each other. I could never be what she is to him.

Draco's gaze falls to her pretty face. I can find no flaw in her when I'm full of them.

I'm ashamed to say I was hoping to find one in her, but there isn't. I could never compete. I could never belong to someone like him.

I'm used.

I'm a woman who sold her pussy for a hundred bucks at a time, taking up the oldest profession in the world. I'm nothing like these people. They're talented. They respect each other and are free to be whoever they want. Gorgeous people who hold their own power.

I'm trapped, damaged, and talentless.

Draco frees his cock, and she licks her lips. Keir stiffens.

He turns to face me, but I'm already turning to walk away. I've seen enough. I know what happens next. They role-play. BDSM. She is his pet. His submissive. It's part of their show and makes sense. It will attract a crowd without the public participating. It's genius. A show after the main show. Who knows what other stuff they are into?

When I walk out, three couples walk inside.

Enjoy the show.

The Circle of Freaks are well...freaks.

When I leave the tent, I walk through the park, glad more people are walking around enjoying the food and rides.

My stomach growls.

I stop at a food stand that sells a tub with a kabob of meat that resembles guts. If I weren't so hungry, I would pass, but the smell has me salivating. It smells like barbecued steak. There is a glaze over the chunk of meat that looks delicious.

I pay for my food and grab the same drink from the guy wearing the jester costume. I place the five bucks on his cart this time and grab a bloody drink.

I ignore him when he calls out, "Hey! Take that back."

I find a spot at a table away from everyone. I was replaying my experience at the circus. It was the best performance I have ever seen in my life. I have to admit the last part I wish I was part of. The sex looked fun. The women were enjoying it. The look on their faces was a reward for the men who gave them pleasure.

Pleasure exists when it's with the right person. I admit I have bad luck. I've never experienced pleasure in a man's hands. Maybe I'm doomed. Cursed. I don't captivate a man or mesmerize a woman. Such bullshit.

"Are you always alone?" I look up. Keir.

I swallow and wipe my mouth with a napkin. "How did you find me?"

He sits, noting he isn't wearing leather pants but black jeans, boots, and a black T-shirt. He has a wallet chain that clanks against the bench when he stretches his long legs.

"Security notified me where you went. Why did you leave?"

I look around, noting that he isn't with his friends. "I saw enough. It's not fun when you're not participating."

His brows shoot up when he turns to face me. "Is that why you left?"

I couldn't stomach the man I fantasized about being pleasured by another woman.

I knew that it wasn't jealousy I felt. It was envy.

I take a sip of the red soda. His gaze falls to my lips. They must be stained red. The last time I drank this, I had to brush my teeth twice when I got home.

"I was interested in the circus— the main show," I point out. "I saw what I wanted."

"Did you like the show?"

I grin. "I loved it."

"I'm Keir."

"I know. You wrote it on the glass. My name is ... Ivy Sloan."

"I like it."

"Huh?"

"Your name. Ivy Sloan. It's nice. Strong."

"Thank you."

You should hear what they call me at school.

"What was your favorite part of the show?" he asks.

The ringmaster, but I don't tell him that. He wants to know what I thought of his performance. I can see in his eyes how important it is to him. What the audience thinks is important to any performer. I would be the same way if I had the talent to perform. I have to say it was his—the illusionist. I also liked the woman who had Draco's attention, but I thought his was the best.

"I liked yours."

"Are you saying that to be nice because I'm sitting here?"

"No. Honestly, I liked yours. The knives were spectacular. I liked all the performers—"

"How about Draco?"

I look at the bucket of meat kabobs in my hands. "He was good."

He was extraordinary, but I would never admit that. I need to forget about him, and fangirling him isn't the way to do it.

"Some say there is nothing like him. The only of his kind."

"Some...but not all."

I flinch when he reaches behind me and produces a black rose like magic. My eyes go wide when he hands it to me. I take the stem and look behind him, but there is nothing. How?

"Don't be afraid."

"I-I wasn't expecting that. I was right." I hold up the rose. "Yours was better."

"Thank you. I'm glad to hear it. It means a lot."

I check the time and decided to get a cab or Uber home. It's almost ten, and it's getting colder. I can't afford to come back to the fair. I'm pushing it as it is with the food I bought, but I have enough to get home.

I get up and toss the bucket with one hand in the trash and then do the same with the cup of red soda. "I should get going."

He looks around like he's waiting for someone to materialize. "You're leaving?"

"It's getting late. If you could thank Draco for me...for the ticket. It was my first time at a circus, and I'll never forget it. When I was a little girl, I would fantasize being part of one,"I admit and pick up my duffel bag. "Bye, Keir. It was nice meeting you."

"It was a pleasure, Ivy," he says, tilting his head, but I don't miss the tinge of a British accent he tries to hide.

When I walk away, I feel his gaze on my back.

I pass through the fog that floats like a chrome cloud of smoke toward the exit with my phone in hand, tracking the Uber driver. Four minutes.

When I look up and the fog clears, I stop.

Draco is bowing before me, wearing his coat and top hat with another ticket. The Butcher and the woman who was sucking him off flank his sides but at a distance.

I take two steps. "Thank you for the opportunity, but I can't take it."

He straightens, eyes dark, face painted like a skull looming over me. It feels like time has stood still.

"Did you not like the show?" He asks in a deep voice.

"I loved the show. You all were spectacular, and I'll never forget it." His gaze falls to the rose in my hand. "You were all so great. "And I meant it. I look between him, the Butcher, and pause on the woman I envy. "You both look great together," I tell her. Her eyes dart to Draco wide like saucers, but his gaze holds something I'm familiar with. Fear. I can't explain why. What could he be afraid of? "Thank you for the other day," I tell him.

I wait for him to say something, but he doesn't. No, *you're welcome.* Nothing. I check my phone. My ride is waiting for me at the exit. I glance at him again, knowing I will never meet anyone like him. "It was nice meeting you, Draco."

CHAPTER 15

DRACO

"I'm sorry," Nyx rushes out. "I didn't know she was there, Draco."

Ignoring her apology, I stare at the empty stage, hating myself for walking in with Nyx. I admit I wanted to forget her. Like I've done since I felt her tremble underneath my fingers. That night on the roller coaster and again in the haunted house.

After the show, I thought she had left to go to the rides and needed to get a grip on the power she had over me. I didn't plan on letting it get that far with Nyx. Not now.

Keir walks in, and I swing at his face with my fist. He didn't see it coming, given the look of surprise on his face. I feel his skin split between my knuckles. I hit him again and feel his lips mash his teeth. Blood drips out of his mouth and down his chin.

"What the fuck do you think you were doing with her?"

He shakes his head, trying to shake off the two blows I landed. He staggers, but I don't give a shit. I lunge at him again, and he takes the blows. I pummel him, and he takes it.

He steps back, and I keep punching. I don't fight him like I would someone else. I can't. He doesn't know. I caught how she smiled at him seated on the bench. A smile she had never given me, and he took it.

He spits on the ground. "I was trying to get her to stay. It wasn't my fault."

"The rose wasn't your fault?"

He raises his hand in surrender. His cheek already swelling and turning purple. It's a good thing we wear makeup for a living.

"Look, look. I was shielding her from seeing you with Nyx, but she already saw and drew her conclusion. You know why I gave her the rose. It's not like that."

"What did she say?" I ask.

"That she wishes she was part of it. We were all great, and she loved the circus. It was her first time seeing a show, and she has imagined being part of one since she was a little girl."

I see it in his eyes. There is more. "Go on," I urge.

His eyes dart to Nyx and then back. "She looked... disappointed. As much as she thought my performance was the best and loved the show, I know she won't be back."

"Your...performance," I say with disdain.

"Yeah, it was mine she liked the best," he says with pride and a busted lip.

I snort. "She was just being nice." But I know she meant it.

It was my performance I wanted her to like the best, but I fucked that up with her seeing me with Nyx.

Nyx walks up to Keir with a first-aid kit.

"Don't ever pull that stunt with me again," I warn her.

"I'm sorry, Draco. I wasn't thinking," she says with hurt in her eyes.

I have myself to blame. Nyx has been in love with me since I saved her all those years ago, but there is only one I want. The one I've been waiting for since I was six years old.

Her name is Ivy.

I tried to tell myself it wasn't her. It couldn't be, but I knew when I saw her with her dark-haired friend. It was real—all of it. I had my doubts but I felt it. I recognized it. I felt her everywhere.

When I held her on the ride, I knew. I knew it even if I denied it a hundred times. Even when I tried to fuck it out of me using Nyx and the others. But nothing worked.

"Go after her," Nyx says while tending to Keir.

"What am I supposed to do? Show up dressed like a ringmaster and sweep her off her feet?"

Her eyes lift. "Maybe...work for it... show her you want her." She pats Keir's cut, and I watch him wince. Shame washed over me for hitting him, but I had to stop him. "Get her to come." She throws back her head and laughs at her own joke.

I roll my eyes but feel my cock thicken, imagining Ivy coming on my tongue.

"I like her name. Ivy Sloan," Keir says.

"Ivy Sloan," Nyx says, testing her name on her tongue. "I love it! It's hot...she's hot," she continues in a syrupy voice, "I want to taste Ivy Sloan."

"Don't get ahead of yourself, Nyx," I warn.

"What..." She pouts dramatically. "You should see her swallow, Draco. She closes her eyes in pleasure, and all I can picture is Ivy Sloan swallowing my cum after she sucks my cock.

Lex walks in and looks at Keir. "Let me guess, he went near her." She walks up to the Butcher seated on a chair, straddles his lap, and looks directly at me. "She's jealous of Nyx. I saw it on her face when we were in the dungeon. It's why she stormed off."

The dungeon is our sex room. A room we have strictly for our VIPs who pay to watch, and we perform. It brings in twenty million a year in the States alone. It's growing. But we cap off how many tickets we sell, or this wouldn't be a circus.

"She's not jealous. She was disappointed," Keir points out.

"Of what?" the Butcher asks.

"Of not being part of it," Keir replies.

"Which part?" Lex asks with a smirk.

"All of it."

AFTER NONSTOP SHOWS, DEVIL'S NIGHT LOOMS, keeping my mind off my blond temptress. I walk into my RV, sit on the couch, and place my top hat on the seat.

My phone goes off, and it's a text.

> L: What hunts a rabbit no one thinks about when they go hunting?

> Draco: That's easy, humans. I taught you that one.

> L: What hunts a human and buys food at the grocery store?

> Draco: Another human trying to save the rabbit.

> L: Why would a human hunt a rabbit?"

My hand tightens around my phone, digging in my palm.

> Draco: To eat wild game or keep them as pets.

> L: Some pets don't like to be caged, but they stay caged because they don't have a choice.

I lock my phone and get up to take a cold shower.

Humans do not have natural-born predators unless they step out of their environment or...take something someone else wants.

CHAPTER
16

I'm at the register, and it's twenty minutes after my shift is over. As I suspected, Kevin keeps me past sunset. The look in his eye when Trisha gave me a ride last week after I snubbed his offer was all I needed to know.

He would do anything to force me to accept his offer for a ride to get me alone. He thinks I will fold because of the news. They haven't found who's behind abducting and killing those girls. It has caused an uproar in the media. The poor victim's parents want answers. They want justice for their girls.

Trisha gives me an apologetic look, stocking the candy shelves in my lane.

She can't take me home today after my shift because her mother refuses to watch her kids later than necessary. Her mother was upset about the last time she agreed to give me a ride to the fair.

"I can take you home if you need a ride, Ivy," Kevin says, passing by the bagging area on his way to his office.

"That's okay. I got it sorted," I reply, wiping down the scanner.

His face falls, and I grin with satisfaction when he turns around. His plan didn't work. I would rather walk in the dark than sit in a car with him. Who knows what else he has up his sleeve, and I don't want to find out. I've dealt with enough creeps hanging around my mother back in South Carolina. Kevin has the same predatory look in his eye as they did.

I need to figure something out. I know I can't walk home on the main highway. It isn't safe, and it would be stupid. My mother gets off at midnight, so calling her isn't an option. I can't leave early because I need the money. I'm pondering the issue when my answer walks in my lane.

Dean.

"Hey, Ivy." He glances at Kevin as he walks back. "How are you doing, Kevin? How's the wife?"

"She's good." He looks at Dean, sizing him up. "Aren't you dating—"

"No. I'm not."

"Oh...I heard different."

Dean sighs, placing a TV dinner on the belt. "Nope. I'm single and ready for what life throws at me. I thought you would be having kids by now, Kevin."

"I don't like kids and not with this job. I work a lot of hours. You run a business. You can understand that."

"I hear ya." Dean pushes the cart down the lane but raises a brow at Trisha because he can't get through with the shopping cart.

Trisha places the gums and the chocolate bars as fast as she can to free her hands. She tries to squeeze in the space between the candy shelf and the next register to let Dean through.

"Get out of the way, Trisha. He's obviously waiting for you to move. He can't fit with you there," Kevin reprimands, insinuating that she's fat.

Embarrassment crosses her features. She grabs the cardboard candy box and looks away. Kevin is such an asshole to her. I hate that he treats her like that.

"It's alright, Kevin. Dean can get through."

It's a tight fit, but he could. Dean is being an asshole like Kevin. Sometimes I wonder who's the biggest one.

Kevin glares at me. "Oh, aren't you the BFF trying to defend her. She's in the way." He opens his arms wide around his waist. "There is no way he could squeeze through with her there."

"She's stocking the candy aisle. Her hands were full, and she was about done. He could get through. There's enough space. You don't have to be so crude about it," I say in a hard tone.

He's pissed off because I won't let him give me a ride home, and his plan didn't work by getting me to stay late.

"Excuse me, miss?" An older woman walks up behind Dean, trying to get Trisha's attention. Her face is wrinkled from age with a worried expression.

"Yes," Trisha asks.

"A big spill in aisle four needs to be cleaned up. I would have slipped if the bottles hadn't been strewn across the floor and gotten stuck on the wheel of my cart."

"How did that happen?" Kevin asks her accusingly.

"I wouldn't know. There was a crash, but it wasn't loud. I was shopping for some wine, and then I saw it. The floor was painted crimson from all the broken bottles of red wine pouring out across the floor. It looks like a bloodbath over there. Like I said, it needs to be cleaned up."

"I'll go check it out," Trish says, walking toward aisle four.

Kevin sighs. "I need to find the idiot who did it. Whoever did it, is going to pay for it." And storms off.

"Dick," I mutter.

I grab the TV dinners and pause. A crisp one-hundred-dollar bill sits near the scanner. A dead president staring at me. Shame and anger bubble inside me. I look up. Dean is watching me.

"I know you need it, Ivy. The same way I know you need a ride home. The last shuttle left half an hour ago, and walking home is too dangerous. I'll give you a ride?"

I grip the cold paper carton over the plastic of his TV dinner causing it to crease. After heating it in the microwave, I know macaroni and cheese tastes like dried-up cardboard. Not even salt can fix the taste.

The same way the hundred-dollar bill staring at me won't fix the sick feeling of Dean fucking me over his kitchen island with his small dick.

My mother was right about me, and I refused to believe her. I was a little girl fantasizing about the circus because I wanted to be part of something great. I want to go somewhere different. But I'm not part of anything, and the show must go on. This is my show, and this is part of my act.

I convince myself I need the money to help pay the rent, or my mother will kick me out. I convince myself I need a ride home from Dean so I don't walk alone in the dark.

I hate Dean, but I hate myself more because I don't have a choice.

"Alright."

"Atta girl," he says and places a box of MyOne condoms near the scanner. Size small.

SITTING IN DEAN'S TRUCK, I CLUTCH MY BAG IN MY LAP like a lifesaver that will keep me from drowning. I convinced myself that I had no choice but to accept what was coming for me. My shame for his pleasure. Every dose costs me one hundred dollars.

The road is dark when he pulls out of the parking lot of the Big H. His house is not far. It's only a couple of blocks, but I wish it wasn't.

He reaches out and touches the screen to play music. The Doors "I Love Her Madly" plays. My head whips in his direction.

"Have you ever heard of The Doors?" he asks. He turns up the volume slightly, making me cringe. "It's not your time or mine, but my father listened to them."

He picks Jim Morrison's voice out of all the artists to play. How ironic. He's a sick fuck.

Especially when the song changes to "Touch Me."

"I know of them," I respond dryly, hating him even more.

I won't tell him I've listened to them on the radio. My mother likes The Doors. She started working at diners that played oldie tunes on the jukebox. Since then, they stuck.

She would find the radio station in her old sedan when she would take me to school that played them. Most people nowadays don't listen to the radio and instead stream from a music app, but I didn't have the option on my mother's radio. It was the only way you could listen to music. I welcomed it when she drove me to school or the store. It was better than static or her talking.

"It's one of my favorites." He glances at me briefly. "You know I still want you, Ivy."

I grip the strap to my bag in a tight fist. My stomach in knots. "I can't stop thinking about you when I'm with someone else." He lets out a laugh, and I want to throw up. "I've wanted your tight cunt since I first laid eyes on you when you were seventeen. I tried to tell myself I was crazy, but I couldn't resist. I couldn't resist wanting to fuck your tight pink cunt, but I had to wait until you were eighteen." I look out the window, trying to blink back the sting from my eyes when I'm thrown forward. Tires squeal, and rocks hit metal. I place my hand on the dash to keep from hitting my head on the windshield and push back on the seat.

"What the fuck!" Dean yells as he blares the horn.

CHAPTER 17

A satin-black Plymouth Barracuda blocks Dean's truck. The windows are tinted so dark you could see the moon's reflection.

Dean blares his horn again, causing me to jolt. "Piece of shit. You fucking psycho!" Dean yells like the person inside the car can hear him.

My hands shake from the adrenaline running through my veins. Dean looks out the truck's rear window, but we're blocked in by the trees at an angle that he can't back up.

The Plymouth engine roars so loud it blocks out the music inside the truck. Dean turns the wheel and moves the car forward but applies the brake. There is no room to drive away without hitting the car.

I focus on the driver's side door, waiting to see who steps out. A second turns into what seems like minutes. I hold my breath, contemplating opening my door to run, but where would I go. How far would I get? I let out a shaky breath and lick my dry lips.

"Motherfucker," Dean spits. The vein in his neck bulges. "Who does this motherfucker think he is?" He opens his door.

"I don't think that's a good idea, Dean."

She glares at me. "Shut up. You stupid bitch."

I lean against my door, clutching my bag, and point behind him. My insides churn with dread, a cold knot forming at the pit of my stomach.

A man dressed all in black with a white mask is there.

He turns around, and the man grips his hair. "Ahhhh!" Dean cries.

"You should have listened to her, Dean," the man says in a raspy voice, dragging him out of the car. Dean tries to swing at him but fails to connect, instead flaring his arms around.

I place my hands over my mouth because I know it's him. I know it's Draco.

"Let me go, you son of a bitch!" Dean yells, trying to get out of Draco's hold.

Draco laughs at his failed attempts.

He bends and looks at me. "Get out."

I open the door, scramble out, not caring the weeds scratch my ankles, and stop in front of the car. I squint from the glare of the headlights, looking down the dark road. He'll catch me if I run. He'll hurt me if I call for help. But who do I need help *from*?

I look back. Draco slams Dean on the hood of his truck, pulling him by the hair so Dean can look at me with his eyes bulging. "Don't you think she's too young for you?"

"Fuck you," Dean snarls.

"You didn't answer my question."

He slams his forehead on the hood. "Fuck!" Dean grunts.

"Let's try again. You like to fuck young girls. You like to take advantage of them."

"What the fuck are you talking about?"

"Look at her," Draco demands. "Are you paying to fuck her?"

"Fuck off!"

Draco slams his head again, denting the hood. When he pulls his head back, big fat drops of blood splatter on the hood. "What the hell, man! You busted my face. Who are you? What the fuck do you want?"

"I'm getting to that, but you won't answer my questions. Let's start over. Are you paying to fuck her?"

"Yes," Dean admits in a strangled voice.

"Hmm...how long?"

"Two years. How old is she?"

"Eighteen."

I'm nineteen, but it wouldn't matter to someone like him. I could be fifteen to someone like Dean, and he still would have done it.

"So you like to fuck underaged girls...prey on the weak and underprivileged. Groom them for your pathetic cock because it's too small."

"Why the fuck do you care? So what, I fucked her. What the fuck is it to you?"

Draco answers with a bone-chilling laugh. "One last question, and I'll let you go." Fear twists in my gut like a coiled serpent, sending waves of nausea through me. "What runs and runs but can never flee? It is often watched yet never seen. When short, it brings fear. What is it?" Dean struggles, but Draco's hold is too strong, and he can't move. It doesn't help Dean that Draco towers over him or that his face is full of blood from the gash on his forehead. "I'm waiting," Draco singsongs. "Come on, you can do it. It's not that hard." Draco leans close to Dean's bloody face, staining his white mask. "Your freedom depends on it."

"I–I—"

Draco makes a buzzard sound, lifting his head, and then says, "Look at her, Dean," in a flat voice.

"A hamster," Dean says with terror in his eyes.

"Time of death," Draco corrects.

Draco slams the door after sliding into the passenger side of his black Plymouth. I try to look out the side mirror but can't determine if he is going to Dean's truck. But I have my answer when the driver's side door opens, and he gets in.

The interior of his car is black with shiny black dials. It's immaculate and smells of rich leather and his scent— citrus, woodsy, and dark like the man. The car vibrates from the massive engine, drowning out the music coming from Dean's car. The air was cool outside, but I was so scared, I didn't notice.

He removes the white mask, and from the corner of my eye, I see his straight nose, full lips, and black hair the same color as his car. His skin is smooth despite wearing makeup all the time.

"Are you going to hurt me?" I ask.

It's a stupid question, but I had to ask. I saw what he did to Dean, but I also saw what he did to Paul and Jason at school.

He doesn't answer and presses the touch screen, which is obviously aftermarket. He grabs his phone from the holder he has installed near the black and white gauges.

A loud thump can be heard coming from the trunk.

I glance at him. His midnight eyes meet mine, hellishly bright and aware, and I'm lost under his spell.

He selects a song and places his phone back on the holder. Depeche Mode's "Enjoy the Silence" plays. The engine roars, adding to the background of the music, as he drives down the road.

I see the bright lights of the fair. The Ferris wheel to the right of the carnival with rainbow lights fading in and out, and the one to the right with its dark red lights and swinging gondolas.

He pulls around back down a dark road. The man manning the gate recognizes his car. He tilts his head and nods when he spots Draco behind the wheel and waves him through.

The road is paved. There are no potholes or rocks. Three red-and-white circus tents are to my right, large and imposing. The car moves at a slow pace and stops behind the tent farthest to the back.

The song changes to "Mouth" by Bush. He turns it up to drown out the noise from the back.

He places the car in park in front of a luxury RV. He glances at me for a beat, then leaves the car on, gets out, and closes the door.

I'm considering getting out, but where would I go? Is he kidnapping me? It wouldn't be kidnapping if I stayed. Right?

A sinking feeling stabs at my core. Is he the killer? I look out the back window when the car rocks, but I can't see anything but the trunk open.

He would have killed me. There is no way he would bring me back to the fairgrounds. There are people. I could scream and call for help.

The trunk slams, and I jolt.

The passenger door opens, and the interior light flicks on. He grabs me gently by the arm and pulls me out.

I move to the side and lean with my back against the car. The curtain from the tent falls closed, and I know that's where they took Dean.

Draco leans inside the car, grabs his keys, shuts off the music, and closes the door. He steps close, and I tilt my head back, lifting my chin. He's fucking tall. Six foot six at least to my five-four. He's wearing a black hoodie that does nothing to hide his broad frame. A tattoo that reads DRACO in big letters is written across his thick neck with flames underneath.

His eyes land on my name tag on the vest of my uniform. He lifts the tag with black-painted nail polish on his fingernails.

"It says Ivy," I say, like he doesn't know how to read.

His eyes lift, like dark liquid pools. He drops his hand, walks to the RV, and pulls the door open.

I walk cautiously up the steps. The inside is pure luxury. LED lights line the floors and ceiling. Black leather covers the seats. There are three television sets with speakers in the living room. The kitchen has a black stainless steel convection microwave oven, a two-burner induction stove, a residential-size refrigerator, and a dishwasher. It even has an electric fireplace with white marble floors. It smells like the perfume section in the department store inside the mall. Expensive.

"Is this where you live?" I ask. He shuts the door and walks to the back. "Are you going to keep ignoring me?"

He opens a door that leads to a bathroom with a spa. It's bigger than the bathroom in my apartment. He removes his black hoodie. He isn't wearing a shirt underneath. His hard body ripples with muscle and tattoos.

My eyes trail down the waves of ab muscles disappearing to the deep V in the waistband of his pants.

"Do you want to take a shower?" he asks.

He speaks.

"I don't...think... that's a good idea. Are you going to kill him?"

I had to ask. I would tell him to take me home. I don't want to shower...I do, but not like this. With him, maybe, but...

"Do you want me to?" He walks toward me slowly, and I can't tear my eyes from his gorgeous body. I can't think around him. His face reminds me of River Phoenix with black hair and dark eyes with the body of a tattooed model.

Get a grip, Ivy. Answer.

"I hate him, but I don't think he deserves to die."

"What do you think he deserves?"

I shake my head slowly. "I don't know."

His eyes caress my face, and I want to melt.

"Did he force you? Did he...touch you when you said no."

I shake my head and look away. "No. He figured out a way so I wouldn't *say* no."

"Are you a whore? Do you sell your pussy for money?"

The letters carved in the wooden desks and written on the walls at school float in my mind. IVY SLOAN IS A SLUT. The one-hundred-dollar bill Dean would give me after he was done.

Draco must think I'm pathetic and asked for it, and is one of the reasons I'm asking him not to kill Dean. Why Jason and Paul thought they could rape me at school. The reason I'm ogling him without his shirt hoping to get something more out of him.

He assumes the same thing all men do when they look at me. I can't tell him no because I have had sex for money. Not because I wanted to but because it was the only way I could survive. A reason he wouldn't understand. Ugly shame spreads like a rash over my skin, reminding me of what I am.

The door swings open, saving me from answering, and it's the girl I saw him with inside the sex room.

She's gorgeous without her clown makeup.

"Oh..." She looks nervously at Draco. "I—"

"It's not what you think," I rush out. Guilt rises to the surface. He doesn't have a shirt on. I'm alone with him, and it looks bad. "I was just leaving."

She steps farther inside but doesn't say anything.

I walk out the small door, purposely avoiding Draco glad I have a good reason to leave.

I can hear them talking inside but can't make out what they are saying, and I don't want to be the cause of them fighting.

I almost reach the back gate when a familiar voice stops me. "Why every time I find you, you're leaving?"

Keir.

"Because you have bad timing," I tease.

"Do I?"

I turn to face him with a smirk. He's wearing black-and-white-striped pants and a matching shirt. It's unbuttoned and looks more like a jacket over his hard body.

I smile because his makeup is amusing. His mouth is painted, giving the illusion of being unnaturally wide with white and black face paint and red shading.

"Did you just perform?"

"No. I was practicing and tending to other stuff."

He means Dean.

"I was heading home," I say.

He looks out the gate. "On foot?"

"It's all I got."

I can't tell him I have a hundred bucks I can't spend on an Uber.

A generator turns on behind him. The smell of barbecue rolls in from the food trucks at the fair.

"Are you hungry? Because I am...it will be my treat."

"Don't you have a girlfriend somewhere?"

He laughs. "I don't, and neither does anyone else here. Maybe Butcher, but I don't know his deal yet."

"Oh...I thought—"

"Nyx isn't Draco's girlfriend."

"Oh...I didn't—"

"You don't have to say it, Ivy. I can see it, and so can everyone else."

"I don't know what you're talking about," I say defensively.

Her name is Nyx. It's cool, and...it fits.

She isn't his girlfriend, but they fuck. That part is obvious, and he thinks I'm a whore. Perfect. He wouldn't have asked if he didn't assume.

"I really should get going."

His expression turns to disappointment, making him look funny because of the makeup.

"What's so funny?"

I didn't realize I was grinning. I thought I was doing it in my head.

"I—"

"Do you always run away when someone asks you a question?"

I turn around, and Draco is wearing a black hoodie, with Nyx at his side.

She rolls her eyes and steps forward. "Hi, I'm Nyx," she introduces herself with a naughty smile.

"Ivy."

Her smile widens, and her eyes land on my name tag. "The Big H, huh."

"Yeah, they were the only ones hiring."

Her eyes slide to Draco and then to Keir. "Keir, I need you to help me with something on stage."

I could tell she doesn't and is trying to get me alone with Draco. "Alright." Keir gives me a wink walking backwards pointing at me. "Don't leave. One of us can take you home." He walks away with his arm around Nyx's waist, disappearing inside the tent.

"Come with me," Draco demands.

"Why?"

"Because I know you're hungry, and we both know I'm not going to let anyone who isn't me take you home."

"On one condition…" His eyes narrow. "If you let Dean go. It wouldn't be good if he disappeared after people saw me leaving with him."

"Alright, but not until I'm done with him. If he goes near you again… his time is up."

I follow him to his car trying to keep up with his long strides. "What do you mean his time is up."

He opens the door and takes out a gray hoodie. "Here," he says, "it's cold."

It is cold. Every day, it gets colder as the fall season settles in. At night, it drops ten or fifteen degrees.

"Where are you taking me?"

"To eat…" I pull the sweater over my breasts, his eyes fixed on the little hole the middle button makes when my shirt pulls. His eyes lift. "I'm hungry."

CHAPTER

18

DRACO

How do you get a woman to like you when you have never had that problem all your life? I should have never asked her if she sold her pussy for money. It was fucked up. She ran out the door.

Nyx showing up didn't help the cause. I wanted to kick her out of my RV but held back. I didn't miss the look of hurt in her eyes when she saw how I looked at Ivy, but I told her the truth.

Accept it or leave.

She stayed.

I admit I was showing off by taking my sweater off when I asked if she wanted a shower. I wanted to see her in my clothes and wearing the scent of my soap on her skin.

I panicked when she was almost to the back gate with Keir afraid of her leaving or him saying something to her that would have her running. I want to know what he said to her but first, I need to feed my little rabbit. She looks tired, hungry and scared.

"Pick a side," I tell her, extending my arms when we reach the crossroads. "The left is dark, and the right is light."

She looks indecisive. Her eyes darted left and right, but surprises me when she says, "Dark."

"Good choice."

I go left, past the entrance, and walk through the gate, bypassing security. She follows me by the employee's side, avoiding the fog. You can hear people screaming from the actors startling them.

"It's different when you're the one scaring them, right?" she asks.

I can see her point. It is different.

"Yes, it's fun if you're into it."

"Are you...into it?"

I pause and stare for a second too long. "I'm always into it. I like to perform."

I like the way my gray sweater swallows her petite body. I wonder how she tastes. If her pussy is as pink as that bastard said it was. I grind my teeth, wanting to rip his arms off for touching her. I take a deep breath and remind myself, in time.

"So what would you like to eat? I tried the bucket of meat kabobs that looked like guts and the smoking blood from the guy wearing the jester costume. That was good."

I smile. The way she talks about the food I selected for the park is amusing. "Have you tried the gelato brains? They are my personal favorite."

She giggles, and the sound sings to the head of my cock. I want to fuck her. I want to fuck her hard. She has nice tits and a nice ass, and I bet the motherfucker is right about her cunt being tight. I want to sink my teeth into it and make her scream. I want to make her bleed from the marks I make on her skin. I bet her blood tastes sweet.

"I haven't." She's so small, I hope I don't break her. "Hey, a-are you okay?"

I tilt my head to catch her gaze. "Huh?"

"You were staring at...nothing," she says worriedly.

I want to break you.

"How loud do you scream?" I ask.

"W-why would you ask me that?"

"Curious. You can tell a lot about the way a person screams."

"How loud do you scream?" she volleys back.

We stop at the food truck. The smell of barbecue floats around us, mixing with the cool air like clouds of smoke. The generators are loud on this side.

"When I kill." I smile when I see the look of terror in her eyes. My cock thickens inside my boxers. "But I'm silent when I fuck."

"How can I help..." Thomas pops his head out, catching the wig on the window's edge. He smooths it down and adjusts it. "How can I help you?" he tries again.

He spots me behind Ivy, and his eyes widen despite the stupid clown costume he's wearing. His makeup is all wrong, cracking near the collar of his clown costume. I don't like it.

Ivy scans the menu from the chalkboard hanging on the side of the truck. "I'll have the human ribs with fingers."

His red nose falls off and floats on the pavement.

"Shit," he mutters, cupping his nose with his palm like it will magically reappear.

"Bad day?" I ask Thomas.

Ivy chases the red nose. She catches it and hands it to him. "Here, you lost this," she says with a laugh.

He takes it and pushes it back on his pointy nose. It's most likely why it won't stay on.

"What do you say?" I tell Thomas like I'm teaching a small child manners.

"Right." Thomas says, "Thank you—"

"Ivy, and you are?"

"Bozo," I answer for him.

She laughs, but I don't. I'm staring at *can't get right Thomas*. He's always fucking up. Comes high to work all the time and screws up everyone's order, and his makeup looks like shit.

"It's Thomas," he corrects.

"It's Bozo," I counter.

He sighs heavily and glances at Ivy. "It's Bozo."

She glances at me and then at Bozo. "Nice to meet you, Bozo. Looks like you need to freshen up."

Good. She sees it, too. He's a mess.

"Make that two of whatever she orders."

"Yes, sir."

We sit, and I watch her eat. How her tongue licks her lips and the sauce off her fingers makes me imagine something else.

"Aren't you going to eat?"

I grab her wrist and bring her fingers to my mouth. She sucks in a breath when the tip of my tongue glides between her index and middle finger, and then I suck.

I close my eyes, savoring the taste of her skin and the barbecue sauce. "Mm..."

She tastes sweet and spicy. I want to lick it all.

She whimpers when I suck the last of the sauce off her thumb. When my eyes open, she's watching me, her eyes the color of dark honey. Hot and full of secrets.

We all have secrets. We all have fears. Wants. Needs. Desires.

I want all of hers, but mine she will fear.

"WHAT MADE YOU WANT TO BE IN A CIRCUS?"

What made you want to fuck losers? But I don't ask her that. I'm sure she has a reason. We all have reasons that make us do things. I turn the heater on in the car to take her home. It's almost midnight.

"I was born to be in a circus. I knew since I learned to walk and what a clown was."

"Most kids are afraid of clowns."

"I wanted to be the clown."

"I can see that," she says.

"Can you?"

"I saw you perform. It was...powerful."

"Did you like it?"

"I loved the main show."

Not disappointed.

"You didn't like the other show?" I press.

She glances at me, clutching her bag to her chest. "I didn't stay to watch."

"I didn't stay to perform," I admit.

"Why not?"

I shouldn't have told her, and I don't know why I did. I didn't fuck Nyx, and she didn't suck my dick. I couldn't.

"I wasn't supposed to be there."

"Oh…" She trails off when I pull into her apartment complex. A run-down shithole full of assholes one paycheck away from getting evicted. I don't want to leave her here, but I don't have a choice.

Soon.

"How come you work at the Big H?" I ask.

"It's just my mom and me, and we need the money."

Typical single mom and daughter story. Where the daughter needs to help the mom because the mom can't figure shit out on her own. Probably makes her feel guilty too.

"How come you were in the bathroom at school?"

"Someone I know goes there."

"Who—"

"It's getting late."

"Thanks for dinner and for not…" She pauses. "You know what I mean. Promise me?"

I glance at her. "I'll do my best."

She shuts the door, and I wait, watching her hips sway up the stairs.

I drive to the back, where I have a clear view of her entering her apartment. Number 206. But I knew that.

Back in the tent, the red light shines on Dean's pathetic form, seated in the chair. He's blindfolded, gagged, and tied by his hands and feet. Nyx stands behind him with a jagged knife in her hands.

I give her the signal to remove the gag. "If you scream or yell, I'll slice your fucking throat," I warn.

I will anyway, but he doesn't know that.

"What do you want?" He asks in a hoarse voice.

Funny he doesn't ask about Ivy. I could have killed her, and he wouldn't have cared.

"I want you to stay away from Ivy. I don't want you around her. I suggest you start ordering your groceries online. Move your business to another state. Give you a head start."

"Are you fucking serious? For a girl? She's no one."

I tilt my head slowly to Nyx. She slaps him with the flat part of the knife across his face.

"Ow!" he howls.

Pathetic.

I step forward cautiously, not wanting to smell him. It's what she's had to smell, and it's an unsettling sensation that turns my stomach.

"I'm going to cut you up and feed you to tigers."

"You're a circus clown." He laughs. "You're part of the Ringling Brothers."

I signal to Nyx. She hits him harder, slicing his face this time.

He howls again.

"Are you done insulting my family? They don't like to be compared."

He is about to respond but hesitates from the pain. Blood drips down his chin.

"You cut me."

"That's how it starts."

"What starts?"

He's nervous. His hands are shaking.

"The time of your death."

"You were serious about that?"

"I never joke when I kill. It's bad manners."

He struggles to pull his hands and feet free. It's amusing.

When he's done, he is out of breath and sweating profusely.

"Like I said, you should find another way to shop and conduct your business of cleaning shit. Have you ever heard of *'you don't shit where you eat'*? I'm the first one to tell you it's bad practice. It *will* kill you."

"You're crazy."

"I prefer to identify myself as insane, but you're not qualified to make that determination. You'll find out when do kill you."

The things I want to do to this man with a hammer and a bone cutter.

"You're going to kill me."

"I am." Why lie? "But not tonight. I like to hunt my kill. I want you to run. I want your fear. I want to see how pathetic you'll look when you avoid the grocery store."

"Why? Why do you want to kill me?"

"You know why. I'm going to drop you off at your pathetic excuse of a white truck. You'll go home and forget any of this happened. If you go near the grocery store or Ivy, I'll cut your eyes out and drain your bodily fluids. Do you understand me?"

He nods frantically.

Keir walks in. "Take him back," I tell him after sending him a text with the location of his truck.

I glance at Nyx and nod for her to begin.

I close my eyes and hear his screams after I shut the door.

I find Lex near the back door behind one of the haunted houses. "Where are you going?" she asks.

"Where I've been going for the past month."

Lex is a gorgeous redhead with long legs and an incredible mouth. She's fun to watch, but there is a blonde I'm dying to see.

"Teach her."

I look back before walking out. "I will, but I need to break her first."

"She's already broken, Draco."

"How so?"

Lex has an eye for these things. She sees things others don't. It's been that way for a long time.

"Nyx was taken by force, and we saved her. Ivy had no choice and accepted what she's had to do." She pushes off the door. "She's already broken, Draco. If you push, you will lose her."

"You're wrong, Lex. She will be what she is destined to become."

CHAPTER 19

I'm sitting on the roof of my apartment building wearing a sweater, black leggings, and a gray blanket I found for five dollars at Dollar General on clearance. I take a seat on the lawn chair I found behind the dumpster and look at the white rectangular screen, waiting for Stephen King's *It* to start.

Not many cars are out tonight. Just a couple of kids from school with fogged-up windows fucking. I spot a couple of cheerleaders with some of the football players from school. I recognize their cars; about four or five are parked in the back row, leaving one row with enough space so the other eight cars up front don't see what they are doing from their rearview mirror.

I was relieved I saw Dean's truck with dirt smudged all over the side this morning when I got into work. Draco didn't kill him, or maybe he was bluffing, but I doubt it. He didn't walk in the grocery store because he probably freaked out. He wouldn't give a shit if I was dead or alive.

No more convincing me to give me a ride.

Those guys at the Circus of Freaks are into other shit I don't want to find out. Dark and dangerous.

The credits roll in as the movie starts.

"Is this your favorite?"

A shiver dances down my spine, and it's not from the cold wind. Draco stands like a looming shadow next to me. The yellow glow from the streetlight by the dumpster makes his shadow stretch to the edge of the building.

"Do you always sneak up on women?" I ask, my heart pounding in my chest.

"No...just you." His voice echoes in my head.

I wake up panting. I look around, and then I hear it. My is alarm going off. I silence my phone and check the time. 9:00 a.m. I fall back on my pillow looking at the ceiling.

It was a dream, Ivy.

I didn't see *It* last night. They don't play horror movies on Wednesdays. Only Thursdays. And Draco didn't show up, and my blanket is in the basket needing to be washed.

"Ivy?" My mother opens my bedroom door. "Are you taking me to work today? If you are, we gotta go now, but remember, you can't pick me up late."

Since I'm working full time this week, my mother has been nice and offered me the car. She's hoping I ditch school and keep working. It's her way to convince me to drop out. She doesn't know I'm planning on going back on Monday.

I sit up. "Yeah, I'll be ready in a minute."

After dropping my mother off at the Moonlight Diner, I head toward the Big H for my shift in her beat-up clunker.

There's another alert on my phone. Another girl missing, Jenny Carson. Seventeen years old. Last seen outside the mall three towns over. More girls have gone missing and found dead.

No leads.

Whoever is doing it knows how to cover their tracks.

When I pull into the parking lot of the plaza of the Big H, I notice a huge sign in front of DTF that says, Moving Sale.

There's some good news.

"Hey, Ivy," Trisha greets me with a beaming smile on her rosy cheeks. "Got yourself some wheels?"

"No. I wish...it's my mom's," I clarify. "She let me borrow it to get to work until I have to get back to school on Monday."

"Oh...well...at least you have a ride now."

After my shift at the Big H, I was relieved when Dean didn't show up. I head out in my mom's old clunker toward the diner. I turn the radio on. The oldie station it's set to plays The Angels "My Boyfriend's Back."I sing along, surprisingly knowing the words like I've been playing it my whole life.

I turn it up and sway to the music.

The sun has set by the time I walk inside the diner with my mom's car keys in hand.

"Hey, Maggy!" Joan shouts from the back. "Your daughter is here." She gives me a wan smile. "Hey, baby. Sorry, but it's gonna be a while."

I look around, and it's a full house on a Thursday night. I'm surprised. My mom told me business has been slow.

"That's alright, Joan. I'll wait."

"How's school? Heard you got suspended." She gives me a wink. "Giving those boys trouble."

"No," I reply in a flat tone.

Joan is an older version of my mom. It's why they get along. Both come from a small town with a shitty upbringing working at diners and gas stations all their life.

I sit on the stool by the counter and watch my mom flirt with a man seated in booth eight. He's heavy set with a trucker hat and scruff on his face. The rig parked out front must be his. He nods at whatever my mother is telling him while staring at the other server's ass. I think her name is Cynthia. She doesn't have an ass by any means, but compared to my mom and Joan, she's the best-looking server here.

"What's your name, darlin'?" I shift in the seat and turn to look at a man with brown hair and a beard.

"Who wants to know?"

I know his type. He likes girls who are barely legal. I took my name tag off my uniform before entering to avoid anyone knowing my name. Moonlight Diner attracts truckers, tourists, and travelers who come through. Mostly sleazy assholes like the one I'm looking at right now.

"My name's John."

He's lying. I catch the white tan line of his ring finger. No one is stupid enough to give out their real name when they are trying to hide the fact they are married.

"I'm Jane."

He chuckles at my obvious bluff. "Jane."

I raise a brow. "John?"

"What do you say we get out of here? I know a nice drive-in not too far from here."

I laugh.

He smiles, but it doesn't reach his eyes. "What's so funny?"

"You expect me to go somewhere with you?"

"Why not? I know your mother works here."

I glance at Joan, but she's busy pulling tickets and fixing plates for customers to notice John sitting next to me.

John's a creep.

I slide off the stool. "Where you goin'?"

Ignoring him, I walk to the women's restroom.

I use the toilet, wash my hands, and fix my hair. When I walk out, I'm blocked by John waiting for me right outside the hallway of the restroom. "You didn't answer me, Jane. How about that drive-in?"

I act like I didn't hear him and go around him, but he blocks me.

"What the fuck, John? The answer is no. Now fuck off."

His nostrils flare, and his eyes are pitch black. His nose is slightly crooked. This close, he looks to be in his late thirties, maybe early forties.

"Well, that's not very nice."

"Neither is some middle-aged creep that can't take the fucking hint when a lady isn't interested. Now move."

He leers at me for a few seconds. My stomach lurches in fear. "Yeah, you're the hard-to-get type who needs a little persuasion." He lowers his voice. "Your mom told me about her pretty daughter who looks just like her when she was young, and we both know your name isn't Jane."

Tears burn my eyes.

I push him out of the way, then march toward my mother and slam the keys on the table of booth eight. "Ivy—"

"I'll find a ride home."And I storm out of the diner.

I swipe furiously at the tears that have escaped and lean on the wall where no one can see me.

"Why does she have to be so stupid," I mumble.

Why can't she be a normal mother? How could she talk about me like that to a complete stranger? It's obvious she gave him more than just service at the diner.

I didn't realize I was walking toward the back of the building when I someone asks, "You need a ride?"

It's John.

"No."

"It looks like you do."

"I don't. Now leave me alone."

"See...I think you need a ride. A long one."

What the fuck is wrong with the men in this town?

I walk toward the back entrance of the diner and open the door. "I'll be here in case you change your mind."

"You had a better chance with my mother," I shoot back and walk inside.

I re-claim my seat at the counter. Joan looks up. "Sorry, babe, it's a busy night."

"I see that,"I tell her, watching my mother. I don't mention John and I don't think she noticed me leave.

Joan opens the door to the carousel, rotating the desserts, and places a piece of cheesecake in front me. I look up, and she smiles. "It's on the house."

"Thanks, Joan."

She knows money is tight for Mother and me, and we can barely keep up with the bills.

After placing my fork down, feeling my stomach cramp from all the sugar, the cook with the apron rushes up to Joan. "Call 911, Joan. Now!"

"What now, Bruce?" she says, placing the dish towel on the counter.

Bruce's eyes have a look of horror. "Tell them to come out back. Blue Ford, Joan. Tell them to send the coroner," he says, out of breath.

"What the hell is going on?" Joan says grabbing the phone.

I slide off the stool and rush out the back door by the bathroom, then pause. Three guys surround the driver's side door, but I hear a familiar song playing on the radio. The Angels "My Boyfriend's Back."

"Jesus,"one man says, gripping his gray hair.

"He was just inside. I saw him," another man with a red trucker hat says.

"His eyes."

I walk slowly. *The song.* All I hear is the song playing in my head.

My eyes go wide when I see John dead in the driver's side. His head on the seat tilted up. His eyes are missing. There is a white piece of paper with SHE HAD ME AT JANE written in his blood and stuck to his forehead. His throat cut. There is blood all over his shirt and the steering wheel.

I can hear the police sirens from a distance.

"Who's Jane?"

"Get her out of here?"

Someone touches my shoulder. It's Bruce.

"You're Maggy's daughter, right?"

"Huh?"

The song. The song.

CHAPTER 20

After three hours of police questioning everyone at the diner, we finally make it home. I can't get the song out of my head or what the note said.

When the cops questioned me, I didn't say anything. I didn't tell him I talked to him except when someone pointed out he was seated next to me at the counter. But all I said was that he knew I was Maggy Sloan's daughter to avoid any mention of the name Jane.

Since the diner is old, there are no working cameras.

"Are you alright?"my mother asks.

I don't mention what she said to him or how pissed off and disappointed I am in her. She is not going to change the way she is because of me. She would have a long time ago.

"I'm fine."

"Who knows if he had any enemies. He's a trucker and passes through from town to town. State to state. Some people have secrets they don't tell. Back home, it happened all the time. People owing drug dealers money. Druggies who couldn't handle their high,"she says in her Southern accent. "You know that's the way of life, Ivy."

She doesn't want to admit that he pays for sex and is a dirtbag. Probably does drugs. She probably slept with him for money. He's a piece of shit.

"What was his name?"

I know it's not John. He is a liar on top of a rapist.

"His name was Steven. All I know is that he was married and drove an eighteen-wheeler."

You knew him so well to give him information about your daughter and screw him for money. He could have a disease. He could have killed his wife or raped someone a few towns over. But I don't tell her that. There is no point in telling her anything because I think I know who killed Steven, and it has everything to do with me.

I PUSH THE SLOT AFTER PLACING THE FIFTH QUARTER to start the wash. One drawback of living in an old apartment complex is the shared laundry facilities. I hate having to wait until I finish all the laundry. You can't walk away or people will steal your clothes by the time you come back.

I hop on the counter and scroll through my phone when a text pops up.

Unknown: It's not safe to be out at night.

Who the hell is this?

Ivy: Who is this?

Unknown: Guess

I look at the entry way but don't see anyone.

Ivy: It is also not safe to talk to strangers.

Unknown: True. But we are not strangers.

Ivy: Who is this?

Unknown: You didn't guess.

Ivy: You texted me.

Unknown: I did.

Ivy: Why?

Unknown: Because you're bored. Waiting sucks.

Fear drips down my spine. I jump off the counter and look out the empty hallway, afraid that someone could be hiding behind the wall on the left. I look at the concrete floor to see if I can see a shadow but there is no one. Whoever this is, knows where I am.

Unknown: You shouldn't be scared, Ivy. Look what happened to the last guy.

Ivy: Who the fuck is this?

"This isn't funny. I know you're there," I say in a shaky voice.

Unknown: I am equally comfortable in your mouth and in your shoe. What am I ?

Ivy: Stop it.

Unknown: Wrong. A tongue.

It's him. The riddles. He likes to mess with people's heads.

Ivy: What loses its head in the morning and gets it back at night?

Unknown: Me. When Ivy touches my cock.

Ivy: Very funny. A pillow.

The washing machine abruptly switches cycles with a mechanical clunk. Startled, I jolt, almost dropping my phone.

Unknown: Have a seat and let's continue.

I hop on the counter.

Ivy: Look at my back, I am no one. Look at my face, I am someone. What am I ?

Unknown: Mine.

Ivy: No. A mirror.

Unknown: Hm…I was hoping I got that one right.

Ivy: Impossible because I don't share.

Unknown: Jealous?

Ivy: I should ask you.

Unknown: Imagine if he touched you.

Ivy: What would you have done?

Unknown: I can't tell you all my secrets.

Ivy: Then I can't tell you mine.

Unknown: But I already know all your secrets, Ivy.

Anticipation claws at my skin, causing my heart to beat faster.

Ivy: What are they?

Unknown: If I told you, they wouldn't be secrets.

When the washer stops, I transfer the clothes to the dryer and notice he's stopped texting me.

Ivy: Where are you?

I check my phone every minute until the dryer stops, and it's time for me to leave.

He never answered.

I SIT IN THE LAWN CHAIR ON THE ROOF. LIKE MY DREAM last night, I stare at the square white screen from the drive-in and wait for the credits to start. Instead of Stephen King's *It,* it's *Friday the 13th*, the 2009 remake, which is the best remake in my opinion.

I grip the freshly washed warm blanket that smells like lavender from the dryer sheets I bought on clearance at the Big H. I hold the small radio to the station so I can hear the movie. This is how I spend my movie nights because we can't afford to pay monthly for streaming apps, a good TV, or purchase movies. When you've lived in a trailer most of your life, there wasn't much we came with.

"Is this how you watch scary movies?"

I jump in my seat. I look to my right, and Draco stands next to me, wearing black boots, jeans, and a black sweater with a leather jacket.

What the fuck?

It feels like déjà vu or my dream coming true. I'm not superstitious, but the fortune teller told me to listen to my dreams. Could she be for real?

"It's the only way I can," I admit. "I don't exactly own a car, and my mother is strict about letting me use hers."

"Have you gone to the drive-in?"

His voice is haunting and mesmerizing. A deep resonance with a hint of melancholy. It has me in his grip. I don't want to tell him the truth, but I can't seem to lie. Not to him.

"Once."

"A date?"

"The first, worst, and last. I'll take my chances on this roof."

"That bad?"

I snort. "Nothing memorable...like everything I've experienced. First times are supposed to be unforgettable. In my case, I wished I could forget they ever happened."

"Your first was bad. Bad date? Bad fuck?"

I giggle. "You know, you could just ask me if it was when I lost my virginity."

"Are you a virgin?" I hear a hint of British in his voice.

I suck in a breath. "No."

"How was your first time?"

I look at him like he's lost his mind. His dark eyes meet mine, and I could tell he wants to know. Not because he's being nosy but because it matters to him. I won't tell him who it was. I'm sure his was better.

"When I first moved here, no one knew me...naturally. I come from a long generation of trailer trash. Every stigma of living at a trailer park, there is some truth in it. Anyway, I never had a guy pay attention to me before in the way it was supposed to be. People knew where I lived at my old school, and my mother had a better reputation with the fathers than with the mothers. When we moved here, I was asked out by one of the most popular guys at school. I was excited. I wanted to live the fantasy until they found out about me. I didn't think it would be a nightmare, but I wasn't thinking. I didn't think he would take me to the drive-in on a first date. Everyone knows you don't actually watch the movies at the drive-in. I thought he was a nice guy. "

"Did he hurt you?"

"No. His dick was small, the seat belt in the back seat of his

Mustang hurt more than him popping my cherry, and he lasted three minutes."

"You didn't come?"

"No. I couldn't wait until he got off me."

"What happened after?"

"He told the whole school I was a slut."

"He didn't want everyone to know he has a two-inch dick."

"I guess. It doesn't change that it was bad."

"Have you ever had a good time?"

I smile. "Are you asking me if I've ever had good sex?"

He towers over me, the movie long forgotten. "Maybe I am." He pulls the blanket off slowly. "Can I take you somewhere?"

"Depends on where you plan on taking me."

"Somewhere unforgettable."

CHAPTER 21

He turns right, goes over an empty road by the beltway. We're in the middle of nowhere. The moon hangs high in the dark sky. The breeze cause the trees to groan.

"Why are we here?"

He shuts the door to his car. "You'll see."

I get out of the car. "What are you going to do?"

He leans on the hood of his car. "What do you want me to do, Ivy?"

"I'm not sure. You asked me to go with you, so I did."

"Do you like me, Ivy?"

"I-I don't know you."

"Did you know your first, your last?"

"Not in the way it counts."

"Do you want me to fuck you, Ivy?"

His face is expressionless, as if he is asking if I prefer regular or Diet Coke.

"Do you want to fuck me?" I volley back.

He grins maliciously. "When you saw me at my show in the enclosed room with Nyx on her knees, did it bother you?"

"If it did or didn't, it's none of my business."

Images of that night cloud my vision, squeezing my chest. I can't explain it.

" I told you. She didn't touch me, Ivy. I didn't fuck her, and she didn't suck my cock. Not since the first time I laid eyes on you."

"Why?"

"I think you know why."

I don't.

"I don't know why."

"Do you remember the first time you had a cock inside your pussy...do you remember what it felt like?"

I shake my head. "No. I can't remember what it felt like when he was...you know...inside me. All I remember was that he was small. It didn't hurt like I thought it would. I didn't come."

"How about Dean?"

"It was small, and I could never come. It felt fake... like... I was being filmed, and the walls were made from cardboard. I felt sick like was... doll in a costume."

"What did he make you wear?"

I look down at my boots for a second and then look up. "A pleated skirt...like a school uniform with the shirt."

His eyes gleam under the light of the moon like a feral animal.

"He was rough?"

I nod. "Yeah," I say softly.

"He paid you?"

"He knew I needed a ride home and the money. It didn't start like that at first, but then it...just was. I'm not..."

"A whore."

Two tears slide down my cheeks hearing that word out loud.

"I want to go home."

He walks to the driver's side door. "Then go home."

Confused, I step forward, and everything happens so fast. He starts the car. I go to open the passenger side door, but the door won't open. It's locked. I keep trying the handle, but it makes a *click, click* and won't budge.

I slap the window with the palm of my hand. "Draco, open the door!" I yell.

The car speeds off, kicking up dirt.

The cloud of dirt hits my eyes like tiny hot needles. The roar of the engine gets farther and farther as he drives off. Hot tears continue to slide down my dirt-stained cheeks.

He left me out here. He left me. He left me in the middle of nowhere, eight miles from home in the dark with no way to get home.

I panic.

"Draco!"I yell in a piercing scream. "Don't leave me! Please!"

My chest is rising and falling as I run toward the two red tail lights of his car. After I can't run anymore from exhaustion, my knees buckle and I fall, skinning my knees and ripping my black tights.

I pull out my phone from the side pocket of my jacket. No signal. I hold it up in the air getting up slowly, but nothing. Not even a bar on the screen.

He planned this.

But why?

None of it makes sense.

After walking for fifteen minutes, I see headlights coming in the opposite direction. Fear curls in my gut. I know not to flag a car down. No one good is out around midnight.

Panic sets in, firing my adrenaline. I run toward the tree line and hide.

The car slows down to a crawl. It's a van. My hands shake. It's dark, and I can't make out the van's color or see the license plate. I think whoever it is saw me because the van stops. I hear a door open.

I take off and run in the opposite direction.

A twig snaps in a subtle crack, shattering the stillness of the night. I freeze, my heart pounding as I try to hear any sign of someone following me. A chill sweeps through the trees. I don't know where I am or if I'm going in the right direction.

I move through the trees, my feet hitting the ground, rustling the leaves like drumbeats.

"Ivyyyyyyy!" I hear my name being called in a plaintive cry, followed by laughter in the distance.

"Ivyyyyy," my name is called again like a sigh in the wind. More laughter and then, "Don't leave me," the voice mocks.

My breath catches in my throat. The pulse in my veins quickens with every second. With every exhale I take, the cold air forms a wispy cloud before dissipating in the dark.

A loud snap from a twig to my right causes me to run.

Something long and hard grabs me around my waist, lifting me in the air.

"No!" I scream.

A large hand covers my mouth. I flail my arms and legs.

I'm slammed on the ground, knocking the wind out of me. I push with my hands and feet. I can't see who it is because it's so dark.

A hand grips my throat and squeezes, but I can still breathe. My tights are ripped to shreds. My skirt shoved above my waist.

"Please!" I plead on a cry.

"Scream my name!" My eyes go wide. " Say. My. Name." His tongue licks me like a dog. "Say it, my pretty little whore," he rasps against my cheek. "Scream my name!"

The grip on my throat relaxes. My body shakes uncontrollably from fear mixed with excitement.

Adrenaline and desire rush in my veins as his name escapes my lips followed by a cloud of smoke. "Draco."

He rips my shirt down the middle. My skirt follows and then my tights.

"Open your thighs, Ivy. I want to give you something you won't forget."

My thighs fall open, and the cold air kisses my heated clit.

Fuck.

I'm so fucking wet. I can come from just the cold breeze. I'm excited like in those porn movies when the man plays a game of cat and mouse with his prey.

His head dips between my legs. The flat part of his tongue swipes my slit.

I whimper at how my pulse pumps between my legs.

He growls, shoves his face between my legs like an animal and fucks me with his tongue.

"Mm," I groan. "Oh my God. Yes!"

His teeth nip at the soft skin of my inner thighs drawing blood. My clit matches the rapid pulse in my veins. I grip his hair and pull hard. I look down and watch as he eats me like an animal.

He lifts me up by gripping my ass and tongues my asshole. I push his face between my thighs, needing to come, but it's like he is in tune with my body and stops when I'm right at the edge.

He pulls away, and I feel a ghostly breeze from the wetness of his tongue. The sting from my knees and the small bites on my inner thighs.

I hear his zipper break through the silence. "Do you think I would leave you, Ivy?" he asks, pulling out his cock.

I can feel it in the inner side of my thighs. I look down as he rubs it where he bit me soothing the sting mixing it with blood. It glistens under the moon. It's huge with a big head and piercings down the underside of his shaft.

He presses the tip of his cock at the entrance of my pussy splitting it open. One hand is flat on the ground as he leans over me with placing his mouth near my ear. "I saw the sparkle in your eye when you realized it was me. The fear disappeared from your lungs. But I'm not a prince. I'm not a savior but I'm the man they all will fear if they so much as touch you. The only name screamed from your lips will be mine."

He strokes the top of his cock over my clit, and I can't take it. I come.

I grab his shoulders, we both watch as he holds the head of his dick and flicks my clit as I come grinding my pussy over the head.

He strokes his cock, once, twice, and then, he groans.

Cum shoots like a jet, landing on the lips of my pussy, more coats my lower stomach.

When he's done, we are both panting. He brushes his lips over mine in a soft kiss and whispers, "I would never leave you."

CHAPTER 22

DRACO

"Fun night?" Keir says in a hard tone when I walk inside the tent.

"Yes."

"Are you insane? If she tells anyone what you did, it could ruin us."

I smile wide. "I am considered"—I twirl my finger in circles over my temple—"a little loose upstairs if you know what I mean." I drop my smile. "She won't."

"How do you know that?"

I walk into our first-aid tent and grab the first-aid kit for her knees. I left her asleep in my bed. I need to bathe her and make sure her knees are tended to.

"Because I do."

He scoffs. "You think she's the one, don't you?" I grab the antiseptic and head back. But he blocks my path. "She isn't," he says, but I see it.

He wants her and I'm not sure in what way.

"You think by pulling a magic trick with a flower, she is going to kneel and suck your cock?"

"Don't do this, Draco. It's too much of a risk. You don't know for sure if she's the one."

She is. I feel it. I can see it in her eyes. She's mine, and deep down, she feels it. Tonight proved more than I could have imagined. She's perfect.

"There is only one way to find out."

I step to the side, and he blocks me again. "I won't let you hurt her."

"That is not your call to make, and besides..." I lean close. "I've already painted her sweet pussy with my cum. If you touch her, I'll shove your teeth down your fucking throat and your magic fingers up your ass before I cut you open and watch you bleed." He pulls away, and I watch the fear burn in his eyes while I suck my lips dramatically. "I can still taste her on my tongue, Keir. Her fear is the fire in my crotch, and the taste of her cum is the scent on my skin. She's here."

"She won't let you kill me,"he says hoarsely, but he's not convinced. I can see the doubt in his expression. He wants it to be her more than anything.

I chuckle. "Are you sure it's her?"

"It's her." I turn around, and Nyx walks in.

"You say that because he won't touch you since she showed up," Keir says.

I see the pained look in her expression. Keir wants to hurt her the same way I hurt him with the truth. I never meant to hurt her, and I told her that anything between us was transactional.

An act of pleasure and nothing more.

I could tell she doubted the day would ever come or that I would feel the need to end it. There was a time I thought it was all bullshit. That it wasn't real. The visions. Whatever tale my mother spilled was a crock of shit, but now that she is here, I believe it.

I believed it when I had my cock in my hand, and Nyx was ready to suck it. It wasn't cooperating. I pictured my blond temptress, and all I saw was a woman who wasn't her. My cock had never malfunctioned before. I never thought it could happen.

That was for fat men who were balding and hated what their life had become.

Nyx told me it happens but not to me. The way she looked seated in the audience and when she caught me with my pants down. I felt ashamed. I felt like I cheated on my girl. I was gutted and knew I had to do anything to get that image out of her mind.

"Nyx knows the rules and so do you,"I tell them and walk out.

I walk in my trailer and hear the shower running. I smile to myself and undress after placing the kit on the table.

I pull the door open, and the steam floats out like an exhaust pipe from the shower stall. Her body glistens under the spotlights. She swipes her hand to remove the fog from the glass. Her eyes dip to my hard cock, jutting out from between my legs. I'm so fucking hard and horny I think my cock will explode. I thought jerking off to her clit would take the edge off, but it has only made it worse.

"What are you doing?" she asks.

"The same thing you're doing, watching the show."

"I'm not a performer."

"You're my performer, and I'm the ringmaster. What I say goes unless you tell me no."

Her tits bounce when she swipes the glass again. "If I say no, it ends?"

"You have complete power over me. Except when I'm inside you."

"What do you mean?"

"Once you give me permission, I do what I want with your body. I fuck you how I want. How deep I want. How many times I want to come inside you. And make no mistake, Ivy, I will come inside you. I don't wear condoms size small."

She lowers her head to hide her grin. "Did you need something?"

"Yes, I need you."

"For?" I look down at my hard dick and then at her. "Oh..."

"Oh," I mock. She pushes the glass door to the shower. "Is this you granting me permission?"

"Yes, but are you nice? Do you think you can be nice?"

"I can be whatever you want me to be when I'm with you, but you also have to let me do what I want."

"Which is?"

I walk inside the shower, the hot water hitting my skin. "Let me show you," I say, pulling at my hard cock and stroking it while my balls hang tight.

I drop to my knees and lift her leg over my shoulder and shove my face into her cunt. She grinds her pussy, seeking my tongue. Her back is arched against the wall in the semi-darkness of the shower, and while I'm sucking her pussy, I fuck myself feeling my ribbed cock in my hand.

I look up, and the water streams down my neck and chest. My nose inhales her sweet scent as my tongue thrusts into her tight cunt, flicking it inside her.

Her tits glisten from the water. Her pink nipples beg for my teeth. I slide her leg off my shoulder and turn her around. I spread her perky ass cheeks and shove my tongue in her ass.

She moans from the pleasure while I slip two and then three fingers into her pussy. I tug on her clit, and she screams my name, urging me on.

"Draco," she moans. "More."

I smile and pump my tongue inside her ass until she comes.

After I shower and dry off, I tend to the scrapes on her knees with antiseptic and gauze. I dry her hair and comb the platinum strands like she's a delicate doll.

When I'm done, she smiles and grips my cock in her hand and sucks on the head, then glides her tongue over each piercing, flicking her tongue over each one.

"I'm fascinated by you," I tell her.

She smiles with my cock between her lips, and it's the greatest show on earth. The most important act in my life. Her fucking me.

I reach around her gorgeous ass, grateful for my height, and slide my finger into her pretty tight cunt. Then I bring my fingers to my mouth and suck on it, tasting the sweet saltiness of her pussy. "God, you are wet, Ivy. You are so fucking wet."

I pull her mouth off my cock and lay her back on the bed with her legs spread open. I push her lips apart so I can see how pink her cunt is inside. I grab my hard cock and stroke it, teasing her a bit. Her pussy clenches in want.

She pulls herself up by her elbows. Her nipples are hard, and her eyes beg me. They beg me to fuck her.

"Say it,"I demand.

"Fuck me, Draco." She bucks her hips like she's possessed. "I want you to fuck me."

I move my mouth between her thighs and divide her body with my tongue, starting with the slit of her pussy to the valley of her chest. I suck her nipple and bite.

She lets out a loud moan, and her pussy leaks on my sheets. I do the same to the other, and more leaks, dripping to the crack of her ass. I glide my tongue down her stomach and lick her wet pussy, sucking it completely in my mouth.

Her fingernails dig in my scalp, and I groan from the pleasure of feeling her body tremble uncontrollably.

Ivy sits up, pulls her pussy away from my mouth, and kneels on the bed. Her lips are on my dick, and she takes it in her mouth as deep as she can go. She hesitates, and my balls are tight hitting her chin. I can tell by the way she hesitates and tries not to gag when the head of my cock touches the back of her throat with every thrust of my hips that it's her first time taking a man she wants.

I fist her hair in both hands like the strands are makeshift handles and fuck her mouth.

She gasps for air, but I hold her steady until her throat relaxes and then keep fucking her mouth until my cock is buried deep and her mouth is near the base of my cock.

I look down and her top lip rubs against the stubble of shaved pubic hair.

"You're fucking amazing,"I praise. "Such a dirty girl." I lean close, causing my cock to slip out of her mouth coated with saliva. "You're my whore, Ivy. My pretty whore." Her eyes flash with saliva dripping down her chin.

She hates that word, but I'll teach her to like it.

Her hands rub over the hard muscles of my abs. Her fingers trace every dip of muscle to the valley that makes up the v that runs down my hips. I push her back on the bed and hold her legs as wide as they can go, digging my thumbs in her inner thighs. I surprise her when I release them and lick the drool from her chin and kiss her deeply on the lips.

My fingers push the strands of hair away from her forehead and look deep in her eyes. My hard cock, desperate to cum, presses between her legs.

"Ivy?"

"Yeah?"she says breathlessly and almost whimsical.

"I'm going to take you how I want now. Is that okay?"

"Will you hurt me?"

"Have I?"

"No, but will you?"

I give her a wicked smile. "There's only one way to find out."

I slide into her with one powerful thrust, causing her back to arch.

The rest happens in slow motion.

The air escapes her lungs. My nostrils flare from the pleasure of her tight cunt gripping my ribbed cock. I don't move so I don't tear her and give her time to adjust to my size.

Her hands grip my arms and slide to my ass, holding me inside her.

She gasps for air. "Draco?"

Her face is a mixture of pleasure and pain.

"I won't move. I'm waiting for you. I will never hurt you unless you like it."

"I'm afraid to move,"she says.

"Play with your clit."

Her dainty fingers find where we are joined.

It's pure.

Raw.

She strums her clit, and her inner walls choke my cock. I grind my hips, pushing deep and slow. She meets my slow, measured thrusts. I suck her nipples, squeezing her full breasts gently like two ripe fruits.

I lift one leg over my arm, place my hand flat on the headboard, and fuck her. The slapping sound of skin adds to the pounding beat of my heart.

"Draco,"she pleads. "Don't stop. I'm...coming."

I continue to fuck her hard. Her tits bounce with each thrust. I'm in heaven burning from the fire of hell from being this long without her. My balls tighten, and I come hard inside her cunt. A loud groan mixes with her sweet cries as I break her apart over and over.

When we are done, I look down at my cock buried in her tight pink cunt. I stare at the thin strip of hair on her pussy and grin.

I look up after releasing her leg. "You're a blond."

She points at her hair, messy from fucking. "I am."

"You're a real blonde,"I add.

Her cheeks flush bright red. "Oh."

"I like it."

There is nothing about her I don't like. I hope she feels the same way when she finds out who I really am.

CHAPTER 23

I squint from the sun streaming through the window, and for a second, I think I'm in my room. Yet it doesn't smell like stale cigarettes mixed with pine cleaner but of citrus and cedar.

I have a pleasant ache between my thighs from being fucked all night. He didn't stop until I passed out from exhaustion. I didn't think one could pass out from coming so much.

The door opens, and I smile, but it fades when I see that it's Nyx. It's not that I hate her or anything, but I was hoping it was Draco. I take that back. I'm jealous of how effortlessly gorgeous she looks with her makeup on. Her eyes are lined with red and a smoky eye that looks hot. Her lips are blood red. She is always dressed and ready to perform. Her skin is white with a hint of pink. She wears a shiny black bodysuit with garters, ripped tights, and laced black heeled boots. Her hair is grayish-white with dark roots, and I love the color of her eyes. They are a mix between violet and blue.

"Good afternoon,"she says with a salacious smile.

"Shit." I reach for my phone, and it's 1 p.m. I have to get ready for my shift soon, and I promised Alice we would hang out. "I have to get ready for work soon."

She angles her head. "Work?"

"Yeah."

I slide off the bed and look at my knees and smile. He bandaged them and put a Band-Aid on with clown faces like I'm five. His black T-shirt hits right above my knees. I look around for my clothes but don't see them anywhere.

She pouts. "You got hurt."She shakes her head slowly. "You can't go to work if you're hurt." She places a finger on her lip. "Draco…" She looks up. "You don't need to work. You can stay here with us."

I walk into the bathroom and find a brand-new electric toothbrush with little clowns on it that says PUSH ME I SPIN.

I pick it up and find it hot that he left it for me.

After I freshen up, I walk out and find Nyx watching me.

I raise my brows with a smirk. "Had fun?"

"Oh… I'm just getting started. I want to suck your pussy."

Well, at least she's honest. I've never had a girl eat me out before. I can't say I have never thought of it or wanted to try it, but it's been in the back of my mind when I think about sex.

The times I've had sex with Dean and the first time with Tommy had me questioning my sexuality at one point. I never liked it, but Draco solidified that I like men. But I wouldn't deny the opportunity to try something new. To explore. In a safe way.

"What would Draco think?"

I wonder if this was a one-time thing. I knew what to expect sleeping with him. I fantasized about having sex with him since I met him, and he touched me for the first time.

When they both said there was nothing serious between them, how could I refuse? He's dangerously hot, and I want him more than I have ever wanted anything in my whole life. The fact that he's the ringleader in a circus makes me want him even more. He says he isn't a prince, but to me, he's more than a prince. To me, he's every dream come true.

"He would watch if you let me. If you say yes of course." She stands, placing a hand on her hip and angles her head to the side. "You must be sore. You two were fucking the whole night." Her eyes dip to my hard nipples protruding from his T-shirt. "I was jealous." My chest squeezes. "Not because of him," she says coyly.

"Because I wanted to taste you, Ivy. I was jealous he made you come, and I wasn't there to lick it from your cunt."

The way she says lick and cunt has my poor pussy throbbing.

"I-I..."

"Have you ever let a girl fuck you with her tongue?"

"No."

Her eyes turn a shade of dark purple. Her fingers play with the hem of my T-shirt. "Can I dress you up so we can play? This is a circus after all," she adds. "I promise to make you... pretty. Sexy. Draco will jerk off all night when they see what I've done with you."

"Draco?"I ask confused.

"Oops,"she says, laughing dramatically. "Did I say that?"

"You did."

She giggles like a little girl. "Draco is craaaazy about you. He can't stop staring at you or talking about you. He warned everyone."

"About what?"

"How he will kill anyone who touches you."

"Why?"

She squeals. "Because silly, you're his woman. The one he's been waiting for and...now you're here, and we should play." She slides clown slippers from the corner of the bed toward me with her boot. I put them on, and she pulls me by the arm out of the trailer. "You'll look amazing in this outfit,"she rambles on. "By the way, your tits look amazing."

I STARE AT MYSELF IN FRONT OF THE MIRROR IN THE dressing tent. She made me into an erotic female ringleader with leather boots over netted tights, my ass hanging out of short black shorts with a bra that has little gold buttons and coins hanging along the edge by the swell of my breasts. It's practically a bathing suit.

My hair is straight, and my makeup is done up like hers, but with more detail and more black smoke around my eyes, plus little jewels stuck to my skin. My lips are painted black with red lip liner. I look like I'm going to a Halloween party at a strip club called Siren Seduction.

"So what do you think?" She leans over my shoulder behind me with her red lips close to my ear. I stare at myself in the mirror. "I think you look hot." Her hand cups me between my legs. "You feel hot too, Ivy." Her breath fans the painted skin on my neck. "Let's give them a show, baby. A special show." I turn my head. "Freaks only,"she says with her lips brushing mine. Her eyes promise me relief from the soreness between my legs.

I follow her to the clear box made of acrylic. I thought it was glass at first, but it isn't. It's huge when I follow her inside and looking out from within. It's big and feels like a room on the set of the movie *The Truman Show* where everyone who wants to watch gets a glimpse of your life.

I stand in front of a leather chaise with chains attached underneath. She motions for me to kneel on all fours with my ass sticking straight up in the air.

"You are so swollen. He's been fucking you hard all night." My pussy is swollen and engorged. I can feel the heat from the cool air hitting my battered cunt. "You have a pretty pussy, Ivy. I can't blame him for fucking you the way he did."

Awareness snakes up my spine. I look over my shoulder, and he's watching like a spectator with no shirt and black pants. He slams his hand on the hard acrylic. His eyes are riveted on my pussy when she spreads my ass cheeks open.

"Nyx,"he warns.

"She needs to be taken care of, Draco. You can't leave her in bed to go train. You don't know what might come crawling in to take a bite," she says with a laugh.

Nyx is a little crazy, but I like her.

"Nyx,"he warns again in a hard tone.

"Just a little taste. She wants it, Draco. Doesn't she look spectacular?" She blows on my pussy. "So soft and delicate. You know how I feel about women—about her." I look over my shoulder. My eyes find hers. "I want you more than I want him, Ivy. He knew what would happen when he found you. I know it all sounds a bit crazy," she says in a childlike voice. "But we're all under your spell. Show him how gorgeous you are, Ivy. Show him why he shouldn't ever leave you alone," she says slowly.

My pussy is heavy and soaked. Draco walks in and lifts my chin delicately with one finger, careful not to ruin my makeup, and says with a thick British accent, "Welcome to the Circle of Freaks, my love. I own you now."He looks up. "Suck her pussy, Nyx." He leans close when my body jerks forward from the pleasure of her tongue and whispers, "Don't get used to this, Ivy. I turn murderous when someone else touches what is mine."

I bite my inner cheek when her mouth sucks my cunt, stifling a moan.

"Does that go for you too?" I ask between breaths.

I don't know why I said that. I don't know what is happening to me. Everything is happening so fast.

He sticks his thumb in my mouth. "You're the only woman who will touch me, and I'm the only man who will touch you. This is to appease your curiosity." Nyx tongues my pussy and then fucks me. I push against her face. She groans. Her mouth feels amazing. I'm about to come. I suck his thumb and moan.

I cry out when she takes her tongue out and glides the tip in my ass.

I pull my mouth from his thumb and moan.

My inner thighs are slick.

"Draco," I plead.

Nyx lets out a crazy laugh. "Mm...poor baby."

I need to come. She's fucking torturing me.

"Fun is over, Nyx."

She kisses my pussy. "I'm sorry," she says in a naughty little voice.

"Go," he demands.

She walks around and tilts my head, then kisses me on my lips. "You're so beautiful," she says and licks my lips and whispers. "He's jealous, and I don't blame him."

Draco doesn't wait for her to leave the room before he spreads my sore pussy with his fingers. I feel something wet that feels like lube, and then he slides his cock slowly in.

I moan on her lips. He pushed deeper.

I close my eyes. "Mm..."

"You like his fat pierced cock inside you...don't you, Ivy?"

I nod, and she drowns out the moan escaping my lips with her mouth when his piercing hits the right spot.

Draco fucks me while she deepens the kiss. My arms shake on the chaise. My pussy makes sucking noises with every thrust. Draco's fingers dig in my hips as he picks up speed.

Little gasps escape my throat, and it's like Nyx and I are breathing the same air. Her tongue licks the roof of my mouth. Her red lipstick smears like blood is dripping down her chin.

I tilt my head back when my orgasm slams into me. Our tongues tangle while she pinches my nipples.

I let out a scream when my orgasm peaks. It feels so fucking good.

I feel alive.

"I'm coming," Draco growls. "Fuck!" He slams into me, gripping my ass in his hands at the same time as he pulls me hard against him with a loud smack. His cock convulses in my pussy followed by the heat of his cum.

Nyx breaks the kiss and says, "You are perfect for him."

CHAPTER 24

fter Nyx touches up my makeup, she smiles. "It's time."

"Time for what?"

"To show you, silly." Her smile widens. "It's showtime."

She has a disturbed look in her eyes. I'm not going to like whatever she is going to show me or rather they are going to show me, but I want to know. I've seen fucked-up things in my life. Things no girl should see but had to accept because there was no other choice. Things I've had to do because it was what my mother said I was destined for.

Nyx takes me to another tent, and it smells like formaldehyde. The same smell the first time I saw the fake body parts in the pickled jars.

We walk through the exhibit with red lights that shine on a shelf with a row of jars. One has eyes, a spine, what looks like a pair of lungs, and another jar with a tongue. That jar reads LIAR in big glowing letters.

"They look so real,"I say distractedly.

She laughs and then stops dramatically. "That's because they are."

"W-what?"I stammer. She's fucking with me, but the way she looks at the jars and then at me tells me she isn't. "N-no. You're joking."

I jolt when a large hand lands on my shoulder. I look up. "You scared me."

"It's what we do here,"Draco says in a calm voice.

He takes my hand and tugs me deeper inside the tent. There is a large box the size of a shipping container with what looks like soundproofing on the sides. It's dark the farther we walk inside. The door slams shut behind us, and I panic.

I whirl around, but Draco grips my shoulders turning me back. "Shh..."

"It's okay, baby," Nyx coos. "You'll get used to it."

Who the fuck are these people? I blink. My eyes sting from the smell. It smells like copper.

A light shines from above, and then there are muffled screams.

I turn around and almost gag from the bile that rises from my throat. Five men are tied to metal chairs gagged and bloody.

The rest of the performers stand behind them. Lex with an ax. Keir with a chainsaw. The Butcher with a butcher knife dressed like they're going to begin a show. But this is a different show. One man has been mutilated. Blood is splattered everywhere. He is missing his limbs. His guts are spilling out of his stomach.

I throw up, not being able to take it. I retch until nothing comes out. "What the fuck?"I back away toward the exit, but Draco blocks my path. "Why?"

"Let us explain,"Draco says. He points at the others, who look like they are an inch away from dying. "They rape and kill girls, Ivy." He steps closer, towering over me. "It's why they can't find who is doing it. There are more." He tilts his head. "So many. They are like a disease that has infected our society. Poisoning the girls who never survive. Their souls scream in pain from the innocence that was taken. They need to be eradicated, not placed in jail so that they have a chance to breathe."

I shake my head. "How do you know?"

"I was one of them." Nyx steps forward. "Draco saved me." She looks behind me. "The Circle of Freaks saved me. They are not just a circus. They are my saviors. I love them. They gave me a home. You see, I don't have parents. The guys who took me killed them and trafficked me from Russia when I was twelve. I was raised by the circus, Ivy. It's all I know. They gave me a home. A place. A new identity."

My chest squeezes. Twelve? I shake my head. I need to get out of here. It's too much. I can't...

"I want to leave. I have work,"I say and step around him toward the exit.

CHAPTER 25

I watch Alice sleeping on my bed. I tried after school, work, and then the bar. I couldn't tell her about Draco or the Circle of Freaks and what I saw. Draco told me not to tell anyone about us and that soon he would come for me.

Whatever that meant.

He forgot to mention that they kill the men raping and killing the girls. They obviously couldn't find the girls after they find out who did it or which one they abducted. I'm sure they get them to talk when they mutilated them.

After he dropped me off at work, I assured him I had a ride home. I could tell by his facial expression he wasn't happy when I asked to leave or the way he drover off when I got out of his car without a backward glance.

There was so much I wanted to ask. So much I didn't know.

My mother called me repeatedly, asking me if I had the rent money. I was worried she would kick me out.

Where would I go? The circus? Be part of their murder crew?

I had to finish school. I had to forget what I saw, but I knew something like that wasn't so simple.

To some, they would be considered them no different from the men who abducted and killed those girls. They had a point about them going to jail and it bot being fair when those girl's lives had been cut short in the worst way.

The authorities would do the same if they caught them and obviously couldn't stop it from happening again. Who would catch the rest? Those men would be set free eventually, and the cycle would continue. It won't change that those girls are dead. The Circle of Freaks didn't kill them, or did they?

I watch Alice while I get dressed for school. The memory from last night in her room floods back. After everything I saw, I needed to feel normal. I didn't want her to feel what I was feeling. I wanted to her to feel wanted. Sexy. Loved.

We all have secrets. I could see that she had them in her eyes last night, and I wanted to do something I never had the courage to do with Nyx. I wanted to taste a woman's pussy. I never expected Alice to be so responsive. So sexy.

It was a one-time thing.

In a way, I felt I was cheating on Draco, but deep down, I knew I wasn't. If he was in the room, he would watch. He would make sure I was able to come.

I push her on the bed after sucking her mouth and tits. I remove my clothes and pull her panties off until we are both naked on her bed. Her pussy is wet and glistening from the light on her nightstand.

I play with my pussy, and Alice watches me masturbate with three fingers. I play with my clit and then take my fingers and slide them past her lips, and she sucks them, tasting me.

She opens her legs. Her pussy is clean and pink. She spreads her lips with her fingers. Her clit is swollen and a shade darker. I press my face into her pussy, licking and sucking her clit. She tastes sweet.

Her fingers slide in my hair, massaging my head while she arches her back, and I make her come. She bites the edge of her pillow to stifle her moans. Her pussy is dripping from her cum, and I suck her clean.

I wipe my mouth with the back of my hand. She faces me, kneeling in the same position on the bed. She dips her head and sucks my tits while sliding a finger in my pussy. Another finger works my clit. I look down and watch her tongue licking my nipple and then the other.

"Alice," I hiss from the pleasure of her tongue and fingers.

She pushes me onto the bed so that my head is toward the head-board and dips her face between my legs and sucks my pussy. I grind my hips, feeling her tongue inside me. She moans and caresses my outer thighs. I play with my tits while my orgasm slams into me. Her tongue continues to flick my clit .

When I think we are done, Alice surprises me by lying on top of me. She kisses me, grinding on my pussy like she has a cock. She cups my face and continues to kiss me with a smile.

She pulls away and lies over me in a sixty-nine position and I eat her pussy. She spreads my legs and eats me out. We fuck each other with our tongues. I spread her ass and suck her clit, then lick her asshole. She likes it because she grinds her pussy on my face, and I slide my tongue in her pussy and fuck her.

She pushes my legs wider and slides her tongue in my ass then sucks my clit. We are both moaning, fucking each other with our tongues until we both come ate the same time.

When we are done, we snuggle in each other's arms and before we fall asleep, we say, "This is our secret," at the same time.

I laugh. "It was a one-time thing, Alice."

"I love you, Ivy," she says and falls asleep.

"I love you too, Alice," I whisper and kiss her temple.

I look at the bedroom door and see the shadow of footsteps retreating. I know he was listening. Fear curls around my heart. Her stepfather is a creep. I know guys like him and what they do.

I have to protect Alice.

AFTER ALICE TOOK ME TO SCHOOL, I THOUGHT THE reporters would have been gone by the time school was out but they are everywhere.

On the sidewalk, parking lot, and bus lane. Mich and his friends were killed last night and mutilated. Body parts were missing. Based on the media reports, eyes, tongues, and their penis were removed. It is big news compared to months of girls gone missing and later found dead.

Unknown: Are you afraid?

Ivy: Of what, the big bad wolf?

I'm standing on the sidewalk, watching the solemn look on girls who knew Mich. It sucks that a group of people died, but some people don't deserve to live if they do things that make people wish they were dead.

Unknown: Aren't you going to ask me?

Ivy: Ask you what?

The first school bus drives off. I rush over to the last one but freeze. The blacked-out Cuda is idling on the curb across the street.

Unknown: Come with me and find out. I'm sure I have something you want.

Ivy: Cocky.

Unknown: It's aching, baby.

I smile, but it dies when Tommy walks up. "Hey, Ivy."
"What do you want? I gotta go."
"In a rush?" he says, staring at my chest.
"Yes."
He grabs my wrist when I take a step to go around him.
"Is there a problem?"
I look behind Tommy as he slowly turns around. "Who the fuck are you?" Tommy says, looking up at Draco.
"Name a place you'll never see your name," Draco replies.
Tommy squares off but doesn't release the grip on my wrist. I

can feel the waves of testosterone flying between them. Draco's gaze dips to Tommy's hand on my wrist.

Tommy smiles. "You think you're funny. Dressed all in black. You look like a wannabe singer in a band from your mother's basement." Tommy lowers his voice. "Did she tell you I was her first? That I fucked her."

"Yes, we talk about it. She told me all three minutes of it. Kinda boring and lame if you ask me." Draco lowers his voice. "But don't worry. Your secret is safe with me. It's okay to have a small dick. She likes mine so much better." He resumes his normal tone. "Back to naming a place. Answer, and if you get it wrong, I'll tell you. It will be a glimpse of your future. I'll be nice and give you a hint. It's a special place."

Tommy looks between us, confused. He isn't sure if Draco is pissed off or not, or crazy.

"I don't know, man," he says, defeated.

"A gravestone."

I finally pull my wrist free when it takes Tommy a minute to let the answer sink in.

"Are you threatening me?" Tommy asks spitefully.

"How can I threaten you with death when we are all meant to die?"

"You're fucking crazy, man."

"We are all crazy about something."

Draco grabs my hand and caresses the spot where Tommy grabbed my wrist like he's erasing his touch from my skin.

Once we are in his car, I look out the window to see Tommy staring at Draco's car as we drive off.

"Are you going to kill him?" I ask.

"What would you like me to do?"

I snort. "If you can get him to stop calling me a slut around school, that would be great. Slut and my name go hand in hand these days."

"I'm sorry."

"For?"

"For what I said. For what I asked. It was...out of line."

"I can't change what anyone thinks of me. I've learned that since I was a little girl. The show must go on, right? I'm just the act."

"Is that what you think of me?"

"If it wasn't... you wouldn't have said it," I say honestly. After a few seconds of silence. I clear my throat, changing the subject. "Thanks for picking me up from school. You didn't have to do that."

He doesn't answer and stares straight ahead. I shouldn't have said that, but it's the truth. I got used to people judging me.

When I was eleven, my mother told me not to cry over spilled milk. I tried to change what people thought of me, but when I couldn't, I learned to accept and stop running from it.

He slows down by the Big H but keeps going.

"You missed the plaza," I tell him.

"I know."

"I can't be late to my shift."

I need Alice to pick me up so I can keep a close eye on her.

"I don't like you working there."

"I don't either, but I have bills to pay."

"Like?"

"Rent, my phone, the light?"

"Your mom?"

"Says she doesn't make enough."

"She's a liar."

"I don't have a choice, Draco."

"We all have a choice."

"What is the real reason?"

"Alice. She's..."

"My brother is taking care of it."

"Your brother?"

He pulls through the gate behind the haunted carnival. Drives around the back near is trailer and places the car in park.

Who's his brother? Then, it slowly dawns.

Lazarus.

"Lazarus is my brother, Ivy. We own"—he waves his hand toward the fair— "all this and more."

"I'm confused? Does Alice know? She's in trouble, Draco. She will be coming to pick me up from work."

Panic sets in. They've been watching us. Alice. Me. The ticket. It was all deliberate.

He turns in his seat and faces me. "Ivy?"

"You're scaring me."

"Don't be afraid. The house. It brought you to me."

"The house?"

A flashback of the house. Me and Alice. The fortune teller Seraphina.

I shake my head, not believing. The killings. The manor. Alice saying her car is charged every morning. The jars. The same ones with the body parts inside them at their exhibit. The old lady buying them every week at the grocery store.

"No."

"The circus calls to you, Ivy, because in another life, you were part of a circus. This circus. With me."

I shake my head in denial. "You're lying. I'm not..."

"You were my wife and will be my wife in this life and the next. Your connection to Alice is strong because she lived in that house with you in another life. The house... brings you back in every life for eternity. Our love is eternal in this life and the next. You will have a son, and Alice will have two. In this life, the way things turn out will depend on certain aspects of free will and... the way the house wants it to be. You will have visions and so will Alice when the time comes. The house will guide you both."

My hands tremble in my lap. "You're crazy. You're going to kill me."

"I'm not, but I will kill whoever touches you."

"I fucked Alice," I confess.

He smiles. "Pity, I wasn't there to watch. My brother will be so disappointed."

"You're not mad?"

"No. If that is what you both wanted. You have a gift, my love. I don't think there is anyone who could resist you. It is *your* gift and I've been waiting for you."

Something doesn't add up. How?

"If this is a gift, then there is a curse, right? There is always a curse."

"We die together. So will Alice and Lazarus. We die young, Ivy. After death, we reincarnate in another life. It is different every time. Our souls are all linked. The house will call us back, but the circus goes on." He caresses my lips with the pad of his thumb. "It will come to you, Ivy. Don't fight it. Our love will come to you. I'll come to you in your dreams, and I will be the nightmare to those who have wronged you. It is all tied to you."

A chill runs up my thighs. "I'm scared. I don't want to die."

"You're not really dead and you don't really die. You want to be part of a circus? Then let me show you. My mother... she wasn't wrong about you."

"What did she say?" I ask curiously.

"She said when I saw my love again, I would fall in love at first sight." His eyes trail over my face. "And she was right. I'm in love with Ivy Sloan, and my biggest fear is the day she stops loving me back."

He gets out of the car, leaving me staring straight ahead.

After two or three minutes, I hear a tap on my window.

I open the door with a smile.

"Keir."

"At your service," he announces with a bow.

I step out and take in his performer's outfit. He's wearing a black and red medieval frock coat over tight leather pants. His chest is smooth and chiseled.

"You must have all the ladies in the audience going crazy."

"As much as I try to impress the audience, I haven't found the one who would give me her heart."

"I'm sure she will be very special. Whoever she is."

"I hope to find her one day."

"You will."

I turn and see Lex and her gorgeous fire-engine-red hair.

"Hi, I'm Lex. Remember me?"

"I could never forget you. You both look gorgeous and spectacular."

"I was hoping you would want to rehearse with us. We would love to have you in our next show."

"Oh," I say with disbelief. "I have no experience. Where would I..."

"It will come back to you," Keir says like we share a special secret. A special bond and I'm supposed to remember.

I'M ON STAGE, AND TO MY LEFT, A CURTAIN ROLLS UP. Draco stands shirtless with black pants and his face painted with black-and-white face paint. I look at my outfit, hoping I look okay. Nyx applied my makeup, and I'm wearing the same outfit I wore Friday night.

"Ready?"

"I'm not sure what you expect me to do. I can't do"—I point at Nyx flying in the air by her hair—"that."

"You're a seductress. You can captivate anyone. All you have to do is walk on the stage and be you. It is in your soul, Ivy. Let it out. Show me what you want."

I want him, but I don't tell him that.

"Later, we have business to take care of. We are not trying to hide anything from you," the Butcher says. "You were the one who started it all, Ivy. We all come back because of you."

I look at Keir, and his eyes are transfixed on me. How could I have started it all? What does he mean?

"Saving the girls," Keir says, quieting my thoughts. "Girls

being abducted and trafficked has been going on for centuries. The 1800s and before that. You and…"

I look at Draco. "It's true," Draco says. "We became a traveling circus because of you. You wanted to find the girls who went missing and hurt the ones responsible. You lured…"

The men. The old me from the past seduced the men who were sick. The ones I knew would rape or had raped and hurt young girls.

"There is a difference between consent and…" Lex pauses. "Nonconsensual sex and being a sick animal."

"Women are beautiful. They should be respected and set free. We…" Nyx stops and lowers herself from the harness. "We are free because of your family. You, Draco, L, and his love."

They don't know about Alice yet. L stands for Lazarus. I have been trying to piece everything together. The signs.

"Stop thinking so much about everything," Draco says, walking up behind me. I can feel his hard cock on my lower back. "Let go, Ivy. Show me your soul."

His voice echoes in my head. I close my eyes, and a flash back to a different time comes into focus.

A woman with a long robe sways her hips while walking on stage.

She removes the robe, and her lips are the shade of bright blood. Her hair is ghostly white. Glitter all over her skin with red sequins on her shorts. There is a crowd in the distant background.

She looks over her shoulder. "Are you ready for me?" she says playfully. She tilts her head back and laughs. "I love you, Draco." Her voice repeats like a ritual.

"You're so gorgeous they are going to love you, Mrs. Hades," the man says. I try to look at his face, but all I can make out is the top hat. The ringmaster.

I jolt, gasping for air. "Ivy!" My shoulders shake. I'm out of breath, my lungs starved of oxygen. "Ivy, are you alright?" Keir asks with a worried expression.

My chest is rising and falling. I nod, trying to swallow.

"Yes," I say, taking another breath. "Hades?"

"Draco Hades."

"Hade's manor?"

The rest of the performers arrive, and everyone goes to the back of the stage to rehearse.

"Yes. It's our family estate. I believe Alice lives there with her mother. Her father is missing at the moment. I don't think he intends to return," Draco says.

He's dead because I told him about Alice. But if he is a Hades, then his brother already knew about him. Lazarus has been watching for Alice. But for how long?

"Where do I fit in all this?"

"Here with me. There is no reason for you to work at the Big H. You'll be taken care of."

"School?"

"By the time we hit the road, you should have graduated. I don't intend to take you until you finish school and we have handled our little problem."

He means the men killing girls.

"You have…"

"What we need. Don't worry, Ivy. I don't intend to stop eating pussy at thirty-five and start collecting two-dollar bills. I don't think we will last that long. "

"You've thought of everything."

"You had a vision, didn't you?"

Is that what that was?

"Yes," I admit.

"The more we are around each other, the more you will have them. It is of all the past lives we have shared. You've always had them since it started."

"How…"

"You will know…in time." He holds out his hand. "I have a surprise for you, but right now, we need to practice. The show must go on, and I'm DYING to be seduced."

CHAPTER 26

At school the next day, I watch as people walk out of the main building laughing and shaking their heads. I'm curious about why I keep getting weird glances, but then I see it.

All over the walls and lockers is my surprise. Posters of Tommy strapped to a chair buck naked with a close-up of his small penis with a large arrow pointed at it all over the school.

In big letters, it reads:

TOMMY HILL HAS A SMALL DICK.

"Holy shit," I whisper with a smile.

When I make it to my locker, I see Tommy trying to pull the posters off the walls, but they fly like leaves all over the floor.

Girls giggle, and guys point at the posters, cackling in laughter.

Principal Miller storms out of the front office, yelling, "Who did this! When I catch the ones responsible, they will be arrested." He pauses when he sees me. "Did you have anything to do with this?"

Anger bubbles in my veins at the accusation. "I don't know, Mr. Miller. I think you should worry about the girls who keep popping up missing. I don't see you distraught over it, but when pictures pop up all over the school of a quarterback who likes to fuck half the school, you seem a little bothered by it." I shake my head in disappointment. "Not a good look, Miller."

"Watch your tone with me, young lady."

"Be careful, Mr. Miller, I'm an adult. I could report you to the school board on how you treat young girls unfairly." I lean close. "How excited you get when you talk to them alone in your office."

His face drains of all color, and then he storms off.

I hear a locker door close and look up. "Alice," I call out.

She smiles. "I have an idea."

"Do you?" I tease.

She gives me a look that says, *I know as much as you*. But does she?

AFTER SCHOOL, DRACO PICKS ME UP, IGNORING JASON'S stare and Tommy's sneer as I walk out to the car. I don't tell Draco the bad feeling I have in the pit of my stomach about Jason but I don't want tell because I don't want to sour the him.

"Where are we going?"I ask.

"Home."

"The circus?"

"No, our home."

He pulls up to the manor, and now it feels familiar. Not like when I've picked up Alice or the last time I was in her room. I squeeze my legs together at the memory. I notice Alice is not home yet. I look over at Draco when he drives around to the side of the house where there is a black metal gate and a door with a knocker with a metal iron mask like the ones you see in medieval times.

When he opens the door, it's part of the house that mirrors where Alice stays. It feels like I've been here before. It smells of citrus and cedar.

"It smells like…"

"Citrus and cedar," he finishes for me.

"How did you…?"

"It's always been your favorite."

I walk into the kitchen, and it looks just like the main house. The staircase. The hallways.

"Is this the same…?"

"It's the same house, but the only access is through a hidden door by the piano. When you walk through, you will be right in the living room like a mirage."

"But you can't see it from the main house."

"The first Hades brother designed it that way when the prophecy began and his brother was born."

"Who started…?"

He turns around. "You did."

"How?"

"I can't tell you that."

"Why?"

"It hurts too much."

"If you care about me and want me to believe all this is real. Why…?"

"You had a daughter. *We*…had a daughter once. She was your second born. The first generation of Hades children. I'm older and so are you compared to Lazarus and Alice."

I walk over to the books on the shelves. Compared to the other side these shelves are full and those are empty. I place my index finger over the spines and notice there are first editions.

"What happened?"

He lowers his head like he is pained to tell me. "She was taken,"he says softly.

My heart drops, and my hands start to tremble. "Taken?"

He cups my cheek. "It drove you to madness. You…It drove me to protect you. To protect this family and everyone you loved." His eyes hold mine for a second. "Performing is what got us through it, and…"

"Trying to save the others from it happening again."

He holds me in his arms. "Yeah."

A wave of dizziness hits me. I close my eyes and hear a little girl's laughter. She's maybe eleven or twelve. *"I'm right here, Momma," she says playfully, waving at me from the old small Ferris wheel.* She throws her head back laughing, and then the image fades away.

A sob escapes my throat. My knees buckle. His strong arms keep me from falling. A pain slices into me so deep. So big, it rips right through me.

"I got you, Ivy," he rasps against my temple. "I have you, baby."

"I saw her," I cry out. "I saw her, Draco."

"I know."

"I'm sorry. It's why I didn't want to tell you." He steadies me. "It brings her back but it also brings the pain."

"I want it. All of it, and don't do that to me again."

I watch his throat work. "I'm sorry."

"Take me back."

He knows I mean to the circus. I want to go back.

I WALK IN THE TENT. NYX GIVES ME A WIDE, CRAZY smile.

"Get me ready," I tell her.

"With pleasure," she says and then giggles madly.

After I'm in costume, I walk out the same side the night Draco took me to get something to eat with Bozo and find Madam Seraphina's booth.

The sun has almost completely set by the time I knock on the wood that says Psychic Readings. FREAK ACCIDENTS DO HAPPEN. SEE ALL KNOW ALL.

"Yes," she calls out.

I walk inside, and when she looks up from rummaging with something from her trunk as she gets dressed before the park opens. Her eyes widen.

"Mrs. H...Ivy Sloan."

"You said I would have dreams, not visions."

She waves her hand. "Dreams. Visions. Same thing."

"So it is true."

"Yes."

"How do you fit in all this?"

"You brought my family here from Europe. Italy, to be precise. Generations of my family are psychics."

"Can you find the girls?"

She gives me a wan smile. "That is like asking me for the winning lottery numbers. If I did know them, I wouldn't be here, and the answer is no. You asked centuries ago the same question, and the answer is still *no*. I'm sorry."

I take a seat and watch her wrap her shawl around her neck.

The gold coins clink when she adjusts it as she settles in her chair.

"It's not your fault. Did we ever...?"

"No. She was never found. My mother warned me you would ask this question as my grandmother and hers before her. They all said the same thing when you asked."

"My son."

"Was one of the best performers and he married his love. The twin soul you and his brother's love carry inside your hearts will split when it is time. It's quite fascinating, I assure you. Your child's love and soul stays dormant in the mother, keeping pure love alive until it's time and you pass . That twin soul reincarnates in another female, keeping your family's legacy alive. When you give birth to your son and your sister-in-law does the same, you dream of how they meet their soul mate so you can prepare your sons for their true love when they find each other. The house."

"What about it?"

"It is the key. It brings you all together. It heals. It destroys all who want to harm you. It is the pact you made with the house and the one you made the pact with."

"With whom?"

"He shall not be named. He is not the God that you pray to or the devil. He breathes in the wind. The keeper of the forest. The tarot guided you. You wanted to be immortal in away. Live young, die young and in return you reincarnate but you had to sacrifice. The loss of your daughter was too great. The love in your heart for Draco greater."

A little girl's voice whispers, "Cernunnos."

"Cernunnos."

She smiles. "She told you. The voice you hear is your daughter. Cernunnos has her. He gave you a way to rebirth and a way to regenerate your bloodline. He is part man. Part stag." She rubs the crystal ball on her table. "In return, you and Draco swore to never use animals out of respect. The lord of wild things granted you a gift. His lover and wife is the goddess of spring, Beltane. Goddess of fertility, which means..."

"We all give birth and die together, but we keep going."

"Sexuality of life and earth. Your husband is eccentric. He is the joker, one might say."

"Did my husband ever love another?"

I don't know why I asked. Maybe because of Nyx and the past.

"Once you meet, he can't. The bond and love is... too great."

"But I..."

"Sucked pussy and had yours sucked?"

I look up, shocked that she would say it aloud. How did she...?

"He came and told me."

"Draco?"

"Jealous, I'm afraid. He's afraid of losing you like he always has in the past. His greatest fear is losing his beloved. Your love is his biggest achievement."

"Does it ever stop?"

"True love never dies, Ivy. It's what you do in this life that affects the next. Always remember that. There is always sacrifice. It's part of it. The good and the bad."

I hear rustling behind me. I turn and find Draco standing in the entrance, looking between me and Seraphina.

"We're ready. The show," he says more to me than to her.

I get up and smile. "I'll see you later."

"Give 'em hell, Ivy. I'll be here if you need me and..." She winks. "Take care of him later."

She means fuck his brains out.

CHAPTER 27

I never meant to tell her about our daughter, worried the pain of our loss would make her spiral into madness. Madness I've spent years controlling with our love.

After Keir and Lex's act is done, she walks up, and I bow dramatically like I've done so many times before. Perfecting it so I would impress her when she saw me again. Like the first time two people meet and they fall in love. Butterflies.

Trembles deep in your bones when you make love, knowing it's the day you conceive your love child.

"Are you ready for the helicopter?"

"Yes," she mouths.

She is so sexy with her red suede boots covering her thighs.

I lift her off the ground. Her legs open wide in a horizontal split. Her arms stretched wide. I turn her in circles, holding her steady. Her pussy is in my face, and the sweet smell is heaven.

I spin her faster, like we are spinning backward in time. To another place. A place I hope she can remember.

IVY

I FEEL ALIVE, THE EXCITEMENT PUMPING IN MY VEINS. The crowd is in awe. I look up and see Nyx flying above, suspended in the air with a seductive smile.

Draco twirls me in the air like a helicopter. The same way we rehearsed, spinning me faster and faster. The crowd fades, then everything around me until I look up and I'm not in the tent. I'm looking straight ahead at a different version of Draco. One without the tattoos. A vintage version.

I look around, and we are seated in the booth at the diner. The same one my mother works except the booths are not shiny but instead have stripes. Red and white like a fifties diner. I look out the window to my right, and all the cars in the parking lot are all sixties classics.

The shiny tabletops catch the light just right. Each booth is separated by slender metal dividers, offering a sense of privacy. The air is filled with the teasing aroma of freshly brewed coffee and sizzling bacon.

Behind the counter is a row of swivel stools. The waitresses, dressed in retro uniforms complete with aprons and paper hats, bustle about with trays balanced expertly on their arms, delivering steaming plates of pancakes and burgers with a smile.

The walls are adorned with vintage memorabilia – old Coca-Cola ads, black-and-white photographs of iconic movie stars, and framed newspaper clippings from the past.

A large chalkboard hangs above the counter, listing the day's specials in colorful chalk writing.

The constant chatter of kids in leather jackets and girls with short hair reminds me of the set of the movie Grease *with John*

Travolta. The mingling with the clinking of flatware and the occasional burst of laughter.

"Do you want to go to the lake, Angela?"

I turn in my seat. Angela? I look out the window and catch my reflection in the glass. My face looks similar but different. My hair a different shade. My lips a different shape.

Music starts playing a familiar song. The Angels "My Boyfriend's Back."

"Your favorite song is playing," Draco says.

I look up and he looks like a sixties version of himself. Leather jacket and dark lashes with a dark line under his eyes.

"Angela?"

Oh shit, the lake.

"Yeah," I say with a smile.

He grins. "You don't have to if you're not ready."

"Your brother?"

"He's home. He doesn't start high school until next year, and he's excited. He is dying to go to the same school as Alex."

"Alex?"

"Alexandria." He winks like we are keeping a special secret. "Your best friend."

"Oh, right."

Alex must be Alice. I look around the diner and smile.

It's a flashback.

The song.

The diner.

Draco.

He slides out of the booth and holds out his hand. I look up, and I know in my heart that this moment is special. It means something. I slide my hand in his. My almond-shaped nails are painted a bright pink. My heavy skirt brushes my ankles as he pulls my arm gently so I can stand.

He leans in and brushes his lips against mine. His lips are warm and familiar.

I can hear gasps and giggles in the background.

"He's so hot,"one girls says.

"So is she,"another girl replies.

"They look so good together,"another girl says.

I keep watching him as he drives through the woods in his classic black Impala. "Runaround Sue"by Dion plays from the radio.

He turns on a dirt road. The tires going over rocks. He parks in front of the lake. The moon reflects off the surface. The stars twinkle in the dark sky.

He turns in his seat and caresses my cheek with his thumb. "I love you, Angela. You're my forever."

I lean into his touch. "I love you too,"I tell him.

I feel like I've never stopped telling him how much I love him. A ball forms in my throat.

"It's okay to be scared your first time." He says with a smile. "But I think you know that."

"I want to. I'm ready."

He leans in and kisses me softly. Our tongues twirl and taste each other.

He unbuttons my blouse. My breasts set high. He pushes my shoulder-length golden blond hair back and slides off the strap of my vintage bra, but I know in this time it's considered new.

He releases my heavy breasts and caresses my hard pink nipples with his fingers. His head dips and sucks one into his mouth.

I gasp, tilting my head back.

"Draco,"I plead.

In one swift movement, he removes his black leather jacket and undoes the button of his black pants to release his hard cock. He pushes my heavy skirt up my thighs.

Suddenly, I wish I didn't have so many clothes on. So much fabric. I'm sweaty and hot. I'm wet. My clit aches.

He manages to push all the layers of my skirt up my waist and pulls my panties down my thighs.

He looks up. I scoot down, so my back is flat on the seat. The palm of his hand slides up my thigh. He settles between my legs. His cock is hot and heavy against my clit.

"Look at me, Angela,"he demands.

His eyes are dark, and I swear I can see my soul reflected inside his. The Chiffons "Will You Still Love Me Tomorrow"plays like a chant between us.

The tip of his cock glides up and down my clit, working me until I'm writhing under him. He pushes in the tip, and I tense. It's tight, and he's big. I feel full, like I'm going to burst into a thousand pieces.

Sweat drips down his forehead. His arms tremble while he holds his weight so he doesn't crush me. I wrap my arms around him. His face falls between my neck and shoulder, and he pushes the rest of the way, breaking through my barrier.

I gasp. "Draco,"I say breathlessly.

It hurts and feels good at the same time. He moves inside me, and I undulate my hips, and he fucks me hard and slow.

"Fuck, you're perfect every time,"he rasps against my skin.

I widen my hips and grip his ass, pushing him deeper inside me.

I moan as he moves faster. Our heavy breaths pant between us as we make love under the pure white stars.

We both come together out of breath. The windows are fogged up. His wet black hair is matted against his forehead as he tries to catch his breath.

He's gorgeous.

"I love you, Draco. I'm lost in a timeless dream. In this time and the next. I love the gift of touching and discovering you again and again."

"I love meeting every version of you. No matter what, I love you and I would do anything for you."

My feet touch the ground, and I look up at the red and black tent. The crowd claps and cheers loudly through the air. I'm out of breath from the exhilaration.

Draco watches me intently as I sway my hips in character down the stage. Something passes between us. Recognition.

"You had a vision?"he asks when I sit in the chair in front of the mirror.

I stare at his reflection through the mirror. "How did you know?"

His mouth inches from my ear when he whispers, "It was one of our first times, wasn't it." I meet his eyes, wondering how he knows. "I can see it in your eyes, Ivy. The memory's attached to your soul. Once the circle begins, it is passed on to the soul that will love the next version of us when the time comes."

"Does it ever stop?"I ask.

He straightens. "I don't know. I'm guessing when it is perfect enough."

"What do you mean?"

"When it's the best version of ourselves. The perfect love story. I think but I'm not sure."

"That doesn't exist."

But every girl wants it to exist.

Villain or hero.

Angel or devil.

We all want the perfect love.

"It exists... with us."

CHAPTER
28

DRACO

"I have a surprise for you," I tell her, handing her an ax.

She's ready. They found one of the girls who was abducted. Dehydrated and starved. Raped and battered. I found the one who took her.

"Show me."

I hand her my phone and wait as she reads the news media article online. She stands with determination in her eyes and the ax in her hand.

Pulling open the door, I watch as her face remains impassive from the smell of death. She walks in, followed by Nyx, Keir, Lex, and the Butcher.

I pull the door closed. "Let the games begin," I announce.

The man hangs from the ceiling by his wrists. Arms spread wide. His ankles are tied together, but he's on his knees, so Ivy can do what she wants.

His beard is matted with blood. His teeth are knocked out and scattered on the floor.

Ivy walks forward, dragging the sharp edge of the ax on the metal floor. It makes a scraping sound as she steps under the light.

She looks magnificent.

"Well, well, well. Look wat wee have here. Another Freak. You're pretty. I bet your pussy smells like that little cunt I fucked until she bled."

"Is that what you did?"Ivy says in a flat tone.

"Oh yeah. I can show you if you'd like." He spits on the ground. "I'll cut you up real nice."

Nyx laughs. "You're in so much trouble, mister," she says in a funny voice. "She's crazier than all of us."

"You should see what happened to the last guy," Lex adds. "That's nothing compared to what she's going to do to you."

Ivy turns and narrows her gaze on the shirt with DTF written across it on the floor.

I lean close. "You didn't think I was actually going to let him move, did you?"

"Come here baby?" The man taunts "I bet you taste nice like them girls."

My gaze flicks to the man. His hair is all sweaty. He's pissed himself about three times already trying to act tough.

His protruding stomach hangs out of his shirt. His pants are sliding off his hip. A ball of pubic hair is stuck to the skin of his lower belly. He's disgusting. A pig. A pedophile. Men like him don't deserve to live.

"You are all a bunch of fucking Freaks. You think you can kill all of us?" He laughs, blood dripping from the corner of his mouth. "You're a pretty whore. I would break you in really good like those little—"

Ivy swings the ax straight into his face, splitting his mouth. His eyes roll upward, looking straight at her and then involuntarily jerk in his skull. Blood doesn't splatter. Not at first. His legs shake convulsively. His eyes fill with blood. He starts crying, but no sound comes out.

Ivy pulls the ax out, and his face splits awkwardly. You could see the roof of his mouth.

Nyx laughs with glee, clapping her hands together. Ivy swings the ax between his eyes, splitting his skull open. Blood shoots out like a spout bathing her hands. There is a hissing noise from his arteries spraying blood everywhere. The Butcher cuts the ropes. Keir tries to take the ax from Ivy, but she glares and pulls it away from his grasp.

This makes me happy for some reason. She's here. It's her.

The man's body falls on the floor, with one eyelid jerking involuntarily. Brain matter oozes from his open skull. His tongue hangs out like a dog. His arms jerk on the floor.

"Who's the Freak now, huh?"Ivy screams and then laughs at her own outburst. "You're all going to die."She swings the ax hard to the ground, splitting the rest of his skull into pieces. It takes forty-five minutes for him to stop jerking and finally die.

She turns around, covered in blood like she came straight from the set of a horror story. "Did I do good, baby?" she says in a naughty voice. "Do you want to play?'

She's back.

My wife is back.

Her madness is music to my ears.

CHAPTER 29

The warning bell rings when I walk in school. I ignore the curious stares at my ripped black tights and short uniform skirt. I'll probably get written up for it.

I walk straight to Alice as she leans on my locker, waiting for me.

"Missed me," I ask coyly.

"Always. How was the show this weekend?"

I tilt my head like I have to think about it. "Bloody fine," I say with a wide smile.

Alice raises a brow. "You're happy they found the missing girl."

"There is more."

"I know." She lowers her voice before Jason and Tommy walk up. "Lazarus told me."

"Well, well. Ivy and the Freak," Jason says slowly.

I laugh. "You mean Alice and the Freak or the Freak and Alice."

"More like the slut and the dyke."

I pout. "I like Freak," I say in a little voice.

"I can be a freak," Jason says, leaning close.

Placing my finger over my black lipstick, I say, "My boyfriend wouldn't like that, Jason."

He finally notices that I'm different. Bolder. I'm dressed different too.

"Who the fuck are you?" Tommy says.

"I'm a Freak. Isn't that what you like to call me or rather—us?"

Jason smiles, and I sense the rapist in him. "I'll show you later."He walks by me and says near my ear, "I'm going to fuck you, Ivy. You're going to like it, and I don't care if you say no."

I giggle, and Alice joins in.

Tommy looks between us like we are crazy. "Dude, what the fuck did you tell her?" He turns away, following Jason. "What the fuck, Jason?" he bellows down the hall over the mob of people rushing to class.

"What are you going to do about them?"Alice asks.

"I'm not sure yet,"I tell her, but I have an idea.

"What did Jason tell you?"

I tell her, and I see the hatred for him in her eyes, but she must see the madness in mine. The one that took over the minute I saw the girl's blurred face and the list of her injuries. It all came back. Memories of the past. Embedded and reincarnated.

"Do you know what we are?"Alice asks.

"Yes."

I do.

"Will it ever stop?"

" I don't know, but the cycle repeats. I just hate the part where it takes time for us to find our way back."

"Do you think we will remember this?"

"I will," I say, caressing her cheek. "I will always find you, Alice. Just like he will."

She smiles. " I love you, and I know."

She knows that when she gives birth to two sons, a soul is created inside us that is reborn upon our death linking us in eternity. I didn't understand it at first, but now I do.

"The house."

"Is the key to it all. It will bring you back, Ivy."

"My son?"I ask, confused.

I had a son. I will have a son. I know about my little girl I can never get back but...

"They didn't tell you."

CHAPTER 30

DRACO

"You didn't tell her."

"I haven't," I say.

"Why? You confused her."

I look up at Keir. "I didn't."

"Then why didn't you tell her about me?" he says through clenched teeth.

"Because you need to believe it."

"I do believe it. I know it's her. I was there. I saw her come back. The way she looked at you. The way you looked at her. It's hard..."

"What is hard?"

"To know that my parents died and they came back to fall in love when I was supposed to die with them the last time."

"She saved you."

"I didn't want to be saved. I want my mother and father."

"She did it because she loved you, Keir. She didn't want children at first because it would slow her down in trying to save the others, but she loved you, and this time, she is going to need you. You have a gift. A chance to find love."

"Are you listening to yourself? You're my father reincarnated into someone else and so is my mother."

"So will you, Keir. The house doesn't bring babies unless you're a Hades. I'm sorry for hitting you the other day. I was afraid..."

"That I would mistake her for the girl of my dreams when she's my mother?"

"Yeah."

"I knew it was her,"he says, grabbing his knives. "I felt it inside."

I SET THE JARS ON THE FLOOR. KEIR TURNS ON THE light. I hear muffled cries from the two assholes tied to the electric chairs I found in the basement at the house. They still do their job.

I adjust my top hat and push my coat out of the way as Keir plays with their heads.

"You didn't think I'd let you call her a slut, did you?" Keir says, making the knives appear and disappear.

I stand and watch the horror in their eyes when they recognize me.

Keir starts cutting them open.

I smile. "You did say you wanted to see the show." Then, they scream in agony. "Now, who's the slut and the Freak?"

CHAPTER
31

Mrs. Hades,

When our eyes first met, I fell in love. It was a bond so profound, so enduring, it seemed to have weathered countless lifetimes. The sort of connection that clings to your soul, refusing to let go. The sort of love worth fighting for, worth sacrificing for, worth dying for. I understood then that this love was relentless. Even death itself couldn't extinguish it. It was compelled to release its hold on us. And what remains now are the most exquisite memories etched into the fabric of time.

In every lifetime, our souls instinctively search for one another, irresistibly pulled by an unbreakable connection that transcends the constraints of time and space.

Our love remains forever, intricately woven into the very essence of being, fated to reunite again. We will find each other...forever.

True Love Never Dies

Eternally,
Mr. D Hades.

"That is beautiful. Who was Mrs. Hades?" I ask curiously. Draco looks up, and I can't get over how gorgeous he is, but he's emotionally unavailable. He's the hottest guy in school. I don't know why he would let me read something so personal belonging to his family. I don't know why he watches me in class.

"Her name was Ivy Hades."

The End

Want more of this world? Want more of Ivy, Alice, Draco and
Lazarus?
Lovers Fate
True Love Never Dies
Coming 12-24-24
Scan the QR code for upcoming releases and links to preorder

ABOUT THE AUTHOR

Carmen Rosales is a best-selling Dark Romance and Latinx author. She loves to write in different genres of Romance and erotic horror under her alter ego, Delilah Croww. Beyond her writing, Carmen is a devoted wife and mother who loves spending time with her loved ones. Join her VIP list and Newsletter- www.carmenrosales.com

Follow her on Social Media and stay up to date with her new releases: